SURVIVING THIS THING CALLED LIFE

S. D. LAURENCE

3/14/15

To   Daria

Thanks for the
Love & Support

First printing 2014

ISBN-13: 978-0692328408
ISBN-10: 0692328408

DEDICATION

THIS BOOK IS DEDICATED TO ALL WHO STRUGGLE TO SURVIVE THIS THING CALLED LIFE

Contact Info
sdlaurence.sl@gmail.com / twitter@sdlaurence
Purchase additional copies @www.sdlaurence.com

Table of Contents

Chapter One

Marva sat quietly in her usual morning pose, a coffee cup in one hand and a lit cigarette in the other. There was a knock at the front door. She knew that if it was a friend they would open the door and let themselves in. As the door opened, a tall almond colored woman with natural short curly hair entered the house and headed for the kitchen.

"Hey Miss Marva, it's me, Cherish!"

"What going on Miss Cherish? Come on back." Marva noticed a hint of stress in her friend's voice. Marva and Cherish knew each other since childhood and their families had the same roots in Greenville, South Carolina, so of course they were cousins!

"Girl, I think I'm due a vacation. There's been too much drama in my life lately. Don't get me wrong, I have a lot to be thankful for but this divorce has really drained my spirit. You know me girl! I was ready to say fuck it! Scott, you take everything and I'll get more. But my dumb ass, let people talk me into a legal battle. But Scott, with his rebellious spirit, refused to cooperate with the process." Marva empathized with her cousin-friend

"Yeah girl you were telling me that he would meet potential buyers for the house with a shotgun at the front door! Cherish, that nigga ain't rebellious. He's crazy!

"Anyway Marva, the divorce is final, the property is being sold and after the lawyers get finished there won't be much left. So I need to go somewhere, spend that little money, and chill."

"Why don't you go to Jamaica child? You could sure use some blue wata and white sands. As a matter of fact, I think you should go to Negril."

"Negril! I don't think so! I heard that Negril is all about White Woman; Rent-a-Dreads and Sex! I'm not up for that kind a trip. Marva. I need to chill. I just got rid of a nigger

1

and I don't want another one, at least not just yet!" They laughed and continued their conversation.

"Now Cherish, all that might be true about Negril, but you're smart, you know how get about on your own. Look here, I have a tour book. Let's look up some place for you to stay." Cherish really didn't feel comfortable with the thought of going to Negril. Traveling alone was not a problem for her. She'd traveled alone many times before and enjoyed every opportunity to be alone with herself. After all, she was an only child and enjoyed every minute of it. But Cherish did respect Marva and their friendship so she cooperated with the investigation.

***

In another space in time, Negril, Jamaica, a Rastafarian is sitting on the white sands beach in deep meditation, when suddenly another Rasta approaches him and speaks in a hurried voice.

"Wisdom yuh waan mek some fast money?" Wisdom thought before he spoke. He knew the runnin's of Negril and fast money could mean anything.

"Wha yuh waan mi fi do, Mon?"

"Rasta deres dis white man from "Foreign" lookin fi a woman named Susan. Mi tell de Mon, dat yuh know de Sista." Wisdom answered him after some contemplation.

"Yes Mon, mi do dat fi yuh, Bredren."

"See him deh soh Star?" The Rasta points to a short fat White Man with a large Cuban cigar standing on the beach as he briskly walks away. Wisdom sensed that this man could mean more than just one fast money deal. Wisdom stood, walked toward the White Man and the two men extended their hands to shake.

"Hello, my name is Simon. Are you the man that knows Susan?'

"Why, yuh de fuckin FBI?" Wisdom spoke in a very harsh tone. He wanted to let Simon know that he was not a person to be fucked with.

"No, I'm not the FBI. I'm looking for a woman named Susan. She left England with some Jamaican man and I was told by reliable sources that they were in Negril. Do you know her?"

"How valuable dis information tu yuh? Five thousand American dollars?" Wisdom just finished praying to Jah. All he needed was a break. Music was his life but he needed money. He didn't even have a guitar but he did have his hopes and dreams.

"I won't pay you that much but I'm willing to give you one thousand dollars for some good information!" Simon reached for his wallet and pulled out a wad of cash. He counted out ten one hundred bills.

"What's your name man? It's not often I give a thousand dollars to someone whose name I don't know."

"Wisdom! Dem call de I Wisdom."

***

"Now that we have your flight booked for Montego Bay, let's get you booked in a hotel. Look here Cherish! This seems like a nice place. It's called Roots and they have small cottages right on the beach!" Cherish stood over Marva's shoulder while reading the hotel's description.

"It's cheap too Marva! Look, there's a telephone number. Let's call!" Cherish felt a sense of excitement. She knew in her spirit that this trip was destined for her. Marva picked up the telephone, dialed the number and hand the phone to Cherish.

"Hello is this Roots?"

"Yes is it. How can mi help yuh?"

"I want to reserve a room for several weeks at your establishment."

"Yes an we lov tu hab yuh!" The voice on the other end of the line was warm and welcoming. Any uneasiness Cherish possessed slowly dissipated as she spoke to the kind young lady on the other end of the line.

"Miss, Yuh must know that Roots a long way from Montego Bay but mi can arrange fi yuh tu git picked up from de airport."

"That's great. So let's make it happen." Cherish continued to complete the arrangements for her much needed vacation.

"Great Nakeda, I'm looking forward to meeting you in person. See you soon, bye." Cherish hung up the phone with a smile on her face.

"Sister Girl, I think this trip is just what I need."

***

The next morning miles away from Marva and Cherish, Simon and Wisdom greet each other on the white sand beach in Negril.

"Mawning Simon. Yuh sleep well inna Jamaica?"

"Yes Wisdom, but I'm anxious to know what you found out last night. I spent a lot of money and time on this Bitch and I'm not ready to give her up yet." Simon had a serious look on his face as he spoke. Wisdom felt his pain and thought to himself, what I am going to say to this man. I'll just open my mouth and say whatever comes out.

"Yes Simon, de truth is Susan was mi woman inna Jamaica an de Bitch leave wit some Rude Bwoy an gone back to England."

"I asked that woman if she would ever fuck a black man and she flat out said no!"

"Simon, she been wit a black man an dat man was de I! Trust mi Mon, de Sistren promised tu tek mi tu England an record mi songs."

"Wisdom, that's all my idea! I want to produce music, not Susan. She got that idea from me! I'll send for you to come to England and record if you help me find that Bitch, Susan!"

"Yes, Mon. Us men must stick together. Us can't let a piece of pussy break us down." Wisdom extended his hand as he finished speaking. Simon returned the gesture and the two men stood in the morning sun on the beautiful

4

white sands of Negril not knowing why destiny put them together.

***

A few weeks later, Cherish arrived at Sangster Airport in Montego Bay, Jamaica. She completed the requirements for customs and headed out of the double doors not knowing what to expect. All she knew was a man named Cowboy was supposed to be there to pick her up. As the doors open, there was a sea of black faces. Everyone was speaking but she couldn't understand a word. As Cherish exited the door, she began to yell.

"Cowboy! Is there anyone here named Cowboy?" There standing at the exit was a tall dark man in a big white Cowboy Hat. He answered in a calm tone.

"Yes Miss. Yuh gwan tu Roots?"

"Yes, I'm going to Roots and I'm glad to see you. I bet they call you cowboy because of your hat." Both laughed as they walked toward the van and headed for Negril. The ride to Negril was breathtaking. The island was filled with lush green plants, blue water and white clouds that danced across the skies. Cherish was beginning to relax from all the stress of her life in America.

"Pardon me Miss. Yuh smoke ganja?"

"As a matter of fact, I do. I heard that Jamaica is known for Rasta's, Reggae and ganja. Can we get some?" Cowboy pulled the van on the side of rode in front of a wooden shack and exited the van. As he exited, Cherish could hear him say.

"Yes Mon, Jamaica no problem." Cherish, Cowboy and the ganja all made it to Roots safely. She paid Cowboy a generous sum of money for the ride to Roots and the ganja.

The resort was beautiful. There were 10 small white cottages neatly placed a few feet away from the Sea. Each cottage had its own veranda, and front yard filled with brilliant colorful flowers. That evening Cherish sat on the veranda listening to the band play and watching as the

5

people began to fill the bar for the evening show. While sitting alone, a tall man with long Dreadlocks approached her.

"Are you enjoying yuhself Sister?"

"Yes I am. In fact, I feel like I'm in paradise." Cherish noticed that this man's accent was understandable.

"Are you an American because I can really understand what you're saying?"

"No Mon. I'm Jamaican but I lived in the States for some time. They call me Africa. Do you know Philadelphia?"

"Yes I know Philadelphia! That's where I live!"

"Yuh mind if I sit and we chat a while?"

"No I don't. Have a seat." Cherish and Africa sat together smoking ganja and exchanging ideas about politics and life. The show was over and people were dispersing to return to their hotels or homes. Suddenly, a flash of light appears out of the darkness and two policemen approach Cherish and Africa. They walked on the veranda and spotted a small piece of spliff left in the ashtray from the evening discourse.

"Whose ganja dis?" A conversation between the angry Police Officer and Africa pursued but Cherish couldn't understand what was going on. She was a visitor in a strange place with a different language. Suddenly the attention was focused on her and the policeman pointed toward her room and yelled.

"Do yuh hab ganja inna yuh room Miss?"

"No sir." As she spoke, the police officer pushed past her and walked inside her little room. Cherish followed. Her heart was pounding. All kinds of thoughts were rushing through her mind. Will they lock me up? Will I be able to get in touch with my family? Why did I come to Jamaica? Jamaica no problem! I don't think so! Jamaica is pure problems she thought.

6

"Miss if yuh hab ganja inna yuh room, yuh must tell. Ganja illegal inna Jamaica!" Cherish began to plead with the Police Officer.

"Yes I do sir!" She quickly went into one of her dresser drawers and pulled out the bag of ganja. She continued to speak to the officers.

"But, I'm a teacher from America on vacation. I love God and I don't usually engage in such behavior! Please accept my humble apology if I offended anyone!" After what seemed like a lifetime the officer spoke to Cherish.

"Mi gwan tu tek dis ganja an mek sure yuh nah git more." The two police officers left her room. Immediately the fear in Cherish changed to anger. She knew that if this were America, her rights had just been violated. But this wasn't America! It was Jamaica! She began to question why she traveled to Negril in the first place. Her fear returned! What if the policemen returned? She was alone.

"Sister dat was close. Dem tek yuh ganja?"

"Yes they did and I'm feeling real fucked up right about now, Africa."

"Yes Mon, de police dem act like dictators amongst the people dem. Don't worry yourself sister. I wish Wisdom was here. He would know what to do."

"Wisdom? Who the fuck is Wisdom and what could he do?" Her anger returned. She thought that Africa should have said more, done more, maybe even told the police it was his ganja. It was surely his country, not hers.

"Sistren believe de I, Wisdom would know wha fi do?" Suddenly a man appeared out of the darkness. He and Africa spoke a few words in Patois to each other and just as suddenly, the man disappeared. Africa turned to Cherish.

"Dat was Wisdom. I told him what happened."

"Alright man! I'm tired. I'm going the fuck to bed. I had enough of Jamaica and its problems." Cherish was upset about the entire incident and could barely sleep. She did finally drop off to sleep but as the sun rose, so did she.

As she woke, Cherish knew it was going to be a beautiful day because yesterday's fears had disappeared. Cherish believed that every day was a gift from God, that's why it was called the present. So, she thanked God for another opportunity to praise him and went to get breakfast at the hotel restaurant.

"Good morning ladies. What's for breakfast today?" She spoke in a cheerful tone.

"Don't worry yuhself Miss. Breakfast soon come. We hab ackee an salt fish. Mi bring it tu yuh."

"Okay but do you have any coffee?"

"Yes Miss, mi hab Blue Mountain coffee. Mi hear dis de best coffee inna de world. Mi soon come."

Cherish returned to her cottage and sat on the veranda. Seeing the blue water and white sands reminded her of why she came to Jamaica. Breakfast was wonderful. The different flavors filled her mouth as the beautiful sights filled her eyes. Things were feeling better. Cherish decided to take a walk, when she spotted a tall, dark and handsome man with Dreadlocks standing on his veranda.

"Good mawning Sista. Dem call mi Singer. I an I de entertainment inna de place. Did yuh hear de I sing last night?"

"I didn't go to the show but I could hear from my veranda. Your music sounds good."

"Respect Sista. Wha ah gwan?"

"I'm going for a short walk."

"Dis mi room. Visit pon yuh return." Singer had a broad beautiful smile on his face as he spoke to Cherish. As she walked away, she thought, I won't be visiting anyone. I had enough with visits. She decided that her time would be spent on the beach and in her room. After a short walk, Cherish headed back to her room. She walked pass Singer's room and noticed his door was wide open. Singer spotted her as she walked by and shouted.

"Sistren, come visit de I now!" Cherish thought to herself, what could one little visit hurt. I am on vacation.

She walked into the room and her eyes scanned everything and everyone. After the experience last night, she decided to be more aware of her surroundings. Maybe if she had seen the police coming, some of the drama could have been avoided.

Singer escorted her to a seat and began to introduce her proudly to the group. She could understand only a few words but she did notice a handsome man with Dreadlocks standing royally across the room. She wondered if that was Wisdom. As Singer called out everyone's names, Cherish heard the name Wisdom. Her heart skipped a beat. It was him.

Wisdom spotted Cherish also. He recognized her as the American from the veranda the night before with Africa. His mind was racing but his body remained calm and still. He looked at Cherish and immediately knew that this was a woman he wanted to get to know. He spoke politely and quickly left the room. Wisdom was on a mission. He thought, if he could get back her ganja that might be the opportunity he needed to get to reason with her. Wisdom went to find Africa.

"Africa, yuh remember de Policeman dat tek de Sistren's ganja?"

"Yes Mon, dat faisty one. Yuh know de big fat one dem call, Bullocks."

"Yes Mon, mi know de Mon. Him go on like he's some dictator. Tek de I tu de police station now."

"Why yuh care so much fi dis American woman?"

"Because she's an African an Africans worldwide must support each other. If yuh nah come, mi go alone!" Wisdom and Africa arrived at the station together but Wisdom walked in alone. As fate would have it, Bullocks was standing near the front desk.

"Officer, mi waan talk wit yuh?"

"Mi?" Bullock looked surprised. "Wha business yuh hab wit mi, Rasta?"

9

S.D. Laurence

"Just a minute sir, yuh know de Black American yuh tek de ganja from at Roots?'

"Yes Mon, wha business is dat fi yuh?" Bullock was annoyed now.

"De Sistren mi cousin from Foreign an she come tu Jamaica tu relax."

"Rasta, yuh must know ganja illegal inna Jamaica."

"Yeah Mon, mi know but yuh must know dat ganja de healing fi de nation. Give back de ganja Mon. Don't mek she go tu America an chat bout de bad treatment inna Jamaica." Bullock thought about it. Wisdom was right. He knew that a little ganja smoking didn't hurt anyone and that any bad talk could discourage people from visiting the island.

"Alright Fireball, mi lik de way yuh talk. Take de ganja an go away!" Wisdom was thankful. He knew the ganja would be what he needed to reason with the American woman. He walked quickly to the car because he also knew the nature of a policeman. He didn't want to be there when Bullocks realized what he had just done.

"Did yuh git through?" Africa was excited.

"Yes Mon, wit no help from de I." Wisdom pulled out the ganja to show Africa and both men laughed as they drove off. Wisdom would spend the rest of the evening thinking about Cherish.

Early the next morning, Wisdom rose with the sun. He remembered his grandmother's advice about the early bird catching the worm. He knew that Singer wanted the American woman too but he didn't deserve her. He did! He searched her spirit while they were in Singer's room for that short time. He loved her confident demeanor. He admired her courage to travel alone to a foreign country, be confronted by the Police and still get up and walk around with dignity. He decided I'll go to her room now. Wisdom took the ganja, went to Cherish's room and knocked on the door.

"Good mawning Miss."

10

"Who is it?"

"It's Wisdom. Mi thought yuh might lik a nice ride tu see de beauty of Jamaica." Cherish's heart stopped for a second. Wisdom, she thought, what does he want with me this early in the morning?

"Just a minute Sistren, mi hab de ganja from de other night." Wisdom quickly spoke again before Cherish could answer. He knew that she would be surprised by his early morning visit. Cherish was dumbfounded. She cracked the door only to see Wisdom holding the portion of ganja high before him like a prize package.

"I don't want to see any more ganja thank you. It has caused me enough trouble for one day."

"Alright Sistren. Mek mi tek yuh tu de river. De mawning de best time tu travel. Mi feel yuh need tu relax an de river's de best place fi relaxation." Cherish thought a moment. It was her vacation. She did want to explore Jamaica. Why not!

"Okay give me about a half hour to get dressed." She needed to relax. She wanted to relax.

"Alright Sistren, mi soon come." Wisdom was joyful. He thanked Jah for this opportunity as he walked away and anxiously waited for Cherish. As Cherish dressed, she thought to herself. What the hell am I doing? I don't know this man. And at that same moment she remembered his royal appearance and finished dressing. Wisdom returned in 15 minutes knocking at the door.

"Yuh ready Sistren?"

"Almost! Give me a few minutes." She finished dressing and joined Wisdom at the car waiting outside. At first they drove very quietly. Cherish had no idea where she was going or what she was doing. Wisdom was the first to speak.

"So Sistren, what brings yuh tu mi island, Jamaica?"

"It was my girlfriend's idea. I needed to cool out and she said that Jamaica was the place for me."

"De Sista was right! Jamaica no problem." They both laughed. As they drove down the long winding road, it seemed like time stood still. They began to relax. They began to talk. They talked about everything. It was as if they knew each other forever, not just the few moments they spent together in Singer's room. Wisdom pulled over and stopped the car at one of the most beautiful places Cherish ever experienced.

"Wow, this spot is beautiful." Her eyes were trying to take in as much of creation as they could. The land below her feet was filled with lush plants and flowers of various colors and textures and in the middle of all this beauty was crystal clear waters dancing along the rocks.

"I knew Jamaica had the blue Caribbean Sea but I never knew about the rivers." Wisdom could feel her spirits fly as she stood and took in the view.

"Yeah Mon, mi waan yuh tu see dis. Mi come tu renew mi soul an talk tu Jah. Come Sistren, tek a dip inna de river." Cherish didn't wear or carry a swim suit. She wore an African wrap skirt and a red sleeveless top. She had just cut her hair because she recently decided to grow Locks. What a fool, she thought to herself. There she was in paradise, standing next to a Rasta with beautiful Locks who wanted to her to take a dip and she didn't have a swimsuit.

"I didn't wear a swimsuit! I probably should have bought one with me because I am in Jamaica" They both laughed and smiled at each other.

"Sistren! Jamaica, no problem. Mi hab a pair of shorts fi yuh. Yuh need a river bath. Please mek mi help yuh relax Sistren." Cherish thought a river bath? A bath involves bathing. Who's gonna bathe who? But she was in Jamaica. The spirit of the place enchanted her. Cherish felt like she was in a dream.

"Okay let me change into the shorts." As Cherish walked away, Wisdom felt nervously happy. Simon was sending for him to come to England and now this! He

12

thanked Jah as he did every day, all the time, no matter what had happened. His life had been full of highs and lows but he always thanked the Father. He thought about how these past few years in Jamaica had been a pure struggle. He thought about America and how quickly things had changed for him there. While Cherish changed clothes, Wisdom's mind drifted back to his time in Philadelphia.

***

Wisdom thought about the things he left behind. He had a few houses that he was restoring, a health food store and one of the first official ganja houses' in Philadelphia. Things were going fine. He even had a band that occasionally performed on South Street, one of the hippest streets in the city. He had some problems with jealousy from his young wife but he never let that bother him. He thought how could Melissa do what she did to him?

"Okay Wisdom. I'm ready for my bath." His mind came back to Jamaica, as Cherish approached him because that was then and this was now. What a beautiful woman Wisdom thought as he gazed upon her long flawless legs and beautiful breast bursting from her bra.

"Yes, Sistren! Mi see dat yuh ready." The couple climbed down the side of a short hill to get to the river. Cherish placed her feet on the earth, she felt grounded, almost rooted to this place.

"The earth feels good Wisdom. I really love this kind of stuff, being outdoors and interacting with nature."

"Yes Sistren, Mi know you was Roots when mi first saw yuh."

"Roots? What's Roots?"

"It's a vibe. Yuh come tu Jamaica an yuh fit in."

"Yes Wisdom. I do feel like I'm at home. Jamaica is an awesome place." They both entered the cool river water. Cherish watched as Widom dipped his locks into the water, threw his head back and the water rolled down his chocolate back. Everything was so perfect. She kept

13

thinking, stay in the moment Cherish! Don't over think anything! Not now, not today! You're safe with this man.

"Come git wet Sistren. De wata likkle cold, but it's nice Mon." Wisdom began to toss a few drops on her body as she slowly entered the river. The water was cold but she needed a river bath and she definitely wanted one.

"It is a little cold and it does feel good!"

"Come sit here. Let de wata massage yuh back." Cherish slowly walked towards Wisdom and sat down in the spot he pointed out. The cascading water seemed to melt away all the years of stress living in America. She thought about what Bob Marley called America, a rat race.

"Yes it's wonderful, Wisdom."

"No disrespect Sistren but yuh must tek off yuh bra."

"My bra, why?"

"Inna Jamaica bathing nude de custom but mi tink yuh must start wit yuh bra." Wisdom had a soft smile on his face as he spoke to Cherish.

"Really Sistren, no disrespect. Mi nah harm yuh or touch yuh. Mi only here fi yuh relaxation. Mi know life inna America stressful." Cherish thought for one moment, when in Rome do as the Romans do. Cherish slowly started to remove her bra.

"Mek mi help yuh Sistren." Wisdom wrapped his arms around her and began to unfasten her bra from the back. Then he kissed her gently on the cheek and let her bar go. Her breasts were free. She felt free. Wisdom began to pour water on her and every drop felt like pure gold on her naked body. Wisdom stood back and looked upon his beautiful queen.

"No disrespect Sistren but yuh hab beautiful breast."

"Thank you."

"Dip yuh head inna de wata tree times. Dis bring blessings pon yuh but yuh mus hab a clean heart. Sistren, mi know yuh heart clean." Wisdom spoke from his heart to Cherish. They both dipped their heads in the river not knowing the blessings that lie ahead.

14

"Yuh mus be hungry. Mek we go tu de caves an git som food. Just leave yuh bra on a carry yuh top. Come now." Wisdom spoke with authority but not dictatorship. Cherish wanted to do what he asked. She put on her African wrap and her bra. She felt like she was in Africa. The sun was hot, lush greenery everywhere and a king by her side. They got in the car and drove to the caves.

"De Parish Westmoreland wit Negril only a small part of de ting." Wisdom would tell Cherish about everything they saw as the pair moved from one beautiful place to the next.

"Jamaica is beautiful, Wisdom. Who wouldn't be roots here?" Cherish felt proud sitting in her bra and by the time they reached their destination, she was no longer self-conscious of her bra and her body.

"See mi Bredren deh sho?" Wisdom and Cherish exited the car and headed across the road.

"Blessings Bredren, glad fi see yuh. Yuh know where de I can git some Ital food?"

"Eat wit de I, Rasta."

"Much Respect!" They joined the party of men gathered around the open fire. While sitting by the fire, Cherish's mind left Jamaica. She thought about how abruptly her marriage ended. Her only son graduated early from high school and was attending college in Georgia. Cherish's husband, Scott, always wanted a PhD. He applied and received a scholarship to the University of Iowa. So when their son left for college, the couple packed up and moved to the small college town in Iowa.

When she got there, she was told that if you want to you see a black person every day, look at yourself before you leave the house. Cherish didn't believe it at first but found the information true most of the time. Cherish didn't like the place. University life wasn't for her. Scott loved it. He loved being a big fish in a small pond. Together they bought a house from the proceeds of their home in New Jersey. Cherish worked to support them both. Scott's

15

scholarship from the University only covered his tuition and books.

After three years, she had enough. She missed the East Coast. She had enough of the Mid-West and took a job teaching in Philadelphia. The job had been offered two years in a row. Cherish was fearful that if she didn't take it this year they may not offer again. Life in Iowa wasn't bad but she wanted something different for herself. The plan was for Cherish to move in with her mother, save money and continue to support Scott financially. When he received his doctorate, there were more than enough colleges and universities in Philadelphia and the surrounding area for him to seek employment. But life had a different plan for Cherish.

"Hey baby. How's the thesis going?" Cherish asked Scott as they chatted on the phone.

"It's going okay but where have you been? I've been trying to get in touch with you for days now." Scott was aggravated. Cherish was hanging out. She married at seventeen and the couple moved to New York. She missed her friends, Philadelphia and its excitement.

"I'm sorry baby. I have been hanging out a little."

"Hanging out!" Scott was yelling now. "Well you better hang out on this thought! Get your ass back to Iowa or you'll be hanging out alone." Cherish couldn't believe her ears. All the years of support and uplifting she had done for him and now he was going to threaten her. She hung up immediately. She and Scott would quarrel for days to come and finally one day he called with an ultimatum.

"Cherish if you don't come back to Iowa. I want a divorce."

"Well you do what you have to do and I'll do what I have to do." In the next few weeks, the divorce papers appeared in the mail. Cherish's response was direct. She signed them and that was that.

"Here's some Ital stew fi yuh Sistren." Wisdom's voice caused Cherish to return to Jamaica. As she ate the Ital stew, every spoonful filled her mouth with new taste experiences: yam, dumpling, potatoes and red peas.

"Yuh lik de stew Sistren?" Wisdom smiled as he watched Cherish enjoy the food.

"Yes Mon, it is good." Cherish couldn't speak or understand Patois but she could say "Mon". They finished their food, thanked the Rasta for his hospitality and walked hand and hand toward the caves. Wisdom felt proud having this American woman on his side. He had captured her early in the morning. He knew the running at Roots. By now, everyone put one and one together and figured out that he stole the American woman. This would be a story that people would tell for years to come.

Wisdom shared very little about his life with Cherish. He wasn't sure she would understand things like being deported, losing everything, not being able to travel and hard times in Jamaica. He wasn't sure if she would understand his dreams of travel and music. Why are you having these thoughts he said to himself. You just met this woman. But he knew this was the beginning of something.

"Yuh gwan lov de caves. Sistren yuh need a dip inna de mineral pool fi spiritual healing."

"If it's anything like the river bath, I'm game!" Cherish was excited. She felt alive and complete. As they entered the caves, the atmosphere was cool and calm. The cave was humongous with various caverns to explore. Water constantly trickled down the walls creating a musical complement to the whole scene. Cherish and Wisdom explored each cavern but now an occasional kiss became a part of the tour. Each time their lips touched both bodies tingled with sensations.

"See de mineral pool. Come tek a dip!" The pool was spectacular. The surface reflected all the colors of the rainbow. The pool was in the middle of a large cavern with walls that spoke if you listened. They spoke of mystic and ancient times.

17

S.D. Laurence

"Yuh mus climb down de ladder an dip yuhself. Nah let go, fi no one knows how deep de pool. Mi nah want fi lose de I cause mi just git yuh!" They both laughed as their voices echoed from the ancient walls.

"You show me what to do first and then maybe I'll try it!" Wisdom stepped on the ladder and lowered himself into the mineral pool. He held on the bottom rung and immersed his body three times. Cherish watched him as her body leaked with excitement. Her eyes followed his body as he climbed out of the pool with his tan athletic body glistening.

"Dat nice. Yuh must try Sistren." This time Cherish removed her bra without hesitation. Next she removed her wrap and there she stood with her bare breast and panties. Wisdom looked at her body and his heart leaped with desire. He had to have her, he thought. She was for him. He was a man who knew Jah and understood that what Jah has for you no man can take away. He knew that he didn't have to worry if she would understand him. He only needed to make love to her. Cherish climbed onto the ladder and slowly dipped her naked body in the water. The water had strange buoyancy. She felt that if she let go, her body would float away to an abyss. She couldn't forget that no one knew how deep the pool was.

"Dip yuhself tree times." As Wisdom watched Cherish dip herself three times. He thought of the holy trinity and his grandmother. He was a Rastafarian with strong Christian roots. His Panamanian grandmother taught him the importance of God's love and mercy. His Grandmother was a short, brown, beautiful woman with long straight mixed gray hair. She spoke Spanish fluently and would often say things in Spanish first then repeat it in Patois. Everyone knew and loved Granny in the yard.

"One, two, three. There you have it. I'm coming out Wisdom!" As Cherish stepped out of the pool her wet naked body caused Wisdom to want her more than he could ever imagine wanting anyone. He only had a few

18

Jamaican dollars but he needed to take her somewhere and pour himself into her. He thought about a Rasta friend that managed a small property with wooden huts that sat on the Roaring River. He would take her there, now!

"Yuh waan tour some more Sistren? Mi love fi see yuh enjoy Jamaica."

"Sure, I can't wait to see more of this beautiful island." As they walked toward the car, Wisdom and Cherish exchanged kisses and intimate touches. The ride was quiet, with Wisdom occasionally pointing out places of interest. Cherish sat quietly and soaked in the calming vibes that Jamaica offered. She was only here for two days but it felt like a lifetime.

Evening was beginning to fall. Wisdom parked the car along the side of the road and called out to a friend. Once again conversations occurred that she didn't understand. The friend opened a wooden gate and there was paradise. Scattered about in the lush surroundings were three wooden huts with bamboo roofs. The property sat on a river called The Roaring River. Flowers bloomed everywhere and birds sang to share their glory. Wisdom entered the car and gently kissed Cherish on the cheek.

"Excuse mi Sistren. De night soon come, yuh don't mind we rest here fi de night, git up early an head back tu Negril." He felt her hesitation.

"Don't worry yuhself, Mi won't do anyting yuh don't want mi fi do?" That was a problem for Cherish. She wanted him to do everything to her. She longed to feel his body inside hers. She didn't want him to think of her as a loose woman because she wasn't.

"I trust you Wisdom. This place is beautiful. In fact, each place is more beautiful than the last."

"Sistren dis only a small tour. Jamaica has some of de most beautiful views on earth. Dis God's country. De people dem struggle an wit struggle come blessings." They got out of the car and began to walk towards the cottages while the beauty all around reminded both of them of God's presence.

As they entered the cottage, there was a large bed in the center of the room with mosquito netting around it. Next to the bed were bamboo tables with lamps. The high ceiling had wooden beams that held a large ceiling fan. And when you stood quiet, the running river seemed to trickle with joy.

"Bathe yuhself inna de river outside Sistren. Yuh hab a long day. De river wata will revive yuh."

"Your right! You did come and capture me at daybreak."

"Yuh sorry yuh come wit de I?" Wisdom gently touched her arm as he spoke.

"No Mon. I wouldn't have missed this for anything in the world." Their lips gently touched. Cherish and Wisdom walked to their separate sides of the hut to disrobe and bathe. She put her clothes on a rock next to the river. She never imagined herself in paradise but it felt like destiny. She had struggled in her life but God's love and mercy continued to bless her daily.

Wisdom bathed on the next side of the cottage. His body was filled with anticipation. He too didn't want this woman to get the wrong impression of him. He was not a loose man either. He was very careful with whom he shared his prize possessions. There were many opportunities for him to fuck a white woman and go to Foreign but he had his pride. Wisdom finished bathing, wrapped a towel around his naked body, lay in the bed and waited for his Empress to come.

Cherish entered the cottage but this time her African wrap draped her entire naked body. Wisdom could see her stiff nipples as she walked towards him and slowly entered the bed. She kissed his lips and pressed her wrapped naked body close to his. She could feel his manhood grow as he gently removed her wrap to suck on her stiff nibbles. Her breast filled his mouth as he caressed them. After

20

completely removing her wrap, his hands slowly reached her hot spot.

Wisdom could feel how wet she was and wanted to enter her then but he waited. He continued to kiss her breast and use his fingers artfully to stroke her clit as she pulsated back and forth to his movements. When neither could wait any longer, Wisdom poured his manhood into her sweet pot and their bodies melted together in pleasure. Once inside, their bodies trembled with passion as they made love through the night. The last thing they both heard before their spirits joined in euphoria was a local youth shouting, "Go Rasta! Git it.

Chapter Two

Cherish awoke early as she did every morning and thanked her heavenly Father for life, breath, and every little thing. Cherish rarely remembered her dreams but this morning was different. She remembered dreaming of Wisdom. She was in love.

Six months passed since meeting Wisdom. During that time, Cherish traveled to Jamaica frequently and spent her entire summer vacation on the beautiful island with her new lover. Things had changed in her life. As she lay there, she began to fondle herself. Cherish liked to pleasure herself, especially in the morning. Wisdom liked that about her also because it took some of the pressure off him.

Cherish was about to climax when the phone rang. At first she started to ignore the ringing and continue stroking her clit, but then she thought maybe it's my baby. She reached for the phone, looked at the name the screen, pressed the talk button and began to speak.

"Baby it's you. Oh Boo, I miss you so much, my pussy misses you, and my whole being wishes you were here inside me." Cherish panted heavily as she spoke to Wisdom. Wisdom was a little caught off guard by the sound of her voice and then he remembered his baby and her morning ritual.

"Yes Babe mi miss yuh too. Touch yuh tits fi mi now. Touch dat pussy fi mi babe. Rub it hard babe. Rub it hard fi yuh babe. Is it wet, baby? Make it wet. Make it wet. Dat's right. Make it real wet fi yuh babe." Wisdom wished he could be there with his lover but he settled for listening as she reached full orgasm over the phone.

"Yuh okay? Yuh feel good? De I always waan mi babe tu be happy. Yuh know dat?" Wisdom spoke in a soft tone because he knew where his woman's head was right now. Cherish panted deeply into the phone, as she pressed hard on her clit. She eventually caught her breath and came back to this planet. She answered Wisdom still a little out of breath.

"Yes Baby, I know you want to make me happy because you do make me happy."

"Yuh frisky dis mawning. Wha up fi de day?"

"Same old, same old. Some people have to work for a living you know." Cherish was back to herself.

"I really miss you. You leave for England today, don't you baby?"

"Yes babe, mi gwan work fi yuh an mek a hit fi yuh." Wisdom was excited about the trip. He hadn't been out of Jamaica in many, many years. He longed to travel again.

"Baby may Jah guide and keep you. I'll see you soon. I'm scheduled to leave for England during my spring break. Love you Wisdom. Call me when you get settled."

"Yes, Mon! Love yuh, Cherish." Wisdom hung up the phone as he heard the driver arrive. Beep! Beep! Beep! The driver yelled.

"Come now Wisdom. Mi don't waan yuh tu be late, Mon." The drive to the airport in Mo Bay was exciting for Wisdom because this time he would be the one saying goodbye to Jamaica. Simon promised to talk more about producing his CD after he arrived but Wisdom knew that Simon only agreed to bring him to England because he thought he could help find and destroy Susan.

Wisdom didn't want to spend too much time on the Susan thing but Simon was addicted to her. The trip across the water was about 12 hours but Wisdom flew first class and anything he wanted was provided to him. While on the plane to England, his mind drifted back to the past.

***

He grew up in Trench Town, Kingston 12 amongst Bob Marley, Delroy Wilson, Joe Hicks and Peter Tosh. Wisdom knew that Jah was blessing him with a good future but he couldn't forget his past. He only finished 6 years of school because his Granny couldn't afford for him to stay. Wisdom was attending school without books and the teachers acted as if he didn't exist. So leaving school wasn't a big thing. It gave him more time to be in the yard and listen to all the music around him.

Being a ghetto youth, he started to follow the expected outcomes of living in the ghetto. He was fifteen when his first child was born. It was a big responsibility for a poor youth in Kingston so his stepmother, Gloria got him a job on a cargo ship that traveled from Jamaica to Miami. On his third trip, when the ship landed in Miami, Wisdom decided he would leave and never return.

"Mon, mi gwan inna de town tu git some tings fi mi Pinckney. Yuh waan anyting?"

"Nah but yuh ask everyone else?"

"Nah." Wisdom didn't want to take anyone's money because he knew he wasn't returning. But he couldn't refuse because that would cause unwanted attention. The result was Wisdom leaving the ship with more money in his pocket than expected. He headed for the nearest train station and boarded a train headed for Philadelphia, Pennsylvania.

Philadelphia was a city with a strong Jamaican presence and he didn't feel alone. Things went well for him in Philly. He and his Bredren got into the ganja business. The money flow was constant but Wisdom wasn't greedy. Granny's voice would remind him that money was the root of all evil. So Wisdom locked his door after he made a certain amount, while his Bredren went on to bigger and better drugs deals. They acquired big homes with swimming pools in Texas and Miami. They drove fine cars, drank the best wine and had multiple women.

Wisdom's life ambitions were different. A young lady named, Melissa caught his attention and he married her. The marriage was not without love but his illegal entrance into the country remained on his mind. He thought that marriage to an American would ensure his stay in the country. They had a son named Malik. He missed his first child, Grace, desperately but knew that he would see and show her love one day in the future.

Melissa was young. Wisdom met her while she was still in high school, took her to her senior prom and soon after they were married. Melissa was jealous but Wisdom didn't let the jealousy keep him from his path. Immigration was now on his back. So he and Melissa hired a lawyer to make the arrangements for the green card interview for married couples.

At the interview, the husband and wife are put in separate rooms. Each is asked a series of questions to help establish if the marriage is a business proposition or the real thing. After his interview, Wisdom waited patiently for the immigration officer to return and tell him to go home with his family. Instead, he was arrested and deported back to Jamaica by the end of the week. He was in shock.

He was shipped back to Jamaica with just the clothes on his back and the little money in his pocket. What had gone wrong? What did Melissa do or not do? Wisdom never saw Melissa again and there he was back in Jamaica with no job and no money.

***

Wisdom reached his destination, and it was time to return to the present. As he traveled toward the exit of the airport, there stood a tall White Man in a black suit with his name written on a small white sign. He approached the man and acknowledged that he was Wisdom to discover that Simon arranged for a limousine to pick him up.

The limousine drove to one of the most expensive areas in London, Chelsea. Simon lived very near the River Thames and the Albert Bridge. Simon was glad to see Wisdom. He and Wisdom talked many times on the telephone. Simon was beginning to think of this Black man as he friend. He was a redneck from America and racist by all accounts. He moved to Europe because he didn't want to deal with the attempt at equality America offered. It was difficult to get away from the other classes in America.

S.D. Laurence

England was different. The society was structured on class. Everyone had their place and didn't mind staying in it.

"Well hello Wisdom. How was your flight?"

"Great Mon! Thanks fi de limousine ride. Glad tu see yuh." Wisdom responded with sincerity.

"We have dinner reservations. I don't want to rush you but take a little time to freshen up and let's be on our way. Follow me and I'll show you to your room."

"Dat fine." Wisdom followed Simon upstairs to his guest room. Simon's home was simple but luxurious. The place was filled with leather, mahogany, glass and books. The guest room had a large bed with four large post. The room looked as if Queen Elizabeth herself may have slept there. There was a telephone in the room. Wisdom was glad to know that he had a Bredren, Actor, who lived in England. He didn't want to be alone in a foreign country with a rich white man. Wisdom quickly went for his phonebook to call Actor.

"Wha ah gwan Bredren? It's Wisdom."

"Wha ah gwan?" Actor answered eagerly. He was glad to hear from Wisdom. It had been a long time for him in "Freezin." Europe had a way of keeping a brother still and unmotivated. It was easy to marry an English woman and get on the Dole. Actor had fallen into that situation. He was looking for Wisdom to save him but Wisdom had to save himself first.

"Actor, mi an de white Mon goin tu dinner. Mi gonna drop de porno ting pon de Mon soon. Yuh far, Rasta?'

"No Mon. Me stayin wit a Bredren inna Brixton so mi come forward quickly."

"Cool Mon, mi soon call. Bless up Bredren." Wisdom hung up the phone, washed his hands, brushed his teeth and changed his shirt. He walked down the stairs and out the door with Simon. Simon owned a large silver Mercedes Benz. It was one of the few cars in England that had air conditioning. After all, Simon was an American in England. He couldn't be without one of the basic

26

American luxuries, air conditioning. As they drove out of the court yard, Simon began to talk about Susan.

"Yeah Wisdom. You see that house across from mine. That's where that bitch Susan lived before she ran away. She lived there with her husband and during the day when he was at work, she and I would fuck all day in my house. Man I spent too much money on that Bitch for her to leave without even a kiss my ass."

"Does her husband still live dere?"

"I don't know. I dare not go and ask any questions but I still watch the place. I even hired a private investigator. That's how I found out that she was possibly in Jamaica." Simon turned into a parking lot of a lavish restaurant.

"I hope you're hungry. This is a great place to eat." As Simon pulled in front of the restaurant, immediately the doors on both sides of the car opened.

"Good evening Mr. Werner. Hope you're having a good evening, Sir."

"Good Evening. My friend and I are having dinner tonight. He is my artist from Jamaica." Simon was proud. It surprised Wisdom that Simon was so proud of him. The entire evening would be spent with Simon showing off his new project, his Jamaican artist. Simon loved the attention and there would be no more talk of Susan for the remainder of the evening.

That night before going to bed, Wisdom prayed to Jah for strength and wisdom. He didn't enjoy the lies and deception. He thought about how he could help Simon. He wanted to rid him of his Susan obsession and also get his CD produced. He needed spiritual guidance for this task. The next morning, Wisdom woke early and called his friend Actor.

"Actor dis Wisdom. Come forward to Chelsea, Star."

"Yes Wisdom. Mi soon come. Gib mi de address now." Wisdom gave Actor the number and went downstairs to greet Simon.

"Good mawning Simon. Yuh sleep well?"

27

"Yes Wisdom. We had fun last night didn't we?" Simon spoke as he sipped his cup of coffee.

"Yes Mon. It was a good time. Wha fi breakfast?"

"I don't know Wisdom. The housekeeper is off today. Would you like to go out for breakfast?"

"Don't worry yuhself, Simon. Mi cook." Wisdom was glad to cook because he needed to know exactly what was going into his body. A Rasta didn't just eat any old thing. He hadn't eaten in the restaurant the night before. As Wisdom prepared to cook, Simon began to talk about Susan again.

"Yeah Wisdom, we must get Susan. I want to blackmail that Bitch. She told me that she never fucked a Black man but we both know she did. One day Wisdom, we'll call that Bitch and arrange a meeting. I'll be sitting close by and won't she be shocked when she sees the two of us together."

Wisdom thought before he answered. It was a good time to bring up the porno film. The plan was to tell Simon that Susan made a porno film sucking a Black man's Dick in Jamaica. Wisdom would tell Simon that he and Actor needed to go to Jamaica to recover the film to blackmail Susan with it. This way he could return to Jamaica and record his CD then bring it back to England for production.

"Simon mi did some investigation! Deres a porno film wit Susan suckin a big black dick inna Jamaica."

"What Wisdom! A porno film! That's perfect! Can we get it Wisdom? What will it take? Whatever it is I have it? Get me that tape!"

"Yes Mon! Mi can git it fi yuh." Wisdom began to spin the tale of Susan, the porno film, the bad bwoy named Rob Garland and Actor as his back up man.

"I don't know Wisdom. I want to get the film but I don't want you to get hurt over this Bitch either. Give me all the information you have and I'll get some people on it right away."

28

"No Simon! Dat's more dangerous! Jamaica is fi Jamaicans. No one else can do wha mi can do. Mi know de people. Remember mi moved amongst them?" At that moment Wisdom remembered that's Simon was a man of money and power. He had to be careful. The intercom rang and Wisdom spoke quickly.

"Oh mi forgot tu tell yuh! Dat mi friend Actor. Mi waan yuh tu meet mi Bredren." Simon pushed the intercom button and spoke to the guard at the front gate.

"He's on his way in now Wisdom." As Actor entered the front door, Wisdom called out from the kitchen.

"Did yuh bring de salt fish, green banana, cabbage, an yam Actor?"

"Yes Mon. Mi bring dem."Actor quickly scanned his surroundings as he extended his hand to shake Simon's hand.

"Glad fi meet yuh sir."

"The pleasure is all mine. Any friend of Wisdom's is a friend of mine. Please call me Simon."

"Okay, Simon it is." Wisdom entered the living room and took the bags from Actor.

"Yes Mon. Mi gonna fix a real Jamaican breakfast fi we."

"Well I've eaten monkey brain so why not a little salt fish and cabbage for breakfast?" Simon walked toward the kitchen followed by Wisdom and Actor. Wisdom began to prepare breakfast for the men.

"Don't worry yuhself. When de I git finished cooking, yuh waan more." While Wisdom cooked, Actor had an opportunity to interview Simon. He wanted to know all that he could. His motives were different from Wisdom's. Although both men wanted to use Simon, each of them had very different motives. Wisdom thought about how to repay Simon without him even knowing a debt was paid. Actor saw him as an external spring of money and opportunity.

Simon didn't like Actor. He wasn't like Wisdom. Simon could sense that Actor was trying to be something that he

29

wasn't. Simon distrusted his falseness. Wisdom was different. Simon knew Wisdom was himself. He didn't need to wear a mask. Simon was old but he wasn't a fool. The Susan thing had gotten a hold of him and caused him to do things he never imagined he would do. As Wisdom would always say, Pussy could lead a man astray and if he wasn't careful he'd never get away. The three men sat down, ate breakfast and discussed the Susan drama.

"You were right, Wisdom. Everything was delicious and I can't eat anymore."

"Dat's okay Simon. Yuh ate yuh fair portion." Wisdom thought it was time to make Simon remember the CD.

"Simon while mi inna Jamaica mi wanna lay de tracks fi mi CD. De musicians an studios dere fi de proper mix."

"Well Wisdom I know I said I would produce your CD and I will. But I want you to do a little project for me first." Wisdom hesitated before responding to the request. He knew that rich people were known to be freaks. They often lacked morals and integrity. Wisdom was poor but not in those areas. His love for Jah caused him to think before he acted. And of course Granny was always there to guide his path.

"Wha de project, Simon?"

"Frankly I never heard you sing and I don't invest in what I don't know."

"Yuh right Simon. Dats de behavior of a fool an mi know dat yuh no fool. So yuh waan de I tu sing fi yuh?'

"No Wisdom. I want you to write an original tune and I'll arrange for you to record in a studio in London. After that, let's see where we go from there?"

"Dat sound fair Simon. Gib de I week tu work de ting fi yuh."

"Now that's settled, what do you guys plan to do today? I need to go to the office and do some work."

"Mi waan look up mi family while mi here."

"You have family here?" Simon was surprised.

30

"Yes Mon. Mi Fada hab two Pinckney inna England. Mi hab a brother an uncle dat mi nevah know. Hopefully mi can link up wit dem."

"Great Wisdom, here's a few pounds to hold you for a while." Simon handed Wisdom 200 pounds.

"Jah bless de I." Wisdom spoke sincerely as Simon headed toward the door.

"The door will lock when you shut it and I should be home any time after 5pm. As a matter of fact, if you're here by 6:00 pm, we can go to dinner together." Once Simon was gone, Actor and Wisdom relaxed and caught up on old times.

"Wisdom dis man has a lot of money, Mon. I an I must take all we can. Remember his people took I an I from Africa."

"Actor some of wha yuh say right, but I an I mus nevah envy rich men." Wisdom finished cleaning the kitchen and prepared to go to Brixton and find his brother, Luke and his uncle, Lion.

This was Wisdom's first trip to London. Everything was old but clean and well kept. There didn't seem to be any homeless people or beggars on the streets like in Jamaica and America. In London, the Underground transportation was called "The Tube". Wisdom and Actor descended to London's Underground and boarded the Victoria Line to Brixton Station. As they disembarked from the train and traveled to the top, they landed in a section of London called Brixton.

Brixton was the neighborhood where mostly Jamaicans and Africans resided. The area reminded Wisdom of Jamaica. There was a market place with shops that held anything you might find in Jamaica or Africa. Music played loudly, as it would in Jamaica and men stood on corners making deals.

"Actor, mi hab tu find de pub called "The Den." Mi old man say, dem know Lion's whereabouts."

31

"Mi know de place, Wisdom." After a short walk, the two men located a small corner pub with a tattered sign that read, "The Den".

As they entered the pub, daylight quickly changed to darkness. Once their eyes adjusted, they could see a bunch of older men sitting at the bar with Red Stripe beer, Guinness Stout or White Rum. Others were sitting at tables playing dominos. Wisdom and Actor headed for the bar and ordered two Guinness Stout. In an English pub, most lagers were on tap and so Wisdom and Actor received two tall glasses of dark stout with a nice tan topping. As they slowly drank their stout, an older man approached them.

"Mi nah see yuh gents here before."

"No Star, I an I just come from Yard."

"Yeah Mon. Glad to see yuh inna Foreign. How's Jamaica. Mi nah been home inna twenty years." Wisdom could see the man's worn face and hands. Jamaica had its share of problems but the people didn't experience the wear and tear this man had his face.

"Jamaica, no problem." All the men at the bar laughed out loud.

"Seriously man mi lookin fi mi uncle. Dem call de Mon Lion?"

"Lion? Mi tink de Bredren at de domino table wit de white beard know de man." The man at the bar yelled at the man with the white beard sitting at the domino table across the room.

"Rubin yuh know one Bredren dem call Lion?"

"Yes Mon give mi a minute while mi beat dis pussy hole." Wisdom and Actor waited patiently while they slowly consumed their stout. Jamaican Ska played on the jukebox as Rubin finished his game of dominoes. After completing the game of dominos, Rubin began to walk toward the bar. As Rubin got closer, Wisdom could see that this man was an old gangster. The scars on his face revealed the remnants of battle.

32

"Who waan know bout Lion an why?"

"Lion's mi uncle"

"Lion has family?" Everyone in the pub laughed.

"How mi know yuh tellin de truth?"

"Trust me Mon yuh don't hab tu tell mi. Tell Lion dat Blacker's son Bruk Foot come from Yard."

"Blacker! Yuh know Blacker? Mi nah hear de name Blacker inna years. Mi know fi sure yuh an Lion family! Drink yuh stout now!" Wisdom and Actor finished their Guinness and followed Rubin to his car parked outside of the Pub. As they drove away, Rubin began to tell Wisdom stories about his father in England.

"Yeah Mon, yuh old man someting else. Yuh know de Mon married some poor white woman who breeded two Pinckney fi him. Mon when Blacker got him pay dat white woman would only gib him money fi cigarettes an transportation. Blacker hustled inna da streets tu make any other money him needed. De Mon beat de white woman, yuh see Mon, but one night him go tu far. Mi know cause yuh father come tell mi an Lion everyting dat go on dat night." Rubin laughed loudly

"Listen tu de storie now." Blacker came home drunk and miserable as he always did. He was tired of living the life he found himself in. He entered the front door as he did most nights, drunk. He barely made it to the sofa. As he laid there in a stupor, his wife approached him with her usual nagging.

"Blacker, can I have a word wit yuh? I hope yuh not fuckin no black woman and then comin home to fuck me. I'll have yuh black dick in me but I won't stand for yuh to bring no stink black pussy in my house." Blacker had enough. Who the fuck did this woman think she was talking to?

"Mi! Yuh talkin tu mi! Yuh Bumboclatt! Yuh betta be tankful fi dis Black Dick inna yuh stinkin white pussy! Get down on yuh fuckin knees Bitch! Bow down tu dis Black Dick!" Blacker's wife was nervous. She knew she had gone too far. She knew a beating was in store but not the one she would get that night. His wife began to withdraw.

"I must be fuckin flippin out or something. I'm sorry baby. Come to bed."

"No Bitch! Mi say git pon yuh knees! Bow down tu dis Black Dick!" He grabbed her by her hair and threw her to the ground. She began to yell for his mercy as he kicked her in her side and head.

"I said bow down tu dis Black Dick Bitch!" He would kick her over and over again as he repeated his slogan. The children, Luke and Joyce, were awake by now. Luke came in first and saw his mother lying in a puddle of blood on the floor. He knew not to say anything because he would risk the danger of being beat himself. Next to come to the living room door was Joyce, his baby sister. He looked at the shock on his baby sister's face and yelled at his father regardless of his fears.

"What yuh doing daddy? Stop Daddy! Stop!" Luke's voice broke Blacker's trance. He stopped kicking his wife and then turned on the boy. Blacker struck him so hard that his little body flew across the room and landed on the floor. The thump of his body against the wall brought Blacker back to his senses. He looked around the room and there was blood everywhere. He didn't know if his wife and son were dead or alive and he wasn't going to wait around to see. There in the living room door stood Joyce, his baby daughter.

"Joyce get yuh clothes on. We gwan tu get a doctor fe yuh Mommy an Luke." Blacker spoke calmly to his daughter. Joyce was in shock but behaved her father and went to her room to dress. While his daughter dressed, Blacker gathered a few things. He then grabbed his daughter, ran out the house, got in his car and drove directly to his brother, Lion. Lion hid Blacker until he was able to get two one way tickets to Jamaica for his brother and niece.

Surviving This Thing Called Life

Rubin's car turned down a small street lined with brick apartment buildings. London began to feel like New York to Wisdom. The street was dark. They parked on the small block, got out the car and walked a few feet to the side entrance of one of the buildings. Wisdom and Actor followed Rubin as he entered into a courtyard and walked up the back stairway of the filthy building.

Wisdom was always aware. His senses became alive. He was not a violent man but when put to the test his was a true warrior. Rubin entered the hallway and walked to apartment number 303. He knocked hard three times and waited for a sound from the other side. The hallway was dark and dirty. After a few minutes, a sound came from inside the apartment.

"Wha ah gwan?"

"Dis Rubin. Tell Lion dat Blacker's son, Bruk Foot, from Yard wit de I." Rubin spoke in a very humble tone. The roughness that Wisdom and Actor had witnessed all evening disappeared. There was only silence from the other side of the door. After about 5 minutes, the door slowly crept open. Rubin entered first and the two men followed.

The apartment was darker than every place they'd been that evening. All of the windows were covered with cloth to keep out any light. In the corner of the room sat a large dark figure. And from that corner came a gruff sound.

"Yuh claiming tu be mi family? Yuh betta be fuckin correct or yuh life will end tonight." Wisdom heard stories about Lion from his father but he never imagined that any of it was true. He prayed for the right words to say because Wisdom feared nothing but God himself. Wisdom thought of Granny.

"Mi Granny from Panama. Mi Granny's hair long an silver gray. She speak Spanish an she live inna Kingston 12. Dem call de I Bruk Foot an mi old man Blacker. Yuh help him leave Foreign an come tu Negril wit mi sista Joyce." Wisdom waited patiently for a response.

35

S.D. Laurence

"Come Closer." Wisdom walked toward the dark figure in the corner. As he got closer, the figure turned on a small lamp and held it close to Wisdom's face. He couldn't see Lion's face because of the glare from the lamp but Lion could see him.

"Bumboclatt! Yuh Bruk Foot. Yuh look lik yuh Fadda. Ain't dis a bitch! When yuh get here an what de fuck yuh doing here? Mon, it's good tu see yuh." The whole vibe of the room changed as Lion spoke happily to Wisdom. Everyone and everything relaxed.

"Peace an blessing uncle. Mi here tu mek mi music. Let mi introduce yuh tu mi Bredren Actor." Lion ignored Actor and continued to talk to his nephew, Wisdom.

"Yuh a singer man? Yuh old man use tu sing a few songs inna de Pub. Dat was til hem beat de shit out of dat white woman." Lion laughed and everyone in the room joined in. The laughter came from several corners of the room. In the corners of darkness sat three armed men. Wisdom thought to himself, Lion must really need protection and he got it from men. Wisdom was protected by God.

"Mi gwan back tu Yard soon. Me hab dis white man dat mi dealing wit. Dis Mon hab money an mi need fi use some of it. Mi need yuh help Lion."

"Yuh family Mon. Me nah turn mi back on family unless dem turn dem back on mi first." Wisdom shared bit and pieces of his plans with Lion. He sensed Lion's tendency to be iniquitous. He needed Lion but he didn't need his wicked attitude to dominate his mission.

"Well Lion now yuh hab it all."

"Wha dem call yuh? Mi know a big Mon lik yuh don't go by Bruk Foot."

"Dem call de I Wisdom."

"Bredren dat's a strong name. Mi know yuh didn't get dat name bein a fool. Wisdom, yuh uncle Lion dere fi yuh. Mi nah called Lion cause of weakness. Do yuh hab somewhere tu stay?"

"Mi stayin wit de White man fi now. Mi let yuh know if mi need a place tu rest mi head." Wisdom didn't really feel comfortable around all the heavy armor. He didn't leave Jamaica to end up in jail like so many other Jamaicans.

Wisdom and Lion spent the evening together talking about old times, drinking Guinness and smoking ganja. Every once and a while Lion would leave the living room, go into the bathroom and take a hit of the white dragon, Heroine. Lion had a gorilla on his back. Wisdom knew from their discussions that his uncle was a very intelligent man, but he chose to use his gifts for idiocy. Lion called his actions being revolutionary. He robbed banks because the White Man stole all the riches in Africa and he murdered to protect the money he stole. What an absurdity, Wisdom thought. Wisdom felt a sense of sadness towards his uncle. He chose the life of a slave. He was a slave to the dragon and a failing lifestyle.

"Bredren, mi waan meet mi brother, Luke." Wisdom stood up to leave.

"Yeah Mon. Luke would love tu meet yuh. Hem lik mi pinckney yuh know. Hem hate Blacker but hem love family. Come tomorrow Mon."

"Mi soon come Lion. Jah's guidance and protection" Wisdom walked towards the door and Actor followed.

"Jah guide Lion." Actor spoke in a soft and humble tone.

"Yes Bredren" Actor smiled because that was first time that Lion acknowledged him all evening. Both men exited the building and walked towards the large main street ahead.

"Where tu now, Wisdom? Yuh waan stay wit de I tonight over me Bredren's place."

"Yes Mon. Mi tired an mi nah waan stay wit Simon tonight." Actor and Wisdom continued to walk down the road together. It had been a long two days for Wisdom.

The next morning Wisdom woke early. He did have jet lag because of the time change but he was also anxious about

S.D. Laurence

all the miracles going on in his life. He woke to thank God as he did every morning. His thoughts went to his friend and lover Cherish. It was too early to call her because of the time difference. He loved and missed her.

His mind shifted to the project for Simon. It was important. The secret that he kept from everyone was that he was not convinced of his own talent. He knew that people envied him when he would record in the studio but he really wasn't sure why. I'll write a song about Susan he thought. He knew Simon would love that because of his obsession with the woman. He worked on the song for hours before Actor awoke.

"Blessings, yuh hab breakfast yet?" Actor greeted Wisdom as he entered the living room to find him working.

"Mi fix breakfast an go we go tu Coventry. De I can work undisturbed an yuh can meet mi queen an pinckney."

"Dat sounds good, Actor." Actor went into the kitchen and began to prepare breakfast for the two men. After eating, they prepared to travel on the bus to Coventry.

They took the Tube to the bus station, purchased their tickets and waited. As Wisdom sat and waited for the bus, he looked around at the advertising on the walls. Most signs dealt with the problem of terrorism in the country. The signs were filled with information on how to inform on your neighbor. They were meant to encourage people not to trust one another. They encouraged fear. Wisdom thought about fear and its power then his spirit reminded him of God's love. He knew that knowing The Father was living in absence of fear. He believed in the God of miracles.

The bus pulled into the station and people lined up in an orderly fashion. The experience was directly opposite to his Jamaican experience. In Jamaica, you hear haggler's yelling destinations and encouraging passengers to board specific buses. People are jammed inside like sardines. Bus and taxi rides in Jamaica could be very intimate. It is not

38

uncommon for butts to touch, breast to lie on neighbor's chest, arms around the neck, and unintentional hugs.

After boarding the bus, he noticed that everyone had a seat. He'd been in Jamaica too long. He didn't want to seem as though the experience was new for him, it wasn't. He loved his island but he also knew that the ability to travel was an education in life. After the orderly loading of the bus, the groups of passengers were on their way to the country. Once on the highways, Wisdom noticed a young woman speaking to each customer and returning with tea and biscuit. He turned to Actor.

"Mon dem serve yuh pon de bus?"

"Yes Mon. This is England, the queen's country. This shitstem do a lot of different tings tu control de people dem. De I will overstand inna time." The ride was pleasant. All roads were clean and the land was separated in orderly plots. It appeared to him that all of England was the same, orderly, identical and clean. Then he remembered Brixton, he would have to return there when he missed the action of home. Actor and Wisdom made is safely to Coventry.

Coventry is the ninth largest city in England that thrives on its small college community and various farm lands. But as in each English Hamlet there is Council Housing and that's where Actor and his family lived. Most people that lived in Council Housing were also on the DOLE. The DOLE was the welfare system in England. Unlike America, it is not a disrespectful position in England. It is more like a choice. Educational training and opportunity are available to everyone. If your choice is to become one of the inevitable unemployed, the government made sure your needs was met so that you wouldn't need to take from the people who made different choices.

Actor had his own one bedroom flat that was about five blocks from his wife and two children. The government understood couples separating therefore it was not uncommon to give housing to fathers to maintain family units. It was also not uncommon to see fathers walking their children to school, both parents spending time in their children's classrooms, yards with flowers and playgrounds where children played and laughed.

Actor and his wife were loving parents but they couldn't get along for more than a few hours. Precious, Actor's wife was gorgeous. She was a mix of Jamaican and Haitian. She was tall, slim, dark and mysterious looking. Actor was intimidated by her beauty alone. His problem was that he could not convince himself that a woman that beautiful really loved him. Their two children were intelligent and charming. Wisdom loved to spend time with the children and they loved to spending time with him.

Wisdom settled into his friend's flat to get a meditation and continue to write for Simon and his upcoming CD. He had a few songs but he needed more. The songs were there he just needed real meditation to write the words and music in his head. Wisdom needed vibes.

It was hard to focus. His baby, Cherish wasn't there even though they talked frequently and Actor kept the drama between himself and Precious going. Wisdom tried not to interfere but friends, family and strangers always consulted him for advice, hence the name Wisdom. Through all the confusion, Wisdom managed to complete the project for Simon. Wisdom picked up the telephone to call Actor and update him on his accomplishments.

"Actor, mi ready tu mek a move. Mi must meet Simon tu record de song. Yuh like de music man?" Wisdom wrote a beautiful reggae and blues mix composition for Simon.

"Yeah Mon, mi love dat. Precious givin mi shit bout gwan wit yuh. She fuckin flippin out cause de kids havin a flippin play at school an she wants me tu go. Is she completely fuckin mad?"

"Yuh wrong Actor. Yuh must support yuh wife an pinckney dem. Dere yuh life an future right now Bredren."

40

"Mi don't see de I wit yuh pinckney!" Actor was upset. He wanted to go with Wisdom and he also thought Wisdom should be supporting him not his wife.

"Yes Bredren, yuh right. But not cause mi nah want to. Mi can't Bredren. Yuh weren't deported an separated from yuh seed like a slave on de plantation. Bredren, mi don't hab tu answer tu yuh. Mi must answer tu Jah. Actor mi soon come." Wisdom hung up the phone. He appreciated the support his friend was giving him but he suspected that Actor was caught up in his aspirations and not his own.

Wisdom packed his bag and proceeded to get the bus for London. He left his friend a nice note informing him of his return, thanking him for his support and encouraged him to love and support his wife and children. Wisdom knew how to get about. He was a traveler although his traveling had been overdue.

He arrived in London with plenty of time to waste. He started to visit his uncle Lion but he gave it a second thought and decided to have breakfast alone in Brixton. He found a small Jamaican restaurant on a busy corner near the famous clock tower. As he entered, the smells of home reminded him of sun and sand. Wisdom took a seat and ordered ackee, salt fish, dumplings and yam. As he dug into his plate, he heard his named.

"Bruk Foot, Bruk Foot, It's yuh Bredren, Yardy." Wisdom raised his head to see his childhood friend. He hadn't laid eyes on him for years.

"How yuh know de I. Mi ain't seen yuh inna years."

"Yuh uncle tell mi dat yuh inna Foreign. Mi hear yuh voice an looked inna yuh eyes an mi knew it was Bruk Foot."

"Sit Bredren, yuh don't mind if mi eat while we talk?" Wisdom continued to consume his food.

"Yeah Man. Foreign been good. How long yuh here?" Yardy was flashy. It was obvious that he had become involved in some form of underground income. It could be numbers, gambling, prostitution or drugs.

"Mi here a month or so. Mi here tu produce mi CD Mon. When mi go back tu yard, mi plan tu record an return tu England tu finish it up."

"Yuh a singer, Mon? Mi nevah know dat. Mi doing a little hustle here. If yuh waan a package to sell while yuh here check wit de I. See yuh later, Mon." Yardy turned and walked out the restaurant to an apple red Porsche. He sped away as Wisdom finished his breakfast. He took his mind from Yardy and his drug selling, back to his morning recording session.

He sopped up the last bit of dumplings and salt fish, wiped his mouth, paid the bill, tipped the waitress and headed for the studio. Wisdom was anxious to record. He reached the recording studio in plenty of time, entered the front door and was greeted by a young blonde receptionist.

"Good day sir. How may I help you?"

"Yes miss. My name is Wisdom. I am here to see Mr. Werner." Wisdom spoke with his best English dialect.

"Yes! Mr. Werner is waiting for you in Studio A. Follow me." Wisdom followed the young lady down the hallway. The place was much larger than it appeared. When they reached Studio A, the young lady opened the double doors an inside was a complete orchestra with strings, percussion, brass and a Baby Grand Piano. There sat Simon with a bottle of chilled Champagne.

"There's my Jamaican artist, Wisdom. How are you? Are you ready to perform your new song?"

"Yes Simon. Mi wrote a song titled," Who's Gonna Love Me Now? Man's dis some set up yuh hab Simon."

"I know Wisdom. I believe in doing things the right way. You need the proper musicians to create the proper sound. Are you pleased?"

"Yes Mon. Let's get started." Wisdom began to discuss with the orchestra leader the sound he was trying to accomplish. He pulled out his guitar and began to play the

42

major cords of the new song. After many attempts, the melody began to sound the way Wisdom heard it in his head. He slowly introduced the lyrics as Simon listened to his artist' creation.

"Who's gonna love me now that you're gone? Who's gonna hold me and keep me strong?" Wisdom sang a few lines as the orchestra played. Simon was very pleased with his new find. He had lost Susan but gained a friend and he was enjoying the adventure. Wisdom finished the song and Simon stood tall and gave him a standing ovation.

"Man you have a good sound. I believe we can make money together. Won't it be funny when Susan sees you and me at the Grammy's winning an award?" Simon opened several bottles of expensive Champagne and everyone drank a toast to Wisdom and Simon's new partnership.

Chapter Three

The phone rang! Cherish quickly picked up the phone. She knew it was her to man.

"Hey baby."

"Wha ah gwan, Empress?"

"Missing you, that's all. How are things with you?"

"Everyting good, Cherish. Mi record de song fi Simon. Hem lov it an waan produce de album."

"Baby, that's great! I knew it would happen for you."

"De ting not fi de I. De ting fi I an I!"

"Yes Baby I know that. I leave in the morning so I'll be seeing you real soon. I love you and miss you. Jah Guide Lover."

Cherish and Wisdom hung up the phone and that night she dreamed about going to England and making love to her man. She couldn't wait to see her lover. They hadn't seen each for several months. During their courtship, she tried not to let any more than three months go by without seeing him. He was a good man but he was a man. Cherish knew he needed some pussy and she wanted that pussy to be hers.

Early the next morning, Cherish turned and looked at the radio clock. She realized that her cab would be there soon so she started down the stairs to head for the porch. As she got to the bottom of the stairs, she heard her mother's apartment door open.

"Cherish is that you?"

"Yes Mom. Remember, I leave for England today."

"Oh that's right, I almost forgot. Have a safe trip and call me when you get a chance. Remember Cherish, I said call me!" Cherish spotted the yellow cab pulling up in front of the house. She opened the front door and began to push her luggage out the front door, yelling back to her mom.

"Okay Mom, I'm leaving. I know, call you when I get there. Love you!" Cherish entered the cab and headed toward the airport. Cherish had never been to Europe. Europe was not on her list of places to see because of her afro-centric view of the world but she was excited about visiting Wisdom.

She was leaving Philadelphia at 7:05 am on British Airways and scheduled to arrive in London Heathrow Airport at 7:05 pm the same day. She was more than on time for the flight, she was early. She got her usual, a cup of coffee and whole wheat bagel. Then she sat down to relax before boarding the airplane.

It was finally time to board the flight and Cherish was more than excited. She was ecstatic. She didn't expect the makeup of the passengers. There were Africans, Jamaicans, East Indians and Europeans on the flight. Her expectation was to be one of the few black people on the flight. Cherish quickly took her seat and waited for the plane to depart. Once in-flight the cabin service began. It was wonderful.

The 12 hours were occupied with food, movies and booze. The seats were roomy and comfortable. The stewardess gave each passenger bag with slippers, eye mask, and tooth brush and tooth paste. The plane landed at Heathrow Airport in London as scheduled. Cherish made it through customs easily and rushed to meet her lover, Wisdom. As she exited from the customs area there he was standing tall and regal as usual.

"Wisdom!"

"Oh Baby it's you." Wisdom rushed toward his woman and embraced her.

"I missed yuh Baby. Yuh know dat right!" Wisdom whispered in her ear.

"I missed you too Wisdom." Cherish looked behind Wisdom and there stood a light skin young man with curly dreadlocks. Wisdom held tight to his baby while he introduced her to his traveling companion.

"Cherish dis mi half caste brother, Luke. The one dat Blacker run away an leave in de Queen's Land."

45

"Please to meet you, Luke. I heard about you before from Blacker in Jamaica."

"The man talks about me, Wisdom?" Luke was surprised

"Yes, Mon. Me tell yuh all de time dat Blacker waan yuh to com to Jamaica."

"Me nah waan see no man that leaves his half-caste Pinckney alone in Foreign."

"He didn't leave yuh alone man. He left yuh wit Lion." Wisdom laughed.

"Yeah look where dat fuckin got me."

"Man mi not here to talk about yuh family problems, Luke. Mi here to welcome mi baby." Wisdom turned to Cherish and gently kissed her on her neck.

"Sorry, Sister In Law but me father drive mi crazy. I'm so glad to see yuh. Me brother talk bout yuh all de time." Luke's accent was a mix between Patois and Cockney.

"Is dis one suitcase all yuh have?"

"Yes, you know that I like to pack light baby." Cherish smiled as she tightly held on her man. The three headed for the parking lot and loaded into a small green car.

"Cute car! What kind of car is this? I've never seen a car so small."

"Dem call it a Mini, Luke borrowed it from a friend to pick yuh up." Cherish and Wisdom sat in the back of the car on the way to Luke's flat. They were engrossed in each other. There was silence in the car except for their nonverbal communication. Wisdom was a loving man but not romantic according to Cherish's American standards. As much as she hated to admit, she was influenced by American movies, magazines and television. But tonight was different. Wisdom caressed her gently, while he passionately kissed her neck, then her shoulders eventually gently caressing her breast. Cherish was wet with anticipation.

"Oh baby I missed you so much." Cherish whispered in Wisdom's ear as he gently licked her exposed nipple.

46

"Mi missed yuh babe. Mi can't wait to be inside yuh." Cherish and Wisdom were finally alone in their room in Luke's small flat. They made love and both passed out. Cherish was exhausted from the long flight and Wisdom was tired from all the hustle of getting his record produced.

Cherish woke up early as usual. She was a morning person. She enjoyed that time alone when everyone else was asleep. Cherish enjoyed being alone even when she was with other people. She made her way to the kitchen and looked for coffee. As she rumbles through the cabinets, she heard someone coming into the kitchen. She hoped it was Wisdom because she really didn't feel like talking to anyone else this early in the morning.

"What de bloody hell are yuh doing so up early?" Luke spoke in a friendly tone to Cherish as he entered the kitchen.

"I'm looking for some coffee?"

"Look in the tin on the counter. Can yuh suss out how to do the rest?"

"Tin? What's a tin? And I don't know what it means to suss out, Luke." Luke looked at Cherish and pointed to the can sitting on the kitchen counter.

"Oh! And I guess you also meant figure out how to do the rest. Is that right?"

"Yeah, Mon dat's right. Yuh happy to see yuh man, Cherish?"

"Yes I am. I'm also happy that you agreed to let me stay in your apartment. I'm sorry, you're flat!"

"No problem, yuh family now! Me can't wait for yuh to meet Lion. Me know we'll see him today." Cherish and Luke drank coffee and ate biscuits quietly until Wisdom awoke.

"What yuh doin wit mi wife, Luke? Yuh tryin to tek her away when mi just got her?" Wisdom still looked tired even after the night of rest.

S.D. Laurence

"Nah, me randy but not dat randy. Dis is me Sista man, not just any old body. Yuh understand brother." Luke didn't like the joke that Wisdom shared so early in the morning.

"Loosen up Bloke, it's only a joke." Wisdom playfully hit his brother on the arm.

"Mi see yuh both already had coffee so mi going tu make mi some tea before mi get ready tu visit Lion."

"Yeah Mon, we must finish up dat business so we can be ready for Simon tonight."

"You have a meeting tonight with Simon, Wisdom? Is it about the album?"

"Kind of, Cherish. Mi tell yuh more later." Wisdom put Cherish off as he did when it was something he really didn't want her to know. After eating and cleaning the kitchen, the three got dressed for the day. Cherish wanted more sex but knew it was out of the question. Wisdom wasn't a day lover. He was more traditional. He needed night and a bed.

Cherish remembered the few times she did get the freak out of the man. Once when he picked her up from the airport in Montego Bay, Cherish was able to convince him to pull over and fuck her in the woods on the side of the road. She loved that shit! She was always bringing the freak out in a man but she really longed for someone to bring more of the freak out in her.

The three headed out the door and headed for the train. The borrowed car was obviously not going to be used today but Cherish didn't mind. She loved traveling on public transportation. It kept her in touch with the people. On "The Tube" individuals bought their ticket electronically for whatever zone they were traveling to. There were several zones and the further you traveled the more you paid. It was mostly an honor system but there were train officials on board who occasionally gave random checks. So of course, Luke brought the cheapest tickets for everyone to travel the farthest.

48

Surviving This Thing Called Life

The three exited the train at Brixton Station. They headed up the steep stairs to a variety of accents and busy streets with lots of traffic. Cherish hadn't seen much of anything yet. She landed at night and headed straight for Luke's flat and then to bed. When she reached the top of the stairs, she was in a place the reminded her a lot of New York City.

"Where are we?"

"Dis Brixton. Dis de part of London where most Africans and Jamaicans live. If dem don't live here, dem must come fi shoppin an partyin." Cherish was trying to take everything in as she, Wisdom and Luke began their walk up Brixton Hill towards Lion's place.

The first thing she noticed as they began their journey was the large clock tower that Wisdom spoke about. The area was filled with lots of people from different cultures and a lot of hustle and bustle in the streets. The scene was a complete surprise. She never expected to be in Europe and see so much diversity.

The area looked as if it was once a wealthy suburb with large houses that were converted into flats and boarding house. About three quarters up the hill, the trio turned down a street called Holmeswood Road. They passed by a quaint park, Bourell Park, filled with trees and well-kept flower beds and shrubberies. They walked up the steps of one of the four story brick homes. Wisdom knocked on the apartment door and a tall, black dreadlock man opened the door.

"You Pisshead's finally made it to mi flat! Mi tell yuh Blokes to come straightaway! Deres tings we must do before we see..." Lion stopped speaking as he noticed Cherish standing in the background.

"Who de fuck is dis? Yuh nevah fuckin tell mi yuh bringin company?"

"Dis Cherish, Uncle. Yuh know mi American Queen."

"Oh forgive mi Sistren. Mi nevah know dat Wisdom an his Queen come. Respect, happy to meet yuh." Wisdom,

Cherish and Luke walked into Lion's flat and sat in the living room. The place was sparsely furnished and messy. Cherish noticed that on the table in front of the couch, there were several pieces of aluminum foil folded in half. She wondered what that was all about.

"Cherish, yuh enjoying yuhself so far in de Queen's country?" Lion said in an authoritative tone.

"Well I only got in last night and I haven't seen much, but so far so good."

"Yuh gonna hab to excuse us men tu talk business." Lion got up and walked into the small bedroom right off the living room and kitchenette area.

"Baby, excuse de I." Wisdom reached over and gave Cherish a hug and kiss. He walked into the bedroom and was immediately followed by Luke. Cherish looked around to absorb all that she could. Her senses were heightened lately. She had to remember to be more observant. She noticed a small wooden box and opened it. The box was filled with pretty green ganja buds. She decided to help herself but remembered that she didn't have any paper so she called out to Wisdom.

"Yo! Wisdom can you come out for one moment please." Cherish waited for a response. She didn't like this we men have to talk shit. It annoyed her and she didn't know or care why. Wisdom didn't answer so she knocked on the bedroom door.

"Wisdom, did you hear me?" Wisdom flew out of the door as if he had an attitude but Cherish paid him no mind because she didn't believe that anyone would have the nerve to have an attitude with her.

"Sorry to bother you but do you have any paper so I can smoke a spliff while you men talk. You know how I like and need my medicine. So can you help a sister out?"

"Mek mi ask if Lion has some Rizla fi de Sista. Sorry fi leavin an not askin if mi can get yuh someting. Soon come." Wisdom quickly returned with the paper for Cherish.

"Thanks Baby. I'm alright now!"

"Yes Baby! Mi soon Come." Wisdom went back to the big meeting. Cherish rolled a spiff and took a long deep draw. The ganja was excellent. She continued to visually explore her surroundings.

It appeared to her that everything and everyplace was modest in England. People didn't over indulge themselves in too much of anything. That included space, furniture, cars or personal belongings. As she continued her visual tour, she heard someone unlock the door. As the door slowly opened, she could see the silhouette of a slim, average height white woman.

"Hello. How yuh doin? Me name Lilly."

"Peace Sister. My name is Cherish. I'm friends with Wisdom. They're all in the bedroom."

"Dem Blots always havin some big meetin and nothing nevah gwan on." Lilly laughed loudly and sat down on the couch next to Cherish. She pulled a small waxy packet of white power from her breast and laid it on the table. She continued to talk.

"Yeah, men act so important but dey ain't nothin but a whole heap of trouble. But dey say, yuh can't live wit em and yuh can't live wit out em." Lilly carefully poured a line of the white powder into a neatly folded piece of aluminum foil as she continued to talk.

"Yeah those bitches git on yuh nerves alright." Then she flicked her cigarette lighter and dragged it beneath the aluminum foil to heat the potion. As the powder heated, Lilly snorted it. Cherish couldn't imagine what this girl was snorting.

"Yuh want some?"

"No thanks." Cherish tried not to act or sound shocked.

"Yuh waan watch some telly?"

"The television? Yes, that would be nice." Lilly turned on the boob tube, sat back on the couch and began to nod. She would wake up from her nod intermittently and say something worthless and clueless to Cherish while she waited for Wisdom to exit the big meeting.

***

"So wha time de meetin wit Simon, Wisdom?" Lion was the first to speak.

"De time bout 9:00 inna de evening. So Lion yuh must act like de bad bwoy, Rob Garland. Remember yuh hab de porno tape and yuh waan 5,000 pounds fi it. Dis money fi yuh alone Bredren."

"Wha yuh mean fi him alone? Wha bout me?" Luke interjected into the conversation. Both men forgot that Luke was in the room.

"Yuh mi son, Luke. Yuh know wha fi de I is fi yuh." Lion spoke with a serious tone.

"No, mi know dat wha fi yuh is fi yuh habit first, den fi me!" Luke was serious also.

"Shut de fuck up, Bredren an listen tu de plan." Wisdom began to share the details of the evening events. Wisdom would take Simon to the Bamboula Restaurant in Brixton to meet Rob Garland and exchange the money for the porno tape. Because the tape is blank, Lion was to bring a young lady to the restaurant that would distract Simon and persuade him to watch the tape later.

By the time Simon discovers that the tape blank, Wisdom and Cherish would be on their road trip. Wisdom would have to use his charm and convince Simon that they were both deceived. He would tell Simon that Ray Gardner had returned to Jamaica therefore, he and Actor would have to go to Jamaica and retrieve Simon's money or the legitimate porno tape. Once in Jamaica, Wisdom would take the opportunity to record the tracks for his CD.

"Mi nah tek too long Baby?" Wisdom sat down besides Cherish and put his arm around her when he noticed Lilly nodding on the other side.

"No, you weren't too long. The ganja helped to occupy my mind while you were gone."Cherish then pointed to Lilly

"And of course I had Lilly to keep me company." Cherish laughed quietly.

"Mi need tu tek care of some business tomorrow night. Yuh don't mind being alone for awhile?"

"No I don't really mind." Cherish did mind but she knew complaining never got anyone anywhere. But Wisdom knew how to turn things around and bring out a good vibe in Cherish.

"Mek we go sightseeing!" Immediately, Cherish forgot about any complaints because she knew that time with Wisdom was always an adventure.

"Mek mi tek yuh tu de place where de Beatles recorded dere songs. Yuh know mi love dem White Buoys." Wisdom grabbed Cherish by her arms and lifted her out of the chair with a sweet kiss and embrace. He turned and looked at Lilly.

"Respect, Sistren. Tell de Bredren dem, dat mi gone." Wisdom held his Queen's hand and headed out the door. They headed down the stairs and walked down the hill toward the beautiful park she'd seen walking up filled with trees and flowers.

"Dem call dis place Bourell Park, Cherish. Yuh lov de place?"

"Yes, Wisdom, I love it." Cherish was happy to finally be alone with her man. They hadn't been alone for some time. The sex wasn't what she loved most about Wisdom. It was his sense of adventure. He had just enough mystery and excitement for Cherish. She didn't like boring. She needed exciting.

"Where are we going Wisdom?"

"Yuh soon find out." Wisdom held Cherish tightly around the waist as they walked briskly down Holmeswood Road.

"Yes mi Princess, mi tek yuh around de place. Yuh know mi yuh tour guide an cook." The two laughed and headed down the steep stairs toward the Tube and boarded the Victoria Line headed toward Oxford Circus. What Cherish discovered later, was that a circus was a circle in England.

"This circus must be here all the time if they named a train station after it?" Wisdom broke out in laughter. He was happy to know something that Cherish didn't know. He knew that she respected him for his street knowledge but her formal education intimated him.

"Nah, Sistren, when dem say circus dem mean a circle inna de road." Wisdom continued to laugh as to couple climbed to the top and exited the Tube. Outside, Cherish was surrounded by rows of quaint shops and historic looking buildings. The circle was filled with several red Double Decker Busses. As the couple waited to cross the road, Cherish watched as one red Double Decker Bus after another came around the circle.

"I really want to ride on one of those Double Decker busses, Wisdom." Cherish was fascinated by the constant movement of the busses.

"Be patient, Sista. Yuh know de I gonna mek certain dat yuh hab a good experience while yuh here. Mi really waan yuh stay wit mi."

"I'm staying with you now. I don't have anywhere else to go." Cherish laughed because she knew it was a language misunderstanding. This was a major issue between them.

"No Cherish, mi don't mean staying wit mi now, but yuh leavin Philly an comin tu live wit mi" Cherish was stunned. She didn't feel it coming. She knew Wisdom wasn't interested in marriage. He never got over the betrayal in his last marriage.

"Wisdom, what are you talking about? All I wanted was a bus ride and how did that turn into me staying in England with you?"

"Yuh know mi shy, Cherish. Mi didn't really know how to ask yuh. Mi know dat mi askin yuh tu give up a lot."

"Let's take one step at a time. I really want to ride on one of those Red Double Decker Buses first!"

"Come Cherish!"Cherish followed Wisdom towards the Big Red Double Decker Busses. They boarded bus number 139 and climbed to the top.

"I'm really lovin this place Wisdom. Be careful what you ask for because you just might get it." Cherish and Wisdom rode quietly on the bus, holding each other tightly.

"Cherish, see de place where de Beatles recorded most of dem music. Yuh know mi luv dem white buoy's!" Cherish and Wisdom climbed down from the bus top on to Grove End Road and walked across the famous Abbey Road zebra crossing to the Abbey Road Studio.

The studio was a splendid 19th century building with an inconspicuous engraved sign that read "Abbey Road Studio." The couple took pictures outside the building and waited for an opportunity to get a photograph of them kissing at famous Abbey Road zebra pedestrian crossing. After a day of excitement, the couple headed back to Luke's flat for the night.

The next day Wisdom woke Cherish early in the morning with a good fuck and a great cup of coffee. These were two things that Wisdom knew would certainly please Cherish. He wanted to make her happy and convince her stay with him. He really didn't know in what part of the world he would be but it didn't matter. He could feel success at his heels and he wanted Cherish to be there with him. In a lot of ways, he felt that his blessings were a result of being with her. She had such a good vibe. She was generous and not too bossy like other African American women he knew.

"Cherish let's get dressed. Me hab a full day fi yuh." Wisdom knew that Cherish would be happy staying in the bed and cuddling all day, but he also knew about his plans with Simon later that night.

S.D. Laurence

"Okay baby, your request is my command." Cherish and Wisdom were both ready to leave in less than 30 minutes. Wisdom loved that Cherish didn't spend a lot of time preparing to leave the house. She was a natural beauty, so there wasn't much more to do that would improve what God had already done.

"Yuh look beautiful mi Queen. Yuh locks, Sistren. Dem beautiful. Mi just love dem an me luv yuh too. Girl, mi luv yuh like cooked food!"

"I love you too Wisdom and I'm glad that God found a way for us to meet. Now let's get out of here." They two love birds left the flat and headed for the Tube toward Westminster station. The couple exited Westminster station and boarded a tour bus. The first part of the tour was a drive past Big Ben and Parliament Square. Next on the itinerary was a visit to the historic Tower of London. The guide on the bus spoke.

"The Tower of London is a historic monument in central London on the north bank of the River Thames. The buildings have the appearance of a pleasant Tudor square, but they were actually the Queen's apartments. The apartments surrounded the place of execution where the Tudors ensured that all noble traitors lost their heads. The Tower of London has served as a place of execution and torture, an armory, a treasury, a zoo, the Royal Mint, a public records office, an observatory, and since 1303, the home of the Crown Jewels of the United Kingdom." The bus stopped and the tour group got off the bus. They walked toward a drawbridge to continue the tour and were greeted in the middle, by all accounts, a Beefeater. Cherish assumed the man was a Beefeater because of her mother's drinking habits. Her mom drank Beefeater Gin and she always remembered the unusual man on the bottle.

The Beefeater led them on a guided tour explaining the history behind the fortress of imprisonment and torture. After the tour, Wisdom and Cherish boarded the tour bus and headed to Buckingham palace. The pair got off the bus at the Mall to watch the changing of the Guard ceremony as one of the Queens Foot Guard Household Regiments marched from St James Palace to Buckingham Palace to military music dressed in their world famous tunics and busbies.

Next they took a short cruise on the River Thames enjoying scenic views of St Paul's Cathedral and Shakespeare's Globe. The boat landed at Cadogan Pier in Chelsea, right down the street from Albert Bridge.

"Wisdom you've really outdone yourself. The day has been beautiful. Where are we now?"

"Dem call dis place Chelsea, London's Riverside Village. Look tu de left, deres de famous Albert Bridge. Yuh must see de bridge inna de night, de ting beautiful. Come Cherish, mek mi tek yuh tu mi friend Simon's house. De walk nice." They walked back down Chelsea Walk for a short piece, made a right on Flood Street to Loo Street and made a left which landed them at the entrance of a small gated community. Wisdom and Cherish proceeded toward the red brick and Iron Gate and was greeted by a security guard.

"We're here to visit Mr. Werner?" Wisdom spoke politely to the guard.

"Gladly sir." The security guard picked up the phone, dialed a few numbers, spoke a few words and allowed Cherish and Wisdom to enter through the gate. On the other side was a most elegant village with neatly groomed English gardens all around. The grass was neatly manicured with red brick paths that led to elegant wooden doors with gold knockers. The small village was obviously a place where the wealthy lived because it was filled with posh Town Houses.

What a swanky place Cherish thought. This Simon must have a lot of cash. Cherish quietly followed Wisdom as he walked toward one of the town house doors and rang the bell. The door was immediately opened and they were greeted by an older big belly gentleman with a large cigar in his hand.

"Wisdom, come in. I'm so happy to see you. I thought we were meeting tonight for dinner but any time with you is great. Who is this beautiful young lady with you?"

"Dis mi queen, Cherish!"

"So this is Cherish? Wisdom talks about you all the time. I wondered if you were real because you sound too good to be true." Simon smiled as he spoke.

"Come inside. Take a seat. Can I get you something to eat or drink?"

"Nah, mi tek de Queen on an official tour today. I an I was inna yuh area so mi decide tu let yuh meet mi princess."

"I'm glad you did, Wisdom. I wouldn't have missed meeting this beautiful lady for the world." Cherish didn't feel sincerity from Simon's comments. She heard sarcasm in his voice and felt fear in his spirit. Why did he fear her she thought to herself?

"I have some cognac, Cherish. Would you like a drink?" Simon went behind his leather bar and prepared Cherish a snifter of warm cognac.

"Here, Cherish. I hope you enjoy the drink."

"Thank you." Cherish decided to show Simon that she knew how to drink a snifter of cognac properly. First, she held the bottom of the wineglass in the palm of her hand to ensure it was warm. Next, she placed her nose on the edge of the wineglass and inhaled the aroma.

"This is lovely." She said as she gently swirled the cognac in her glass and gave the cognac another sniff. Finally, Cherish took a small sip.

"You like?"

"Yes! I do!" As Cherish sipped the cognac, the pleasant smell dried apricot flowers and cinnamon filled her nose.

"This is $5000 Courvoisier." Simon said proudly.

"I apologize for not having an open bottle of the $55,000 Remy Martin Cognac Black Pearl Louis XIII to share with you. How about next time? I'm sure there will be one." The two held their glasses up to acknowledge the invitation.

"Wisdom, I didn't ask if you wanted a drink because I know you don't indulge in the strong stuff."

"Yuh right, Simon. Mi nah mess wit de strong stuff but mi waan de beautiful bottle."

"Oh, so you noticed! The decanter itself cost a couple of hundred dollars. No two are alike. Each one is hand blown and numbered by Lalique, a famous French crystal maker. You may have this decanter my friend."

"Blessing pon yuh, Bredren." Wisdom was truly grateful for the gift.

"So Cherish, are you enjoying England? And Wisdom, are you showing Cherish a great time?"

"Yes, Mon. I an I went tu de London Towers an did all de royal stuff. De cherry on top was de dinner boat ride down de Thames."

"That sounds like a perfect day. I couldn't have done better myself." Simon was proud of Wisdom.

"Cherish, are you dining with us men this evening?"

"I don't think so Simon. I realize it's a business meeting and I've had a real busy day today. Tonight will be a good time for me to rest because we're leaving on our road trip tomorrow."

"Is that right? Where are you two going?"

"Mi gonna drive up the M1 and stop in Coventry, Manchester and stay a couple of days in Liverpool. Yuh know how mi love de Beatles!"

"That sounds like a wonderful time Wisdom. I know you will enjoy yourself Cherish."

"Simon, mi nevah waan keep yuh long. Mek mi tek Cherish tu de house an mi soon come."

"Do you want the limo driver to drop Cherish off and bring you back here afterwards?"

"Yuh know dat sound great Simon." In fact, the ride went right along with Wisdom's plan. This would be the

59

excuse he needed for Lion meet them at the restaurant. Cherish and Wisdom said goodbye to Simon as they loaded into the Limo and took a leisurely ride to Luke's flat.

After arriving at the flat, Wisdom escorted Cherish inside and made sure she had everything she needed for the evening. He made his way back to the Limo. Before getting into the Limo, Wisdom pulled out his cell phone and dialed Lion's number.

"Peace Bredren dis Wisdom. Yuh must meet mi at de restaurant."

"Yuh nah waan de I tu go tu de restaurant wit yuh? Lion sounded more hurt than anything.

"No, Mon. Mi hab Simon's limousine an mi must drive an git de Mon." Wisdom was gentle with his uncle. He knew that underneath all the gangster stuff there was a man with a big heart.

"Mi overstand, Wisdom. Mek mi hear de plan" Wisdom reiterated the plan to his uncle. He finished his call and hurried inside the Limo so the driver could pick up Simon. He was anxious to get this bandulu business out of the way.

The limousine reached Simon's home safely, he entered the Limo and the two men headed for the Bamboula Restaurant at the bottom of Brixton Hill. As Simon and Wisdom reached the restaurant, they were greeted by the most beautiful brown Jamaican woman that both men had seen in a long while.

"Respect Bredren. Yuh wanna sit inside or outside. De outside nice. Mi recommend dat fi yuh." The two men were mesmerized and followed the young woman to an area filled with bright colors and thatched roofs over small tables that gave you the feel of a real native Jamaican restaurant.

"Tek a seat an de menu. Mi soon come tu tek yuh order." Both men stared at the bodacious booty on their waitress until it disappeared.

"Wisdom, I love this place. It reminds me of the restaurant in Negril except for the white sand, blue seas and warm breezes." Both men laughed remembering their short time together in Jamaica.

"What time is your friend supposed to get here with the video? I've been waiting patiently all day for this moment."

"Relax Simon. De Mon soon come. Mek we enjoy de evening an de structure of de waitress." Wisdom sat back and began to roll a spliff. He'd been to Bamboula before and he knew it was cool to burn a spliff in the backyard.

"You mean her body Wisdom. I knew I wasn't the only one who knew perfection when he saw it." The waitress returned to the table ready to take the men's order.

"Dere anyting mi can get yuh from de bar." The waitress had a sexy Jamaican accent.

"I'll have a chilled bottle of your best Champagne. What time do you get off this evening my dear lady?"

"Mi! Mi git off work bout midnight when de place closes." The Bamboula was an after hour spot when the restaurant closed. Wisdom knew it was the perfect spot to get Simon relaxed and off guard. But Wisdom would also protect Simon under all circumstances. No one was going to take advantage of Simon but him and he had his limits.

"Then you better chill a few more bottles because I'm not going to stop drinking until you're able to have a drink with me."

"Dats fine wit mi Bredren. Mi love tu hab a good time an yuh seem tu enjoy life. Mi soon come wit de Champagne. Yuh waan drink, Rasta?" Wisdom knew the waitress was interested in him and not Simon but he needed her to pay more attention to Simon.

"Git de I a Guinness." Wisdom was not friendly with the young lady when he spoke. As the waitress walked away, both men took the time to watch the beautiful scenery.

61

"I hope you order food for me Wisdom because I have no idea what's good here. I'll have to trust your judgment. You've sure trusted me a few times or more."

"No problem. Mi love dat!" The waitress returned, popped the bottle of Champagne for Simon and served Wisdom a Guinness with a smooth, creamy white head that sat just above the lip of the pint glass.

"Yuh ready tu order, Bredren?"

"Yes Sistren, mi waan some red peas an rice, callaloo, escovitch and bammy. Sistren just bring some large bowls filled wit de food an plates. Mek we serve ourselves. Deres gonna be more company later in de night. Dem call de I Wisdom if someone ask."

"Nice tu know yuh Wisdom." The waitress was very aggressive with Wisdom. She liked Simon for the money but for sex she wanted a Jamaican. Wisdom was tired of being used by women.

Over the years, he felt he was getting over fucking woman but to his surprise it was the woman that were taking advantage of him. Plus he was satisfied with Cherish. His only discontentment in life was his inability to attain fame. It has always been his dream and he was determined to see it to the end.

"Sistren, keep de drinks comin an if yuh don't mind, keep yuh focus pon de old man. Do dat an mi mek sure yuh git a big tip."

"No problem Bredren. De Rasta waan meet later dis evening?

"No disrespect Sistren. Trust mi, yuh beautiful but mi hab mi Queen an mi cook an curry." Wisdom and Simon ate and drank for hours before Lion showed up with Lilly, the thin dope addict white woman from his living room.

"Wisdom mi glad fi see yuh." Lion briskly walked toward the table acting too anxious. His addiction was evident now because in the old days money didn't excite him. He literally robbed from the rich and gave to the poor. He never kept anything for himself. It was the thrill

62

he loved but times were different now. He craved the dope and he knew money could get him more of what he needed.

"Respect. Pull up a chair fi yuhself an de lady." Wisdom coughed as he made the lady statement. Lion looked over at the next table and grabbed two chairs for himself and Lilly. He knew that Wisdom wasn't pleased with him bringing Lilly but she turned a trick and made enough money to get the two of them real high. Also, he didn't want to leave Lilly alone in the flat with the drugs they hadn't consumed yet.

"Simon, dis Ray Gardner."

"Please tu meet yuh Mr. Gardner. Glad you could join the party. Can I get anything for you and the young lady? There's food and plates on the table. Would you like me to have the waitress get you something else?" Lion and Lilly were high on heroin and the last thing a heroin addict wants is food.

"Mi tek a Guinness Stout." Simon called for the waitress.

"Ruby, Ruby will you bring two Guinness and another bottle of Champagne to the table?" Simon lit his cigar and sat back in his chair. He took a good long look at Ray. His inner sense told him that Ray was not a trustworthy man. In his business, there was honor among thieves but he knew Ray wasn't the type of thief he wanted to do business with. Ruby quickly returned to the table with the requested libations.

"Is dis everyting yuh waan Simon? Mi be free in another thirty minutes. Keep a seat fi mi now!" Ruby looked toward the skinny, dope fiend at the table as she spoke.

"Baby you have the best seat in the house! I guarantee that Ruby." Simon smacked Ruby on her hard, round ass as she passed by the table.

"Well back to you Mr. Gardner. I never like to draw out a business deal so let's get to it. First of all, I don't know your girlfriend so she can to go to the ladies room while

63

we talk?" Wisdom was impressed with Simon's skills. The old man wasn't a straight push over. Even after a few drinks, he still had his wits about him.

"No problem, Mr. Simon." Lion quickly turned to Lilly and briskly waved his hand. Lilly knew the hand wave meant for her to get ghost. Lilly picked up her skinny bones, glass of Guinness and headed toward the door. She didn't give a fuck. She knew there was more dope at home anyway.

"Do you have the item with you Mr. Gardner?"

"Yes Mon, mi hab de tape." Lion wasn't excited any longer, he was thinking about the package he left at home.

"Are we still talking about 5,000 pounds?" Simon was frank and to the point.

"Yuh, Mon." Lion was getting nervous again. The mention of the money made him forget about the little piece of dope he had at home.

"Wisdom, how do you suggest we made this exchange? I'm really enjoying my evening and I want to get back to just that, enjoyment."

"Wha ah gwan, Simon?" Ruby joined the conversation and smiled as she spoke while rubbing on Simon's bald head.

"Nothing lovely Ruby. Are you coming to join me?"

"Yes, Mon. Mi feel Irie. Mi need a drink, Simon." Simon leaned over and spoke to Wisdom in his ear.

"Wisdom, I'm going to give you the envelope with the money and I want you and Mr. Gardner to go outside and make the exchange. I'll look at the damn thing later. Right now all I want to look at is this brown sugar next to me.

"Ruby, mek mi git yuh some drink. I an I gwan wait pon yuh." As Wisdom was speaking, Simon placed the envelope between Wisdom's thighs under the table. Wisdom picked the envelope up and slid it under his shirt as he exited the table with Lion following quickly behind. Wisdom and Lion went to the inside bar and quietly made the exchange.

"Wha up wit yuh bringing Lilly? Yuh must know dat Simon nah waan no dope woman?" Wisdom was upset but happy that there was a beautiful waitress there to fill the role. He didn't expect a response from his uncle so he proceeded with his conversation. He needed to get back to Simon.

"Lion yuh know de money is fi yuh an Luke. Don't fuck up de Bwoy's money pon dope fi yuhself!"

"Mi nah do dat, Wisdom. Yuh waan keep de money fi yuh brother?"

"Mi glad yuh say dat cause mi nevah waan tell yuh what fi do."

"Mi soon come." Lion left the bar, went into the men's room and returned with rolled up money wrapped in paper towels. He gave the bundle to Wisdom and he quietly put it in his jacket pocket. Before returning to the table with Simon, Wisdom returned to the bathroom and distributed the money safely in various areas of his body.

"Yuh feelin good Simon?"

"Yes, Ruby and I are enjoying ourselves." Ruby was sitting on Simon's lap rubbing his balding head while squirming her big ass on his penis. Wisdom didn't want to interfere with what was going on. Everything had gone as planned so far. He wanted to get out of there and head home to Cherish. But, he also wanted to make sure Simon was okay in the process.

"It's getting late Simon. Mi waan git some rest fi mi road trip inna de morning." Simon turned to Ruby.

"Ruby, you want to take a ride in the limo with me? Let's go together and have a few more drinks at a special place I know." Ruby looked at Wisdom before she spoke. He gave her the nod of acceptance that she needed to say yes.

"Yes Simon, mi waan spend more time wit yuh. De night's still young an so are we."

"Wisdom, you want us to drop you off at home?"

"No, Mon. De I tek a cabby tu de flat."

"Then let me give you some money for the cabby. My business brought you here so it's only right that I make sure you get home." Ruby moved from Simon's lap so that Simon could rise to get the money he wanted to give to Wisdom. As Simon fumbled to retrieve the money from his pockets, Wisdom moved closer to Ruby and whispered in the ear.

"Tek de man wit yuh. Git paid but nah rob de man." Ruby nodded to Wisdom to let him know that she agreed. She knew not to mess with a Jamaican man and his money. She knew that Simon was some sort of cash cow to Wisdom and that she could capitalize on the situation also.

"Here Wisdom." Simon handed Wisdom a wad of money.

"Get home safe my brother. I know I'll be safe with Ruby."

"Mi know yuh will." Wisdom gave a final look at Ruby to let her know that he really didn't want no shit out of her. The trio walked to the door together. Simon and Ruby entered the limo and Wisdom slipped the tape to Simon. After saying his goodbyes, he entered a cab waiting at the curbside to head home. Wisdom was happy that part of the plan was complete.

"Is this the flat, sir?"

"Yes, Mon." Wisdom exited the car and headed towards the arms of Cherish. When Simon viewed the video that next day, it was blank. Cherish and Wisdom had already begun their road trip when his cell phone rang.

"Wisdom what kind of shit is this. I'm old Wisdom but I'm not dumb."

"Wha ah gwan?"

"You know what the fuck is going on Wisdom! I always thought you were a man of integrity?"

"Mi don't know wha de word integrity mean but mi know dat mi a man of Jah."

"Well, your damn Jah must be money because you sure as hell took my mine."

66

"Mi nah tek no ting from yuh Bredren."

"Wisdom, the video tape is blank."

"Dat fuckin Ray Gardner! Simon! Mi know dat a Mon must nevah buy someting hem can't see. Forgive mi Simon, mek mi tek care of dis fi yuh."

"You damn right you're going to take care of this shit!" Simon was livid, but Wisdom managed to convince Simon that he and Actor would find the scoundrel, Ray Gardner, and retrieve the money or another tape. So as destiny would have it, after Cherish returned home, Wisdom and Actor were on a plane headed for Montego Bay, Jamaica to retrieve the tape or money from Ray Gardner.

S.D. Laurence

Chapter Four

Wisdom was on the airplane heading back to Jamaica. Things were going well. He felt blessed. He had the love and support of a beautiful woman and his music was starting to bust wide open. Even though he had to be a bit devious to achieve his goals, he knew his blessings were coming.

"Welcome to Jamaica, ladies and gentlemen." The stewardess proudly announced as their plane landed in Montego Bay and the passengers applauded. Actor hadn't been home in more years than he cared to remember.

"Wisdom mi can't thank yuh enouf fi de trip. Mi can't believe dat mi back inna Yard, Mon."

"Yes Mon. Yuh home."

***

Cherish was back to her normal busy schedule. The thought of her living with Wisdom in Jamaica was enticing! Plans had changed! He no longer wanted her in England. He said he needed her in Jamaica!

Why not be daring she thought! She could take a leave of absence for one year and still be assured of a job when she returned. Besides, she'd accumulated a few bucks in her pension. Scott, her first husband had robbed her blind and she knew she had to work until the end of time. She never really shared that with too many people, so when asked about retirement, her response was always.

"Me retire! The only retirement I'll ever get is being taken out of here in pine box." Then she would laugh hardily. Cherish felt she would never be able to afford to retire so why not enjoy some of what life had to offer now!

"What you thinking about Cherish?" Dee asked in a quizzical tone.

"Man, I don't even know. There's so much shit going through my mind right now, I don't know what to think."

"Try me Cherish! You always giving advice and listening to other people's problems. Talk to me Sis! Besides, I

68

know your problems are going to be more exciting than mine." Dee and Cherish both laughed as Dee shut the office door.

"Put the Do Not Disturb sign on the door knob, Dee. You're right I need to share."

"Well share girl!" Dee sat down put her fist underneath her chin and listened intensely as Cherish spoke.

"You know I've been dating this Jamaican guy for some time now and he wants me to move in with him. And I don't know what to do! I've been real happy being single. It's given me an opportunity to focus on my work. These children are like my own. No, they're not like my own, they are mine. I love them like I love, Tyreek. There's not nothing I wouldn't do for him or them. Tyreek is doing great and I want the rest of my children to have a chance at success also. If I'm in Jamaica how can I be helpful to any of my children?"

"Wait! Wait! Cherish! Did you say Jamaica?"

"Yeah, Wisdom wants me to move to Jamaica with him while he records and produces his CD." Cherish answered in a matter of fact tone.

"What the fuck do you have to think about? You see what I mean? Your problems ain't shit! Go with him girl. You like him, he likes you and you get to leave this shit hole!"

"Don't say that shit, Dee. That's real fucked up. You know I love this school and this town. You know that!"

"That's because your ass is crazy as shit! In a good way! You live on the good side of town and only hang out with us when you want too!" Dee laughed.

"Fuck you, Dee! I really don't know what to do? I know Wisdom but I don't know him. Our cultures are very different and I know that can be a problem. It's not unusual for me not to understand a thing he says and I know the same thing happens to him! I also feel some kinda way about moving to a place where I have no family or friends."

S. D. Laurence

"Y'all got the universal language, LOVE! And if something goes down, you know your people will get the first thing smokin to Jamaica!" Dee was smiling now. She was happy for Cherish.

"That's it Dee! I don't know if I LOVE, LOVE him. I might love him but I really love everybody. The impulsive part of me wants to go but I was trying to control that part of my spirit."

"What type of spirit do you want Cherish? You want a spirit of fear? I don't know that much about your life because you're a private person. Yeah, you love everybody else but do you let them love you in return?"

"You know you just might have something there, Dee? Thanks for listening. I love you. You really gave me something to think about." The two women embraced and went their separate ways. Cherish sat at her desk and thought about her impulsive self. It was as if she was always trying to fill something in her life and she didn't understand what the emptiness was all about.

***

Wisdom was elated to be home. The air still smelled sweet and the Sea was still blue. When Wisdom and Actor disembarked from the plane, they quickly made it through customs and out the door of Sangster Airport. Wisdom looked around and there stood his beautiful daughter Grace standing with her new husband, Rashaun. Wisdom walked toward his daughter with open arms. As they embraced, Wisdom felt everything he needed at once. He was home and in the arms of someone he loved and love him.

"Grace, mi glad fi see yuh."

"Me too Daddy. Meet my husband, Rashaun." Wisdom extended his hand and gave Rashaun and stern shake. It wasn't that he didn't like him but he wasn't really happy about any man marrying his daughter.

The two, Grace and Wisdom held hands and walked toward the car while Rashaun and Actor trailed behind

70

them. Their closeness was one that couldn't be intruded upon and everyone who saw them together noticed it right away. She loved her dad and he adored his beautiful, strong and intelligent daughter. They all loaded into the car and exited the car park to head toward Grace's house.

As they pulled into Grace's driveway, he remembered when he somehow found the money to send her to cosmetology school and the investment paid off tenfold. She owned her own home complete with housekeeper and nanny for her son. Rashaun wasn't the child's father but from all that Wisdom witnessed no one would ever know.

"Mi lov de new house Grace. Yuh know how fi manage yuh money. Yuh didn't go to America an lose yuh mind buyin clothes an tings. Yuh brought yuh money back an built a house. Mi need fi follow yuh an come back home when mi mek mi fortune."

"You better do that! I don't want you to act like everyone else and lose your roots, Daddy. I miss you and you have a grandson now that you need to get to know. You can always come and go for business." Grace smiled at the thought of having her father close again.

"Enougf talk bout business. Wha bout mi dawta? Mi see yuh hab de American accent?"

"Daddy you know I spent two years working in the states and I like the American accent. Mi can switch back an forth yuh know." Grace was on top of the world. She had her father, son and a new husband. How blessed I am she thought. His daughter's home was in Iron Shore and only twenty minutes from the airport in Montego Bay. She was also very near the Caribbean Sea but most of the beach in this area of Jamaica was owned by hotels. Grace worked at the Riu, a new hotel chain.

Riu hotels are Spain's second biggest international hotel chain with 102 hotels in 16 countries. Grace, like her father had the urge to travel and planned to take advantage of her new employer's international status.

71

S.D. Laurence

"Daddy don't worry about the beach. You can use the beach where I work and of course you can eat and drink all day if you want." Grace was holding on to her father's hand as if she let go he would be gone.

"Mi nah worried bout noting, dawta. Mi jus happy tu be wit mi family. Come, mek we go inside an see yuh new house." Wisdom toured his daughter's beautiful home with pride. He was happy about his daughter's success. It was now time to focus on his own success.

"This is your room, Daddy. I hope you like it. I decorated it especially for you."

"Mi love de room dawta!"

"Rest Daddy! I know you had a long flight. I will show Actor to his room."

The next morning, Wisdom was awakened by the bright Jamaican sun. His bedroom had a beautiful view of the sea. He missed Jamaica. As he laid in bed and felt the sea breeze from the window, he thought about Cherish. He wanted her here in Jamaica but there was a lot to things to do in the meantime. Grace and her new husband had taken care of everything. He and Actor had access to a car and money. He heard a knock at his bedroom door.

"Grand Papa it's me, Kyler. Wha yuh doin?"

"Come in Bredren. Wha happenin tu yuh?"

"Mi jus waan see yuh." Wisdom was happy to see that his grandson didn't have the American accent that his daughter inherited.

"Yuh being good fe yuh Nana?"

"Yes, Oh dats right, Nana waan know if yuh waan some food dis mawning?"

"Yes, Mon. Axe Nana if she gwan fix de real Jamaica breakfast wit ackee, salt fish and dumplins."

"Mi tink dats wha she's fixin. Yuh comin, Grand Papa?"

"Yes pinckney, mi soon come." Kyler left the room and Wisdom began to prepare for the day. As he headed down the stairs, he could smell everything good coming from the

72

kitchen. Wisdom pulled his chair up to the table to wait for his plate.

"Nana, mi couldn't wait fi get down de steps fi yuh food." Actor entered the kitchen and took a seat next to Wisdom and waited for his share of breakfast also.

"Yuh sleep well Bredren?"

"Yes, Mon. Dis de best rest mi hab en long time. Yuh nevah know how much yuh miss a place til yuh come back!" When Wisdom finished eating breakfast, he got ready for the day's work. Wisdom wanted to get things going to lay down the tracks for his CD. He called one of his Bredren.

"Delroy, dis Wisdom."

"Bredren, wha ah gwan? Yuh back from foreign?"

"Yes, Mon. Mi back inna Yard an glad fi dat."

"Where de I stayin?'

"Iron Shore wit mi dawta. Mi here tu lay down some tracks fi mi CD an mi know yuh hab de proper vibe! Dats why mi checking yuh Bredren. Mi waan yuh help. Organize a band fi de I."

"Don't worry yuhself, Rasta. Mi tek care of de ting. Make mi hab yuh number an mi call yuh when everyting done."

"Much respect, Rasta. Mi tek care of de transportation. De number is….." Wisdom was relieved. He knew that Delroy would get a band together for him. His now began to focus his mind on his other mission. Simon and the video tape.

He couldn't depend on Actor to organize anything. He had been in Foreign so long that he was behaving more like a tourist than a Jamaican. He only saw the beauty. He forgot about the poverty. Most Jamaicans weren't as fortunate as his daughter, Grace, most were unemployed and depended on odd jobs or money from friends and relatives in the States or England. Wisdom dialed his Bredren in Trench town.

"Blessings"

S.D. Laurence

"Respect King Fyah, dis Wisdom. Wha ah gwan Rasta?"

"Yuh in Foreign, Rasta?"

"No, Mon. Mi inna Jamaica. Mi come fi some important business. Mi know yuh can help de I."

"No problem Wisdom! Wha yuh need?" Wisdom explained that he needed a video of a white blonde girl sucking a big black dick. He had a picture of Susan. She was a plain looking blonde girl. It would be easy to find a look alike.

Thousands of white women came to Jamaica all year round to get fucked by Black men. Often times their white men paid to watch the action! King Fyah's hustle was to create videos of white girls fucking black men and selling it to the boyfriend or husband before they left the island. As a result, he had thousands of tapes to preview. And if need be, he'd find some white girl to tape.

"Call de I when everyting cook and curry, Bredren." Wisdom felt another brick removed from his brain. For him, it was all about the vibe. Now he could think about Cherish. He loved her but having her in Jamaica could make this whole experience much more relaxed and comfortable.

After visiting England, he didn't want to go back to living on the move. He had the experiences, now he needed constant shelter, food and love to write and create. What better way than to bring Cherish to Jamaica. She could rent a place. He did want her around but he could also use her economic help. Simon would send money but he wanted to spend that money only on the music. If he had rent and food to worry about that would be less for the music and he didn't want that to happen at all. He didn't feel as if he was taking advantage of her. She had a career and lived in America. She could always make more money.

This was the opportunity of his lifetime. It was survival for him. He did love Cherish but there were things about her that turned him off. She had an attitude of superiority

74

and she thought she knew everything but most of the time she did. Plus, he didn't think she recognized his talent or respected his street knowledge. But that was neither here nor there; he wanted her in Jamaica with him. He picked up his cell phone and called Cherish.

"Blessing Sistren, mi pray dat mi nah wake yuh?"

"No Wisdom. I'm glad to hear from you. Glad to know that your flight landed safely. I was a little worried but I knew you would eventually call." Wisdom wasn't use to checking in. He not only lived alone but he lived anywhere and everywhere. Cherish use say he was like the song, "Papa was a rolling stone wherever he laid his hat was his home." She never told him the part "but when he died all he had was alone".

"Yuh must know de I by now Cherish. Mi hab tings tu tek care of. Yuh tinkin bout comin tu Jamaica. Mi mus hab yuh wit de I! Yuh know mi need yuh vibes!"

"Is that all you need from me Wisdom, vibes. What about love and affection?"

"Mi need dat too, Cherish."

"I'm really considering coming to Jamaica. I love you and Jamaica. It seems to be a win, win situation. I do have some reservations because I don't really know you. I mean, we've been in a long distance relationship for some time but we haven't really spent a whole lot of time together."

"Is dere anyting de I can say or do tu make yuh mind up Cherish?"

"Not really Wisdom. I'm gonna pray on it some more. I'll let you know in a few days. How are things?"

"Everyting Irie. Mi gettin de band together."

"That's great Wisdom. I know you will get everything together for your music. I pray you give me the same amount of attention if I decide to come to Jamaica. I'm going to hang up because you know time is money."

"Jah guide Cherish. Mi pray de next time mi talk tu yuh. Yuh gonna say yuh comin tu be wit de I."

75

"Jah guide Wisdom. Talk to you soon."Cherish hung up the phone and rolled a spliff. She needed to relax and chill. She decided to retire and think about things again tomorrow.

***

"Hey Miss Davis!" Cherish's thoughts were interrupted suddenly by one of her students walking next to her. She'd reached her destination unknowingly

"What's up? How are you doing this morning Miss Davis? Can I go in the building with you? I have something to talk to you about."

"So talk while we walk and try to keep up." Cherish knew that this was a common ploy students used who wanted to get into the building early and avoid the wait outside.

"I have a lot to tell you. It's no way possible I'll be finish by the time we get to the front door. And look how fast you walk Ms. Davis?" The student slowed down because he couldn't keep up and accepted his outside situation.

"Get a pass during homeroom and come talk to me. It better be important too! Don't waste my time! Love you! See you later!"Cherish entered the bright red wooden doors into the elegant marble entrance hallway. She walked up the stairs, greeted the office workers, got her cup of coffee and retreated to her office. She prayed that things wouldn't be too hectic because she didn't feel emotionally up to it today. The phone rang.

"Hello, this is Ms. Davis, how may I help you?"

"Cherish, this is Jill. How you doing girl?"

"Jill! It's so good to hear from you. I'm good. How you doing?"

"Just thought I'd hit up a sister and see what's been happening. When you coming to New York so we can hang out? I really miss you."

"Actually Jill I'm thinking about moving to Jamaica." She hadn't made up her mind but thought she'd tell her friend and get her reaction.

"Jamaica! Now that's the Cherish I know! What's going on in Jamaica?"

"Well you know I been dealing with this guy in Jamaica, Wisdom?"

"Yeah"

"Well he wants me to move there with him."

"I thought he was in England? Didn't you just visit him there?"

"Yeah but he went back to Jamaica to record his CD."

"So you would live in Jamaica forever? I mean, what's the plan?"

"The plan is for me to move to Jamaica, that's it. I can take a year leave from my job and still keep it. So it'll be like a year vacation, if nothing else." There was silence in the air for a moment or two.

"Well, you just take care of your ass in Jamaica. I don't want to have to come down there and fuck somebody up." Jill had a serious tone now.

"I'll be okay. You know God protects babies and fools so I guess I'm the fool! But I haven't really decided what I'm going to do."

"I know you Cherish. You're going to go. Just visit me before you leave and keep in touch." Jill had a resolved tone now. She knew her friend.

"I'm gonna see you real soon girl because I miss you too." Cherish heard her telephone beep. It was another phone call.

"Jill, let me go. There's a call on the other line. Let me get that and I'll talk to you real soon." Cherish took the waiting call from a parent and continued her work day. The day was over sooner than she anticipated. Thankfully the day wasn't filled with the drama that Cherish so desperately needed to avoid. She began to collect her belongings and start her walk home when her cell phone rang. She looked at the caller ID and it was Wisdom.

"Hey baby what's up? I was just getting ready to walk out the door and go home."

S. D. Laurence

"Mi wanted tu hear yuh voice, Cherish. Yuh think bout coming tu Jamaica tu be wit yuh lover?"

"I miss you too Wisdom. You know I want to come but it is a big move for me. The problem is that I don't want to leave my kids."

"Wha kids? Yuh only hab de one boy, right?"

"I'm talking about the children where I work. I really love them and feel responsible for them. I don't want to leave them."

"Yuh not leavin dem, Cherish. Yuh spirit is wit dem. Mi need yuh now Cherish. Jah put yuh inna mi life fi a purpose. Come an be wit mi! Mi luv yuh girl."

"Wisdom, I need to put things together in my mind. It would be a big change for me. Moving to a different country. I do love Jamaica and feel at home when I'm there. Look, I'm leaving work. Let me call you when I get home and we'll talk some more."

"Cherish, mi call tu tell yuh dat mi going tu Kingston."

"So call me when you reach. Jah guide, Wisdom."

"Blessings Cherish." Cherish ended the call and continued to prepare for her walk home. Maybe an extended vacation wouldn't be bad so bad she thought.

***

Wisdom ended the conversation with Cherish. She's coming, he thought and that would be a good thing for him. He told Cherish that his trip to Kingston was about music but it was about the video that Simon wanted so desperately.

"Respect Bredren, dis is Wisdom. Wha happenin King Fyah?"

"Mi hab de tape fi de Bredren hab de funds?"

"Seen! Mi on de way tu Kingston. Little more." Wisdom had smoothed things over with Simon and was able to get more money from him. His plan was to get the tape and have Actor take it back to England. Actor was in his way. He required too much attention. Wisdom wasn't use to

78

being responsible for anyone's happiness except his own. He was driven by his need to be a superstar in the music.

Success to Wisdom meant money and recognition. He was a sufferer and music was his ticket out of Jamaica and poverty. He hadn't really shared with Cherish the shady part of his relationship with Simon. She only knew that Simon had in interest in producing his music.

Wisdom reached his destination in Kingston and pulled up in front of a 5 foot zinc fence chained locked shut. The fence was painted with large images of Bob Marley, Haile Selassie, Peter Tosh and numerous bible verses written in red, black, gold and green. He honked the horn and waited for the gate to open. Once inside there was a large cleared dirt area with several cinder blocks for seating and a one room cement buildings. Each building had a small porch with an outside toilet and two basins for washing dishes and clothing. Wisdom exited the car and greeted King Fyah.

"Wha happenin, King Fyah?" Wisdom looked around as he greeted King Fyah.

"Jah guide, Wisdom. Mi hab de tape. Yuh hab de funds?"

"Seen! Mi need fi see de tape, Mon."

"No problem! Follow de I." Wisdom followed King Fyah into his one room. Inside was a bed, table with two chairs, television and DVD player. Wisdom sat down and waited for King Fyah to load the video for review.

"Ras, mi know dat de I gonna luv dis tape. De white woman pon dis tape look jus lik yuh need fi she tu look." Wisdom viewed the tape of a blonde woman fuckin and suckin two black men. The woman looked like Susan and he knew that Simon would be convinced.

"Yes Mon. Mi luv dat. Mek we tek care of dis bandulu bizness." The two men exchanged money and tape. Wisdom proceeded out the yard.

S.D. Laurence

***

Cherish wrapped things up, gathered her belonging and started her walk home. But today her spirit was leading her in a different direction. Her walk home was usually straight down 48th street until she reached Windsor Ave, make a right and landed at her door step. But today was different. She walked down 48th street but made a left on Haverford avenue to 46th and turned right. She passed her three favorite small streets, Mandela Way, St. Malachy's Way and Nehemiah Way. She often wondered about how and when these streets were named.

Cherish was being guided by spirit alone. She had no idea why she was taking this route. Her mind wasn't filled with thoughts of the past. She was fully present and enjoying the gift. Cherish crossed Market Street and 46th Street which change to Farragut Street. On the corner of Farragut and Chestnut Streets stood a BP gas station. She knew the quick mart had the paper she used to prepare her medicine. Cherish didn't really like stopping here because the West Park projects were close and her students often used the gas station to get their hustle on. She decided against stopping and continued her walk home. As she reached home, she saw her mother standing on the porch.

"Hey mom. What's up?"Cherish said cheerfully.

"Hi Cherish. Did you have a good day?

"Why don't you come inside my apartment and let me fix you a cup of tea." Ellen walked through her apartment door and Cherish followed her into the kitchen.

"I have peppermint, Cherish. Is that okay?" Ellen put the kettle of water on the stove to boil

"I'm moving to Jamaica." Cherish didn't want to waste time with her mother.

"What are you talking about now, Cherish? I don't know where you come from. Maybe you should check out who your real mother is because you sure don't act like my child. What the hell you gonna do in Jamaica? Follow some nigga there? That's your problem, your ass followed

80

Scott and look what that got you, nothing. When you gonna learn that men ain't shit! You keep lookin for love in life and what you gettin return, nothing!"

"Well, Mom! That's how we're different. I believe in love."

"Well you better believe this! These Jamaican men don't want nothing but an opportunity to come to America. And don't you dare put my property in jeopardy!"

"What are you talking about? I'm going to Jamaica! He's not coming here!"

"I know but like I said, coming to America is what he wants. And marrying you can get him an American citizenship and possession of this property."

"I'm not marrying anyone, Mom. And no one could take this property because what I bring to a marriage stays mine. I don't even know why I'm talking to you right now!"

"You don't have to talk to me! But you have to listen to me. I'm not going to let anyone take what I worked for all my life and that includes you Cherish!"

"I'm going upstairs Mom. God bless you." Cherish got up from the kitchen table and headed for the door.

"You think you so smart, Cherish. If it wasn't for me you wouldn't be anything!" Her finger was in Cherish's face. Ellen had a lot of built up frustrations towards Cherish. She thought that Cherish had wasted so many opportunities in her life for the sake of love.

"Look mom, we can talk about this later. I'll do whatever it is you want me to do to make you feel comfortable about the whole thing. But, we can't talk now. So please excuse me, I'm going upstairs to my place." Cherish walked out the door and headed for her apartment. She entered her apartment and thanked God for the peace that surpasses all understanding.

"Cherish, think about all that shit later." She said out loud to herself

"Right now, you need a spliff!" She sat down on her window ledge and observed her beautiful tree. The season was changing and everything in her life was changing again. Change never bothered Cherish. The phone rang and brought Cherish back to the present. It was Marva.

"Hey Marva, what's goin on? I was going to call you this evening."

"I'm okay, Cherish. I was just checking in. I haven't heard from you in a while. Is everything okay? " Marva had a little sarcasm in her voice.

"I'm good and Wisdom is fine. He asked me to move to Jamaica with him." Cherish didn't sound excited. Once she decided something in her mind it was already done. The incidentals were secondary.

"Jamaica! I thought he was in England?" Marva was upset. She didn't think Cherish deserved a life in Jamaica. She did!

"No, Marva. He's in Jamaica recording the music for his CD and he wants me there."

"How long would you stay, Cherish? Where would you stay? Does Wisdom have a house?" Marva was more curious now. She'd lived in Jamaica before. In fact, she married a Jamaican man. The marriage ended when on an unannounced visit, when she found him in bed with a little girl from the same yard.

"I don't know any of that Marva. I just decided to go about five minutes ago. I haven't even thought about any details." Cherish was getting irritated. She didn't want to talk about things she hadn't thought about.

"What made you decide Cherish?"

"Mandela, St. Malachy and Nehemiah."

"What are you talking about Cherish?"

"My spirit took me on a trip home this afternoon. I passed those three small streets. You know they're one right after the other off 46th Street?"

"Yeah, I know the blocks. They're all kept really nice and clean. But how did clean streets help you decide to move to Jamaica?"

"Well Mandela stands for freedom. St. Malachy saw visions of the future and Nehemiah didn't care whether he impressed other people. But he always wanted to please God." Cherish was silent. She wanted to hear what Marva would have to say.

"So you telling me that Jamaica is a vision of freedom for you and by going your pleasing God."

"You got it girl. Jamaica is freedom for me. I don't know what that means I just know what is. Look, I'm tired, Marva. I had a big day today and I need to rest. We'll talk soon."

"Okay Cherish. Talk to you soon. Let me know how I can help with your move."

"Thanks Marva. I'll definitely be in touch and I'll definitely need your advice."

***

Cherish entered her home and was greeted by five brown barrels. For the past few months, they were a constant reminder of her moving to Jamaica. She knew that everyone thought she was crazy including her mother, son, friends and anyone else she might share her story with.

It seemed like people couldn't imagine leaving America, the land of opportunity, to live in a small third world country where telephones, running water and electricity were still a luxury. She quickly ran upstairs to her apartment and waited for her phone call from her love, Wisdom. He usually called this time of the day. The phone rang, it was Wisdom.

"Hello Wisdom."

"Yes baby, mi miss yuh bad Mon. How tings wit yuh?"

"Great, it won't be long before we are together in Jamaica. Baby I can't wait."

"Mi know, see yuh soon. Jah guide and protect you love."

83

S.D. Laurence

"Jah guide Wisdom. Mi soon come." Cherish looked at her life possessions up till now. It wasn't much. Everything seemed to be packed and ready to go. She didn't really know what to do or what to bring but she packed as if she had a purpose.

The barrels were living memorials of her past, present and future. Cherish was leaving the old to find the new. She was considered by some to be a runner. At least that's what people said about her way of surviving this thing called life.

Chapter Five

Cherish left for Jamaica early in the morning. It seemed as though the entire world was asleep. The cab was waiting for her but this time her mother was not at the door waving good-bye. Cherish felt very alone. What she didn't know was that loneliness was about to become her friend.

When she reached the airport, the world was awake and alive. Traveling to Jamaica was always a unique experience. There are two types of travelers. The Jamaicans returning home for a visit and the tourist going on vacation. You could distinguish between the two by the amount of luggage they carried. The returnee's baggage consists of overstuffed luggage and boxes filled with thick strips of tape to secure the goods going home to family and friends. It's not acceptable for come back to "Yard" from "Foreign" and not have gifts for family and friends.

Cherish had suddenly become a returnee by appearance alone. Her luggage was now filled with things that Wisdom asked her to bring and Marva insisted that she needed in Jamaica. She was finally checked in for the flight. She wanted to relax and get something to eat. Cherish found her way to the International terminal and located a spot to get a coffee and whole wheat bagel. As she settled down, her cell phone rang. It was Jill.

"Her girl! What's up?" Cherish answered with a smile on her face. She was glad to know that someone was thinking about her this morning.

"What's up with you? Are you still going through with the move?"

"What you talkin about Willis?" Cherish and Jill both laughed.

"You know what the fuck I'm talkin about Cherish. Are you still takin your ass to Jamaica to live?"

"I'm at the airport as we speak. And yes Muthafucka, I'm still going." Both women could feel their mutual love and respect.

85

"You be careful Cherish. I know how you feel about life and love but not everyone functions in the world like you. Just remember that Cherish and be safe. Call me if you need me and be sure to call me when you don't. Keep in touch. I mean that Cherish!"

"I will keep in touch Jill. I promise. Thanks for calling, Jill. I was feeling a little alone this morning." There was a silence on both ends of the telephone line.

"We are alone, Cherish, except for God. But we always have God and that's all we'll ever need. Cherish you realize that you're leaving for a different country and you only know one person there?"

"I know, Jill. I've thought about all that but I'm going for more than Wisdom. I'm going for myself too. If this thing between me and Wisdom works out, all good, but if it doesn't I'll be happy with the experience of a different way of life."

"Okay different way of life!" Jill laughed. She wanted to lighten the tone of the conversation.

"Alright girlfriend, I'll talk to you soon and see you later. Come to Jamaica!"

"Oh, I'll be there. Love you girl!" Both women hung up the phone at the same time feeling the love of a lasting friendship. It was time to board the plane and Cherish was feeling butterflies in her stomach. It wasn't the flight. It was the anxiety of not knowing what to expect. This feeling was new for Cherish. This time she really didn't know what expect. She always knew what to expect about most things in life based on other people's experiences. But she hadn't known anyone to go live in another country. She'd read about people with similar experiences but she never really personally knew anyone.

The plane ride was pleasurable as usual. It was the Champagne and breakfast flight. The waitresses were lovely and everyone on the flight was anxious to reach Jamaica, returnee and visitor. As the airplane reached the island, Cherish sited the Dead End bar where she and

86

Surviving This Thing Called Life

Wisdom always visited when he picked her up and dropped her off at the airport. Cherish knew they would stop there today. She'd have a hot Guinness stout, escovitch fish, callaloo and red beans and rice. She and Wisdom will bathe in the blue wata and make love under the bright stars and moon. She couldn't wait.

As Cherish exited the plane, she could feel the heat as she walked down the stairs onto the tar-mat. She followed the crowd toward the doors to enter the airport and begin the long wait through customs. There were two lines. One line was for people bringing nothing into the country except for their clothes. These people were usually on vacation. Then there was the line for people bringing things into the country. This was the line Cherish found herself in for the first time. In this line, every bag was thoroughly investigated for items not claimed on your immigration form. This was a means for the Jamaican government to attain taxes from individuals living outside of the country.

Cherish had learned from former visits to the island how to hide things in her bag that would hopefully be overlooked and avoid the added taxes. She waited patiently for her turn at the immigration station. She'd learned a little about patience from her former visits to the island, so she was putting those lessons into practice today. As she reached the immigration officer, she handed him her paper work.

"So I see you're visiting Jamaica for a year, Miss. Have you brought any gifts for anyone?" The immigration officer smiled and looked Cherish straight in the eye as he spoke. She'd overcome her fear of Jamaican officials after her first visit to Jamaica. From her initial encounter with the police, she realized that most officials were motivated by money and fear. It was up to you to let them know respectfully that you were not intimidated by their presence, so Cherish returned the smile and the look.

"I have the few gifts. I've listed on my paperwork. Most of the things, I've brought to enjoy my stay in Jamaica and I plan to bring back when I return."

"Are you Jamaican, Miss Davis."

"Yes, Mon. Mi not born upon de island but mi hab cousins an aunties dat liv inna St. Elizabeth." Cherish tried out her Jamaican accent and also followed Wisdom's advice to always claim St. Elizabeth as her home because of its German influence. The Parish was filled with an abundance of "Brown" Jamaicans.

"Yuh look like yuh come from St. Elizabeth. Yuh play de guitar Miss?" Cherish had an electric acoustic on her shoulder. It was a gift for Wisdom.

"I use to play a little when I was younger. So I decided to try my skills during my stay in Jamaica. Cherish smiled as she spoke and the immigration officer stamped her papers. Cherish was on her way to meet her new life. Once outside, the familiar crowd was waiting for friends, relatives and tourist. But this time, she wasn't leaving in a few weeks. She was staying.

"Yuh need a ride Miss?"

"No thanks. I have someone picking me up." Cherish answered to that same question over and over again until she set eyes on Wisdom.

"Wisdom! Wisdom!"

"Wha happenin, Sistren?"

"What's happening is your woman is here. Are you happy?" Cherish had her arms around her man's neck and looked him directly in his eyes.

"Yes, Cherish. Mi happy. Mi more den dat Cherish. Mi feel blessed." Wisdom grabbed Cherish's arms and put them by her side.

"Are you telling me that's enough public affection?"

"Cherish, mi hab de driver waiting. Let's git yuh suitcases tu de car." Wisdom quickly dragged her luggage and Cherish followed dutifully. She was in Jamaica. A new chapter was about to begin in her life. She didn't know what the end result would be but she was praying for a happy one. Cherish knew deep in her heart that she really didn't know Wisdom but that was not an issue for her.

He was different from Scott. He was a spiritual man. He talked about God and his mysterious ways. He was a man of faith. He lived a life based on faith. She would later discover how faith would work in her own life. She felt happy as she rode down the rough roads of Jamaica with Wisdom headed to she didn't know where.

Cherish and Wisdom headed out of Sangster Airport in Montego Bay in a well preserved old Toyota. Wisdom sat in the front of the car next to the driver. The two men talked excessively about things she couldn't understand. Cherish sat in the back seat looking out the window and wondering what life would be like here. Jamaica was God's land to Cherish. There was beauty all around. Having lived in cement jungles all her life, being closer to nature made her feel closer to God.

Cherish didn't grow up in a religious family. She had a few memories about church but the memories were never about what was said in church. Cherish remembered the images of church. She remembered Jesus always having blonde hair and blue eyes. That's what she liked about Muslim Temples. There were no images. You could imagine your creator in the way you wished. She knew The Almighty was unimaginable so she was always looking to discover more about the Creator's goodness and faithfulness

"Everyting crisp Sistren?" The driver spoke to Cherish loudly to overcome the sounds of the radio and the wind rushing through the window.

"Cherish, yuh still wit de I?" Wisdom spoke to Cherish because she did not respond to the driver.

"What did you say?" Cherish's mind returned to the backseat of the car. Her mind was everywhere else but in the car.

"De driver ask yuh if yuh okay?"

"I'm sorry. I didn't hear him. I was just admiring God's beauty. But I'm okay."

"Yuh need a drink Cherish?"

"Yes, I could use a Guinness?" Cherish was a little regretful that she and Wisdom didn't go to the Dead End bar for their traditional meal and swim.

"Driver, mek we stop at de shop near mi dawta's." Wisdom continued to talk with the driver and Cherish went back to her thoughts. Jamaica was an opportunity for her to quiet her spirit. All her life she searched for some kind of inner peace. She was just always missing something and in Jamaica she found that inner peace she'd searched for. The driver pulled up to a small shop on the side of the road. He and Wisdom exited the car and headed toward the shop. Wisdom returned with a bag full of groceries and a hot Guinness for Cherish.

"Mi didn't know if yuh wanted de Guinness hot or cold. So mi got yuh a hot one. Dat suit yuh Sistren?" Cherish hadn't asked Wisdom much about what living in Jamaica would be like. She didn't know how to pose that question to him. She didn't know if he'd understand her concern. Wisdom lived his life the Jamaican way by faith and Cherish lived the American way by works.

As the car made its way up the winding hills heading toward Grace's house, Cherish sipped her hot Guinness waiting for the day to unfold. She had three large pieces of luggage with her and 4 barrels waiting at the airport to be picked up. The barrels were filled only God's knows what because the last few months became an exercise in mindless purchasing of various items from rice to toothpaste. Marva told her of the expense of purchasing certain items in Jamaica so Cherish made sure she was fully stocked in all those areas.

The car finally pulled up to a large locked iron gate and honked the horn. Wisdom got out the car, walked up to the gate and released the lock to open the gate. As the gate opened, out of the front door ran Wisdom's grandson, Kyler.

"Mi miss yuh grandpapa." Kyler jumped in Wisdom's arms as he flung him in a circle.

"Mi miss yuh too Mon. Kyler mek mi introduce yuh tu mi wife, Cherish." Wisdom walked Kyler to the car and opened the back door of the car for Cherish.

"Hello Kyler. How are you?" Cherish leaned over and spoke to Kyler in his face.

"Mi fine Miss. Yuh from American?" Kyler had a look of excitement in his face.

"Yes, Kyler. I'm from America but I'm coming to Jamaica to live with your grandfather."

"Yuh hab a gift fi me?"

"Dat's not de right ting tu ask, Kyler." Wisdom was angry.

"I do have something for you Kyler. But I have to unpack first.

"Yuh don't hab tu git dis boy no ting, Cherish. Mi apologize fi mi grandson behavior." Wisdom seemed to be really embarrassed by the question.

"Wisdom, it's okay. He's only a child. It's very normal for children to ask for gifts."Cherish was speaking softly into Wisdom's ear.

"Mi know Cherish but dis wanti wanti can't getti getti attitude mi nah waan dat fi mi grandson." Wisdom wasn't soft and reasonable but harsh and loud when he spoke. Cherish immediately stepped away and had nothing else to say. It was an attitude from Wisdom that she was seeing for the first time. She looked to the door and noticed Grace walking out to greet everyone. Grace and Cherish really loved and respected each other. They got to know each other from all her prior visits to Jamaica.

"Cherish I'm happy to see yuh! Yuh look as beautiful as ever. I tell Daddy all de time dat him must marry yuh in order to keep yuh. Has he listened Cherish?"

"Grace, I'm happy to see you also. But you're the beautiful one, not me." Cherish didn't want to speak about the marriage issue. She wasn't interested in marriage.

"Welcome to my home Cherish. Feel free and relaxed. Follow me and I'll show you to your room." Cherish followed Grace up the tile stairs as she opened the beautifully crafted wooden doors of her home. Upon entering, Cherish could see how Grace spent the money she made while working in America. Her home was a duplicate of any extravagant American home Cherish had ever experienced.

"You have a beautiful home Grace."

"Thanks. I'm going to give you my best guest room. It has an ocean view from the veranda. I know you and daddy will enjoy it." Grace continued to up the staircase heading for the room. The room was absolutely gorgeous. Everything was coordinated and elegant. From the Sealy Posturepedic mattress to the coordinated vertical blinds and bed spread. It didn't appear that anyone stayed in this room.

Cherish wondered where Wisdom stayed while in Jamaica. It obviously wasn't here. Wisdom entered the room as the two women made idol conversation.

"Yuh like de room Cherish?"

"Yes, everything is beautiful." Cherish headed for the veranda to admire the view.

"Where yuh waan de suitcase, Cherish?" Wisdom dragged the heaviest piece of luggage behind him.

"Put it near the closet, please."

"I'm going to leave you two alone. You can get the other luggage later Daddy. Why don't you two rest for now?" Grace walked out of the room as she spoke.

"Mi gonna tek yuh advice dawta." Wisdom closed the door. He turned around headed for the bed to lie down. Cherish left the veranda and headed toward the bed to lie next to her lover.

Surviving This Thing Called Life

"Well Wisdom, we're in Jamaica together. I'm happy to be here. How do you feel?"

"Mi feel great Cherish. Mi glad yuh come tu Jamaica. Mi hab a great responsibility tu tek care of yuh. Mi can't call yuh son an tell hem someting happen tu hem old lady."

"Nothing's going to happen Wisdom. This is Jamaica. Remember, Jamaica no problem."

"Cherish, don't let dis likkle beautiful island fool yuh. There is as much danger as deres beauty. Yuh know de ackee plant?"

"Yes"

"Dis plant de national dish of de island an a good way fi de I tu see de island. When de plant is ready to eat it opens an Jah know de ting is good to eat. But when de plant nah open an de person fix de ting, de ackee sick yuh. So Jamaica is de ackee plant. De ting can be bad or good fi yuh." Cherish was thinking to herself. He never mentioned how bad Jamaica was when he was asking me to come! What's this all about? Cherish changed the subject.

"Grace has a beautiful home. I really love this room too. What room did you stay in Wisdom?"

"Mi nevah really stay no one place Cherish. Deres a room an bath behind de garage where mi keep mi tings dem."

"Oh, you know I always thought you were staying at your daughter's house." Cherish was curious.

"Mi guided by mi spirit Cherish. Life is all bout de vibe yuh know."

"Well, what if the spirit guides you to stay out all night? What would you do?"

"Cherish, mi can only gib yuh mi luv and faithfulness. Mi can't promise dat mi be dere by yuh side all de time lik mi some youth." Wisdom had an serious tone to his voice.

"Don't stress yourself Wisdom. I don't know all of what you mean but I can feel your vibe and it's not all that positive. Remember, it's all about the vibes!" Cherish was a bit upset herself now. She was just asking questions and

93

that really seemed to bother Wisdom. She couldn't understand the source of his annoyance. As a matter of fact, she hadn't really seen this him annoyed at all in him on their short visits together.

"Mek we get some rest Cherish. It's been a long day. Mi tired yuh know." Wisdom took his shoes off to lie down. Cherish did stress him. It wasn't her but her American habit of needing to know so much. Wisdom did things with little thought involved. Most of his life was spent in the survival mode and that didn't leave much time to question what was going on.

"We didn't even go to our favorite restaurant today. I'm not really tired. I really want some ganja. Do you have any?"

"Mi sorry Sistren. Mek mi git yuh some ganja. Yuh waan travel wit de I?"

"Yeah, you know I wanna ride. I wanna see the island. Do we have a car to use?"

"No problem wit taking Grace's transport. Come Cherish, mi know yuh luv Jamaica more den de I. Come see yuh first luv, Jamaica!"

"I love you Wisdom but I can't deny my love for Jamaica. I feel close to God here."

The two loaded into Grace's Toyota van. The island had just become flooded with thousands of Toyota's straight from Japan. They headed toward the rocky roads of the island. First stop was to the corner shop where Wisdom purchased a portion of ganja, rolled Cherish a healthy spliff and the couple headed for the Dead End bar. Wisdom lit the spliff as they pulled off. He puffed it and released the smoke as if he were a dragon and handed it to Cherish. Cherish felt heavenly. She was in her Jamaican uniform, an African wrap and a bathing suit. She was ready this time.

The ride to the Dead End Bar was quiet except for Wisdom on the CD player. Wisdom listened to himself more than anyone else. He did listen to other music and a lot of his new found musical variety was from Cherish's influence. Cherish brought him the music of Stevie Wonder, Sam Cooke, Curtis Mayfield, James Brown and Luther Vandross. Cherish drew on her spliff and relaxed as she smelled the sweetness of the countryside and sea. Her mind drifted away and she didn't mind the silence. In America, it was as if the goal was to fill all time with speech In Jamaica, moments of silence was usual and expected.

Wisdom didn't mind the silence either. He smoked but not as much as Cherish, so his one puff had him where he needed to be. He knew once he passed the spliff to her the rest was history.

He was in his own meditation now, asking Father if he'd made a mistake. Could he take this questioning American woman who doesn't even realize their differences? But she was so sweet and loving toward him and helped make life much more livable. No one believed in him as much as she had, so all the work was worth it. But top on the list was his career and his dreams. He was the sufferer and he deserved Jah's blessing more than her because she was already blessed. She was an American and at the end of the day, there's always opportunity for her.

They pulled up to the Dead End bar and sat at their usual table. She ordered ackee and salt fish with a side order of callaloo and he ordered escovitch and two orders of rice and peas. Both had a bottle of Guinness Stout. Cherish had a hot one and Wisdom a cold one.

"Wha happenin Star?" A short Rasta spoke as he walked up to the couples table.

"Respect Dup. Good tu see de I. Yuh brother dere about?" Wisdom watched as Dup pulled up a chair and joined the table.

"Hem inna de yard. Blessings Cherish. Yuh still wit dis old Rasta?"

"Yes, Dup. I'm still with this old Rasta but I'm happy to see you. How you been doing?"

"Mi jus tryin tu survive Babylon. How long yuh en Yard fi dis time Cherish?"

"I've moved to Jamaica, Dup. Today's my first day." Cherish was smiling from cheek to cheek.

"So Wisdom yuh get tu hab de fullness of dis beautiful Sistren."

"Yes Mon. Jah blessed de I. Dup yuh know dat mi workin pon de tracks fi mi CD?"

"Yes Mon, mi know dat."

"Mi waan de I tu sing some background pon dis ting, Star. Yuh know mi luv de Bredren not de Sistren as mi background singers.

"Mi luv dat Wisdom. But yuh know mi hab no transport?"

"Yes, Mon mi know. Mi move forward first light, Rasta an pick yuh up at de bar."

"Everyting, Irie. Little more, Dread." Dup walked away with a bigger smile on his face. He was about to get some food tomorrow.

"You going to record tomorrow, Wisdom?"

"Yes, Mon."

"When were you going to tell me?"

"Mi gonna hab tu get use tu yuh." Wisdom reached over and put his hand on Cherish's hand.

"Wisdom, we are both going to have to get use to each other. Remember my days were full with teaching and children. I'm going to have to find something to do or I'll go crazy and drive you crazy also." Cherish and Wisdom both smiled and quietly finished their meal.

***

Back in Philadelphia, Vince Barnes was leaving the after-hours spot at his usual time, daybreak. He was tired. Tired of his life and how things changed. As he entered his blue Buick regal and put his key in the ignition, he wondered where he would sleep tonight. He didn't feel like hearing Phyllis' mouth this morning. He knew he wasn't bringing money into the house but she was supposed to understand. She knew all the ups and downs he endured. She was legit now and had a nine to five and he didn't ask her for anything so he really didn't understand all the drama. Vince knew that if it weren't for him, her son Weldon would be on the corners instead of an "A" student. Vince headed for his mom's house. He could rest there without being disturbed. When he pulled up in the driveway, he could see the kitchen light was on.

"Hey Mom." Vince yelled as he opened the front door with his key.

"Hey son. Are you just getting in from work?" Mona continued her kitchen project.

"What you doing?" Vince didn't answer her question. He took a seat as the kitchen table.

"I'm making some tea. Do you want some?" Mona was worried about her son. She was one of the few people that knew the struggles he endured.

"No mom. I'm tired and sleepy. I worked all night and I need some sleep."

"Well, you know your room is always there for you. Did you talk to Phyllis this morning and let her know you're staying here so she won't be worried?

"Trust me mom. She's not worried about me! She's only worried about how much money I bring in the house!" Vince was heading toward the stairs as he spoke.

"Your effect on Weldon is worth it all. You know that God puts people in our lives for a reason. We're here to do his work on earth." Mona was a Godly woman and always let Vince know how she felt about things. Even though she knew he didn't pay too much attention. She spent her whole life trying to protect her son's from the world with little success.

"Yeah mom, I know. I'll talk to you later. I'm gonna lay it down right now." Vince entered his room and plopped on the bed. He was drunk and tired. Tired of his life. His mind drifted to the day Elaine informed the police where his money stash was located. He never wanted her to know about the stash but she stumbled upon his hiding place one night after a long night of gambling.

***

"What you doing out here in the backyard so late, Vince?" Elaine heard the noise in the backyard, put on her robe and slippers to see what Vince was doing in the back yard. She'd noticed him in the backyard several nights before and was curious to see what he was doing back there. Vince was very generous with her and her daughter but Elaine always wanted more. She longed to find his stash because she knew he had one. He couldn't use banks because that's who he stole the money from. He wasn't a bank robber. He was an identity thief and used various identities to get money fraudulently.

"I thought I heard some noise outback so I was checking things out. Everything's okay baby. Let's go back in the house." Vince had just finished putting a big bag of money in his secret spot.

"I was awake with the bedroom window open when you came home. I didn't hear any noise out back before you. How did you hear noise from the front of the house?" Elaine knew that was all bullshit. Plus he called her "Baby" and that had stopped some time ago. She and Vince hadn't been on the best of terms lately. He was always on the road, gambling or running the streets. Vince's solution to the problem was more things and more money.

"Girl, let's go in the house. It's late and I'm not up to a whole bunch of bullshit tonight." Vince changed his attitude now. He knew being nice to Elaine and he knew that wouldn't accomplish anything. The two entered the house and went to sleep.

But the next day when Vince traveled out of state to cash some checks, Elaine went out back and found to the hollowed underground area with only God knows how much money. Elaine was in heaven. She wanted to leave Vince but didn't want to leave the money. Having access to his stash was an opportunity to siphon off enough funds to be set for life without him.

***

The next morning Cherish woke to the bright Jamaica sunlight pouring into the window. The veranda doors were left open all night so there was also an awesome sea breeze coaxing her back to sleep. She looked over at Wisdom sleeping next to her. She rolled back over and tried to return the sleep. This new life was going to be different she thought.

"Yuh sleep Cherish?"

"No, I'm awake."

"De sun rise wake yuh?"

"Yes, but you know I love the morning."

"Mi know Cherish. Feel free tu do wha yuh want. Yuh home now." Wisdom appeared to go back to sleep. Cherish got out the bed and headed for the veranda. Everything was beautiful. She thanked God for all this beauty and for having the opportunity to wake up one more day.

On the way to the veranda, she noticed a small glass top round table with a small coffee maker, fresh ground Blue Mountain coffee and raw brown sugar. Cherish was ecstatic! Coffee and a beautiful morning view, who could ask for more. Cherish held the coffee mug to her nose as she poured a large cup of Blue mountain coffee. There was nothing like it. It reminded her of Negril when she met Wisdom.

As she sat on one of the white cast iron chairs, she noticed they were very uncomfortable but they did look beautiful. She wondered if life in Jamaica would be like that: beautiful but uncomfortable. She put the thought out of her mind and continued to admire the view when she heard the shower in the bathroom. It was Wisdom.

"Mawning Sistren. Mi see yuh hab Blue mountain coffee." Wisdom was standing on the veranda with a large

bath towel wrapped around his waist flipping his thick
locks back and forth to let them dry in the hot Jamaican
sun.

"Good Morning, Wisdom. Isn't it a beautiful day?"

"Yes, Mon dis a great day Father God has sent de I tu
travel tu Kingston. Mi feeling de fullness of dis work
Sistren. Yuh waan beach wit Grace?"

"Yes, I would like that. But why can't I go with you to
Kingston?"

"Yuh hab plenty time tu visit Kingston. Trust mi, de city
hot as hell an de studio's hotter an filled wit Bredren. Mi
nah return til morrow, seen?

"That's alright with me. I'll enjoy the beach with Grace
today."

"Trust mi, deres a betta times on de beach. De hotel hab
private beach wit all de food an drink yuh can tek."
Wisdom was dressing now. He knew Cherish would enjoy
herself much more at the beach than with him.

"You leaving so soon, Wisdom. It's still early."

"Yuh must remember how long de ride tu Kingston,
Cherish?"

"Yeah, I do. It's my first day and I thought we would
spend it together."

"Yesterday was yuh first day an de day was spent
together. Dis day mi must do a whole heap of work."
Wisdom walked away and continued to prepare for his
day. Cherish continued to sit on the veranda and admire
the beauty around her. As she sat, her spirit spoke to her.
She really didn't need to go to Kingston. She should stay
and chill on the beach. It didn't take Wisdom long to get
ready.

"Cherish mi pon de rode. Mi soon come. Jah guide."
Wisdom walked out the bedroom and closed the door
behind.

***

Vince woke early to the same life he fell asleep to. He
needed a drink before the past began to enter his mind

again. As he headed for the bathroom, his cell phone rang. He didn't answer it and he knew he wouldn't answer until he had a beer.

Vince headed downstairs trying not to disturb his mom. He could not take a morning lecture. He knew what he needed to change in his life. He just wasn't ready. He managed to make it to his car without disruption and headed straight to the bar.

"Hey Joanne, give me a cold Miller draft sister." Vince went into his pocket and pulled out a ten dollar bill and laid it on the counter.

"You payin for last night's tab with that ten dollar bill, Vince?" Elaine's betrayal had resulted with him losing every material thing he ever owned. He had acquired some things through his illegal ventures and he had earned some of his belongings legally. But the law didn't agree with him and took everything from him. Vince spent a few years in federal prison and 7 years on probation. It was all coming to an end but was he ready? He didn't think so.

"What the hell you talking about Joanne"? Lately, Vince rarely remembered much about the night before.

"You musta forgot to pay or something because there was a note on the register that said you owed five dollars." Joanne spoke in a very matter of fact tone. She and Vince both knew that he owed the money because he usually got so drunk and out of control that he was put out before paying his final bill.

"Y'all full of shit but take the five bucks and give me another cold draft beer." Vince was feeling better after the first beer and he would feel much better after the second. He knew that Phyllis would be calling soon and he needed at least two beers to deal with her attitude. Vince thought to himself that he needed a change in his life. He had given up on himself and his relationship with God. He wanted change. He needed change but didn't know how to go about it.

"You seen Wayne and the boys this morning, Joanne"?

101

"No but it's early yet."

"You right." Vince took out his phone to call Phyllis. It would be better for him to get it over with now.

"What you want Vince?" Phyllis answered with much attitude in her voice. Phyllis remembered how things use to be when Vince brought lots of money into the household. She was tired of him. The money and prestige was gone and she was stuck with a poor alcoholic. She tolerated a lot of his bullshit because of her son be she couldn't do it any longer.

"Just checkin in to let you know I'm okay." Vince motioned to the barmaid to fill his beer mug one more time. There was silence on the other end of the phone.

"You there Phyllis?"

"Yes, I'm here but I'm tired of your shit! I want you to get your shit out of my place by Monday. I'm going away for the week-end and when I come back I'm going to change the locks and throw out anything you don't take."

"Phyllis, I don't have the energy or the desire to argue with you. I agree it will be best for the both of us. But you have to let me stay in Weldon's life. You know how much we love each other." Vince had a defeated tone in his voice. He would have to move back home in his room that his mother always kept available for him.

"You have my word Phyllis; I will be out by the time you get back in town." Vince hung up the phone without saying goodbye because there was nothing else to be said. He left the bar to relieve himself in the bathroom. When he returned, the bar was no longer the lonely place he left.

"Hey man." Walt was standing at the bar with the permanent smile he kept on his face.

"What you drinkin? Give this man a cold brew, Joanne."

"Hey Walt. Y'all just leavin the yard?"

"Yeah man. You wanna meet us in a few hours and put in some work before we go in tonight?"

"Yeah man. I'll meet you guys later. I'm gonna finish this drink, get some food and more rest. See you later." Vince pulled himself from the bar stool, exited the bar and headed back to his mother's house to get some more rest. He needed to work and get the money to move his stuff out of Phyllis' place and back to his mom.

***

Cherish's first full day in Jamaica was spent without her love, Wisdom. She and Grace loaded her Toyota 4 Runner and headed for the Riu hotel. The hotel was lovely with wonderful pools, gardens and a white sand beach. Grace hooked Cherish up with an all-inclusive band that gave her access to all restaurants and unlimited drinks by the pool or on the beach. Cherish pulled out her mp3 player and her assortment of books that included, "The Bluest Eye" by Toni Morrison and "The New Jerusalem Bible".

She felt like she was in heaven. It was as if all her stresses from the past were taken out to sea with the back and forth flow of the waves. She didn't mind that Wisdom wasn't there. She didn't mind being alone. Cherish closed her eyes and let the music take her away for an afternoon of total rest and relaxation.

Wisdom picked up Dup at the Dead End Bar and headed to Kingston. It was an important day for him. He had arranged recording time at Tuff Gong studios where the late Bob Marley produced the music that still inspires and motivates peace and love in the world. His plan was on track. He gave the porno film to Simon. He was laying the tracks for his CD and Cherish was in Jamaica.

Wisdom tried to clear his mind as he entered the studio. He wanted to be focused only on the music. He had plenty of songs, the right musicians and backup singers. The only thing left was to get everyone in the right vibe to record. Wisdom looked around the recording studio to make sure everyone he requested was there. To his surprise no one was missing probably because there was money and other extras involved in the deal.

"Bredren, mi waan thank yuh fi comin tu mek mi CD. Dis music food not only fi de I but all yuh Bredren. Mi pray dat yuh come on de concert tour. So light up de spliff's an gib thanks to Jah an let us git tu work." Everyone in the room prepared for a long recording session. All the men knew Wisdom and understood that they were not leaving until all the music was completed and satisfactory to him.

The recording session ended three days later. As Wisdom prepared to leave and return to Montego Bay, he remembered Cherish. He was totally involved in the music, his first and true love, and forgot about his American love, Cherish. He knew she would be angry but he thought it was better to get her use to the way things would be now that she was not in Jamaica on vacation.

What Cherish failed to realize was that when she visited, Wisdom took time out to just focus on her. But when she wasn't on the island, he spent his days and nights here and there doing whatever he could to make a buck or a connection. His survival lifestyle was very different from her daily routines and constant flow of money.

"Dup, yuh ridin wit de I back tu MoBay?"

"Yes Mon but mi waan check mi pinckney dem."

"Dup, yuh know mi hab Cherish?"

"Jah know Wisdom but mi nah hab no transport tu Kingston, Bredren."

"Mi soon come!" Wisdom walked away from Dup and headed toward the back of the property where there were a few one room cinder block homes. Georgie lived in one of the properties. It was the same Georgie from the song,

"No Woman, No Cry." The Georgie that made the fire light. Wisdom walked up on the porch and yelled through the open door.

"Wha happenin, Georgie. Its Bruk- Foot!" Wisdom sat down on the porch as a mocha colored, tall, frail older man appeared. His beard was white and braided down to the middle of his chest. His head was tied loosely with a long piece of white cotton cloth to cover his long white dreads.

104

"Mi nah overstand wha mi hear. Yuh nah say, Bruk-Foot!" The elder moved gracefully out the door using a long wooden stick for a cane and gently landed in the rocking chair positioned on the porch. Bob Marley guaranteed Georgie a place to live for the rest of his life. So when the home on Hope Street was changed to the museum and recording studio, Georgie was given a place to live on the back portion of the property.

"Yes, Star, Bruk Foot but dem call de I Wisdom."

"Mi glad fi see yuh. Now mi know dat mi grow a God fearing youth."

"Mi an Dub goin tu yard, yuh waan catch some breeze wit de I"?

"No Mon. Mi old an done wit dem tings dere. Mi more homely. Hale up de Bredren fi mi, Wisdom." Georgie raised from the rocking chair using his wooden stick gracefully and gave Wisdom a full embrace. The two men hugged exchanging no words but sharing their love for each other because they were both survivors. Wisdom released the embrace first. He felt himself getting emotional. He knew there was no time for emotion only action. His mind flashed to Cherish and his spirit could feel her discontent. But his spirit was telling him to stick with the flow and continue to First Street in Trench town to get some vibes from de Bredren in Culture Yard.

***

Three days passed and no sign of Wisdom. Wisdom didn't have his cell phone with him. Cherish found it ringing in their room when she asked Grace to call to check on him. The two women took an early morning drive and about an hour later landed at the beach in Runaway Bay.

It was one of Cherish's favorite beaches and Grace knew it. She wanted Cherish to enjoy herself. Cherish always loved this beach because in addition to the usual blue water and white sands there was always Reggae music playing from the nearby Flavours Beach Bar and Restaurant. The beach was surrounded by resorts but this part of the beach belonged to everyone. Cherish was sipping on a hot Guinness with a spliff in her other hand.

"Don't trouble yourself, Cherish. This is usual for my dad. I'm sure he's okay. He just got caught up in the music. Cherish you're going to find out that Jamaican men are different from American men and my dad is more different than that. I can tell you that he's a faithful man so you don't have to worry about other women but his other woman is the music." Grace and Cherish rested peacefully under a palm tree out of the sun as they discussed the situation.

"Grace, I am really finding it hard to be angry with your dad because I am having such a good time without him. Perhaps you are right. It's probably my American expectations. I only hope your dad can adjust when he has to deal with his Jamaican expectations"

"What's that Cherish?"

"The expectation that I won't take off and do me in Jamaica. I know that's not what Jamaican men expect from their woman." Cherish took a drag from her spliff and looked out toward the beautiful sea water while she spoke

"You mostly right about that Cherish. But you see what kind of Jamaican man I ended up with. One that gives me the freedom and liberty of a working woman." Both woman lied quietly and let the day quietly drift by with the sounds of Reggae music and the gentle flow of the sea.

***

Wisdom didn't want to make Cherish unhappy and at the same time he knew how important it was for him to follow his spirit, not the expectations of others. His spirit was telling him to go to Trench town. Wisdom hadn't been to the yard where he grew up in a long time. When he left Georgie, he found Dub standing in the front near the tall bronze statue of Bob Marley.

There were tourist everywhere but that didn't stop Dup from smoking a big spliff as he meditated on his children only a few minutes away. He hadn't seen his children for some time now. He loved his children dearly but Jamaica was an old slave island and its economics and politics made it almost impossible for men to stay with their families. There was nothing to do in the ghetto but sell drugs and die. So men who wanted to survive, left for the country. In the country, they could grow and sell ganja to the tourist. If they got lucky, meet an occasional foreign woman to support themselves and their children.

"Dup" Wisdom spoke softly as he approached his friend.

"Wha happenin? Yuh goin tu yard?"

"Yes Mon, mek we go tu yard." That was all conversation needed and the two men entered the car and headed west on Hope Road toward Hagley Road then on to Waltham Park Road and right on Spanish Road. The car made a slight left onto Collie Smith Drive. The men drove by the wall of honor where pictures of Bob Marley, Peter Tosh and Delroy Wilson were brightly painted and made a right turn onto First Street. They parked on First Street right in front of Culture Yard, and was greeted by an elder Rasta.

"Wha happenin! Welcome to Culture Yard. Mek mi tek yuh pon de tour". The elder stopped talking when he realized that the men where Dup and Bruk Foot.

"Rastas! Wha happenin?" The men began hugging and greeting each other.

"Dutty Money, yuh nah know yuh Bredren?" More people began to gather as news spread that Bruk Foot and Dub were in the yard.

"Yes Mon, mi know de I? Jah know de I is happy tu see yuh." Wisdom and Dub walked around the neighbors who came out to greet them and gave them all love. Dutty Money was one of the Bredren who ran the Culture Yard Museum. The Culture yard museum consisted of two long rows of tin roof houses with four doors along each that led to one room with enough room for one or two small beds.

Tourists were able to see the room where Bob and Rita slept on a single bed like in his song lyrics.

"We'll be together, with a roof right over our heads; We'll share the shelter of my single bed; We'll share the same room, for Jah provide the bread." The tour also included seeing Bob Marley's original guitar and the bucket where Ziggy Marley was bathed as a baby. In the middle of the yard, was a wide open space where everyone would gather, build a fire to cook and interact. Everyone in the yard shared a common cooking space, bathroom and washing tubs. The tour demonstrated what the yards in Trench town use to look like long ago when Bob was a young man and Wisdom was a boy.

Behind Culture Yard was how the residents lived in Trench town today. There were rows and rows of small alley ways lined up with makeshift tin walls. On the other side of these tin walls, were more makeshift housing constructed from anything available. There was no indoor plumbing and as a result it was not unusual to walk up and down the allies and run into a resident taking a leak.

"Dutty, dem call de I Wisdom. Mi jus finish recordin tracks fe mi CD at Tuff Gong. Georgie asked mi tu hail yuh up."

"Jah know yuh gwan break out Wisdom. Yuh been blessed by Jah wit knowin dem Rasta's, Bob, Peter and Delroy."

Wisdom spent the rest of his time in the yard catching vibes from the past memories. Dub went to his baby momma's shack to make love and see his children Wisdom made a stop in Cutty's kitchen for some fish and rice and peas before bedding down on Dutty Money's floor. He would leave for Mo Bay first light. He'd only been gone for four days. He was sure Cherish would understand.

When Wisdom got home four days later, Cherish and Grace were nowhere to be found. The nanny had Kyler and Rashaun, Grace's husband, had no idea of the women's whereabouts. The woman decided to stay the night at Breezes Runaway Bay Resort. Grace knew people who worked at many resorts and if rooms were not taken for the night, she could easily take advantage of the opportunity. The women spent the evening at Reggae Café in Breezes, an all-inclusive resort, drinking, eating, and dancing.

Wisdom was happy that Cherish was out with Grace. He knew his daughter would keep her happy and show her a good time. Wisdom took a long shower. He hadn't really showered in the past four days and he really appreciated the indoor plumbing in the bathroom. After his shower, he headed downstairs to see what he missed these past four days.

"Wha ah gwan,Bredren? Yuh waan Guinness?" Rashaun greeted Wisdom as he entered the room.

"Yes Mon. Wha happenin, Star?"

"Mi jus relaxin, Rasta"

"Wha happenin wit de Sistren?"

"Dem left fi de beach de other day an mi nah seen dem yet." Yuh know Grace no drive inna de nite. Yuh must know dem stay overnight."

"Mi know Mon. Mi nah worried. Mi jus relaxin." The men fell asleep on the couch watching football.

"Hey baby. You made it back home I see." Wisdom was awaken by Cherish's sweet lips. Cherish was over it all. She had a great time while he was among the missing and hadn't really missed him. The first few days were spent alone on the beach at the Riu with servers who took care of her every want, yesterday at her favorite beach and an evening of entertainment at Breezes. Cherish took a seat next to Wisdom on the couch. She was horny and really didn't want to argue because an argument would cause Wisdom to withhold sex.

"Jah know mi missed yuh Cherish."

"I missed you too but honestly, I didn't miss you too much. You know I was with my other lover, Jamaica. Grace made sure I was treated like a queen at the Riu and

109

we had a beautiful day on the beach at Runaway Bay with an excellent night's stay at Breeze's." Cherish was cheerful as she shared her adventures with Wisdom.

"Hope you accomplished all that you wanted to get done with the music?"

"Yes, Mon everyting cook an curry. Mi tired. Yuh waan come tu bed, Cherish"?

"Yes baby. Let's lie down." The couple climbed the stairs. Upon entering the room, the lovers laid on the bed. Her positive attitude about his time away helped to promote his feelings. He tenderly kissed her lips and gently suck her breast while slowly rubbing her clit. Cherish was soaking wet. Wisdom's kissing moved down from his lover's breast to her stomach and then headed toward her Punany. Wisdom had never tasted Cherish's sweet pot or any other woman's. But during the past four days, Wisdom heard more about eating pussy than he'd heard in his entire life. From all he could gather, American woman really loved it and expected to have their pussy eaten from time to time. He wanted to taste his lady. He knew her sugar pot was nothing but sweet. Wisdom wanted to please Cherish and make her as happy as he could.

Cherish was shocked as her lover moved his lips toward her precious jewels and the closer his lips moved toward her Punany, the wetter she got. She didn't know what changed and didn't care. Wisdom ate her pussy better than any of her lover's and she enjoyed every moment. Afterwards he made passionate love to her and they both fell into a deep rewarding sleep.

Chapter Six

Cherish and time was moving forward. She had lots of plans for her stay in Jamaica and was beginning to relax in her new life. It wasn't everything she expected. She expected to spend more time with her man. That wasn't happening but it was more time than she spent with him while living in Philadelphia. She was okay with that and decided to put some of her own plans into effect to fill-up her alone time. Wisdom had his music and she needed a passion also. She tried to share her ideas with him but he was only processing information that affected his own dreams. The two were moving forward but neither one knew if the other was headed in the same direction.

The first thing Cherish did was rent a six bedroom furnished home in Retreat, nestled within the hills of "The Three Courts" in the Parish of St. Mary. Ocho Rios was fifteen minutes to the west and to the east was Oracabassa and Port Maria. The next step was to purchase a computer because the island had access to the internet and she knew that would be helpful in many different ways. Finally, Cherish purchased two vehicles, a car and a truck, because in Jamaica you needed both.

Cherish and Wisdom sat on the veranda of their new rental property which overlooked the green canopies of the valley below with picturesque scenes of eastern St. Mary and a breathtaking view of the harbor and the Caribbean Sea. The property was a three storied house located on about ¾ of an acre of land with plush trees and various fruits and vegetables. One side of the property had a gentle slope bounded by a stone retaining wall with a well paved access road to the car port and front door. The ground level had a large living room and kitchen with three bedrooms and three full baths. The middle level had a moderate sized living room and kitchen, with two bedrooms, and bathrooms. Finally, the top level was studio

111

S.D. Laurence

apartment with a separate entrance that included a small bedroom and bath with a small kitchenette.

Cherish and Wisdom was both enjoying the silence and beautiful flora of Jamaica. She was learning that it wasn't always necessary to have something to say all the time; sometimes it was cool to just listen to the silence. Maybe in America everyone talked to overpower the sounds of the city.

"Wisdom, when are we going to Kingston to register the car?" Cherish broke the silence. She usually did. Wisdom could sit for a day and not feel the need to say anything about anything.

"Dis morning Cherish. Dis a good day tu travel." The couple prepared for the long ride to Kingston. The ride to Kingston was awesome but the registration process was horrendous. She couldn't believe all the bull shit they had to go through to pay money and register a car. In addition to the unbearable lines, every time they got one piece of paper another one was required. Three days later, Cherish had enough and demanded to see the supervisor.

"This wouldn't happen in America! I don't understand why it takes so much paperwork to give the government money!" Cherish spoke rudely to the official.

"How can I help you Madame." Mr. Bailey spoke with an English accent. He wore a hot black suit and a white shirt with a collar that was obviously too large.

"Can you help me register this vehicle I just purchased? This is my third day at to the motor vehicle registry. I live in St Mary and the ride is too long to come back and forth. So I've had to stay in a hotel for the past two nights and all this is not making me happy." Cherish calmed down a little.

"I understand Madame but we have our procedures and necessary paperwork attached to vehicle registration in this country." Mr. Bailey spoke with a very patient tone.

"I do understand but what I don't understand is why couldn't anyone tell us everything we needed at once?"

112

Cherish settled back in her chair more relaxed and willing to tell Mr. Bailey a few things about Jamaica's shitistim.

"Well Sir, let me explain what happened to me." Cherish gave a step by step account about coming to the office for information to register her vehicle and was initially told that she needed the certificate of title, registration certificate, proof of insurance, certificate of fitness, and a discharge of lien if necessary, to register the vehicle.

What she didn't tell Mr. Bradley was that Wisdom was no help at all. He never owned or registered a vehicle in Jamaica. Wisdom drove and had access to vehicles all the time but never bothered with the paperwork. He couldn't take the government vibes. The only times he did tolerate the vibe was to attain a driver's license, visa, or passport.

"Mr. Bailey, I returned with all the papers and the clerk informs me that proof of insurance is not the receipt stamped paid with the dates of coverage but a specific piece of paper from the insurance company called an insurance cover note." Cherish was really sick of the entire conversation now. She didn't want to talk about it any longer.

"Well Madame, I apologize but the insurance cover note is very important." Mr. Bailey was beginning to feel that Cherish didn't respect the Jamaican way of doing things.

"Okay, I get the cover note and then I'm told about having a Taxpayer Registration Number." As Cherish spoke this time she raised her hands dramatically in the air. Wisdom sat quietly during the conversation.

"Well, Miss, I must inform you that most Jamaicans understand that a TRN is needed to do any type of business so I know the clerk assumed you knew that." Mr. Bailey looked toward Wisdom as he spoke this time. Dreadlocks were not accepted in Jamaican society and the remnants were still alive today especially in the old time English Jamaicans.

"The final draw Mr. Bailey was asking me to have the previous owner present for the registration of the vehicle.

113

Bottom line is that I have washed out my panties in a hotel sink for three days now because I never imagined registering a car would take so long." Cherish spoke with finality to her voice. Without a word Mr. Bailey quickly picked up the phone on his desk.

"Miss. Henry, may I beg you to find the paperwork on vehicle registration for Miss Cherish Davis?" Cherish felt the ordeal was coming to an end. In the next 30 minutes, Miss Henry would walk into Mr. Bailey's office with the papers Cherish waited so long to attain.

Although most of their hot days in Kingston were spent in traffic going from one office to another and waiting in lines, their evenings were spent in a pleasant hotel and nights on the town. Wisdom and Cherish stayed at the Chelsea Hotel on Chelsea Avenue in New Kingston 10. Kingston is Jamaica's capital city that lies between the southeastern coastline of the island and the towering Blue Mountains, Red Hills, and Long Mountain. The bustling city of over 700,000 people is a combination of a shanty town and modern metropolitan city. New Kingston, the metropolitan area, is situated between the downtown and midtown areas and the suburbs of St. Andrew with the soaring Blue Mountains as a backdrop. The nearby hillside suburb of Beverly Hills has luxury homes gracing its cool slopes. Not even Beverly Hills, Los Angeles can boast of the elaborate architecture found in its Kingston namesake.

The New Chelsea Hotel had over 50 rooms. Each room had cable TV, air conditioning and hot & cold water. The added luxury of hot water was always mentioned as an attraction because it was a luxury. Most Jamaicans didn't see the need for hot water in their homes. First of all, the cold water was never really cold, only in the morning, because the hot sun heated the water daily. The hotel was within walking distance to several restaurants and shopping plazas. There were pool tables, game machines and a beautiful indoor lounge with a rooftop garden bar. What put the cherry on top were the nightly rates, 35

American dollars. So when Cherish and Wisdom finished the paperwork, they decided to stay in Kingston for the remainder of the weekend. The next morning, Wisdom woke Cherish early to get ready for the day.

"Come Cherish, mek we go tu de beach." Wisdom knew to have a cup of Blue Mountain coffee in hand if he decided to wake Cherish earlier than her usual time. Cherish yawned and turned to see Wisdom standing with a white cup filled with hot coffee.

"Thanks baby." She grabbed the coffee and took a long hard sip.

"What you talkin about Willis?" She started to laugh and looked in Wisdom's face only to discover, he had no idea what she said was a joke

"Wha yuh say, Cherish?"

"Oh nothing." She didn't feel like an explanation.

"Cherish yuh must know Hellshire beach? Mek we go." Wisdom had taken her so many places on the island it was often hard to remember all the exotic locations.

"That would be nice Wisdom. I could use a day at the beach." Cherish finished her coffee while Wisdom showered. The couple prepared for their day on the beach. Hellshire beach is the favored beach for the locals in Kingston. It's a place to relax all day while eating fresh fish, or snacking on festival and barbeque lobster while drinking fresh coconut water. The beach is located west of Portmore in Hellshire Hills.

Portmore is the suburb of the two cities, Kingston and Spanish Town, located on the southern coast of Jamaica in the Parish of St. Catherine. The drive to Hellshire Hills took about 35 minutes from the hotel. As the two drove down the Kingston Causeway, Cherish caught glimpses of fishing shacks and women tending their stalls preparing to sell their wares to stopping motorist. The drive along Kingston Causeway lead them through the seaside town of Port Henderson.

115

S.D. Laurence

Port Henderson is a shore town lined with restaurants, guest houses and motels that Jamaicans from nearby Kingston drive to and enjoy the fresh fish prepared in varied ways. Continuing along the Kingston Causeway, they came to a large roundabout with large neon video boards indicating you have arrived in the city of Portmore. To the right was the Portmore Mall, the largest indoor mall of its kind in the Caribbean. Further on is the Mega Mart, the largest superstore in Jamaica similar to Costco and BJ's in America. At the T-junction, Wisdom turned left toward Greater Portmore with Hellshire Hills at the end of the route.

The day was perfect. Cherish and Wisdom took a horse ride along the beach, bathed in the blue water and rested on the white sands. The two ate and drank as much as they possibly could that day and of course, Wisdom ran into someone he knew. It appeared to Cherish, there was no place on the island where someone didn't know Wisdom. Wisdom decided to take a walk and get some ganja for Cherish to complete her day.

"Cherish, mi soon come." As Wisdom walked away, Cherish was thankful for the time alone. Wisdom wasn't annoying at all. He rarely engaged in useless conversations. It was the being alone part Cherish was learning to enjoy. She was realizing that time alone was very important. She didn't quite understand why but recognized that the need existed and decided to go with it. Cherish laid on the beach watching the still blue water of the Caribbean Sea, children and families enjoying a day at the beach. Cherish could see Wisdom returning with another Rasta in tow.

"Cherish, meet mi Bredren Knowledge." Cherish looked behind the two men and saw a tall husky white woman with a Red Stripe beer in one hand and a cigarette in the other attempting to catch up with the men.

"Knowledge, introduce yuh girl tu mi queen, Cherish."

"Zerby dis Cherish." Knowledge quickly made the introduction as he and Wisdom quietly walked away to talk

116

without disruption. Zerby took a seat next to Cherish on the beach, pulled out a large spliff and lit it with the cigarette she was smoking. She put the cigarette out in the sand and that disgusted Cherish.

"I'm from New Mexico. Where you from Cherish?" Zerby took a long draw of the spliff and passed in on to Cherish.

"I'm from the east coast. You know New York, Philly, and New Jersey." Cherish responded after drawing on the tall spliff. The ganja was excellent and the draw mellowed Cherish out enough to deal with this American White woman.

"Wisdom tells me you just moved to the island. That's great! I come down often to visit my baby and business. I'm here for at least seven or eight months a year. Where do you and Wisdom stay. Knowledge and I are always here and there on the island." Her story sounded familiar to Cherish. It appeared that Wisdom was not the only man on the island that had no one place to call home.

"We just rented a pretty large property in St. Mary up in the hills. I'm hoping to use it as a guest house and make some money during my stay."

"That's a great idea. Knowledge is looking for a piece of property for me to build a place to stay when I'm on the island. Yuh want another Guinness, Cherish?"

"Yes, that would be nice." Cherish watched as Zerby walked toward a vendor to purchase a Red Stripe for herself and a cold Guinness for Cherish. Zerby returned to Cherish and handed her the cold Guinness.

"How many rooms are in your rental property?" Zerby sipped on her Red Stripe as she spoke.

"There are six bedrooms with six baths in total with a studio apartment on the top floor."

"Do you have any guest yet?'

"No, we just moved in a few weeks ago."

"How much you charging?" Cherish hadn't thought about rates yet.

117

"How long are you interested in staying?" Cherish was trying to think of a figure while Zerby gave her an answer.

"Well, I'm staying on the island for another seven or eight months. I would like to stay in the studio apartment if that's okay." Zerby sat quietly as Cherish dealt with her own thoughts. The silence was broken with Wisdom and Knowledge retuning to the beach spot.

"Cherish, mi hab de first guest fi de house." Wisdom sat down next to Cherish and waited for a response.

"That's a coincidence; Zerby just asked me how much it would cost to stay at the place." Cherish wanted to see if Wisdom quoted a price for the property. She didn't mind him acting like they were in everything together but she did want Wisdom to respect that everything was her investment.

"Mi nevah say how much, Cherish. Mi tell de Rasta hem must talk tu mi queen." Wisdom leaned over and gave Cherish a quick peck on the cheek.

"Well, I was thinking about $500.00 a month for the studio." Zerby was excited.

"I'll pay 500 dollars. Roaming the island with Knowledge will cost me much more than that." Zerby rose up and grabbed Knowledge by the cheeks and kissed him on the lips. Cherish was happy to have her first guest. She knew that Wisdom would come through with the guest but she was also depending on some of her family and friends visiting.

"Rasta, mi an de Sistren stayin at de Chelsea Hotel inna New Kingston. Yuh know de place, Star?" It was getting late and it appeared that Wisdom was preparing to leave the beach.

"Yes Mon, mi know de place. Yuh tink dem hab more rooms tu rent?" Knowledge and Wisdom were old friends and it was obvious they didn't want the end their time together just yet.

"Yes Star, mi know dem hab more room tu rent. Come Rasta mek we drive tu Kingston." Wisdom and Cherish packed up their belongings and headed back to the Chelsea Hotel. The two were followed by their new found tenants. Knowledge and Zerby got a room right down the hall from Wisdom and Cherish.

The four planned an evening out on the town at the Quad, one of the busiest nightclubs in Kingston. The admission is $600 Jamaican dollars (about $7 US dollars) for men and free admission for the women. It's frequented by locals and foreigners alike. There was a jazz bar on the ground floor and three floors of dancing upstairs. One floor played predominantly Jamaican dance music and the other more mainstream. The very top floor had a more intimate dance floor, and a small terrace where the group went to avoid the crowds and take in the pleasant view of Kingston by night.

"Cherish, I can't wait to see your place in St Mary. I am a little familiar with the area." Zerby was rolling a giant spliff as she spoke.

"Careful, Sistren." Wisdom spoke softly to Zerby.

"Careful for what Bredren?" Zerby spoke as if she were insulted.

"Careful bout de ganja Sistren. It is illegal an dis not de place tu light a spliff." Wisdom changed his tone. He avoided trouble as much as possible but was more than willing to deal with it if it came his way.

"Come now, Sistren. Respect de Bredren. Do lik hem ake." Knowledge intervened immediately. He knew his friend Wisdom; he didn't take no shit from anyone especially not a White woman. Zerby put the spliff in her small purse.

"Cherish, I hope we can smoke at your house and it won't be a problem?"

"Wisdom is just looking out for us. You know that's how we met in Negril?" Cherish recounted to Zerby how Wisdom managed to get her ganja back from the policeman who took it from her at Roots.

S.D. Laurence

"That's a sweet story. Okay, I'm not mad at you Bredren." Zerby held out her arms for Wisdom to embrace her but Wisdom hesitated.

"You don't want to hug me and make peace?" Zerby said in a course tone.

"Sistren, mi luv an respect yuh but mi respect mi queen. Mi nah disrespect she." Wisdom really didn't hug up on women. Cherish hadn't noticed until one day he called her attention to the fact that she would always hug his friends when she met them.

"That's true, Zerby. Wisdom doesn't hug up on the opposite sex like we Americans do." Cherish was telling the truth more than defending her man. She was confident that Wisdom could take care of himself.

"Can't we just all get along!" Cherish added in an attempt to end the episode.

"Yuh waan drink, Zerby?" Knowledge was trying to change the subject also. He didn't want this white woman to rub his friend the wrong way. Knowledge knew about Wisdom's temper. He didn't know if Cherish was aware because Wisdom always showed a cool exterior. But Knowledge knew different.

"Yes, get me a shot of that Wray & Nephew over proof white rum and a red stripe. You want anything Cherish?"

"Yes, I'll have white rum also. I need to kill some germs inna mi body!" Everyone laughed and the group continued to enjoy their evening together drinking and dancing. Wisdom was not known for dancing except for on the stage but this night Cherish was enjoying a dancing man. She tried to keep her mind in the moment. Life was teaching her there is no past and no future, only now.

The next day the couples headed for more adventure. What Cherish was discovering that her experience was not that unique? She thought she was the only woman on the island that enjoyed the company of a Rasta man to escort them around. After talking to Zerby, she realized that Zerby's dreams were the same as hers. Relocate to Jamaica,

120

run some kind of business and relax in Jamaica with her man. Another thing Cherish noticed was that the two men didn't spend their time talking about staying in Jamaica. It was always about leaving.

"Cherish, Cherish" Wisdom whispered in his lover's ear as she slept through the early morning. She had a little too much white rum the night before. After returning to the hotel, they sat at rooftop garden bar and smoked spliffs till the morning.

"Empress, mi waan tek yuh tu de mineral baths." Wisdom was gently rubbing Cherish's ass as he spoke. Cherish was enjoying the moment and hoping it might end with a great morning sexual encounter. She didn't want to get too excited because if Wisdom didn't complete the task, she would need the time to masturbate before they left.

"Cherish, yuh gonna luv de mineral baths an mi waan tek yuh tu Port Royal. Come now." Wisdom stopped rubbing her ass and began to tap it lightly. Wisdom thought he was getting her to wake up but in reality the tapping was getting her more aroused.

"What baby?" Cherish turned over to give Wisdom another opportunity to taste her sugar pot. He hadn't made a visit down south since the first time.

"Mi soon come, Cherish." Wisdom stopped abruptly and stood up.

"Mek de I go git Knowledge ready fi de day." Wisdom was walking toward the door.

"Why don't you call his room, Baby. There's no need for you to go anywhere." Cherish sat up on one elbow to poke her boobs forward and push her ass out in a sexy pose.

"Mi need de air an mi git de Blue Mountain coffee fi yuh. Get ready now." Wisdom walked out the door. Cherish decided to finish the job Wisdom started. She rolled over on her back, and began to engage her clitoris to orgasm. Cherish was becoming proficient in pleasing

121

herself in many ways. Her sexual satisfaction was only one way she was learning to satisfy herself.

"Yuh comin, Cherish?" Wisdom called out as he returned to the hotel room.

"I came after you went." Cherish was walking toward the bathroom with a towel wrapped around her body.

"Knowledge an de Sistren, dem soon come." Wisdom ignored the comment made by Cherish because he didn't understand what she was talking about. Cherish finished her shower and began to dress for the day.

"Where are we going again, Wisdom?" Cherish didn't bring many clothes but she did have a few bathing suits and several wraps. She called them her Jamaican uniform.

"Tu de mineral bath an Port Royal. Wear yuh bath suit an yuh wrap." Wisdom and Cherish were ready for the day.

"Hey yall!" Zerby yelled as Cherish and Wisdom walked toward the car.

"Good morning, Zerby. You sleep good last night?" Cherish said cheerfully

"As a matter of fact, I did. How about you?" Zerby responded.

"Great! The rum and ganja helped a lot!" Both women laughed as they entered the car. It appeared that Knowledge returned their rental car early that morning so this time the two couples loaded into one car for the excursion. The two women were directed to the back seats and the two men sat up front. Cherish never liked the idea of men in front and women in the back. It was really much safer in the back because Jamaican drivers were known for speeding and not observing the rules of the road. Additionally, the men were able to sit together and talk while traveling. In Jamaica, the culture included sexual segregation. Men spent time with men and women spent time with women. Cherish never liked this because she was always interested in everyone's opinion.

The couples headed east on Golding Road toward Studio One Blvd and made a left. When they reached Retirement Road, they turned right and then left onto Half Way Tree Road. Half Way Tree Road is the unofficial marker that divides the urban, inner-city commercial areas of downtown Kingston, and the quieter, residential suburban communities of St. Andrew.

The name "Half Way Tree Road" came from a huge cotton tree that dominated the intersection until 1866 when the tree died. The tree was a major meeting place for travelers and traders coming to and from Kingston, Spanish Town, St. Thomas or St. Mary. Even though the tree is gone, it remains as a place where people stop to refresh themselves. From Half Way, they landed on Arthur Wint Drive and drove pass the Edna Manley College of the Visual and Performing Arts. Cherish noticed the sign and got excited.

"How long has Edna Manley College been established? Can we stop and have a look, Wisdom?"

"Yuh hab enougf of school Cherish! Mek de I tek yuh tu de Mineral Baths!" Everyone laughed and the group proceeded to their destination. The car continued down Arthur Wint Drive and turned right onto Mountain View and left onto Windward Road for a short distance turning left onto the A4 exiting on Windward Road heading for Rock fort. The Rockfort Mineral Baths were located on the road leading to Jamaica's International Airport and Wisdom drove past the baths and headed for the airport. Cherish noticed that Wisdom missed the exit for Rockfort Mineral Baths and spoke out as if she spent her whole life in Kingston.

"Wisdom you missed the exit to the baths!" Wisdom did not respond and continued to drive.

"Wisdom you missed the exit to the baths!" Cherish spoke again not believing that Wisdom may be ignoring her.

"Mi know Sistren. Cherish, yuh must know dat mi know wha mi doin an where mi goin." His tone was quiet and stern. His attitude displayed how he felt about having anyone question him about where he's going. Especially Cherish because this was his Island not hers.

"Where are we going"? Cherish spoke in a normal tone realizing that Wisdom did know what he was doing and where he was going.

"Cherish yuh messin wit mi vibe, Sistren!" Cherish and the passengers in the car all sensed Wisdom's tension and shut up. Cherish didn't know what the fuck was wrong with this man and didn't care. She reminded herself of her goal for her time in Jamaica. The car continued to the Kingston Airport and Wisdom parked the car in the car lot.

"Mi gonna pick up Simon. De flight soon come. Mi need tu check upon de arrival time. Mi soon come." Wisdom walked away and of course Knowledge obediently followed.

"What de fuck are we supposed to do in this hot fuckin car?" Cherish was angry. Who did Wisdom think he was? Or did he forget who she was?

"Hey man. I don't know what just happened but I know these Jamaican men are temperamental." Both girls laughed loudly and quieted down to realize that they were stranded in a hot box at the Norman Manley Airport for God knows how long.

"This shit is not fun Zerby. We can't smoke a joint cause there's too many police around and there isn't anywhere we can take a walk to. What you waan do?"

"You know what there are a lot of Cherish?"

"No, what?"

"Taxi cabs, Cherish! There are plenty of Taxi cabs!"

"And?" Cherish didn't catch on right away.

"We can take a cab to the baths! They're not that far from the airport and it shouldn't cost much. Anyway, I got plenty of money. Money is not an issue for us!" Zerby

124

laughed as she reached over to give her new found sister a tight hug.

"Let's go then girl. You're my kinda Bitch. We gonna have fun roommate. You have a pen? I got some paper." The women composed a simple note for the boys informing them of their cab ride to the baths and instructions for them to pick them up after they retrieve Simon.

Cherish and Zerby grabbed a cab and headed for Rockfort Baths. Cherish couldn't believe that her new friend was a White American girl from New Mexico. Cherish had given up her prejudicial attitude while living in Iowa where she became dear friends with a White woman she closely worked with. She thought to herself how funny it was for her to come all the way to Jamaica and meet up with a white girl from America as a best friend.

"Hey driver?" Zerby hailed a cab and the two women headed for the mineral bath.

"Yuh mind if de Sista lite up a spliff? Deres a tip fi yuh."

"No Problem, Miss." The driver continued to the destination.

"How you think the boys gonna feel when they find us gone and read the note?" Zerby was filling her pipe with ganja as she spoke.

"I don't really give a fuck. Do you? I wonder if either one of them will be able to read the note?" Cherish and Zerby laughed and smoked on the short ride to the baths. The car drove down a back road toward a beautifully manicured garden and pulled up in front of a wire fence. Cherish and Zerby exited the cab and walked toward the fence that enclosed a large pool filled with blue water surrounded by small enclosures where people placed towels, food, drink, and necessary items for the day at the pool. The place was loaded with locals enjoying the day. As the two entered the gate, they were immediately greeted.

"Good day ladies. Welcome tu de Rockfort mineral baths. Yuh been here before?" The young black Jamaican greeter was beautiful. Cherish was happy that she came to Jamaica as a more matured woman because in her younger days, the days without AIDS, she would have fucked as many of these lovely young men as possible.

"No, I haven't been here before. Have you Zerby?" Cherish turned to see that Zerby was pulling on her small pipe.

"Yes, Cherish mi been here before. Cherish you're hooked up wit de right Bitch. Mi know Jamaica. Mi a rebel and don't need a man tu tek mi around." Zerby laughed her hearty laugh and proceeded confidently down the walk toward the private baths. Cherish followed closely behind Zerby and thought to herself how she needed to stop being so judgmental. When she met Zerby, she had no idea how this relationship would affect her life. Once again, everything happens the way it's supposed to happen, so don't judge a person or a situation. Wait on the universe to reveal its meaning and purpose. The perspective tour guide followed the two girls catching up with Cherish telling her about the historic importance of the place as they walked.

"No one know jus who discovered de healing wata. Some say de wata come from de earthquake in 1907. But de wata is certified as healing an de people dem come from around de world to soak. Yuh can tek a bath an a massage, Mon." The three reached the private bath area and were greeted by friendly young lady that guided them to a small private room with a large Jacuzzi-type bath and two massage tables.

"Yuh hab de room fi de hour. De masseuse soon come. Enjoy." The young lady quickly exited the room. Cherish and Zerby quietly resorted to opposite sides of the room and changed into their bath suits. Cherish was happy that Zerby wasn't one of these let's get naked together white girls. She liked Zerby. Cherish didn't easily make friends with woman but Zerby was different.

Cherish entered the hot springs and settled into a relaxing position to feel the mineral water encircle her body while the heat melted away years of tension and stress. Zerby was busy preparing a large spliff to accompany the bath experience. Neither woman had spoken or thought about the men for some time now.

"What you think the boys are doing Cherish?" Zerby lit the spliff as she spoke.

"I told you, girl. I don't give a fuck." As Cherish finished her statement, a blue-black gorgeous young man walked into the room. His walked with prominence and had the build of a supernatural human being.

"Good day Miss. Mi come tu gib yuh a massage." He spoke with a low soft tone and brushed back his long locks back as he handed both Cherish and Zerby a white cotton robe and began to place clean white sheets on the massage tables.

"Deres a masseuse fi each of yuh. Mek yuhself ready an mi soon come." The gorgeous man exited.

"Zerby, I hope the next one is a fine as the last one." Wisdom wasn't what you called Jamaican fine. He was short with a small frame and a worn but interesting, spiritual face. Zerby's man on the other hand was young, black, tall and muscular and she wasn't as interested in the eye candy as much as Cherish seemed to be.

"Girl, I don't give a fuck how fine these Jamaican men are they're all lookin for the same thing, a ticket out of Jamaica to anywhere but here. They all have a kind side and a rude side. Kindness and rudeness are necessary to survive in Jamaica. Stick wit me girl. I'll teach you a few things." Cherish felt there was something different about her new found girlfriend. She wasn't a shy, weak White American woman. Cherish thought, maybe it was her New Mexico upbringing. Cherish had never been to New Mexico but it was on her list of places to visit. Cherish ended her thoughts and returned them to the fine Jamaican man that was about to attack her body with his strong and powerful healing hands.

The massage time was spent quietly. The masseuses were so through in getting the job done that when they left the two women were knocked out and snoring on the tables. The two women slept for over an hour and awoke hungry and peaceful. They dressed and proceeded to the cafeteria and juice bar. Cherish had a veggie patty with carrot juice and Zerby had ice cream and a red stripe beer.

"How long you think we been here Cherish?"

"I guess two hours or more. Why?"

"How long you think we should wait? I can't do another bath and massage and I can't smoke my spliffs in this area so I think we should make a move."

"What you mean make a move? We can't take a cab back to St. Mary. That's a long way to ask somebody to drive!"

"Cherish, I got cash, so as long as there's cash there's somebody to drive us the fuck where we want to go on this island. But no, I'm gonna call one of my friends to bring my Hummer to me. I was gonna tell them to bring it to St. Mary but fuck it. I'll drive us home. The Bredren had to do some work for me up in the mountains and needed to use the Hummer. He dropped me and Knowledge off at the beach and we rented a car until the Hummer returned and then we met you guys. So shit has changed and the Bredren will go along wit de change."

Zerby pulled out her phone and proceeded to make the call. She walked away as she spoke and talked in quiet tones she hadn't used since she and Cherish met.

"Okay, Cherish. We should be out of this place soon. Let's walk into the gardens out in the parking area and wait for our ride." Zerby confidently walked toward the parking lot. She knew Jamaica, what she wanted, and she made it happen.

***

Wisdom and Knowledge entered the airport and shortly after Simon appeared from behind the immigration doors followed by a tall, slender blonde blued eyed Australian. Wisdom sited Simon and quickly called out to greet him.

"Simon, wha ah gwan Mon? Long time no see. Welcome, Jamaica no problem." Wisdom and Simon reached out and hugged one another. The feelings the two men shared were genuine. Wisdom truly felt Simon was his angel and treated him as such. There wasn't anything Wisdom wouldn't do for Simon because he had unknowingly done do much for him. Simon thought only about this Susan thing that didn't really exist. Wisdom managed to get the Susan thing off Simon's mind and replaced it with, I'm a producer kinda guy and Simon was lovin it.

"Wisdom, meet Aiden. He's a videographer from the other side of the pond, Australia. He's come to shoot some scenes for your video and some other shit." Wisdom and Aiden shook hands and Simon walked ahead as if he owned the airport and everything in it. Aiden rushed ahead to look after the luggage because a lot of it included his valuable equipment.

The two men gather all the luggage and equipment, while Knowledge went to get car. Knowledge returned and Wisdom noticed only Knowledge in the front seat. It was so noticeable to him because he was looking to see, as the car drove up, if there was enough room for everyone and everything. Where were the woman? Knowledge exited the car and motioned to Wisdom to come closer.

"De Sistren left a note. Dem gone tu de mineral springs."

"Jah blessed de I, Bredren! Deres no way mi gonna git all dis and de Sistren in de car. Yuh must know Zerby's number. Call de number now." Wisdom walked back to Simon and began small talk as they prepared to load the

129

car and Knowledge walked away to make the call. The phone rang a few times and Zerby answered.

"Wha ah gwan, Sistren?" Knowledge spoke in his normal calm tone. He was use to Zerby doing whatever the fuck she wanted to do. Zerby was a business woman first. She was a big ganja smuggler and did business all around the world.

"So yuh alright? Blessings, mi soon come." Knowledge ended the conversation. Zerby told Knowledge that she was having her Hummer brought to her at the mineral springs and she and Cherish were driving to St. Mary. That all sounded cool to Knowledge and he immediately shared the good news with Wisdom.

"Tings cooks and curry, Bredren. De Sistren dem drivin tu St. Mary." Knowledge proceeded to help load the car.

"Mi know dat Zerby knows de place! But Zerby wit Cherish mi don't know bout dem tings, Rasta!"

"No ting stops Jah's plan yuh know, Rasta!" The conversation about the woman ceased and the two men went back to the present moment of loading the car. The four men and all their belongings were packed and loaded.

"Where tu, Rasta?" Knowledge was just a surprised as Cherish about the plan change. Wisdom hadn't bothered to share anything with anyone. He wasn't use to sharing what he was going to do and when it was going to happen. Knowledge was surprised but not shocked. Rasta follow their spiritual vibes so for Knowledge it was things as usual.

"Yuh mus know de Courtleigh inna New Kingston on Knutsford Blvd."

"Yes, Mon mi know de place." Knowledge pulled off and headed for Norman Manley Highway. The four men back tracked pass Edna Manley College and Mountain View Road, and within 25 minutes they were pulling into the driveway of the Courtleigh Hotel & Suites.

The area was covered with the beautiful lush flowers of Jamaica and the group was immediately greeted by two

130

extremely polite Jamaican doormen that opened all doors and supplied hot towels for their immediate refreshment while being guided inside to a cold Jamaican rum punch and exceptional front desk service. Simon began to light his Cuban cigar as the one of the doormen quickly managed to light it before Simon could complete the process.

"Wisdom, so far so good, man!" Simon was pleased. His last stay in Jamaica was different, this time his focus was on pleasure and Wisdom seemed to understand the type of service he required. His instructions to Wisdom were cost is no problem, just make my stay pleasurable.

"Blessings, Simon. Jah know yuh gwan luv de room!" Wisdom was happy that Simon was happy. His greatest pleasure in life was to make people happy. Wisdom had planned a full three weeks for him and Simon. He hadn't shared this information with Cherish. It hadn't crossed his mind to share. Wisdom knew that having someone else around to consider was going to be something he had to get use to. But he also thought maybe Cherish would have to get use to him because he didn't see how he could change his soul.

***

Zerby and Cherish waited in the garden for her vehicle to take them trip home to St. Mary. Suddenly, a brand new cherry red Hummer pulled in front of the gates of Rockfort mineral baths. Zerby yelled out to get the drivers attention.

"Scooby!" Zerby slowly walked toward the Hummer and Cherish obediently followed. Another tall, black, muscular Jamaican Rasta with long luxurious locks jumped out the Hummer to give Zerby a hearty greeting.

"Sistren, mi so glad fi see yuh! Wha happenin tu yuh an tell de I bout dis beautiful Sistren wit yuh!"

Cherish had just begun to grow her Locks. Her hair was curly, blondish brown and beautiful, while her mocha skin glistened in the sun.

"Dis Cherish. She's Wisdom's Empress. Yuh know Wisdom?"

"No, Mon! Mi only know Jah an Jah know dis Sistren is beautiful." Scooby finished hugging Zerby and quickly ran to kiss Cherish on the hand.

"We ain't got time for that shit Scooby. We tryin tu git tu St. Mary."

"Yuh waan de I tu be yuh driver?" Scooby was looking at Cherish as he spoke. He didn't care about Wisdom. He didn't know Wisdom and in Jamaica every woman was fair game. It was up to the man to keep his woman happy enough to not go out and find another baby daddy.

"Mi nah waan de Sistren tu travel upon de road alone."

"Come with us Scooby that way we can enjoy ourselves on the ride home. Okay, Scooby let's get going but stop off at the Tastee Patties on Knutsford Blvd. Get plenty of patties, Guinness and Red Stripe for the ride to St. Mary. How bout ganja? Yuh got ganja, Scooby?"

"Wha yuh tink, Sistren! Mi a Rasta an Rasta nevah wit out ganja! Come now! Jah guide us to St. Mary safely." The three loaded up on food and drink and proceeded on their trip to St. Mary.

Cherish found herself in another interesting situation in Jamaica. What her experiences in Jamaica taught her was to live more in the moment and not to worry. As Bob Marley would say, "Don't worry about a ting, cause every little thing gonna be all right." She settled in the back seat of the Hummer and allowed herself to become absorbed in the relaxing scenery on the trip back to St. Mary. The ride back could take anywhere from two hours to all night. It all depended on who you ran into and what was happening in the moment.

***

Simon and his entourage made it to the Presidential Suite at the Courtleigh hotel, where they were greeted by the personal butler hired for their stay at the hotel.

"Sir, my name is Dudley. I'm here to serve you during your stay at the Courtleigh." Dudley had the complete butler decorum down to the white gloves.

"Good man." answered Simon "So you must have some good aged cognac on hand?"

"Yes sir. We have an 80 proof French Martell Grand Extra Cognac. Does that suit you sir?"

"Of course! Hey Wisdom, you're hitting a home run so far. This guy has a $300 bottle of French cognac on hand. I like that shit!" Wisdom was looking around the suite to see what the accommodations really looked like. He knew of the Courtleigh but never had the pleasure of seeing the inside of the place. A friend that worked at the hotel guaranteed him this was the best place for his rich friend from England.

The suite was just over 1200 sq. ft. with three large bedrooms with balconies for each of them. The dining and the living area offered a panoramic view of Kingston, revealing the beauty of the Blue Mountains and the azure Caribbean Sea. There was also a fully equipped kitchen with butler service that already impressed Simone.

"Check out the view in de livin room, Simone. Yuh see de Blue Mountains an de Sea." Wisdom stretched out on the couch and prepared a spliff as everyone got settled. He wasn't interested in choosing a room. He'd found his spot in the living room to catch both views of the sea and the mountain. Wisdom didn't like to smoke when he had things to do, but now he felt he had a short time to rest before the evening fun began. The hotel was close to all the great nightclubs and restaurants in New Kingston.

***

Cherish spent her time sleeping in the back of the Hummer on the way home. She was tired. The massage, ganja, veggie patties, Guinness, and fresh air blowing from the large rear window of the soft top all hit her at once. She could vaguely hear Zerby and Scooby talk and laugh about old times but she didn't care about them and their

133

lives right now. She was in a groove and enjoying it. Her ride home was a mystic journey with dreams and glimpses of trees, flowers, hills and mountains.

It was dusk when they drove up the hill at Three Courts in St. Mary. The drive reminded her of what she loved most about Jamaica, the hills, mountains and its eternal green. The three drove into the car port and Scooby got a look at how the property overlooked the green valley.

"Jah kissed dis place fi real, Sistren. Mi stay in de city too much. Mi tink bout comin tu de country more ofen." Scooby and Zerby got out the Hummer followed by Cherish. She was happy to be home.

"This place is wonderful. Are you hiding from somebody Cherish? Because nobody could find your ass here unless you want them too. I love the spot. I can't wait to see inside." The entrance was on the top floor of the property. There were two doors on the front porch. One let you into the one bedroom studio apartment and the other to the other two floors that seemed to be nestled inside the hill tops.

"You wanna see your place first or my place first?"

"Yuh place, Sistren!" Scooby answered quickly.

"Fuck no Scooby! I wanna see my place first." Zerby had a Red Stripe in her hand. She was still hanging tough throughout the entire day. Cherish found her keys and opened the wooden door in the left that opened to a living area, small kitchen with a full bedroom and bath. The place was filled with tall open windows that shared excellent views of the open blue skies with a massive green backdrop.

"The place is beautiful. I love all the handmade wooden furniture, Cherish."

"Yeah, I lucked out. The place is beautiful isn't it? The lady didn't want too much considering the space. She really wanted someone in the property during her year in the states. I knew it wouldn't be a problem finding people to share the space and the cost."

134

Surviving This Thing Called Life

"She has a beautiful home, Cherish. I bet your spot is better than this."

"As a matter of fact it is. Come on down and see!" Cherish opened the door on the right and led the two down a small flight of circular stairs that opened to a full living and dining rooms with beautifully tiled floors and elegant handmade aged wooden furniture correctly place throughout.

"There's a living room, full kitchen, and two bedrooms with full baths on this floor. The bottom floor has a full living room, kitchen, master bedroom with full sitting room and veranda, and another bedroom with full bath."

"I don't want to stay in the small apartment, Cherish. I want to stay on this floor. How much more? It doesn't matter. I'll pay you whatever you want. You're a business woman and I like that." Zerby walked around to feel the vibe. It felt like she found a home, at least for a while.

"Get the shit out the Hummer Scooby." Zerby instructed Scooby to bring her things inside. So Scooby took out two large leather duffle bags filled to the brim and brought them into the house.

"And don't pick a room until I pick one. Let's go see your place Cherish?"

"Yuh nah wait fi Scooby?"

"No, Scooby! Cherish is my fuckin friend. Yuh de driver, remember!" Scooby shut his mouth while Cherish and Zerby proceeded down the next set of circular stairs to the lowest level of the house. At this level, on the veranda of the master bedroom you felt as if you were sitting in the mountain foliage.

"Cherish, this place is the shit. Wisdom found it?"

"Yes, he knew the people that owned the property and sent the Brown American girl to rent it."

"I understand. Well, as least he found a nice and secure area for you to stay while in Jamaica. But I'm glad we found each other because I really wouldn't want you stayin here all by yourself. Although the people in the country are

135

really friendly and peaceful but there's always a fool in the bunch."

"I'm glad you're here too. I had no idea how much I would be alone and without Wisdom. I'm thankful for the company and the adventure. You seem to be a lady after my own kind but the difference is I don't know enough about Jamaica to get around. Thank you for releasing me from feeling dependent on Wisdom."

"No thank you. I can't stand these Jamaican women and I hang with the men all the time. You're what I needed. A black American not afraid of shit. I know we can hang. I'll put Scooby on my floor so he won't bug the hell out of you tonight."

"Here's the door key, Zerby. Feel free to come and go as you please. We're not stuck to each other's hip!"

"Cool! See you in the morning. Me and Scooby might go out. I know you waan stay in? Don't you?"

"You know it! I'm tired from all of today's activities. Jah guide, Zerby. I'll see you in the morning for breakfast."Cherish walked Zerby to the stairway and headed to her bedroom. She prepared herself a hot bath to relax before going to bed.

***

Simon, Aiden and Knowledge consumed the bottle of cognac on the balcony in one of the bedrooms while Wisdom slept in the living room. Wisdom woke to Simone speaking in his ear.

"Wisdom I want to go to the stripe club. I need to see some black pussy. I don't know who said that, once you go black you never go back but he was right." Simon still had his signature cigar in his mouth as he spoke. That cigar reminded Wisdom of Clint Eastwood and the Good, the Bad and the Ugly. He wasn't sure yet which one Simon was.

"Jamaica, no problem. Mek mi put wata pon mi face tu wake up. Wha bout food? Yuh, Bredren eat food?" Wisdom was standing to stretch and noticed the food tray on the table. He grabbed a plate and filled it with mango, pineapple, papaya, and pear.

"Wisdom, no disrespect. Is that how you say it Bredren?" Simon burst out laughing as he tried his new Rasta saying. He was a little drunk by now.

"No disrespect taken Bredren. Wha happenin?"

"Your Suzuki is fine but I needed more space. So, I rented a Hummer Excursion Limo with the help of Dudley." Simon took a seat on the couch that Wisdom was sleeping on.

"Dat good, Bredren but de vehicle gwan be tu big fi some places."

"Then we don't need to go to any of those places! To the stripe club gentlemen." Wisdom didn't like strip clubs but Simon did. The strip club was less than five minutes away, so there was no need to rush. Wisdom was missing Cherish and wondering if she was missing him. He didn't have his cell phone but Knowledge did. Cherish hadn't bother picking up her phone to call Knowledge and ask about him, he thought. Maybe, he should try to call her, but it was late and he knew she would be sleep.

"Yuh hire a driver too, Simon?"

"Fuckin right. Wisdom thinks I hire cars without drivers! What the fuck you think about that Aiden?" Simon lived in England but he was basically a redneck from Texas, and Aiden was a man of few or no words.

"Simon, tell de driver we goin tu de Lucky 38 Stripe Club on Old Hope Road!" Wisdom yelled the destination as a way of getting the attention of all the drunks. The men quickly gathered themselves and headed to the club for a night of pussy, dick sucking, lap dancing, alcohol, and cocaine consumption.

Wisdom would be the only sensible one at the end of the evening. Wisdom found a seat, burned a spliff, drank cold Guinness, and thought of more songs to record for his next album.

Chapter Seven

Simon's three week visit to Jamaica was a success for Wisdom. Aiden got all the footage in Jamaica needed to complete the video for the single to be released from the album and Simon paid all the musicians and studio time needed to complete the tracks for the album. During the three weeks, Wisdom was able to sneak away and spend several nights with Cherish only to leave at the break of dawn to head back to Kingston.

Cherish was being very understanding about the whole situation. It appeared to Wisdom that she had plans of her own while residing in Jamaica. On one of his visits home, he spotted colorful business cards with the slogan "Retreat to Retreat." He and Cherish didn't talk about it because his time was limited so the lovers spent their time doing what lovers do, making love. When Wisdom returned home another time, he was surprised to see Cherish up so late in the evening working on the computer.

"Wha happenin mi Empress!" Wisdom kissed Cherish on her neck as she focused on the computer screen.

"Hey Baby, you surprised me!" Cherish turned around and gave her lover a big hug. Wisdom glanced at the computer screen and it read Retreat to Retreat- For a Royal Vacation in the hills of The Three Courts" St. Mary, Jamaica, WI."

"Wha dis, Empress?"

"What's What's?" Cherish was still engrossed in the embrace.

"Di ting pon de computer. Wha yuh planning cause mi know dat yuh always tinking bout doin someting."

"Oh, Retreat to Retreat! That's my new tour business. I'm putting together a website for people to come and stay at the place with optional tours to take with us once they get here."

"Did yuh say wit us?"

138

"Yes, with us. I can take the people some of the places but not all of them because I'm not that good of a driver. I thought we would do this together. I mean we rented this large property to make money and I'm getting the ball rolling."

"Mi know but mi music important Cherish. Simon took care of all de studio time an mi mus spend mi time inna de studio." Wisdom waited for Cherish's reaction. Wisdom knew Cherish was finally getting a dose of reality about him and his music. Besides Jah, nothing else but the music was really important.

"Wisdom, I know your CD is important but in the mean time we need to find a way to bring in more money. Your expenses are largely taken care of by Simon now but what about the future?"

"Sistren, mi nah tink bout dem tings dere! Mi pon de music! Yuh must hire a driver fi yuh business!" In the back of his mind, Wisdom knew this would be a good opportunity to tell Cherish about leaving for England to produce and manufacture the CD. But then again, it wasn't a good time because he didn't feel like having a discussion and with Cherish everything was a long discussion. Wisdom was use to Jamaican women from the ghetto who understood the rules of survival! Everybody has to get what they need for themselves!

"What are you talking about Wisdom? I think we need to discuss our future plans so we are both on the same track."

"De same track? Well, Sistren, mi track is headin straight fi yuh sugar pot fi a nice taste." Wisdom began to squeeze her breast together as he gently sucked on her nipples.

"Yuh waan talk Cherish?"

"No baby. Let's make love! There's always time to talk!" The two made it to the bedroom and made love

***

Vince woke in a cold sweat. He looked around to see where he was because he had no idea. He was having a nightmare about the fatal night that the FBI broke down the front door and ran into the house. It was guns pulled and everybody on the floor. Vince was relieved that he and Elaine were the only people home that night. They handcuffed Vince and put him in one room while they ransacked the house and focused their scare tactics on Elaine. As Vince waited, he prayed his stash was not discovered because without it there was no evidence in the house that could cause him harm. But as he sat, he heard the men escort Elaine down the stairs and the back door slamming. That's when Vince knew the jig was up. He woke from the nightmare realizing his present situation, back home, living with his mother, no income to speak of and an addiction to beer and cocaine that he could no longer deny. Vince managed to return to sleep while he prayed to God for a new beginning.

***

Things weren't going as Cherish planned. Wisdom left her home alone most of the time and in his absence, one of his Rasta bredren stayed at the house to cook, clean and protect Cherish. It was a nice gesture on his part but Cherish wasn't excited about the entire arrangement.

The Rasta didn't sleep in the house because that would not be acceptable. Wisdom hooked up an area on the property for the brother to sleep but Cherish had no idea where he bathed and took care of his personal needs. Only thing she knew was the Rasta woke early, prepared a full breakfast with a cup of hot Blue Mountain coffee, cooked all the meals and kept everything clean and tidy for Cherish. This morning Cherish was being graced with Zerby's company for breakfast.

"So what's up Cherish? You heard from Wisdom?" Zerby sipped her coffee as the two women sat on the veranda and took in the still of the morning.

"Yeah, he remembered to take his cell phone this time and called me. He's getting so civilized." Both the woman laughed heartily.

"Oh Cherish, I forgot to tell you. My nephew is scheduled to land in Montego Bay in the morning. I was hoping he could stay here."

"Sure! I don't have any guest scheduled yet but I'm still working on it. I would love to have some more company in this house. Does your nephew live in New Mexico?"

"No, he's from Los Angeles, California. He's sick. I'm not quite sure how sick but my sister says he's not doing well. Unfortunately, I don't see my family much. I spend so much time traveling and taking care of my business. I make a lot of money Cherish but I have to sacrifice a lot to get it."

"Well, Jamaica will be good for him. If he's young, he's probably just needs some rest from partying in LA."
"You're probably right, Cherish. My sister and mother said they might come later. Would that be okay too?"

"Sure!" Cherish felt a little better. It may not be her friends or family but she could use the company and she needed the money. It was funny because it didn't matter that her company was white! What mattered was she had company and more importantly they were American! Cherish was gaining a new Patriotism living away.

"It's business so I will pay you well for his stay." Zerby went into her purse and pulled out a roll of hundreds and handed them to Cherish.

"Count it later Cherish and let me know how much more I owe you for me, Knowledge and my nephew staying here for the next six months." Zerby was a blessing to Cherish. Money didn't seem to be an object for her. Zerby had an import-export business. Cherish didn't know just what she imported and exported and didn't care. Her monthly rent took care of the bills and adding the nephew would mean a profit for Cherish.

"What time is he scheduled to arrive?" Cherish was eating her ackee and dumpling right about now and enjoying her favorite morning meal.

"Early, he's gonna travel all night."

141

S.D. Laurence

"How long is the flight from LA to Jamaica, Zerby?"

"It took me about seven hours on Delta with a one hour stopover in Atlanta, Ga. It will probably take my nephew about seven or eight hours depending on the stopover time in Atlanta, Georgia. Cherish lets go to Reggae Beach today and relax." Knowledge was at the studio in Kingston with Wisdom so the ladies spent a restful day on the beach and returned home to a home cooked dinner from the Rasta, a few drinks and a good night's sleep to prepare for the three hour drive to Sangster Airport in Montego Bay in the morning.

Cherish retired to her room and sat on the veranda to enjoy the stillness, and the brilliant sky of Jamaica. In Jamaica the stars and the moon lit the night. There were little to no streetlights and the result was real darkness, something she never experienced until Jamaica. Cherish decided to sleep on the veranda tonight. It was too beautiful to go inside.

When she first moved into the property, Wisdom would sleep on the veranda all the time but Cherish was too timid. Her attitude changed. She felt safe and free. Cherish stretched out flat and gazed at the sky while thanking God for all his grace and glory. She wasn't worried about all the stuff she use to be worried about. She felt that God was trying to tell her something and she was willing to listen and learn.

***

The next morning the two women rose early to take the ride to Montego Bay to pick up Zerby's nephew. The Rasta fixed an early breakfast for the trip and the two women jumped in Zerby's truck and headed for MoBay. The ride to MoBay was beautiful. The new road had not taken away the picturequest views as it had in some areas. Zerby and Cherish were quiet for the first 30 to 35 minutes trying to awaken themselves for the day.

"Cherish, you feel like getting me a spliff out my bag. I prepared a few for the ride today." Zerby was awake by

142

now and her morning hit of ganja was wearing off so she definitely wanted another. Cherish turned to the back and grabbed Zerby's bag and began to look inside to retrieve the spliff. Zerby always rolled big giant spliffs that looked like an ice cream cone only filled with ganja and twisted at the end. Cherish pulled out a spliff and a lighter. She lit the joint and watched as the white smoke created interesting swirls as it drifted away.

"Pass de Dutchie Sistren!" Zerby glanced over to see Cherish mediating on the white smoke. Cherish passed the spliff.

"So you don't know what's wrong with your nephew? Did you talk to anyone last night?" Cherish was concerned because by now, she thought of Zerby as family and therefore her nephew was also family.

"Yes, in fact I did talk to my sister. She told me that my nephew has liver cancer." Zerby's tone was softer than usual as she spoke this time and Cherish noticed the change.

"Well what the heck is our new patient's name? It's not "my nephew" is it?" Cherish laughed. She always tried to make people laugh when spirits were low. Zerby did laugh.

"Oh you a nurse now! His name is Justin, sweet Justin. You'll like him. He's a lovely and gentle person."

"Oh so you sayin he's not like you?" Both women laughed and proceeded to quietly drive to the airport in MoBay to pick up Zerby's nephew, Justin. Cherish did have a lot more questions for Zerby. But decided not to bother Zerby with them now because she could feel how upset Zerby felt about this whole issue. Jamaica was teaching Cherish a valuable lesson. There is more peace in silence than in unnecessary chatter.

***

Wisdom awoke after a short nap and looked around to see where he was. Before Cherish relocated to Jamaica, he would be anywhere at any time and often awaked not remembering where he had parked his body for the night.

143

He hadn't been home for several days. He tried to make it home a few days out of the week and hopefully on the weekends but it didn't always work out that way. Wisdom moved by his vibes not by what was expected of him. His lifestyle had worked for him so far and he wasn't willing to give it up. Cherish would understand after the CD was a success and money was flowing.

"Wisdom, yuh still dere, Rasta?" Jam Prince spoke out loud as he entered the studio and saw Wisdom sleep on the couch.

"Yes, man. mi still dere bouts. Mi nevah waan drive home." Wisdom didn't get up to speak to Jam Prince. He lay in the same position to gather himself for a new day of mixing music. Mixing the tracks was a very important part of the production process and Jam Prince was the best. He had mixed many songs for many people and was honored to work with Wisdom. He loved his sound and good vibes.

"Rasta, mek we do dis ting here." Jam Prince headed toward the mixing board while Wisdom started to gather himself for the day. He thought about Cherish and knew he should have called her over the past three days but he was so busy with his music and he couldn't include Cherish in the mix this time.

***

Cherish and Zerby made it safely to Sangster International Airport. They parked the Hummer and made their way to the outside bar to wait for Justin.

"What you drinking Cherish." Zerby already caught the attention of the bartender and signaled for him to make his way to her and Cherish. The bartender was another gorgeous Jamaican man kissed by the sun.

"Wha can mi do fi yuh beautiful ladies?"

"I'll have a Red Stripe. Tell de Mon wha yuh waan Cherish." Zerby added her Jamaican accent to let the bartender know she wasn't a newby to the island.

"I'll have a cold Guinness young man." Cherish said in a polite tone. The bartender brought the drinks quickly and the two women drank without speaking to quench their thirst after the long drive.

"Is that your phone Cherish?" Zerby motioned the bartender to return because she had already chugged down her nice cold Red Stripe. Cherish took her phone out her bag and answered.

"Hello."

"Greeting Empress! Yuh miss de I?" Wisdom couldn't get Cherish off his mind. He had to call her so he could work on mixing the track with Jam Prince

"Who is this? Do I miss you? I don't even know who this is?"

"Wha yuh mean Cherish? Dis Wisdom!" Cherish laughed loudly over the phone,

"I know it's you baby. I'm just playing with you. But I could forget who you are because I hardly ever see your ass."

"Yuh know mi workin pon de music! Mi soon come." Wisdom was starting to feel like he shouldn't have called Cherish but he also knew he would be off the phone soon and back to his business.

"I know de Music! Me and Zerby at the airport in Mobay. We pickin up her nephew from L.A. He's gonna stay with us for awhile." Cherish noticed that Zerby was gathering her things as if she had spotted her nephew coming out of the airport.

"Dat good! Mi nah keep yuh. Jah Guide."

"Jah guide, Wisdom. When am I going to see you?" As Cherish spoke the last sentence she realized that Wisdom had already ended the conversation. She thought fuck it and joined Zerby as she left the bar and headed toward the airport exit area.

"You see Justin?" Cherish was walking fast trying to keep up with Zerby's pace.

"Yeah, I see him. You see that good looking blonde kid with the blues jeans and knapsack on his back? That's Justin." Zerby was excited. She began to run toward Justin.

145

As Cherish approached the couple, she got a good look at Justin. He looked undernourished even though Cherish had never set eyes on him before. Justin turned to give Cherish a hug as Zerby introduced them and as she looked in his face she noticed his yellow skin and dark eyes.

"Welcome to Jamaica Justin. How was your flight?" Cherish held him tight and felt his fragile bones.

"The flight was good but my back is killing me from sitting for such a long time." Justin was supporting his back with his right hand as he spoke to Cherish.

"You want to get a drink before we get in the Hummer and head back Justin?" Zerby spoke as if she was more concerned about her nephew now that he was here in her presence.

"Well I would like to chill a little before getting in another form of transportation. Man, it's beautiful here." Justin was looking around now and beginning to notice his surroundings.

"You haven't seen anything yet wait till you see where you gonna live for now." Zerby headed back to the bar. Cherish and Justin followed. Cherish was very observant but because of her casual demeanor people often thought that she didn't hear everything that was said. Cherish was stuck for a moment on Zerby's words, "we're you gonna live for now." She wasn't quite sure what about the words or why they struck her but they did. Cherish decided to shelve the thought and get back to enjoying the moment.

"Justin, where's your luggage?" Cherish just noticed as they returned to the bar that "my nephew" didn't have any luggage.

"Oh, I'm a light packer." Justin laughed and Zerby quickly cut in.

"I promised Justin a shopping trip when he got here! Look at him Cherish! Isn't he sweet and gorgeous?"
"Stop it Auntie! Cherish, she did promise me a shopping spree but I also wanted to get out of L.A. quickly for some

rest and restoration." Justin's tone was serious so Cherish left it alone.

"Bartender!" Cherish called out to the handsome chocolate server.

***

On the ride back to St. Mary, Justin stretched out in the back of the Hummer and fell fast asleep. The trip from Los Angeles, California to Montego Bay, Jamaica was long and tiresome.

He dreamt that he was back in L.A. at his Hydroponics Operation inspecting the marijuana plants when suddenly tear gas canisters burst through the windows and numerous Drug Task Force men in black ran through the abandoned factory destroying everything and arresting everyone in the place. Ganja was legal in the state but there were many laws to abide by and Justin adhered to none of them. The dream was so vivid it woke him from his sleep.

"Where are we?" Justin jumped up and looked around to see the beauty of Jamaica all around him.

"We are almost there." Cherish made a right turn and began to climb the hill of Three Court. As the trio, rode to the top of the hill, the air became cleaner and fresher to Justin. Everything was so green and couldn't compare to the oxygen levels he received at home. He was feeling like he could breathe more freely. Lately, he had been experiencing wheezing and shortness of breath, but not today. He was breathing fine and wondering if this would keep up when he got out the Hummer to walk.

"Wow, this place gets more beautiful and more beautiful." Justin was smiling now.

"Justin, I want you to relax, eat, enjoy and get strong in Jamaica." Zerby felt better because she could see that Justin was feeling better. The three exited the Hummer and headed toward the main entrance of the house.

"Okay Justin this is your apartment." Cherish dug inside her purse, pulled out her set of keys and opened the wooden door to the left that revealed a spacious living area

147

with tall open windows and excellent views of the open blue skies and the lush green trees.

"It's beautiful!" Justin was almost in tears. He made his way to the couch to take a seat because he thought he might pass out. So much had happened in the past year and to end up here was overwhelming. He was feeling grateful. A feeling he hadn't felt in many, many years.

"You okay, Nephew?" Zerby was concerned again.

"I'm more than okay, Auntie. I'm ecstatic! I couldn't be happier than I am right this moment." Justin got up from the sofa and started to explore his new residence.

"Your bedroom and bath is over there Justin. Man the breeze is wicked at night. You gonna love it." Cherish was happy that Justin was so happy.

"Here's your key young man." Cherish put Justin's key on a chain with an outline of the Island of Jamaica.

"I love the furniture, too!" Justin was still in a state of ecstasy.

"Now that's enough of looking at your apartment. Let's go to your place Cherish, sit on the veranda, smoke a spliff and have a drink. Where's that Rasta man of yours? Tell him to get us some food too." Zerby walked out the door and opened the other door that led to her and Cherish's space. Everyone followed behind as Zerby headed down the two set of stairs and straight to the veranda. Cherish went to find the Rasta and have him prepare dinner for three. Zerby and Justin sat on the veranda preparing to smoke a spliff and relax.

"Justin, you feeling okay?" Zerby was pulling on her Spliff.

"Auntie. I was feeling like shit when I got off the plane but this place has made me feel better immediately. Plus, Auntie who could ever find me here!"

"Shh…I haven't told Cherish the whole story yet. She's square you know." Being square meant that Cherish was not involved in any illegal activities.

Surviving This Thing Called Life

"I know. I could tell and I'm thankful for her." Justin was sincere when he made that statement. Cherish walked into the room and noticed the silence as she entered.

"The Rasta is preparing our meal. What you guys talking about?" Cherish sat and joined the couple.

"I was just telling my Auntie how grateful I am to you for offering your home to me." Justin yawned at the end of his statement. He was still tired from all the travel and stress.

"Justin, after you eat. Go to bed and get some rest." Both Cherish and Zerby cosigned on that statement.

***

Wisdom and Jam Prince spent the day mixing the music tracks. There wasn't much more work needed to complete the mixing of the tracks and then it would be ready to take to England. Making a CD involves four steps and Wisdom had completed the first two: recording and mixing. The next steps were getting a digital audio master and a glass master to prepare for replication. The digital master of the CD had to be done in England because it's one of the most important steps toward making the product musically and commercially competitive.

Wisdom didn't know how to tell Cherish that either he or they were going to England. He hadn't decided which and didn't have any idea how these changes would affect their relationship. He thought, "She'll have to understand." He decided to head home in the middle of the night. He quietly entered the house, got into the bed with Cherish. He kissed the back of her neck softly to awaken her gently. She turned and the two embraced and kissed passionately. Neither one thought of anything but the moment. These were the moments that kept them loving and caring for each other. That night the two made passionate love and slept soundly until the brilliant sun rose over the hills and the birds sang their songs of appreciation to the Universe.

Wisdom woke before Cherish and went outside to pray and thank the Rasta for his assistance in taking care of his

149

wife. He also planned to tell Rasta that he might be going to England for a few months and would he mind staying on indefinitely. He knew Rasta would agree. He cooked, cleaned and took care of the grounds but he was really a Roots man. He knew every bush and its purpose. He loved living there in the hills because he had access to a lot of herbs not found in other places.

Cherish woke to an empty bed. She wondered if making love to Wisdom was a dream because he wasn't there now. She knew he had been there because she could still feel the wetness in her Punany. She got out of bed and went to the bathroom.

After taking care of her morning rituals, Cherish carried her Bible and went to the veranda to inhale the sweet air and thank God for waking her up to this beautiful morning. She opened the Bible and began to read whatever verse she opened to. This was her morning pattern and it set the tone for her day.

"Sweetie, look wha mi hab fi yuh." Wisdom had two large mugs of Blue mountain coffee for himself and Cherish.

"Mi yuh new server!" Wisdom had a big beautiful smile on his face. He was happy to see Cherish.

"I was wondering where my lover took off too. I was beginning to think I had a dream last night." Cherish was smiling too. She loved Wisdom and missed him.

"How are things going with the music, Baby?"

"Tings goin good. De mix pretty much cooked and curried."

"What's next, Wisdom?"

"De next ting de digital master." This was another good opportunity to share with Cherish but he didn't want to destroy their present moment together.

"Will the digital master be done at Tuff Gong too?"

"Nah" Luckily their conversation was interrupted by the Rasta bringing the morning meal of Cornmeal Porridge.

150

Rasta sat two hot bowls of porridge on the table and immediately left the room.

"So, yuh picked up Zerby's family from de airport?"

"Yes, we picked him up yesterday. Zerby said he has cancer. I don't know what kind because I didn't want to ask too many questions. I figure it will come out as the days go by."

"Hem look sick?"

"Yesterday he looked tired but he did travel from L.A. and that's a long trip."

"Mi don't know Cherish. Why de Bwoy come all de way tu Jamaica an hem got cancer?"

"Maybe it's just a short trip to help him feel better. But Zerby did give me a lot of money. She gave me two thousand dollars the other day and said when I need more just ask."

"Cherish you do know what business Zerby is involved in don't you?"

"Something about import and export!"

"Zerby exports ganja. She hab connections en de government, the airport and customs. Her family has been en de business fi years." Wisdom waited to see Cherish's reaction to the news.

"She's not putting us in any danger?" Cherish was concerned but she knew that Wisdom didn't involve himself in such things but in Jamaica it was difficult not to be around people involved in all types of hustles.

"No, Mon!" Wisdom stopped talking because he could hear someone entering their space.

"Cherish, you up?" It was Zerby.

"Yes Zerby. Wisdom and I are on the veranda. Come." Zerby sauntered onto the veranda. Wisdom got up from his seat and yelled to the back of the house for the Rasta to bring more food and coffee. Immediately coffee and food appeared for Zerby.

"Rasta, de next guest soon come." Wisdom spoke politely to the Rasta. He was not a servant but a person who loved to serve people with love.

"So yuh nephew dere bouts?"

"Yes, Wisdom. I would like to thank you and Cherish for your hospitality."

"Cherish say de Bwoy got cancer."

"Yes, he has liver cancer." Zerby had tears in her eyes as she spoke.

"It's only stage one, so there's hope. He had a lobectomy where they removed a part of his liver. He's fortunate because his liver was well enough and the doctor's said it would grow back and work normally again. They only perform this type of surgery when the tumor on the liver is small and the cancer hasn't spread. So my sister and I are hoping that time in Jamaica might help him heal so things look good."

"No, Sistren. Justin nah fortunate! Hem blessed! Comin tu Jamaica de best ting. Yuh know de Rasta a Roots man, Zerby!"

"What?" Cherish was curious.

"Cherish a Roots man know all de herbs dat cure yuh ills. Hem must mek some tings up fi yuh nephew. Mi tek de Bwoy tu all de healing places mi know." Wisdom thought this would be a good time to take a road trip. He could help the young white boy and give Cherish a wonderful vacation while his spirit revealed to him what to do. Take Cherish to England or leave her here until he returned in a few months.

"We gonna take a road trip? What about de music, Wisdom?" Cherish wasn't sure whether to be happy or annoyed with Wisdom.

"Cherish, mi tell yuh dis mornin dat de ting cooked an curry! Mi git de Rasta workin pun de roots den pon de road." Wisdom got up from the table in case Cherish wanted to start the conversation about finishing the music.

152

The two girls were left on the veranda to keep the conversation going.

"When did Justin have his surgery?" Cherish was more curious than ever now.

"It's been about a month and a half ago. My sister said he healed very well."

"Oh!" Cherish wanted to know more but for right now that was enough information.

***

It was the day of the big road trip. Wisdom had Rasta man prepared a special root remedy for Justin to take during the road trip. The remedy was made from the Soursop tree in the backyard. The Soursop tree was about 25 feet high. Its bushy branches were filled with smooth, glossy, dark green leaves. The Soursop fruit is shaped like an irregular heart-shape with a leathery looking green skin covered with protruding stubby, soft bristles. It has a strong and pungent odor when crushed and its spiky green skin is not edible.

Rasta prepared the Soursop fruit for Cherish many times in different ways. At night he would make juice that relaxed her and gave her a good night's sleep. He also made a delicious frozen dessert for Cherish that tasted like strawberries and pineapple.

To prepared the Soursop fruit for Justin, Rasta took branches from the tree and washed them thoroughly. He broke the branches in smaller pieces and put all the leaves and stems in a large stainless steel pot filled with boiling water. After boiling the portion for 20 minutes, he left to cool and soak overnight. The next morning, he bottled the Soursop potion in glass bottles and put them in the refrigerator.

"Wisdom mek de Bwoy drink de ting tree times a day." Rasta took the bottles out the refrigerator and gave them to Wisdom.

S. D. Laurence

"Yes, Mon." Wisdom carefully placed the bottles in a separate nap sack. He went back to the bedroom to see how Cherish was doing preparing for the trip.

"Yuh ready Baby. Yuh need mi fi do anyting for yuh?" Cherish turned to look at her lover. She was happy about the road trip. It was the first real road trip since she came to live with Wisdom in Jamaica. They always took short trips but for Wisdom and Cherish a road trip is usually two or more weeks going from place to place around the island.

Wisdom wanted this trip to be memorable. He wanted to make up for all his days in the studio and his departure to England to complete his music project.

"Where we going Wisdom? Or is this a totally vibes trip?" Cherish knew that Wisdom didn't usually plan their trips but this time might be different.

"De Bwoy need healing so mi tink Port Antonio an St Thomas." Wisdom was going to surprise Cherish with a few days in the Blue Mountains. She'd been everywhere on the island but the Blue Mountains.

"Oh, the Blue Lagoon and Somerset Falls, that's fantastic. What about Bath? Wouldn't that be good for Justin also?" Cherish had finished up everything and was putting her Dreadlocks up in a ponytail. Her Dreadlocks had grown quite long. She and Wisdom loved them. Wisdom didn't answer. He had enough talk about what, where and when they were going.

"Mi soon come, Cherish." Wisdom kissed Cherish, picked up the bags and headed to the Hummer. Zerby and Justin were finished packing and waiting inside Justin's apartment for Wisdom and Cherish.

"Justin how do you feel?" Zerby could see that Justin was sick. He wasn't the same bright, energetic boy she once knew.

"Okay, Auntie. The surgery went well. The doctors said all the tumor was removed with part of my liver and they

154

think they got all the cancer." Justin rubbed his head as he spoke. He rubbed his head when he was stressed.

"You worried about your other situation, Justin?"

"No, I'm worried about not being able to return the U. S. but I don't want to spend the rest of my life in jail either."

"Justin, don't worry. I'm going to build a house in Jamaica. I should've done it a long time ago. You can live here with me. Your mom and sister said they would come down and stay for a few months every year. Hell, we can fly down any piece of pussy when you want too. Just get well, Justin. Going to jail would have killed you. So thank God you had a choice. A whole lot of people have no choices in their life. Just relax and get well." Zerby heard Wisdom outside and ended the conversation but Wisdom made noise to let them know he was there. He already heard the entire story.

"Wisdom, we getting ready to leave?" Zerby yelled out the window, got up from the chair and walked outside to talk with Wisdom.

"Knowledge dere bouts Sistren?" Wisdom hadn't seen Knowledge since they were together in Kingston.

"He went up in the hills to take care of some things on the farm. You know its harvest time and there's a lot of work to be done. I stay away anymore. The men seem to respect Knowledge and the crew he put together. I'm happy. Why didn't you ever work for me Wisdom? You could have made a lot of money." Zerby always wondered why Knowledge never brought Wisdom into the business.

"Sistren, mi nah judge yuh but mi nevah waan be involved inna no Bandulu business." Wisdom lit a spliff and took a pull.

"No disrespect taken Rasta. I just always wondered that's all."

"Zerby, why de Bwoy come tu Jamaica?" Wisdom looked into Zerby's soul to try and understand why she was hiding things from him.

155

S. D. Laurence

"He's sick with cancer and I thought Jamaica would be good for him." Zerby lit her spliff and drew on it nervously.

"Nah, Rasta. I an I tink more den dat." Wisdom continued to look Zerby in her eyes.

"Okay Wisdom, I can't lie to you. I'm not sure if Justin is ready to share with everyone but he got into some legal trouble and was facing a lot to time in jail in the U.S. And on top of it all, he was diagnosed with liver cancer. So his mother and I decided that if Justin went back to jail he may die from lack of treatment. So Jamaica was the next best thing." Zerby turned to make sure that Justin was still inside the house. It was his business she was sharing with Wisdom.

"Mi nah git loud pon de ting, Zerby. Dis tween I an I." Wisdom tossed his spliff in the bush and continued to prepare for the trip. Justin appeared on the porch.

"Don't forget I need to go shopping Auntie?" Justin couldn't believe how much better he felt after a good night's sleep.

"Yuh git food Justin?" Wisdom was concerned about the White boy too.

"Yeah, Rasta knocked on my door and left a plate of fresh fruits and juice outside my door. Where is he? I want to thank him." Justin looked around for the Rasta. He always seemed to appear and disappear out of nowhere.

"Yuh must waan thank de man fi more. Rasta fix yuh a Soursop potion tu tek tree times a day." Wisdom held the bottle up for Justin to see.

"Come tek some, Justin." Justin walked over to Wisdom. Wisdom opened the glass bottle and filled the cap with the liquid for Justin to consume.

"What is it?"

"Tea mek from de Soursop tree inna de yard dere?" Wisdom pointed to one of the Soursop trees on the property.

156

"So why am I leaving my cure if it's right here?" Justin was smiling.

"Don't worry yuhself Bredren, deres lots of healing tings pon de Island. Mi soon come." Wisdom went into the house to get Cherish.

"Yuh ready baby? Zerby and Justin waitin at de transport." Everyone loaded into the Hummer anxiously anticipating the road trip.

Chapter Eight

The first stop on the road trip was the market in Port Maria to shop for Justin. It took about 15 minutes on the main road to get to the market. The building was a large concrete structure with two floors. The food vendors were located on the bottom floor and the top floor was filled with lots of people selling clothing, shoes and all sorts of items. Justin and Zerby ventured into the marketplace while Cherish and Wisdom waited outside for them to complete their mission.

"Wisdom you see Zerby and Justin trying to cross the street? I think you better help them." Wisdom quickly came out of his meditative state and ran to help the duo. Everyone reloaded into the Hummer and prepared for the journey. The next stop was Buff Bay and then the Blue Mountains. Wisdom figured it would take them about one hour to get to Buff Bay where they would stop to eat, drink and revive themselves for the grueling 2½ hour ride to the Blue Mountains.

Buff Bay is located on the northeast coast of Portland Parrish. The ride to Buff Bay included driving through acres and acres of banana plantations that seemed to stretch forever. Eventually, the road left the hills and headed toward the coast of the Blue Caribbean Sea. The first small, coastal highway town is Annotto Bay and then Buff Bay. The coastal town of Buff Bay is nestled deep in rural Jamaica with the spectacular Blue Mountains as its backdrop.

The cherry red Hummer pulled up in front of Jah Bingi's Cook Shop. The shop was full of beautiful conch shells, ice-cold jelly coconuts, other cold drinks and an assortment of food. Wisdom exited the car and the others followed behind him.

"Bruk Foot! Bruk Foot!" Jah Bingi was smiling from ear to ear as he hugged Wisdom. Jah Bingi was a massive Blue

Black man with long Dreadlocks. Cherish thought that's probably how Samson from the Bible story appeared.

"Mi nah Bruk Foot! Mi Wisdom, Rasta!" Wisdom stood proudly. He was small in frame but strong with determination and self-preservation. He was also proud of his African-American Brown Dreadlock woman.

"Brethern dis mi wife, Cherish."

"Nice to meet you." Cherish spoke politely. She also tried not to stare at the man's protruding muscles and blue velvet skin.

"Wisdom mi glad fi see de I. Come mek mi prepare some food fi yuh friends." The group followed Jah Bingi inside his restaurant.

"Sit and relax, mi soon come." Wisdom's wandering spirit and condition of poverty resulted in him traveling the entire island so he knew people wherever he went on the island.

"Mi know yuh hungry after being pon de road." Jah Bingi returned to the table with a tray of fruit and a tray of cooked food. The fruit tray included sliced mangoes, tangerines, oranges, jackfruit and Jamaican apples. Justin recognized the mangoes, tangerines and oranges but the jackfruit and Jamaican apples confused him.

"Auntie, what's this?" He pointed to the jackfruit.

"Yuh must know some de tings pon de tray but yuh nevah know jackfruit an dis type of apple." Jah Bingi waited for a response from the Foreigners at the table then when on to describe his presentation.

"Everyting pon de trays grown inna Buff Bay. Di long fruit wit de dark red skin an white flesh, dats a Jamaican apple. Dis apple good fi yuh constipation. Di green ting wit de thick spiky skin an sweet yellow flesh around de seeds is jackfruit. Dis fruit yuh must suck de seeds tu git de sweet flavor.

Di next tray steamed cabbage wit carrots, callaloo, tomatoes, dasheen, and fried bread fruit." Jah Bingi stood proudly as he served some of best food in Buff Bay.

S. D. Laurence

Everyone dug in and began to fill their bellies with the delicious foods. As each person began to slow down from gobbling up the food, Cherish had a question.

"Are we close to the Blue Mountains?" Wisdom and Zerby laughed but Cherish was serious. She hadn't been to the Blue Mountains and really wanted to go and Wisdom hadn't mentioned that as one of their destinations.

"Yes, Cherish! Yuh gwan tu de Blue Mountain!" Wisdom laughed because he was happy that he was able to surprise Cherish.

"Cherish inna 2 ½ hours, yuh be inna de Blue Mountains. From Buff Bay I an I go straight up de Blue Mountain." The group finished their meal and sat on the veranda of Jah Bingi's Cook Shop. Jah Bingi gave Wisdom's some beautiful bud for himself and his friends. Wisdom rolled a spliff for each person and passed them out.

Zerby was happy to get a spliff because when you rode with Wisdom there was never any ganja in the car. Wisdom's theory was there was too much ganja in Jamaica to carry it with you and be molested by the police. His policy was to get ganja everywhere you stopped to chill because everyplace you stop in Jamaica ganja is always just a few feet away.

The veranda, where the foursome smoked their spliff, faced the Blue Mountains. The mountain peaks were surrounded by a sapphire mist. The Blue Mountains are one of the steepest slopes in the world. The mountains shoot out of the coastal plain with their summits rising and falling for 24 miles with the widest distance between them being 14 miles. The awesome sounds of nature and the breeze whistling through the leaves beckoned the group to acknowledge the existence of God.

"Wow, the Blue Mountains are beautiful!" Justin was astounded. He was from California and witnessed many mountains but none ever so close and so steep.

160

"Aren't they beautiful, Justin? This is where the great tasting coffee in Jamaica is grown." Cherish though about the coffee beans and then thought about the weather.

"Wisdom, I didn't bring the proper clothes for the Blue Mountains. You know it gets cold up there." Cherish was concerned now.

"How cold Cherish?" Justin was curious. He wanted to know how cold the Island could get?"

"At the mountain peak, the temperature is about 5°Centigrade or about 40°Farenheit." Wisdom broke into the conversation.

"Baby mi hab warm tings fi yuh."

"Thank you Wisdom but what about Zerby and Justin?" Cherish always thought about everyone not just herself.

"Cherish yuh de only one surprised. Zerby knew all de time." Wisdom laughed again.

"I was wondering why Aunt Zerby was buying long pants and jackets." Justin sounded as if a mystery was also solved in his mind.

"Well, at least I'm not the only one that didn't know?" Cherish got up from her seat to kiss Wisdom and thank him for the surprise.

***

The 2½ hour drive up from Buff Bay to the Blue Mountains was beautiful, long and scary. The road followed the river straight up passing through miles of banana trees, various wild beautiful plants and flowers with several waterfalls sprinkled along the way. The first turn off the main road, was the road that was in the worse condition. The rough road lasted for about 2 miles before the group reached their destination, the Starlight Chalet and Health Spa. It was a beautiful Chalet nestled 5000 feet up in the Blue Mountains. The group exited the Hummer and headed for the check in office.

"The ride was really scary for me you guys!" Justin was really shaking in his shoes. It wasn't the height that frightened him. It was the bad roads that often appeared as if you might just drop off the side and disappear.

"Be thankful that you had the best driver in Jamaica, Wisdom. That's why I need him for my tour business!" Cherish grabbed Wisdom by the cheeks and kissed his lips.

"Dat enouf Cherish." Wisdom was embarrassed. He did not really like public displays of affection. As they entered the Chalet, they spotted an African –American woman standing behind the desk with her head down. The open door caused her to raise her head and notice the visitors.

"Wisdom is that you?" The woman made her way from behind the desk and gave Wisdom a healthy embrace.

"I am so happy to see you! It's been so long!" The woman released her embrace and began to notice the other people with Wisdom.

"Rhonda, mi waan yuh tu meet mi wife Cherish an mi friends Zerby and Justin." Wisdom pointed to each person as he introduced them.

"Any friend of Wisdom is a friend of mine. He helped me find this property and start a new life in these mountains. I will always be grateful to him for that." Rhonda was an older, hardy looking African-American woman.

"Where are you from Rhonda?" Cherish was curious. This woman achieved what she wanted to achieve. If she was able to establish a tourist business she may not have to return to American either.

"I'm from Minnesota. You know, one of the really cold states!" Everyone laughed.

"I don't have that problem and many others any more. Let's get you guys settled in. I know you're all tired after the ride up." The sun was beginning to set and the clouds coming over the mountains were beginning to engulf the Chalet.

"Yuh hab de tree bedroom suite fi I an I?" Wisdom seemed to know the place. Cherish use to get jealous when she met women that Wisdom knew but not anymore. She was use to it now and he always let everyone know who she was and how much he loved her.

"Yes, I do. Follow me guys." Rhonda took the group outside. They walked to the back of the property toward a set of stairs. During the walk to their accommodations, birds, butterflies, fruit trees, wild flowers, and coffee plants surrounded the foursome. The set of stairs lead to a private wing of the hotel with the three bedroom suite. The suite opened to a large nicely furnished living room with a TV and a balcony that wrapped around the entire suite overlooking the Blue Mountains. There was a full kitchen and each bedroom had its own private bath.

"Beautiful!" Cherish was impressed.

"I will have to add you to my tour but we'll talk about that later."

"Let's see the bedrooms." Rhonda continued the tour. Each bedroom was decorated nicely with, what looked like, an extremely comfortable four-poster bed. After the tour, each picked a room for their stay at the Starlight Chalet.

"Let me know if you guys need anything. I'll leave you alone to rest. See you in the morning for breakfast." Rhonda closed the door to the suite and everyone retired to their rooms.

Once inside his room, Justin walked out on the balcony that overlooked the deep mountains. He knew this place provided the peace and serenity he so desperately needed. It was getting cool but he was prepared. His auntie had given him everything he needed and more. He looked at the sky and thanked God for having her in his life. Zerby was settled in her room. The only thing she lacked was ganja. She hadn't smoked a spliff since Buff Bay. She heard a knock at her door. It was Wisdom.

"What's happening, Star?" Zerby greeted Wisdom as she opened the door.

"Yuh lik de place, Zerby?" Wisdom stood in the doorway. He hadn't planned to stay. He was really tired

163

and needed to rest. No one knew but he was leaving for Kingston early in the morning so he wanted to make sure everyone was happy.

"It's beautiful here Wisdom. I've been to the Blue Mountains but never at the Starlight Chalet. Only one thing would make it better!" Zerby gave Wisdom a look she knew he would understand.

"Mi know Zerby." Wisdom handed Cherish a nice portion of ganja. He picked it up at the local store where they purchased Red Stripe and Guinness for their stay. They were close to the Chalet and he wasn't worried about the police stopping them on the bad roads in the Blue Mountains.

"Thank you Wisdom. You're always thinking about everyone!" Zerby was sincere. Wisdom was the most thoughtful man she'd ever known.

"Di lady dat run de place can git yuh more ganja. Good nite, Sistren. Mek Justin know deres Red Stripe and Guinness inna de place." Wisdom's next stop was to his friend Rhonda.

"Rhonda" Wisdom called out his friend's name as he knocked on her office door.

"Come in." Rhonda answered in a polite tone from her desk. As the door opened, she could see that it was Wisdom. There were two other couples at the Chalet for the evening and she didn't think it was any of them.

"Wisdom!" Rhonda was always physically attracted to Wisdom. But when they met, he was married and everyone knew that he was faithful to his wife.

"Wisdom I am so happy to see you. I can never thank you enough for all that you've done for me." Rhonda met Wisdom in Negril. She was seeing a man called Butter. Butter was "brown" and wore his hair in Dreadlocks but was not a Rastafarian. He was a Rude Bwoy. He looked for woman to give him money for the time he spent with them.

164

Surviving This Thing Called Life

One night Butter and Rhonda went out on the town drinking and partying. Butter took Rhonda to a friend's house up in the hills. Later that night, Butter and Rhonda were passed out from drinking. Rhonda was awakened by the homeowner attempting to rape her. She ran out of the house crying. Wisdom's sister's house was the neighboring property. Wisdom was staying with his sister that night. He heard Rhonda crying outside in the morning dew and rescued her from the bad situation. Later, he took her to the Blue Mountains and the rest is history.

"Sistren, mi leavin fi Kingston inna de mornin. Mi beg yuh tek care of mi wife an friends. Mek dem go pon de coffee plantations an de Blue Mountain peak." Wisdom knew that Rhonda would make sure Cherish had a good time while he was away.

"Wisdom don't worry yourself. Take care of your business and I'll take care of your beautiful wife and her friends." Rhonda reached out and gave Wisdom another hug and the two parted for the night. Wisdom returned to his room. He opened the door and heard Cherish from the balcony.

"Was Zerby happy to see you and the ganja?" Wisdom could hear the joy in Cherish's voice. He prayed that his departure wouldn't ruin her happy mood.

"Di Sistren was overjoyed!" Wisdom walked on the patio where Cherish was smoking a spliff and drinking a Guinness.

"Wow! Wisdom we are really high in the mountains. It's so blessedly quiet and beautiful. This is definitely the handiwork of God." Cherish was in a state of bliss.

"Mi know Cherish. Come tu bed, Sweetie." Wisdom left the balcony and headed for the shower. He was tired but he was going to make exquisite love to Cherish tonight because he was leaving in the morning. The plan was to wake before dawn and whisper into Cherish's ear that he had to go to Kingston and try to return that evening.

165

S.D. Laurence

"Okay Baby! I'll come and take my shower after you finish." Cherish knew she wouldn't get no love making tonight because Wisdom had to be tired from the long drive. But she would be surprised tonight; they made love better than they had in a long time. Cherish went fast to sleep. She was tired from the travel and the enthusiastic love making session.

Before first light, Wisdom gently whispered into Cherish's ear and quietly slipped out of bed to prepare for his trip to Kingston. The birds filled the air with songs of joy. Wisdom was joyful also. The music tracks were probably already mixed and ready for his review. Wisdom had tried to call Jam Prince but cells phones didn't work this high in the Blue Mountains and he didn't want to bother Rhonda to use the Chalet's land phone. It would take him about an hour to reach Kingston in the Parish of St Andrew. He was taking Zerby's Hummer and hadn't informed her but Wisdom knew she would be alright. But to be sure he left two notes, one under Zerby's bedroom door and the other on the bed next to Cherish.

"Gone tu Kingston fi business. Soon come, Wisdom." He got behind the wheel of the Hummer and headed down the mountain. About a half an hour later, Cherish was awaken by the bright sun rising over the mountain peaks and the songs of the more than 200 species of birds that lived in the Blue Mountains.

She rolled over to find herself in bed alone with a note in the place Wisdom should have been. She read the note. She was shocked but not surprised. This was definitely a Wisdom move. He avoided confrontation with Cherish. He'd rather not talk about what he was going to do because the conversation with Cherish would be an hour. And when it was over, he was going to do what he needed to do anyway. Cherish knew this about Wisdom and it did bother her. She felt his actions were often very selfish, but his many acts of kindness often made up for times like this. Cherish was not going to let this disturb her good

166

mood. She was going to enjoy her time in the Blue Mountains with or without Wisdom. The phone rang in the suite.

"Hello?" Cherish couldn't imagine who was calling. She knew it wasn't Wisdom. After a move like this, she knew she wouldn't hear from him for a few days.

"Cherish, this is Rhonda. Did I wake you? I know it's early but I also know that the birds and sun would awaken you. I have some hot Blue Mountain coffee for you and your guest. May I send it up to your suite?"

"Yes, that would be great." Cherish hung up the phone. It seemed that the bright sun and the singing birds awakened the entire party. Zerby was the first to come out of her room and was quickly followed by Cherish and Justin.

"Is Wisdom still sleep?" Justin looked around and saw everyone but his new best friend. Zerby was quiet. She saw her note but wasn't sure what Cherish knew or didn't know.

"He got up early and went to Kingston for some business. He'll be back tonight or tomorrow." Cherish tried to sound confident and undisturbed by Wisdom's latest actions because she was determined to enjoy her stay.

"Rhonda is sending up some Blue Mountain coffee for us." There was a knock at the door.

"You want me to get that Aunt Cherish?" Justin liked his new title for Cherish. Justin opened the door and standing there holding a large tray with coffee and cups was a beautiful chocolate brown young lady.

"Coffee Sir?" The young lady waited for instructions.

"Let me take that heavy tray from you." Justin put the tray on the large table in the living room. He had grown fond of the Blue Mountain coffee during his short stay in Jamaica but he was also growing fond of the young lady serving it. Justin went to his room to get 10 U.S. dollars for the beautiful young lady.

167

S.D. Laurence

The young lady was very happy with the tip and left the room smiling. She would definitely serve these Americans again. The threesome relaxed on a terrace sipping coffee, watching the hummingbirds drink from hibiscus flowers and the lush panoramic view of the Blue Mountains. Zerby pulled out three already prepared spliffs and passed them out to her friend and nephew.

"Did you drink your roots this morning Justin?" Justin looked 100% better in a few days but Zerby didn't want him to forget to take his Soursop tea. Zerby knew about the potential health benefits of Soursop. It was said to cure diabetes because it regulates the blood sugar levels in the body. The Soursop tea is also considered especially effective as a cure for liver problems, and improving the function of the pancreas. Additionally, it's the best sleep aid you could ever drink. There was a knock at the door. Justin, being the man in the group, got up to answer the door. It was Rhonda.

"Good morning, Justin. Hope you guys are enjoying the coffee." Rhonda waited to be invited in.

"Come in Rhonda. We're sitting on the veranda enjoying the view and the coffee." Justin led Rhonda to the veranda.

"Good morning, Rhonda." Cherish was happy to see the African-American woman running a successful business in Jamaica and she was doing it without a man. Cherish had a lot of questions for her but not this morning. She would tap her brain later.

"I have some tours planned for your guys." Cherish knew that Wisdom had spoken to Rhonda about being gone for a few days. Even if he wasn't there he made sure everything was always taken care of.

"I've taken the liberty to plan a trip to Holywell National Recreation Park." Rhonda looked at Cherish to try and detect if she was happy about her plans for them.

"That sounds perfect." Cherish was smiling.

Surviving This Thing Called Life

"Hey girl, do you have the time to go the park with us this afternoon? I would really love your company. The truth is I really want to start an adventure tour business in Jamaica and spending time with you today would be very valuable to me." Cherish put her crossed fingers in the air so Rhonda could see that she really hoped she would agree.

"You know, I just might take you up on that offer. The other guests are leaving soon and there are no reservations. I haven't left the property in a while now. I'd love to spend some time with a few good old American women. Let me check out some things and I'll let you know after breakfast. What about breakfast? What can I get for you guys?" Rhonda was excited about the picnic too.

"Surprise us Rhonda." Cherish was in the Jamaica with her new no problem mood. Whatever she fixed would be alright with her.

"Okay, I'll take care of breakfast as soon as I leave. I would suggest that after breakfast, you guys take a walk around the property. It's really beautiful. Also guys, we do Swedish and deep tissue massages, manicure and pedicures. We'll meet in the lobby about 1 o'clock. I've arranged for a driver and tour guide but it looks like I might be the tour guide."

"That all sounds sensational, Rhonda. Everyone I've met in Jamaica has been so considerate and kind." Justin was sincere.

"Not everyone is nice in Jamaica. I had to learn that the hard way. Just stick with Wisdom, he'll protect you. Alright, let me go take care of breakfast and I'll see you all later." Rhonda left the group to prepare breakfast. Rhonda hoped that Justin didn't have to find out the hard way that everyone in Jamaica was not so kind. A short time later, there was a knock on the door. It was the beautiful young Jamaican woman that served the party earlier. Justin opened the door.

169

"It's you again. Hello beautiful. What is your name?" Justin focused intensely on the young lady as she began to tell him her name.

"Mi name Kizzie." The young lady was standing with the tray when Justin noticed her discomfort.

"Let me take the tray for you, Kizzie." Justin grabbed the large tray and placed it on the living room table. Justin went to his room while Kizzie was still waiting at the door. This time he came back with 20 US dollars and gave it to Kizzie. She was shocked.

"Change, sir? Mi hab tu go tu de office tu mek change."

"It's for you Kizzie! That took a lot of work to carry that big tray up to us for breakfast."

"Blessings, Sir." Kizzie was truly grateful.

"I'm not anybody's sir! Call me Justin, please! Maybe later today can you show me around the property?"

"Mi workin Sir. Mi mean Justin."

"Oh I forgot about that. What time do you get off?"

"Mi stop work bout 7 or 8 o clock."

"You go straight home?"

"No, mi stay pon de property. Mi live inna Kingston." Kizzie was getting nervous. It was too many questions and she needed to report back to the kitchen and get breakfast to the other two couples staying on the property.

"Do you think you can give me a tour around the place later this evening?" Justin was smiling at Kizzie. He could sense her discomfort and wanted her to feel more relaxed with him.

"Mi don't know. Mek mi check wit yuh later." Kizzie quickly left before the young White Boy had more questions for her.

"Okay Kizzie. I hope I can spend time with you later today or any day!" Justin closed the door to the suite, picked up the breakfast tray and walked it to the balcony where Cherish and Zerby sat observing the beauty and peace around them.

170

"Food!" Justin was happy. He was excited about the possibility of spending time with Kizzie. Justin placed the tray on the table. The tray had three serving dishes covered with stainless steel tops including plates and other necessary eating utensils.

"What's good?" Zerby asked Justin as if he knew the food. Zerby took the tops off the three serving dishes. There was ackee and salt fish, fried breadfruit, and fresh fruits.

"I know what that is?" Justin pointed to the Jamaican apple. He was proud of himself.

"Is that ackee and salt fish?" Cherish really didn't look at the food. Her focus was on the mystic Blue Mountains.

"Yes it is and I'm gonna fill my belly this morning." Zerby began to fill her plate. Cherish got up from her seat and went to the table and fixed herself a plate also. The trio quietly consumed the meal. Cherish was the first to speak.

"You know we have to meet Rhonda and the driver for the picnic today?" Cherish was really enjoying the balcony view. She couldn't imagine anything better.

"Let's see the rest of the property you guys!" Zerby stood up.

"I'm going to shower, change and meet you guys in the living room in an hour or so. Does that sound like a plan family?" Zerby did feel like Cherish was her family. She embraced her and her nephew with no hesitation and not a lot of inquisition. Zerby was use to people being ultra curious about how she spent her life and her money but Cherish wasn't like that. She minded her own business. Zerby walked out the room without waiting for a response. She knew it was alright. Justin sat down next to Cherish.

"Cherish I like that beautiful young lady that's been serving us. I asked her to take me on a tour later but she acts real shy. What's up with these Jamaican women?"

"Well, Justin there's two basic types. One is real street wise and survives off her ability to seduce men for money, clothes, and what not. Then there's the shy girl that either grew up in the country or the church. But her goal is likely to get married and pregnant or just pregnant to get your support for the child. This is a very poor country and people are more about survival than emotional love. So yeah, she probably is shy but be sure to wrap up for two great reasons, AIDS and pregnancy. And if you get the pussy, be nice to her and stay her friend even after you leave because she won't expect much but she'll give more in return if she has a kind heart. You'll know." Cherish was serious. She spoke to Justin as if he were her son.

"Cherish why do you think I want to fuck her?" Justin acted like he was shocked.

"Because you're a man!" Cherish laughed

"Anyway, thanks for the advice! Love you!" Justin gave Cherish a big hug and walked out off the balcony. The trio gathered in the living room of the suite to begin their tour of the property. As they exited their suite, before them was a breathtaking cloud that covered the mountainside and its gardens.

The beautiful gardens were paths lined with wild flowers, tiny impatiens, wild orchids, bromeliads, and other green tropical plants. As the trio walked through the garden, their lungs were filled with the wonderfully scented air of the flourishing plants and flowers.

"Everything smells so garden-fresh and unpolluted up here!" Justin said out loud as he took deep breaths of air. He remembered that just a few days ago he could hardly catch his breath. Another highlight of the garden was the many hummingbirds that were encouraged to feed there. The peace and tranquility of the property could not be explained. Everything was breathtakingly beautiful.

"I knew I would love the Blue Mountains! That's why I love Jamaica so much because when you think you've experienced the most incredible thing there's something more incredible." Cherish was ecstatic.

Surviving This Thing Called Life

***

Wisdom made it safely to the Tuff Gong studio in Kingston. He thought about Cherish a lot during his drive to town. He couldn't call her because there was no cell phone service in the Blue Mountains but he could call the land phone in Rhonda's office. He wondered if she was still upset with him but knowing Cherish she was going on about her business.

"Jam Prince! Jam Prince!" Wisdom called out into the studio as he entered. Jam Prince entered from the back room. He was excited to see Wisdom. Jam Prince loved the final product and was anxious for Wisdom to hear the tracks.

"Rasta, mi happy fi yuh. Di tracks dem nice. Mek yuh hear dem!" The two men sat at the mixing board, put on his headphones and listened to his new mixed tracks for this CD.

***

The group entered the driver's Jeep and headed for Holywell National Recreation Park. The park was one of the best venues to enjoy the majestic Blue Mountains. It is a 330 acre area, park in a park, located about 3,500 ft above sea-level. After the entrance fee was paid, a short distance beyond there was the ranger station, orientation center, bathroom facilities and picnic areas with barbecue pits. The driver parked the Jeep and the foursome got out to look around.

"So far so good!"

"Driver, take the stuff out for the picnic and start the grill. I'm going to take the group on the waterfall trail. We'll be back in an hour or so to eat." Rhonda wanted everything to be right for her new American friends.

"Trails, waterfalls, and Bar-be-que! Sounds like heaven to me!" Justin responded to Rhonda's instructions to the driver.

"Yeah, Justin there are four well-maintained trails to choose from but if we take the waterfall trial we can see a

173

waterfall that leads to a river with a few watering holes. It's pretty warm so we can take a swim. At the end of the trail, there's a spectacular view of Kingston, Portmore and Port Royal." Everyone could tell that this was not Rhonda's first time at Holywell National Recreation Park.

When her business first began, she gave the tours because she couldn't afford any help. But her driver, Big Boss, knew she needed help and offered to drive for free until she could afford to pay him. He did get tips from the tourist and that was better than nothing. In Jamaica, you had to create your own way to make a living and Big Boss knew that. Cherish, Zerby, and Justin followed Rhonda to the entrance of the trail.

"Before we start, I want to share with you several things you should look for while on the trail. First, the Giant Swallowtail Butterfly. It is the largest Butterfly in the Americas and mostly found in Jamaica. They're dark in color with yellow and blue bands and spots. Swallowtails feed on the leaves of trees and flowers, so look for them there. Next is the Jamaican Yellow Boa." Rhonda spoke in a matter of fact tone.

"Jamaican Yellow Boa!" Zerby was from New Mexico and to her any snake meant danger.

"I thought there were no plants or animals harmful to humans in Jamaica." Cherish chimed into the conversation.

"I thought that's why they imported the mongoose from India to devour the snakes, rats, lizards, and other creatures not in harmony with humanity?"

"It's not a poisonous snake! You're right Cherish. In fact, no animal on the island is poisonous or harmful. The Boa is actually extraordinarily beneficial because its major diet is composed of rats. So when a farmer finds one coiled in a coffee tree or banana plant, the farmer's happy because he knows that the snake is eating something that might be eating his crop. The Blue Mountain's is one of the only environments where you can find the Jamaican

Boa." Cherish and company was impressed by Rhonda's knowledge.

"The Blue Mountains are one of the largest migratory bird habitats in the Caribbean with 200 species of resident and migratory birds. Look for the national bird of Jamaica, the Doctor Bird or the Swallow-Tail Hummingbird. Its feathers are a shimmering emerald green and black color and when it flies backwards, it causes their feathers to make a humming sound. The Doctor Bird is indigenous to Jamaica and its main source of food is the nectar from plants. They feed during the daytime and hibernate at night so they're easy to sight."

"Didn't the Taino Indians believe that the Doctor Bird had magical powers and they called it the God Bird?" Cherish wanted Rhonda to know that she'd done her homework too.

"Yeah, Cherish that's right. Let's start the trail so we can still catch the warm weather for our swim in the river." The group followed Rhonda on the beautiful waterfall trail. They enjoyed the waterfall and swam in the crystal clear watering holes found in the river. Afterwards they made it to the remarkable view of Kingston, Portmore and Port Royal.

"You guys, the Blue Mountains are Jamaica's last remaining rainforest. Its home to the world's tiniest Orchids and a plant called, Jamaican Bamboo that flowers once every 33 years. The next flowering will take place in 2017. The cool climate of the Blue Mountains is the only place on the island where you find wild strawberries and raspberries." Rhonda paused and allowed everyone to take in the outstanding view.

"Anyone ever heard the story of the Maroons?" Rhonda asked the trio.

"Didn't the Maroons hide in the Blue Mountains?" Zerby wanted the group to know that she also knew some things about Jamaica.

S.D. Laurence

"Your right Zerby. The Blue Mountains are very tough so when the Spanish fled from Jamaica, their freed slaves escaped to the Blue Mountains. The Winward Maroons, as they later became known, were led by Nanny. She was a legendary Chieftainess who was said to have magical powers. They harassed the English for decades before signing a treaty whereby they were allowed to live in relative autonomy." Rhonda was finished. She had talked enough. It was time for the group to walk back to the picnic area and eat.

***

The mix on the music tracks was perfect. Wisdom wanted to have something to say but there was nothing he could say but job well done.

"Bredren, yuh feel mi spirit. Di mix perfect!" Wisdom was excited.

"Di ting ready fi yuh tu tek foreign, Wisdom." Jam Prince was happy for Wisdom. He knew his struggle. He also knew that when Wisdom got food so would he.

"Mi know Rasta. Mi mek de move soon. Play de ting fi mi now!" The two men listened to the tracks over and over again.

***

When the group returned to the picnic area, the barbecue was finish and ready to be served. Big Boss prepared Jerk chicken with several side plates of rice and peas, Jamaican cole slaw, veggie patties, and spicy shrimp. The neighboring orientation center was sponsoring a group of Maroon musicians to play music and entertain. The Americans enjoyed their time together. The night was over when the delightful fireflies began to appear with the nightly unearthly noises of frogs and insects. They all loaded into the Jeep and returned to the Chalet for a restful night's sleep.

***

Wisdom awoke early to head back to the Blue Mountains. He couldn't decide whether to tell Cherish during or after

176

the trip that he had to go to England to finish the project. Telling her during the trip would give him the time and opportunity to make up to her before leaving. Neither was a great choice but he wasn't worried because he would trust his spirit.

"Jam Prince, mi waan thank yuh fi yuh help an support. Mi gonna tek de master tape tu foreign. Jah Guide Rasta." Wisdom embraced his friend as they departed.

"I an I go wit blessing!" Jam Prince knew the mixed tracks that Wisdom had in his hand were all a hit. It was just a matter of time before they would all be eating food from this CD. Wisdom got into Zerby's red Hummer and headed up the mountain to see his lover. He hoped they all had a good time without him yesterday.

***

Vince was headed to his uncle's after hour spot. It was about 3:00am and Uncle Tommy's spot would probably be off the hook by the time he got to North Philly. After Hour spots are bars, usually in someone's home, that people attended after the regular bars closed. After hour spots provide liquor, food, drugs, music, and other illegal activities for its customers. They are considered private clubs. They are allowed to stay open after the regular bar are closed because everyone that attends these establishments pay an annual fee in addition to the nightly cost of having a good time. Vince reached his destination and headed inside.

"What's up Vince?" The security at the door knew Vince because he was Tommy's nephew but also because he usually caused problems when he visited the spot.

"Nothing, Chaz." Vince didn't want to deal with his shit tonight.

"You got your card nigga!" Chaz didn't want to deal with Vince either.

"No nigga! Why you always fuckin with me over the same old shit?"

177

S.D. Laurence

"Because I'm your uncle's security! If he's busted for letting someone in without a membership card, he'll lose this club." Chaz took his job seriously because Tommy was good to him and his family.

"You fuckin see anybody else here but me? You a stupid Muthafucker!" Vince walked pass Chaz and entered the club. He spotted his uncle sitting as his usual spot at the main bar.

"What's up Uncle Tommie?" Vince spoke to his uncle in a calm tone.

"Same old same old! What's up with you nephew? You still giving people a hard time at the door?" Tommie spoke in a serious tone.

"Boy you must know that these pigs is always trying to close me down. I don't have time for your shit." Tommie looked around for one of his helpers.

"Uncle Tommie, I'm not trying to cause trouble. I just can't seem to keep that damn membership card on me." Vince didn't want to cause problems with his uncle tonight because he was going to ask him for a favor.

"Johnnie Boy! Come here for a minute!" Johnnie Boy responded quickly to his boss's request.

"Yes sir." Jonnie Boy waited for his commands.

"Get this Nigga a membership card now please!" Johnnie Boy quickly responded to the request and was back in a few minutes with the membership card for Vince.

"Give me your wallet. I know you don't have any money in it so you don't have nothing to worry about." Uncle Tommie laughed.

"Here, Uncle Tommie. What's mines is yours!" Vince handed his wallet to his uncle. He took Vince's wallet and placed the membership card inside.

"Now you have no excuses!" Uncle Tommie turned back to the bar and requested the bar maid to serve his nephew.

178

Surviving This Thing Called Life

"What you drinking Vince?" Bunny asked politely. She knew Vince could be a pain in the ass when he wanted to.

"Give me a cold Bud and a shot of Henny." Vince turned to his uncle Tommie.

"You know I'm back home with mom. Phyllis asked me to leave. I was glad because I was tired of her shit. Ever since she got square, she changed." Vince was tired of his life and his uncle could hear it in his voice.

"I'm sure she's tired of your shit too, Nephew. You ain't the easiest person to live with either. I hope you know that?" Tommie was worried about his nephew. Ever since all his legal troubles, his drinking and drugging was out of control. Uncle Tommie made sure that his nephew didn't serve a lot of jail time but he had no control over the amount of probation he received. He also couldn't help his nephew much with money because he finances was still be watched by the Feds.

"I know! I'm trying to improve my life, Uncle. I been going to work every night. I'm trying to save enough money to move into my own place."

"How can I help?" Tommie could sense Vince's serious attitude.

"I want to do some work for you on the weekends to make some extra money." Vince was hoping his uncle would give him a chance to work for him.

"I don't know Nephew. There are two things that present a problem for me and you. You leaving town while on probation and your excessive drinking and drugging. I can't afford to send you somewhere to do business and you get locked up for DUI or being in a fight." Tommie was raising his voice so his nephew could hear him over the loud noise in the club.

"Uncle, I'm working on my drinking, drugs, and attitude. If I can make some extra money, I can move into my own place and begin to feel a little happier." Vince was almost pleading with his uncle. Tommie didn't respond. He sat for a moment to think.

"Vince, let me make this shit clear to you. I'm gonna call your probation officer and give him some bullshit about you working for me and having to travel on some weekends. Now when I do this you have to give me your word that you will act right!"

"I promise Uncle. I will be on my best behavior." Vince was smiling now.

"You need to clean yourself up and get a good woman, Vince." Tommie was concerned about his sister's son.

"I don't need no woman. They're a pain in the ass and I have enough pain in my life right now!" Vince motioned to Bunny for another drink.

"Son, let me tell you something right now. A good woman is what you need. Why you always get those woman who after your money not your heart? That's because you ain't trying to give your heart to no one. The only thing you've given women is your dick and your money that's why you can't keep one." Tommie thought he was giving his nephew good advice.

"Well I don't have no money and my dick don't work like it use to so it seems like the only thing I have left to give is my heart." The conversation was depressing Vince.

"Okay you can start next month. I have to hook up all the contacts and let everyone know about the change. I'll start you in Virginia Beach, Virginia and Ocean City, Maryland. It'll be a nice change of scenery for you." Tommie called Bunny to refresh his drink.

A young lady with long blonde hair, green eyes, and bootie shorts came over to Tommie and kissed his cheek. The two engaged in a long embrace and Vince knew that his uncle had spent enough time with him. Vince got up from the bar and disappeared into the crowd to begin his departure from reality.

***

Wisdom made it to the Starlite Chalet in good time. He headed straight to the suite to greet his favorite girl,

Cherish. He opened the door and hoped they hadn't left for today's tour.

"Cherish, Cherish!" He was happy to be back and happier that his finished product was about to blow up. Everyone heard Wisdom come in and was happy to see him. Cherish walked into the living room.

"Look what the cat dragged in!" She was happy to see Wisdom but wanted him to suffer.

"Yuh happy tu see de I?" Wisdom opened his arms wide for Cherish to exchange an embrace with him. Cherish didn't move from her spot.

"Come Sweetie! Yuh know mi luv yuh!" Wisdom spoke sweetly to Cherish.

"Get over there and hug your man!" Zerby responded to the conversation.

"You hug him if you love him so much!" Cherish spoke with a hint of laughter in her voice.

"Alright then!" Zerby rushed to Wisdom and gave him a great big hug.

"That's enough, Zerby! I'll take over now." Cherish gently pushed Zerby to the side and embraced her man.

"Yuh hab a good time Cherish!" Wisdom held on to his lady longer than usual.

"Yes, baby!" Cherish was okay now.

"We having a good time too Wisdom." Justin wanted attention from Wisdom also.

"Dat good. Wha happenin?" Wisdom released his embrace.

"We suppose to go the Marley Coffee Farm today." Cherish wasn't really looking forward to visiting the coffee farm. She enjoyed her time in the Blue Mountains but she was ready to move on.

"You don't sound so happy about today's agenda." Zerby was curious to see if her feeling were correct.

"For real, I'm ready to move on. I want go to the Blue Lagoon." Cherish was excited again.

181

"Aunt Cherish, you keep saying the Blue Lagoon. Is that the same place that Brooke Shields made that famous movie? If so, that's where I want to go too."

"Well, two against one wins. Let's just drink some Blue Mountain coffee before we leave." Zerby walked to the phone and called the front desk. Rhonda answered.

"Good morning, how may I help you?" Rhonda knew the call was coming from Wisdom's suite but wanted to remain professional.

"Hello Rhonda. It's Zerby. Would you send some coffee and breakfast to the suite? I think we're leaving today." Zerby looked around to confirm with her people and it appeared everyone agreed. Rhoda assured Zerby that breakfast and coffee was on the way.

"You think that pretty young lady, Kizzie, will serve us today?" Justin smiled.

"Wisdom, Justin has a crush on the young lady that's been serving us." Cherish nudged Justin as she spoke.

"Di Bredren gettin betta!" Wisdom softly tapped Justin on the back. Wisdom thought about the situation with Justin and the young lady at the Chalet. He saw the young lady. She was a beautiful black pearl.

"Let's go on the veranda for a final look at the breathtaking view." Zerby walked on to the veranda and everyone followed. After a short time, there was a knock at the door. It was Kizzie with the food. Wisdom opened the door.

"Mawning Sistren."

"Mawning, Rasta." Kizzie felt more relaxed with Wisdom. He was a Rastafarian and he was kind. She could tell.

"Put de ting pon de table." Wisdom waited while Kizzie placed the large tray on the table.

"Yuh hab pinckney in Kingston, Sistren?"

"Nah, mi hab no pickney." Kizzie was wondering why Wisdom wanted to know so much about her life. Maybe he wasn't as kind as she thought he was.

182

"Where yuh stay inna Kingston?"

"Lizard Town." Kizzie knew that Wisdom understood the dangers of living in Lizard Town. It was home of a violent criminal gang known as the Posses that had strong connections to U.S. drug-traffickers.

"Yuh ever know de Blue Lagoon in Port Antonio?" Wisdom smiled

"Mi know de Blue Mountains an Lizard Town." Kizzie was more curious.

"Sistren, I an I on de move tu Port Antonio. Yuh waan com?" Wisdom was still smiling. He didn't want to frighten the young lady.

"Mi nah overstand Rasta?" Kizzie was confused. She couldn't understand what this man was asking her to do.

"Mi askin yuh tu go wit mi family. Yuh only do wha yuh waan do. Mi mek yuh share a room wit Zerby. Come, Sistren." Wisdom was hoping Kizzie knew the opportunity he was presenting to her. The majority of Jamaica's residents live in extreme poverty. This extreme poverty creates circumstances that sometimes seem unusual. This was one of those circumstances.

Justin liked Kizzie. Kizzie could come for the trip and if things didn't work out for her and Justin, she could return to her life. But if things did work out, she would have an American friend that would be more helpful to her than any poor Jamaican man. Kizzie paused for a long time to think about the opportunity Wisdom was presenting her. She knew other girls that worked at the Chalet who met American men and their lives improved financially as a result of it.

"Mi waan go. Wha bout mi job?" Kizzie was scared but knew that this might be the opportunity she needed to escape Lizard Town and its violence.

"Mek mi talk tu Rhonda." Wisdom and Kizzie headed to Rhonda's office. Wisdom hoped that Rhonda would share her story with Kizzie and that might convince her that it was safe to travel with Wisdom. After Wisdom, Rhonda and Kizzie discussed the entire situation, she decided to take the trip. Wisdom and company loaded into Zerby's Hummer and headed for Port Antonio. The group added a new member, Kizzie.

"How long before we get to the Blue Lagoon?" Justin was excited. He and Kizzie were seated in the far rear seats.

"De trip tek bout one hour. Relax Bredren!" Wisdom could see the improvement in Justin's health since he'd been in Jamaica. The group made it safely to Port Antonio.

"I know we're in Port Antonio but how far before we reach the Blue Lagoon?" Cherish was anxious to reach the beach.

"You know that the Blue Lagoon is one of the renowned beauty spots in the world. The water is a mix of fresh and saltwater! They say the lagoon is bottomless but in reality the world famous Jacques Cousteau dove beneath the 171 foot deep 'Blue Hole' to discover that it opens to the sea through a narrow funnel, but is fed by freshwater springs that come in at about 131ft deep." Cherish was doing her tour guide thing again.

"Dat good Cherish. Yuh know a lot bout Jamaica." Wisdom really wanted Cherish's business venture to be a success but he didn't have the time right now to drive her friends and relatives around the island. He needed to go to England and finish the CD to realize his dream not Cherish's dream. About seven miles outside the town center, Wisdom pulled in the driveway of a lovely three story white villa with large veranda on each floor overlooking the Caribbean Sea.

"Is this where we're staying?" Justin was blown away.

"Yes, Star. Dis de place." Wisdom got out of the Hummer and walked to the front door. Everyone else stayed in the car. It was as if the traveling party didn't believe they were going to stay in such elegant accommodations. Wisdom knocked on the front door and a tall middle aged White man answered the door.

184

"Wisdom! So happy to see you. It's been a long time. Come inside." Wisdom entered into the house and the tall White man closed the door behind him.

"Alex, mi glad fi see yuh. Blessings fi lettin mi stay at yuh place! Mi nevah remember how grand de place is!" Wisdom looked around in awe. The living room was full of white wicker furniture television, DVD player and stereo. The place was open and spacious.

"Wisdom invite your friends into the house so they can get comfortable." Alex met Wisdom in Negril many years ago. Alex relocated to Jamaica after selling his business in the states. He was looking for property in Negril but Wisdom brought him to Port Antonio. He fell in love with Port Antonio, brought the property for a good price and built this beautiful villa. Wisdom walked back to the Hummer.

"Come now!" Everyone exited the Hummer and walked into the large three story white house.

"Come in! Come in!" Alex was happy have Wisdom's friends stay at his property. Wisdom had done so much to help his transition to Jamaica. He was ripped off by many individuals before he met Wisdom. Wisdom made Alex rethink his negative opinion about Jamaicans. He loved Port Antonio. The north end of the island had less tourist and the people were friendly, honest and kind.

"Alex! Dis Cherish, mi wife. Justin, Zerby, and Kizzie mi friends!" Wisdom was proud to introduce his wife and friends.

"Welcome! The villa has five bedrooms, five baths, two dining rooms, a living room, and two decks overlooking the Caribbean Sea. Every room has a cable TV and air conditioners. The villa is one hundred feet from the sea and approximately three hundred feet from the entrance to the world famous Blue Lagoon. Let me show you around!" Alex took his visitors for a tour of the property.

"There is a full staff here that will take care of all your meals. Additionally, I will give you guy's free passes to the

185

African Star boat for snorkeling and sightseeing, and the Blue Lagoon. I hope everyone is happy."Alex smiled.

"I'm more than happy!" Cherish shared in an excited tone. Everyone but Kizzie shared with Alex their appreciation for such a beautiful property. Kizzie stood in silence. She couldn't believe that she was going to stay at such a beautiful place and not have to serve anyone. There were four bedrooms to choose from because Alex lived on the property in the master suite.

Wisdom and Cherish chose one of the second floor bedrooms with a veranda. Zerby chose the bedroom on the other side of the second floor with a veranda. Justin and Kizzie were assigned to the two bedrooms on the bottom floor. There was no veranda but there was an outside porch that the two bedrooms shared.

"Go to your rooms and freshen up. I'll have the kitchen staff prepare dinner for you. It will be served in the outdoor dining area." Alex exited. He was being very professional. He had no idea who Wisdom's guests were. They could return without him or recommend him to their friends. Everyone settled in their rooms to prepare for dinner.

Wisdom and Cherish quietly showered and began to dress for dinner. After his shower, Wisdom laid across the bed to allow himself to dry naturally. He didn't use towels often. Cherish exited the bathroom and began to dry her naked body while Wisdom lay on the bed. He loved Cherish's body. Every morning, Cherish awoke early and performed a series of Yoga stretches. Between exercise and diet she was tight.

He made his way over to her and began to kiss the back of her neck. Cherish was always excited by Wisdom's gentle love making. She didn't resist. The two made passionate love. While lying in the bed after lovemaking, Wisdom decided to make his move. His plan was to stay in Port Antonio for two days, return home and leave for

England the next day. Simon had already made the reservation and he needed to be at the airport in four days.

"Cherish, mi need tu talk tu yuh!" Wisdom was holding Cherish in his arms. He could feel her heartbeat increase as he made the statement.

"Oh, Wisdom! This sounds like trouble for me because you never want to talk." Cherish was serious. She vacated her lover's arms, sat up and looked him in the face.

"Cherish deres no trouble fi yuh! Yuh nevah hear de CD! Jah know de ting gwan take off!" Wisdom was excited. He waited for Cherish to respond but she said nothing. She wanted to hear all that Wisdom had to say. She knew that wasn't what he wanted to share with her.

"Mi gwan tu England."

"When?"

"Inna four days mi leave." Wisdom knew that statement would get a response from Cherish.

"Four days! Why did you wait so late to tell me?" Cherish had tears in her eyes.

"Mi nevah know til now. De music just mixed. Mi hab tu tek de ting tu England. Simon mek arrangements to press an release de ting." Wisdom spoke softly. He didn't want to upset Cherish anymore than he had. He wanted her to understand that this was for them.

"What am I suppose to do?"

"Com wit de I!" He knew Cherish didn't want to go to England with him and he really didn't want her to go with him either. He was taking a chance.

"I didn't come to Jamaica to go to England. What about the house, and the cars? I should just leave everything and go with you." Cherish wasn't crying anymore.

"Mi nah stay fi long, Cherish." Now Wisdom was trying to negotiate. He had no idea of how long he was going to be in England.

"How long?"

"Two, tree weeks!" Wisdom hoped this ended the conversation. He couldn't take much more. He was going

187

no matter how the conversation ended. He prayed that Cherish would understand.

"Well, I know there's nothing I can do about it. I know that everything happens the way it's supposed to happen. Go follow your dream. I'll stay with my other love, Jamaica." Cherish and Wisdom prepared for dinner and spent the next two days enjoying each other's company. But, the road trip was over. Everyone made it safely to St. Mary, including Kizzie.

Wisdom woke early the next morning. He arranged for Delroy to pick him up before everyone in the house awoke. He hated goodbyes. Wisdom got in the car with Delroy and headed for the Sangster International Airport in Montego Bay. He prayed to Jah for strength and guidance.

Chapter Nine

Cherish was on the airplane headed back to the United States. She could wait no longer for Wisdom to return from England. Wisdom's couple of weeks in England extended to over three months now. After the CD release, he was busy with interviews, performances and photo opportunities all over Europe. The music was taking off and he couldn't leave. This was something he'd dreamed of all his life.

He asked Cherish over and over again to join him in England but she refused. Her length of stay in Jamaica was about to expire. Wisdom said there was nothing to worry about because people always extended their stay with no problem when they decided to leave the island. Additionally, her one year leave of absence from her job was about to expire so she had to return if she wanted to keep it. She wasn't that stupid or so in love that she forgot to cover her own ass. She was a survivor not a failure but she knew that a lot of people would think that about her. When she thought about it all, this last year with Wisdom was more positive than negative. Everything changes; nothing stays the same, that's what she kept telling herself.

When the plane landed, there was no one there to greet her. But that was all good because Cherish didn't really feel like a lot of conversation. She still owned the apartment building with her mom so she had a place to live but Cherish thought she was out of America. Cherish loved Wisdom but she loved Jamaica more.

She got in a yellow cab and headed for Southwest Philadelphia. As the cab entered the Schuylkill Expressway, she remembered her life in the States. There were many beautiful places in America but most of her life was spent in the concrete jungles. The cab got off at University City exit and drove across the Grays Ferry Ave Bridge to head straight toward Cherish's house. The block she lived on was still lined with trees.

189

S.D. Laurence

Philadelphia use to be a city filled with trees but when the neighborhoods changed from White to Black, most of the trees were cut down. Cherish always said it was so the police helicopters could see the so called criminals they chased through the community. Now that the White folks were coming back, the trees were returning. As the cab parked by the curb in front of her three story brick house, she remembered how lovely the place was. She opened the cab door and saw her mother and cousin, Dana, standing on the porch.

"There she is! The world traveler! There she is!" Cherish's mother called out as her daughter climbed the front stairs of the house.

"Hey Mom. Hey Dana. What's going on, y'all. It's good to be home." Cherish dropped her luggage to reach out to hug her family.

"Hey Cuz! I really missed you. You know I didn't have anybody to party with while you were away! You know nobody can hang like me and you!" Dana was obviously happy to see her cousin.

"I know Dana. I missed you too but right now I'm real tired. I need to get some rest. What you getting ready to do Dana?"

"Girl I'm goin out! It's Saturday night and Kimon is having a party at the bar. You wanna come Cuz? It's still early! Get some rest and Junior can come around and pick you up later." Dana used her entire body as she spoke. She was truly a "down the way" girl.

"Now Cherish you just got off the plane and you really should rest. You know that if you and Dana get together, you two will be out until the next morning." Ellen knew her daughter and niece.

"Aunt Ellen you know I always want to come home. It's Cherish that refuses to leave the place. You know the apple don't fall too far from the tree and your daughter party's just like you use to party." All three of the woman laughed as they picked up the several pieces of luggage.

190

Surviving This Thing Called Life

"Okay Dana help me with the suitcases. I haven't hung out in a really long time. I'll get some rest and be ready for Junior to pick me up around ten."

"Okay girls. Just be careful out there in those streets. Cherish I'm going inside. If you need me call. I had Joe clean your apartment and put a little food in the frig. I hope everything is alright for you." Ellen walked toward her apartment door to go inside. She was happy her daughter was back home.

"Thanks Mom. I'm sure everything is okay. Come on Dana. Can you still take the stairs?"

"Can you?" Dana said as she smiled. Dana loved her cousin Cherish. Cherish had a couple of college degrees but she never forgot her family in the hood. There were some members of the family who attained success, moved out the hood and tried to forget that they ever lived there but not Cherish. She worked in the hood, hung in hood and was respected by her cousin Dana because of that.

The woman managed to get all the luggage up to the third floor apartment. As Cherish opened the door, she really felt glad to be there. The apartment was beautiful. The building was at least 100 years old and in excellent condition. When Cherish saw it for sale at an unbelievable price, she knew she had to live there.

"Man I'm tired. Dana I hope I can wake up at ten to go out."

"Aw Cherish! Don't back out! Come and go out with me! Everybody's going to be there and you've been gone for a year. Come on and go out Cherish." Dana had a very sad look on her face.

"Alright, girl. So get the fuck out of here so I can get some sleep." Cherish began to push Dana out the apartment door.

"Ok I'm leavin but later on tonight you must tell me everything. I wanna know where you been and what you did. You know you a crazy ass? You the only Black woman I know that just picks up and lives in another country with

191

some foreign Nigga. I'll see your yella ass later Sista." Dana closed the door and headed down the stairs.

Cherish could hear as Dana headed down the steps and exited the front door. She looked around the place. It was just as she left it. Her friend, Geraldine, sublet the apartment while she was gone. When she told Geraldine she had to leave, she was a little upset. Now Cherish understood why.

The apartment was filled with large windows that allowed the wind to blow freely. There was a large old tree in the front yard that filled the entire front window. The tree helped Cherish to forget that she was living in a concrete jungle.

Cherish headed for the bathroom to shower and then rest in her bed. She set the alarm clock for 9:00 pm because she knew that she was too emotionally and physically tired to wake up on her own. She wanted to go out. She needed to go out. She had to get back into the groove. Being out of the country and being involved with Wisdom had gotten her out of the night life. She decided to put her emotions to the back and put fun to the front of her life.

She hadn't really told anyone about her and Wisdom's situation. They relationship was over and she knew it. Stardom was on his horizon and Cherish wasn't quite sure if she fit into his new life. She and Wisdom parted as if they would see each other again but Cherish knew better. As she lay in the bed, she wanted to cry but she didn't want to feel sadness. She was home now and she trusted God. She knew that her heavenly Father had a plan for her life. She knew that his ways was not hers and now she was learning to live by faith.

BRRINNG! BRRINNG! The alarm clock rang loudly. She hadn't heard the sound of an alarm clock in a year. For the past year, her life wasn't about time schedules. It was about the vibes. But she was back in the states and when in Rome do as the Romans do.

Surviving This Thing Called Life

She opened her eyes and looked around. At first she was unsure of where she was then she remembered, Philly and cousin Dana. She jumped up because she knew that if she lay there any longer she wouldn't get up to go anywhere. What she would wear she thought, she was going to party in the hood. Her cousin Dana worked at the bar where the party was being held. It was an old neighborhood bar where her family members hung out for several generations. Cherish heard her house phone ring and it reminded her that she needed to get her cell activated the first thing Monday morning.

"Peace" Cherish said as she answered the phone.

"Cherish, you up?" Dana said shyly.

"I'm up and I'm getting dressed. What you wearin anyway?"

"I'm wearin a sexy top and some cut out jeans. What you wearin?"

"Probably some jeans too. I hope you didn't cut out too much of them jeans, Dana?" Cherish knew her cousin. She was built like a brick shit house and used every opportunity to share it with the world.

"Yes I did girl. You know I'm shaking my ass and showin what I'm workin wit" Both women laughed. Cherish knew she would enjoy herself this evening. She needed a change of pace.

"I'm going to hang up now and finished getting dressed. Tell Junior to get here about eleven thirty and bring some weed. I need a draw desperately."

"Okay cousin. See you soon." Cherish finished dressing just as Junior was ringing the doorbell. The old intercom system worked but you could only hear a voice. Cherish needed to see a face so she ran down the steps to open the door.

"Hey Cuz! How you doin? Boy I really missed you? Where you been anyway?" Junior was one of Cherish's younger thug cousins.

193

"I been chillin. I been out the country for a while. You got something for me?"

"Oh yeah! This shit is tight too Cuz!"

"Come upstairs for a minute." Cherish and Junior climbed the stairs to Cherish's apartment.

"You got any paper Junior? I want to smoke a joint before we go."

"Naw Cuz. You know we only smoke blunts now days. I don't even know how to roll a joint but let me roll you a blunt. You'll like it. I know you will. I got some coke. You want a hit?"

"Naw man. My thing is ganja. Always is and always will be." Junior took out a large cigar and emptied its contents into an old newspaper. He carefully replaced the tobacco with beautiful green ganja.

"Look at this bud, Cuz. It's pretty ain't it? I got the best shit in town."

"Yes man. It's nice." Cherish lit the blunt and took a deep draw. Smoking a blunt was not the same as a joint for two reasons. One there was more ganja to inhale and second the outside was not paper but tobacco so in addition to smoking ganja you inhale tobacco. The combination of the two went straight to Cherish's head. It wasn't the head she liked but she was going to party at the bar tonight.

Cherish jumped into Junior's car and before she knew it they pulled up in front of the bar on the corner of 42nd and Lancaster Avenue. The place looked the same. There was an old tattered sign that read, Sir Richard's.

"Okay Cuz. I'll check you out later. I have some business to take care of. You goin to the afterhours spot?" Cherish thought for a second. She didn't really like the afterhour spots because that's where the real Gangstas hung out.

"I don't know. I'll have to see if I can still hang."

"You know you can hang Cuz! It's the old heads in the family that taught me how to hang. There's a new

194

afterhours spot at 40th & Girard and it's tight. The sound system is banging and the DJ is dope." Junior was excited. He loved to show off his fine old head cousin to his young friends. Everyone said his family had good genes and as he thought about it, he had to agree. In his mind, everyone in his family was fine.

"Alright Junior, I'll see you later." Cherish gave her cousin a kiss on the cheek and exited the car. She opened the door to the bar and it was packed with people. She looked around and spotted her family gathered at the end of the bar. Everyone was there.

"Hey Cuz!" Dana yelled.

"Hey y'all" Cherish yelled out as she headed toward her family. She went around to everyone and gave out hugs and kisses.

"We got food on the table over there if you want some Cherish." One of her other cousins said.

"What you drinkin, Cuz?" Another cousin asked.

"What you think man? Tequila! Patron, if they have it."

"Whatever the fuck you want Cuz! You know how we roll!" The rest the evening at Sir Richard's was spent drinking, smoking and dancing. Cherish was having a ball. She had forgotten everything. The only thing she knew was the music. Cherish loved to dance and never needed a partner. She would spend most of the night on the dance floor with occasional breaks to drink Patron and talk shit.

"You goin to the afterhours spot, Cherish?" Dana asked as the other bartender yelled!

"Last call for alcohol!"

"Yeah, I promised Junior I would check him there later. Order me a drink, Dana, before the bar closes."

"Don't worry about the bar closing. You know I run this place and if we want a drink I'll go the fuck behind the bar and fix one!" Dana laughed as she ordered their last drink and prepared to head for the afterhours spot. They all loaded into three souped up cars with spinners and loud sound systems. The rap was thumping as they drove down

195

Lancaster Avenue heading for the afterhours spot. They pulled up in front of the place and there was a crowd of people standing outside. The cars parked and the entire clan got out of the three cars they arrived in.

"Follow me y'all!" Everyone did just that. With Dana in the lead the entire Jefferson Clan headed for the entrance to the joint.

"Jabo, they got you at the door tonight?" Dana knew everyone from the night scene.

"Yeah Sis. They got me pickin cotton tonight. But I'll be in there soon to dance with your fine ass. My God! Look at them jeans. You couldn't have cut anymore could you?"

"Yes the fuck I could have but I didn't want to upset you anymore than I already did! Now let me and my family inside this Muthafucka." Dana smiled and flirted with Jabo as she spoke.

"And by the way, you know my cousin that I told you was in Europe some fuckin where?"

"Yeah, what about her?"

"Well she came home today and she wit us tonight."

"Is she as fine as you Dana?"

"Cherish! Cherish! Let this Nigga know that all females in the Jefferson family is fine." Cherish walked to the door and introduced herself to Jabo.

"You right, Dana. All of y'all is fine. Now get your fine asses inside and party like a Rock Star. The Jefferson clans entered the afterhours spot and once inside were greeted by more family and wanna be family members. Cherish forgot how big her clan was and remembered why she kept her business to herself. Her family was ready and willing to defend her honor at a drop of a hat.

"Junior was right, Dana. This place is tight and the sound system is booming. They got the right place to put the spot because there are no residents to disturb during the night."

"Let's go upstairs Cherish. You ain't seen nothing yet." Cherish and Dana climbed the stairs for the second floor.

Both first and second floor had long bars with large couches and cozy chairs scattered about the massive rooms. The second floor was for ganja smoking and Reggae music.

"I thought you'd like this floor Cuz."

"You were right Dana. This does suit my style."

"Cherish, I'll be back. You cool? I'm going to see if my new friend Kayon came out tonight." Dana walked away and disappeared in the crowd. Cherish pulled out the little weed she had left and rolled a joint. She opened her purse and began to look for a lighter when a young man walked up to her seat.

"Let me light that for you Sis." Cherish looked up and saw a tall, fine young man with deep dimples and full kissable lips.

"Yes I would like a light. Do you have one for me?"

"Yes I do. I have a light and anything else you might need." The young man lit Cherish's joint and then asked.

"Do you mind if I join you? I see you came in with a lot of people. Are any of them your man because I know someone as fine as you didn't come here alone?"

"Well no, I didn't come alone. I came with my family and it's a free country. So feel free to take a seat."

"The Jefferson's are your family?" The young stranger asked as he pulled his chair close to Cherish.

"Yes. Why? Do you know any of my family?"

"Why yes I do. As a matter of fact, our families know each other. By the way, my name is Vince. Vince Barnes."

"Well my family might know you and your family but I don't know you." Cherish looked into the young man's eyes as best she could in the dark. She knew that a man's eyes were the key to his soul.

"I don't think I've seen you before either. You must not hang out with your family that often."

"Well as a matter of fact I just got back in the country today. I've been away for a while."

S.D. Laurence

"You haven't been locked up have you?" Vince smiled as he spoke. Cherish admired his beautiful smile, lips and dimples.

"I guess that is what some people might say if they just got out of the joint but trust me that's not me. I love my freedom too much to put it in jeopardy." Cherish smiled back and thought, this man is too young for you Cherish so leave him alone.

"I love your Locks, Sister. I love a natural woman and a natural beauty is more better. Where were you if you don't mind me asking?"

"I was in Jamaica. I'd love to talk to you but I really didn't come here for that Brother. I came to dance." Cherish kept her eyes on Vince. She was cautious of him for some reason. He was fine and young but she knew it was more to him than that.

"Well excuse me! If dancing is what you want then dancing is what you get." The couple danced and laughed for about an hour before the Jefferson clan realized that one of their own was missing. When you rolled with the family, everyone was expected to check in from time to time so if anything went down no one was too far away to be protected.

Junior spotted Cherish on the dance floor with Vince. He knew Vince's family connection. He wasn't from "The Bottom". His family connections were all in North Philadelphia. But Vince did have some small parts of his family that chilled "Down the Way" and they hung with the Jefferson clan.

"Hey Vince. What's goin on? I see you met my cousin." Junior spoke in a deep aggressive tone to Vince but it didn't mean much. It was only to let him know that Cherish was family and fuckin with his cousin could be a serious thing.

"Yeah man. I saw this beautiful lady come in with you so I decided to be her protector until you came. That's okay with you, right Junior?"

198

Surviving This Thing Called Life

"It's okay with me if it's okay with my cousin. You just remember who her people are that's all." Junior took his attention off of Vince and looked towards his cousin.

"We gettin ready to jet Cuz. You ready to go?"

"What time is it Junior?"

"It's about 3:00 am. We gonna go to another spot on 52nd and Girard. You game?"

"Well, I was kinda enjoying myself here. If I go anyplace, I was hoping it would be home."

"If you don't mind Junior. I will make sure that your cousin gets home alright. That's if it's okay with you pretty woman?" Cherish could tell that Vince was accustomed to getting his way in life. He used his boyish features in addition to a begging tone when he spoke.

"Yeah Junior. If it's okay with you, I'll let Vince take me home because I'll be ready to go in a few."

"Then I'll drop you off now, before we go to the other spot." Junior knew the rule; never leave a family member behind without protection.

"Man, I'll take care of your cousin. You know how I roll man." Vince's tone changed from begging to aggressive as he spoke to Junior.

"Muthafucka, I wasn't talking to you. I was talking to my muthafuckin cousin and family business in none of your business!" Cherish knew that anything could jump off between the two men because both men wanted the same thing, Cherish. So Cherish solved the problem.

"Vince, take my number and give me a call. We can finish our little party together later. I'm really tired and need to get some rest."

"So let me take you home. You said you live in Southwest and so do I. I'm ready to leave if you're going anyway." Vince took Cherish by the hand as he spoke and continued to look in her eyes his boyish smile.

"Okay Junior, I'm leaving now but I'm going to let Vince drive me home. You guys would have to go out of your way to take me home anyway."

199

"Alright Vince. I'm putting my cousin's safety in your hands. If anything happens to her, you're a dead Muthafucka! Cherish call me later here." Junior walked away while Cherish and Vince finished their dance.

"I'm ready to go anytime you are Cherish. I wouldn't want to upset Junior and keep Cinderella out too late!"

"Well let's go then Vince. I'm really kinda tired anyway."

"I know how travel can be Cherish. I use to model for several European designers but that was then." Vince seemed to have a sad tone as he spoke of his past. Cherish and Vince left the afterhours spot and headed for his car. Vince's car was not new or stylish. It appeared to be a working man's car with tools and such.

"Excuse the car Cherish. It's kinda dirty inside. I didn't expect to meet the woman of my dreams tonight." Vince flashed his beautiful smile again. Cherish couldn't resist that smile.

"You want to get something to eat princess. I'm a little hungry. How bout you?"

"I am hungry now that you mention it. I haven't had much to eat since I got off the plane. But I'm a vegetarian and at this time of night where would I get something to eat."

"Leave that up to me. I know a spot in North Philly that has collard greens and potato salad. You can eat that can't you?"

"Okay Vince let's get something to eat." Vince and Cherish drove down Girard Avenue towards the Zoo and across the Girard Bridge that led to the north side of Philadelphia.

"I love Fairmount Park Cherish. If you don't mind, can I take you to my favorite spot? It's not far from here."

"I don't mind. I haven't been in the park for a very long time. Fairmount Park is one of my special places also." Vince made a right turn at the end of the Girard Bridge

200

and drove down a small winding road. At the end of the road was Kelly Drive. Vince pulled to the side of the road.

"Look to your right Cherish." Cherish knew the place. It was Rock Garden. She was shocked.

"Vince you won't believe this but this is my favorite spot also. As a little girl, I use to say this was where I would like to have my wedding. We could say our vows right next to the waterfall."

"You can still do that. Marry me there because I also imagined myself saying my vows in the exact spot. I feel so close to God here." Vince and Cherish were both quiet for a moment.

"Okay Vince. I've done enough sightseeing for the night. How about that food?" Cherish tried to lighten the moment because things were feeling too serious and that's not what she wanted. She was through with serious.

"You're right Boo. Let's get some food and maybe some more dancing. I see you love to dance." Vince and Cherish returned to the car and as they entered he placed his juicy lips on her forehead and kissed her gently on the forehead before starting the car. He made a U turn back up the hill and an illegal left turn to drive down 33rd street. When Vince reached 33rd and Berks Street, he parked the car and the two exited the vehicle. The car was located on the park side of the street. The other side of 33rd street was filled with large three and four story brick building. Cherish was beginning to like Vince. She liked his spirit. She followed him across the street and down Berks a short distance to a brightly colored three story house. They both climbed the stairs and Vince rang the doorbell.

"Vince! You got your card with you man?" A tall young man spoke as he opened the door.

"Card! Man I don't need no card! You Muthafuckas know who the fuck I am. Move man! You got my lady standing outside." Vince pushed the young man to the side and ushered Cherish inside the door.

S.D. Laurence

"Man it's not me. It's the boss. He told me not to let anyone in without a membership card. You know I wouldn't say that to you man." The tall young man looked worried. It seemed as though he didn't want to offend Vince.

"Alright Muthafucka, I won't hold that against you. You know I'm a man of peace not war." Vince shook the young man's hand as if to calm him down.

"Go inside! You and your babe have a drink on me." The young man opened the door and yelled at the bartender,

"Give Vince and his lady a drink on me!"

"Muthafucka, you ain't paid your own bar tab! How the fuck you gonna buy another Muthafucka a drink?" The bartender yelled back and everyone at the bar laughed.

The place was jammed, the music was loud and everyone was live. There were several more rooms but Cherish couldn't see beyond the front bar, kitchen and dining area. Vince walked past the front bar speaking to everyone. He was obviously well known in the spot. As he spoke to each of them, he introduced Cherish as his future wife. Cherish was a bit overwhelmed. She thought to herself, this man is talking a little bit too much shit.

"Uncle Tommy you must talk to the Muthafucka you have at the front door." Vince stopped to talk with an older gentleman at the bar.

"Nephew, you need to have your membership card because this is a private club and I don't want nobody fuckin that status up. Who's the beautiful lady you have with you?" Vince's uncle looked Cherish up and down as he spoke.

"She's going to be my new wife but she just doesn't know it yet. She is beautiful isn't she uncle." Vince gently stroked Cherish's hair as he spoke to his uncle.

"What do you have to say about that pretty lady? You're mighty quiet."

202

"Well I just met your nephew a few hours ago and I'm not sure what he's talking about but we are having a good time together." Cherish smiled as she spoke.

"Well, Miss you've just met a member of the Barnes family and what Barnes men want Barnes men get." Tommy spoke in a very serious tone.

"Well, no disrespect but you just met me and I do what I want, get what I want and give what I want to give!" Cherish spoke with an attitude because she didn't want to hear what the old man was saying.

"You have sassy one on your hands, Vince. Maybe, that's what the fuck you need to get your shit in order. She don't seem like she takes no shit." Tommy was smiling and patting his nephew on the shoulder. You two young people sit next down and have a drink with this old man." Tommy waved his hand and the seats next to him were cleared immediately.

"We gettin ready to get something to eat Uncle. We'll make sure to have a drink with you before we leave." Vince led Cherish to the kitchen area. Cherish could see that men feared and respected Vince while woman loved him.

"What you havin Boo?" Vince asked as he found a small table for the both of them.

"Oh that's right, collard greens and potato salad. I'll be right back. Relax." Vince walked toward the kitchen and continued to greet people in the place. He returned to the table with two platters of food. Vince had chicken on his plate but that didn't bother Cherish. What he ate was none of her business.

"Is the food good Cherish?"

"Yes I'm really enjoying it. I didn't know how hunger I really was."

"When we finish Cherish, we can go downstairs to dance if you like."

"It's getting late and I need to get some sleep, Vince."

"Tomorrow is Sunday. I mean today is Sunday. You don't have to work today do you?" Vince was smiling with those thick luscious lips.

"Well you got a point there but when I get tired I want you to take me home." Cherish spoke sternly to Vince trying to ward of the hypnotic effect of his smile and dimples. The couple danced, drank, talked and laughed until 5:00 am. They were about to leave the club when Tommy, Vince's uncle, called to them to have a drink before they left. Cherish was tired. She wanted to leave. She'd had enough partying for one night but Vince seemed as though he could go on for a few hours more.

"I'm tired Vince. You promised that we would leave when I was tired." Cherish was speaking sheepishly to Vince. She didn't really know the man. It was early in the morning and two of them consumed a considerable amount of alcohol.

"Now come on baby. This is my uncle. He's a powerful man, not many people refuse to have a drink with him." Vince was smiling again. He knew how to invade her space with his charm.

"Okay Vince. Just one drink." Cherish sat down and the two men began to reminisce about good times together.

"Well young lady, I want you to know that you got a good dude here. Treat him well and he'll treat you better." Cherish was a tired of all this couple talk. She just met this man. She knew nothing about him except that he was a good time and a good time was what she wanted and needed. When Cherish and Vince finally left the club at 6:00 am.

"My goodness! I've never been out this late or early in my life." Cherish was shocked at her ability to stay awake so long. She wasn't a night owl. She didn't even stay up all night for the one year she lived on a college campus.

"Did you have a good time? That's what's important Cherish!"

"I had a good time Vince but I'm tired. It's all coming down on me at once." Cherish was yawning now and trying to keep her eyes open.

"You want to stop somewhere and get some breakfast, Cherish?"

"Are you some kind of mechanical man? How do you manage to stay so alive?" Cherish spoke in a very quizzical tone.

"No Baby. I'm just so excited about meeting you that I don't want to let you go yet." Vince was at a stop light when he reached over and laid a fat juicy kiss on her forehead. It shocked her. She didn't know what to say or do. So she sat quietly.

"You got food at your house. I'll cook for you. It's better to go to sleep with food on your belly after drinking. You'll sleep longer in the morning. You game baby?"

"I don't know what's in the house. Remember I just got back into the country today or should I say yesterday."

"If it's food you need then its food I'll get." Vince made a right turn and pulled down a tiny street off Baltimore Avenue. He parked the car half on the sidewalk and half in the street and opened the door to get out.

"Wait here a minute baby. I'll be right back." Vince returned quickly with a can of beer and a bag of groceries.

"What kind of store did you go to so early in the morning?" Cherish asked as they drove away.

"Just another afterhours spot. I needed stop by there for some business and decided to raid the refrigerator while I was inside." Vince laughed. "So where do you live now?"

"I live on South 44th Street. I'm right off Baltimore Avenue. We're not far away." Vince and Cherish proceeded down Baltimore Avenue toward 44th Street and made a left.

"Drive down one more block and you'll see a three story brick house with a large green porch."

"That's your crib. I've always admired the place. It reminds me of my grandmother's house in North Philly. I use to stay on the third floor when I traveled to and from Europe."

"Well I live on the third floor so get ready to climb the stairs." Vince parked his car almost in front of the house. Cherish was glad that he couldn't park directly in front because she didn't want her mother to see them. They both exited the car quietly and headed toward the house. Cherish opened the door quietly. She wanted to get the third floor as quickly and as quietly as possible. Vince and Cherish made it to the third floor without disruption. As Vince entered the apartment, he could feel the peacefulness.

"You have a beautiful home, Cherish. Who lives here with you? If you don't mind me asking?"

"My mother lives on the first floor and a cousin on the second floor." Cherish took her shoes off as she spoke and dropped on the sofa.

"A real family affair. I like that. Where is your kitchen? Never mind, I'll found it. Sit down and relax. Let me fix you a good breakfast." Vince made himself at home while Cherish slept on the sofa.

"Cherish. Cherish." Vince whispered as he spoke.

"Breakfast is ready. Wake up and eat." Cherish yawned and looked around to see where she was. She dreamt of Wisdom and Jamaica but she woke to Vince and Southwest Philadelphia.

"Thanks Vince. Everything looks good."

"I remembered that you were a vegetarian and fixed grits, eggs and potatoes. You like?" He kissed her on the forehead.

"Yes I like. Aren't you going to eat?" Cherish felt a little uneasy about the forehead kisses but she was getting use to it and starting to like it.

"I ate while I was cooking. I'm getting tired Cherish." Vince sat in a plush comfortable chair in front of Cherish.

206

Surviving This Thing Called Life

"You have to be. I did have a little nap while you cooked. Do you live far, Vince?"

"Not too far. I live closer to the airport."

"That's far man. Why don't you rest a little before you try to drive home?" Cherish didn't want the man to hurt himself driving home after treating her so good all evening.

"If you don't mind, I'll just lay here on your hardwood floors. I have a bad back and this floor will help me a lot."

"You don't have to sleep on the floor. The sofa opens to a bed."

"No, trust me Cherish. The floor is what I need. Do you have any music I can listen too while I sleep?"

"Of course. Let me put on some Earth, Wind and Fire for you." Cherish walked toward her stereo system and began to search through her music collection. Vince looked at Cherish's sexy body as she stood in front of the stereo system.

"Why don't you join me on the floor, Cherish? I won't touch you. I promise. I won't even take off my clothes. I just want to be near you. I can't explain it but I feel close to you."

"Vince, I wasn't born yesterday. In case you haven't noticed, I am an old head."

"I'm not trying to get over Cherish and you're the prettiest old head I've had the pleasure of knowing. Someday I'll tell you about me and old heads. But what right now, how about a little hugging. We all can use a hug. I know that I can surely use one and I would like to share a hug with you."Cherish thought about it. She could use a hug. He definitely wasn't getting any pussy and there was nothing he could do to change that.

"Okay friendly hugs for a good day's sleep. Is that what you're proposing, Vince."

"Yes Cherish. Oh and one other thing."

"What other thing?"

"Can I have one more kiss on your forehead?" Cherish gathered all they needed to be comfortable on the floor

207

and laid down next to Vince. He placed his juicy lips on her forehead and kissed her gently. Cherish turned her back and backed her ass close to his body. He wrapped his arm tightly around her waist, removed her hair from her neck and gave her another gentle, sweet peck on the neck. In a matter of seconds, Vince was asleep. Cherish soon followed.

Cherish and Vince woke to a ringing cell phone. It reminded Cherish that she needed to get her own cell phone activated. Vince picked his cell phone up from the floor next to him and answered it.

"Hey Joey, how's my oldest son? Yes boy! I'm comin to get you today. What you doing right now? Put your mother on the phone. Yeah, I'll be there in a couple of hours. Yes! Yes! I'll make sure he gets home early. Yes, I know that he has school tomorrow! He's my son too and I care about his education! Look I can't talk right now. I'll see you when I pick up Joey in a few." Vince hung up the phone. Cherish had already gotten up to go to the bathroom and brush her teeth.

"You need a toothbrush, Vince. I think there's a new toothbrush here you can use. I'll use my old one."

"Thanks Goldie Locks. Don't throw it away because I may need to use it again." Vince was smiling again. Cherish looked at his attractive smile and thought he can't help himself. He's just a natural cutie. When Vince came from the bathroom, Cherish was fixing a pot of coffee and toast.

"Thanks, Goldie Locks. Good lookin out."

"You looked out for me. It's the least I can do." Cherish smiled as she poured coffee for her new friend and herself.

"What you doin today, Cherish?"

"I don't have any plans. I'll probably sleep. I don't think you remember that I just got back in town yesterday."

"I haven't forgotten Cherish. Remember I told you that I made that trip many times myself. You have to work tomorrow?"

"No, I'm a school teacher."

Surviving This Thing Called Life

"A teacher! Good, that means that I have you a few weeks before you go back to work! Cherish, you been away from Philly for one year or more let me take you to your favorite place today, Fairmount Park."

"I don't want to impose on your time with your son Vince."

"Trust me, it's not an imposition. I'm sorry but I'm not ready to leave you yet." Cherish thought about it. She really loved the park and suddenly she didn't feel tired.

"Okay Vince, that sounds like fun. Why don't you go home, get dressed and come back to pick me up?"

"I said I'm not ready to leave you. Why don't you shower, dress and come to my house while I dress? You can meet my mother. She'll love you. I know she will."

"Vince, how do you know your mother wants to be bothered with company today?"

"Because it's Sunday and she'll be praising the Lord and cookin dinner. Come on Cherish." Vince gently brushed her hair and kissed her on the forehead.

"Okay, man. You are a persistent Nigga. You sure know how to get what you want."

"Does that mean you're coming with me and we're not going to separate us yet." Vince was smiling wider than ever. Cherish headed for the bathroom to shower and dress. Vince made himself at home. He put some smooth jazz on the stereo and cleaned the kitchen from the morning coffee.

As Cherish showered, she thought about what happened over the past 24 hours. She hadn't had a moment to think. She usually used her evening to go over her daily actions but this man hadn't given her any time to be alone and think. She didn't mind because she didn't want to think. She was having fun and that's what she wanted most right now.

"Boy you're more beautiful today than you were yesterday. Boo, I love your hair. What color is it anyway? It seems to change with the light. That's why I call you

209

S.D. Laurence

Goldie Locks because you are my girl with the Golden Locks." Cherish knew why her hair changed color because she dyed it but she didn't feel like sharing the details of her life with this man. He was just a good time and she had to keep it like that.

"Thanks, Vince. You ready to go?" Cherish opened the front door and they left the apartment for a day in the park. Cherish and Vince headed down 47th Street towards Elmwood Avenue. Vince pulled the car over in front of a local bar, parked and opened the door to get out.

"I'll be one minute. Do you want to come inside for a minute?"

"No, that's okay. I'll listen to the radio while I wait for you." Cherish wasn't a person who hung out in bars. She wondered what kind of business this man could have on Sunday afternoon in a local bar. It wasn't her business. She had to remember that this was all supposed to be fun. Vince returned to the car in about thirty minutes. Cherish didn't mind because she was occupied with the sights and sounds of Southwest Philly.

"I didn't take too long did I, Boo?" Vince said as he started the car and headed uptown.

"No, I was just enjoying being back in Philadelphia." Vince entered the car and drove to his house. He pulled up in front of a pink and white house and parked. Vince got out the car and opened the door for Cherish. She liked his manners.

"Come on, let's go inside."

"Did you tell your mother that you were bringing company home this afternoon?" Cherish felt uneasy about the entire situation.

"It's okay Goldie Locks!" Vince opened the door to a small quaint living room. The only sound in the house was gospel music playing on the radio.

"Hey sweet woman! Your handsome son is home! Where are you? I have someone I want you to meet" Vince yelled up the stairs.

210

"Alright sweetie. I'll be down in a minute." The voice from upstairs was sweet and soft.

"Have a seat Boo. My mom will be down soon. I'm going to go upstairs to dress. You okay? Can I get you something?"

"No thank you. I'm okay." Vince ran up the steps to dress while Cherish waited in his living room. She looked at the family pictures displayed around the room. There were several pictures of Vince in high fashion poses and pictures of another young man in prison attire.

"Sorry to keep you waiting. It's very nice to meet you. You are pretty. Vince said you were."

"You don't have to apologize to me. It's me who imposed on your time. It's very nice to meet you also Mrs. Barnes."

"Oh my last name isn't Barnes. It's Harris. Can I get you something to drink? I didn't start Sunday dinner yet."

"I'll take a cup of tea if you don't mind."

"It's not a problem at all. So you and Vince are out for an afternoon in the park. Are you two going to pick up Joey?"

"I'm sorry. All I know is that Vince is picking up his son today." Cherish felt nervous. Mrs. Harris was an attractive woman. Cherish could see where her sons got their good looks. She quietly prepared the tea for Cherish as soft gospel music played in the background.

"That would be Joey, my grandson." She said as she placed the china tea cup in front of Cherish.

"Here's your tea. Did you see the pictures of my two handsome sons?"

"Yes, I did. I took a quick look while waiting for you to come downstairs."

"I have a photo album here. Would you like to look at it?" She was already getting up to take photo album out of the bottom of the china cabinet.

"Of course!" Cherish didn't really like looking at, taking or owning pictures. She never understood why she felt that

211

way. At one point, she blamed it on her Native American heritage. It is said that Native Americans don't allow pictures taken of themselves because they capture your soul. She quickly browsed through the photo album. It was filled pictures of Mrs. Harris' baby boys. Vince was obviously the older of the two. His brother was taller, darker and all of his pictures, except for the very young ones, were taken in prison. Vince, on the other hand, had pictures taken from many different places around the world.

"Do you have any children?" Mrs. Harris inquired of Cherish.

"Yes I have one son." Cherish prayed that Vince would return soon. She didn't feel like answering any more questions.

"Only one child! You didn't want to give him company?"

"I was his company!" Cherish answered in a matter of fact tone. Mrs. Harris and Cherish drink their tea in silence until Vince returned.

"Did my two favorite girls have a good time while I was getting dressed?" Vince walked over to his mother and kissed her on the forehead.

"Why yes we did, Vince. I pray you guys have a great day. Are you picking up Joey and Sheila?" Mrs. Harris was in the kitchen now and starting to prepare Sunday dinner.

"I'm definitely picking up Joey but I couldn't get Sheila on her cell phone today. Okay mom, I'll see you later." Vince headed toward the front door and Cherish was right behind him.

"Nice to have met you Mrs. Harris. Enjoy your day." Cherish was glad to be out of there. She didn't want Vince's mother to think that she was one of her son's women. Vince had stayed out all night and came home with her. Cherish understood why his mother may think of her that way.

Surviving This Thing Called Life

Vince and Cherish headed up the Schuylkill Expressway toward Northeast Blvd. Vince talked the entire ride. He made Cherish laugh and that made her happy but she didn't like that all he talked about was himself. By the time they arrived at his son's house, Cherish heard more than she really wanted to know about Vince. He attended Howard University. He was an electrical engineer. He had modeled in Europe when he was a young man. He had five children, three girls and two boys. He also had five baby Mommas. He never married or had a serious relationship.

Vince pulled up to a two story white house on a tree lined street. His son lived in the Northeast section of the city. For many years, Black folks were not allowed to buy houses in this part of town. But with White folks moving back to the city, the Northeast neighborhoods changed to Black people and Section Eight rentals.

"I'll be right back." Vince got out of the car and headed for the house. In a matter of minutes, he was exiting the house with a chubby young man that looked like his twin. Standing at the front door was an obese woman yelling at Vince as he walked toward the car.

"Vince, don't take Joey in any bars today. I mean it Vince and remember to bring him home by eight. I have to go to work tomorrow and he has to get up early to go to his grandmother's house." Vince never turned around to acknowledge the woman at the door. The two reached the car, opened the door and got inside.

"Say hello to Miss Cherish, Joey. Cherish, this is my son Joey.

"Hello Miss Cherish. Are you going to the park with us today?" Joey spoke like an older child but looked much younger.

"Yes I am Joey. I hope you don't mind if I tag along with you and your dad?'

"No, I don't mind. Any friend of my dad's is a friend of mind. Dad are we going to get my sister, Sheila?"

213

"I called her earlier Joey but she didn't answer her cell phone. Why don't you try and get her now?"

"Okay Dad." Joey pulled out his cell phone and quick dialed his sister.

"Hey Sis. It's your brother, Joey. Me and Dad are going to the park today. Do you want to come with us?"

"Give me the phone, Joey. Let me talk to her." Vince took the phone from Joey and began to speak to his daughter.

"Sheila, I tried to call you earlier. I'm leavin the Northeast as we speak. Will you be ready in the next half hour? Okay, see you soon. Love you."

"We're going to pick up my daughter first. Is that okay with you Goldie Locks?"

"I'm with you today, Vince."

"That's what I like to hear." Vince didn't head toward the expressway. He was driving in the city streets. Cherish hadn't really spent a lot of time in the Northeast but she knew enough to know how much the neighborhood had changed. The area looked depressed and dirty. Vince pulled up in front of another local bar and parked.

"I have to take care of some business inside, Cherish. I won't be long. Joey behave yourself while I'm gone and don't talk Miss Cherish ears off."

"I won't Dad." Vince got out the car and headed toward the bar.

"How long have you known my dad, Miss Cherish?"

"We just met, Joey."

"So that explains why I never met you before." Joey and Cherish talked in the car until Vince returned. Cherish wasn't very happy. She hadn't planned on all these stops.

"Cherish come inside the bar a minute and meet my uncle. He owns the bar."

"What about your son. Who'll watch him while we're inside?"

"He can come inside with us. We won't be long." Cherish remembered what the fat women at the door said.

214

Cherish thought, he must do this often but it's not any of my business.

"I don't really feel like it. I want to go to the park like you promised. It's getting late and I'm really tired from last night."

"Alright, I guess Uncle Clyde will have to wait." Vince entered the car and headed toward North Philadelphia. The ride back was no different than the ride up. It was filled with Vince chatting constantly along the way. Cherish used the time to site see. She barely heard anything he said. By the time they picked up Vince's daughter, it was getting late.

"Is anybody hungry?" Vince announced to the members in the car.

"I am!" Yelled Joey

"You're always hungry, Boy. That question was really not for you."

"Yes, I'm hungry." Cherish was happy to see that some else was thinking about food beside her.

"Dad, why don't we stop at the pizza shop on the corner?"

"That's a good idea. It's getting late and we won't have much time in the park if we don't hurry up." After eating pizza, they all loaded in the car again and headed for the park. Cherish was ready to go home. There was too much stopping and picking up for her. She was use to doing things alone.

"Are you okay, Goldie Locks? I'm sorry it took so long to get to our destination but we're here now." Vince parked the car in the same location he had parked earlier that morning. He went to the trunk of his car and pulled out two blankets and a cooler.

"Come on kids. Let's go." Vince found a nice spot near the small waterfall and neatly laid the blankets on the grass.

"Dad I'm going to climb the hill. Are you coming with me?" Joey was excited.

"No, not today. Sheila, would you climb the hill with your brother? Your dad is a tired old man.

"Sure Dad. Come on Joey. Let's go." Vince's children headed for the hills that surrounded that area of the park. Vince opened the cooler and it was filled with cans of beer

"You want a beer?" Vince asked as he took out a can.

"No but if you have some water I'll take that."

"Sorry but no water only beer."

"Okay give me one then." Vince spent the next hour talking and drinking beer. But Cherish spent her time admiring the beauty around her and trying not to pay attention.

"Vince it's getting late. I want to go home and get some sleep." Cherish was ready to go home. She was tired and wanted to rest.

"Are you tired?" Vince was gently stroking Cherish's forehead and getting ready to kiss her when the children arrived from their hike.

"Okay, I guess it's time to go. Joey, fold up the blankets and take them to the car." Everyone piled in the car. Cherish really didn't feel like riding with Vince to take his children home.

"Vince do you think you could take me home first? I'm really tired." Cherish was hoping that she didn't have to become adamant with him. He seemed to be a man that wanted his way under any circumstances.

"You think that I'm going to try to kidnap you again. So you're going to go home first in order to get away from me. But I'm telling you now Miss Cherish, you'll never get away from me. I'm yours forever." Vince was looking at Cherish directly in her eyes as he spoke.

"But I will take you home because I want you to be happy." Vince drove up Girard Ave and made a left turn on 48th street to go across town. He passed Mayer Middle School and that really reminded Cherish that she was back to her old life.

216

Surviving This Thing Called Life

***

Cherish woke to the telephone ringing. She turned over to look at the clock. It was 2:00 am.

"Hello" Cherish said in a sleepy tone.

"Hey Cherish. It's me. Wisdom!"

"What's going on Wisdom?" Cherish spoke with a flat tone. She hadn't heard from Wisdom since her return to America.

"Blessing! Mi been real busy baby, dats why mi nah call yuh."

"Yeah, I know."

"Wha happen to yuh? Why yuh talk so?"

"I'm tired Wisdom and it's early in the morning here."

"Oh, Mi forgot bout de time difference. Mi call yuh later."

"Okay, talk to you later." Cherish hung up the phone. She knew she wouldn't hear from Wisdom any time soon. She tried to return to sleep but sleep had already deserted her. She thought about the last six months. She'd spent most of that time with Vince. They hadn't been together sexually. Their time was spent hanging out together and having fun. He made her laugh and he loved to travel. Vince always had business out of town on the weekends and included Cherish when he made his runs.

His business would take them to Virginia Beach, New York, Pocono Mountains, Myrtle Beach and many other places. She didn't know what the business was and she didn't care because she enjoyed the trips. It wasn't Jamaica but it was fun. She tried sleep again but sleep wouldn't come and join her. Her mind kept wandering. She thought about Wisdom and how that relationship was over for her. She couldn't take the loneliness. She thought her business and friends would be enough to occupy her time and sooth her mind in Jamaica but it wasn't.

Vince was different. He spent a lot of his time trying to make her happy. He worked at night during the week so he and Cherish often traveled together on the weekend. He

217

S.D. Laurence

hadn't pressured her for sex. When they went out of town, having her own room was never a problem. Cherish couldn't figure out what this young man wanted from her and she didn't spend much time thinking about it. She knew that he treated her well and didn't pressure her at all. She tried to remember what day it was. It was Sunday. Cherish had joined a neighborhood church with very young congregation.

She wasn't really into organized religion much but this church was very active in the community and very non-traditional. Cherish loved that the church occupied her mind and time. So between Vince and the church, she hadn't thought much about the past. She wondered why Wisdom called. Why wouldn't he just leave her alone? Cherish woke again to a ringing phone. She obviously had fallen to sleep. She looked at the clock and it was almost time for her to leave for church.

"Hello." Cherish said as she answered the phone for the second time this morning.

"Hey, Goldie Locks! It's me, Vince. You going to church today?"

"Yeah, I'm going. Why?"

"I was going to join you if you don't mind?" Cherish thought about it. She really didn't want Vince in all parts of her life. Although he tried very hard to include her in his life and he always introduced her as his future wife. At first it bothered Cherish, but after a time she got use to it and paid it no mind.

"It's a free world. I can't tell you not to go to church. What kind of person would I be?"

"No, Cherish. I want to go to church with you. I mean pick you up and walk inside together. Maybe afterwards we can go get something to eat." There was silence on the other end of the line. Cherish didn't know what to say or do. She really didn't want Vince at church with her because he might start talking that "ying-yang" about his future wife.

218

"I can't hear you Cherish. You still there? What about me, you, church and brunch today?"

"I'm here. You know that I walk or bike to church. It's a part of my weekly exercise routine."

"I know Cherish but it's cold as shit today. You shouldn't be walking and you damn sure shouldn't be riding a bike. I'm sorry Lord for the language. I almost forgot it was your day. Come on Goldie Locks! We'll have a good time together. I promise you." Cherish thought about it. It was unusually cold today and she wasn't really going to walk to church today. Her plan was to take a cab there and by the end of service the sun would warm things up and she would walk home.

"Well okay but I'll be leaving soon. Can you come in the next half hour?"

"I'll come right now if you want me to." Cherish could hear the smile on Vince's face.

"No not now. Call me in a half hour and I'll come down to meet you on the porch."

"Alright Baby. See you in a half." Cherish really didn't want Vince to go to church with her. So far she had only gone places with him. She never took him places with her. She didn't want too many people to see them together because they might get the wrong idea that Vince tried so hard to perpetuate. There was a 12 year difference between them. He was a handsome, intelligent man and Cherish did feel physically attracted to him on occasion. Just as she finished dressing for church, her phone rang. It was Vince.

"Good morning gorgeous. I'm down stairs waiting for you, okay?"

"Yes Vince. I'll be right down." Cherish wished she hadn't invited Vince to church but she hadn't invited him. He invited himself. Cherish headed down the stairs and out the front door to meet Vince.

"You look beautiful as usual."

"Thanks. You know I teach Sunday school today so I won't be in the sanctuary with you." Cherish didn't really

219

have to be in Sunday school this morning. She supervised the operation and every Sunday was assigned to different members of the congregation.

"That's okay, Baby. Is there any place in particular you want to eat afterwards?"

"No, not really but let's make it local because I want to get in a work out today at the gym and it closes early."

"Then local it is. I have some place in mind that I know you'll love." Cherish and Vince arrived at the church and found a parking place right in front. After parking, Vince politely opened the door for Cherish as he always did. Together they walked toward the church doors and there stood Pastor Kane greeting everyone as they arrived.

"Good morning Cherish. It's always good to see you, Sister. I see you brought someone with you today."
"Yes Pastor. This is my friend Vince Barnes." Pastor Kane extended his hand to shake hands with Vince.

"Good morning, Pastor Kane. Cherish has spoken so much about your church that I had to come and feel the spirit myself."

"Brother this is not my church. It's God's house and we're happy you came to worship with us today." Pastor Kane's attention turned to Cherish. He had his usual big smile when he spoke to her but today his smile seemed larger.

"Cherish you're not in the Sunday school room today are you?"

"Well, Sister Pat and Brother Ben are assigned but I really want to go over the lesson that I planned for the children with them this morning."

"Sister Cherish, you stay in the sanctuary today with your guest. Everyone knows you're a soldier for Christ but even a soldier needs a break from time to time. God will supervise Sunday school today. I know there's a word for you today, Sister." Cherish wanted to challenge Pastor Kane but decided not to create a scene and go with the flow.

220

"Thanks, Pastor Kane." Cherish and Vince climbed the stairs of the church and headed inside. Everyone knew Cherish at the church but Cherish never really paid attention to anyone. She knew the names of all the children and some adults who worked with her but other than that she knew no one. Cherish spoke politely to everyone but that was about it.

The sermon was about marriage. Pastor Kane read Ephesians 5 verses 25-33. The passage talked about husbands loving their wives just as Christ loved the church. As usual, when Pastor Kane finished reading and interpreting what he read the entire congregation would agree that everyone needed to be married. After the sermon, there was always something to drink and eat but Cherish headed for the exit. Vince had a different idea.

"Cherish, I need to go the men's room."

"Okay Vince, walk towards the back of the sanctuary and make a left." As Vince walked to the men's room, he stopped and introduced himself to everyone. Cherish was irate. Why did this man constantly push himself into her life? What was he saying to these people? Why did she let this man into this part of her life? When Vince returned, Cherish was outside waiting at the car door. Her cell phone rang.

"Cherish, where are you? I'm inside the church looking for you."

"I'm outside waiting at the car."

"I'll be right there." Vince walked toward the car with a big grin on his face. He was always happy and sometimes that disturbed Cherish because happiness was infectious and Cherish didn't want to be happy with him.

"Why you look so glum?"

"No reason. I don't really feel like brunch, Vince. Would you please take me home?"

"Baby please have brunch with me! I'll get you to the gym in time to get a good workout."

"I don't feel like eating, Vince. I'll grab something after the gym later."

"Cherish, I really want to talk to you about something that's very important to me and I want to do this today." Vince had a serious look upon his face. It was a look that Cherish hadn't seen before.

"Okay Vince but please remember that I want to visit the gym before it closes today."

"I'll remember Cherish." Vince gently kissed Cherish on the forehead and the couple drove quietly to a small restaurant with outside seating in the winter. The restaurant was a refurbished old house with a large wooden porch that surrounded the place. There were large heaters strategically placed to insure enough heat for a comfortable meal.

"You like the place Cherish?"

"Yes I do. I've never noticed it before and it's right around the corner from my house." The hostess seated Cherish and Vince at a table near one of the large heaters.

"There's a brunch buffet inside if you like but also have a look at our menu. Can I get you something to drink?"

"Yes you may. Do you have a bottle of Champagne at the bar?

"I'll have to check for you. The waiter will inform you when he takes your order." The hostess walked away and left Cherish and Vince alone again.

"Champaign! Why are you ordering Champaign, Vince?"

"Because I brought you here to share something very serious."

"But Champaign, Vince. What could be so important to order Champaign? As Cherish finished her statement, the waiter appeared at the table.

"Have you guys decided what you having this morning and yes we do have Champaign at the bar. It's Don Perion and the cost is 125 dollars."

"Yes, we've decided. We'll definitely have the Champaign and I'll have the buffet. What are you having?" Vince asked smiling proudly.

"Let me have the fruit tray please and a cup of coffee."

"It may take a little time to chill the Champagne Sir. In the mean time, serve yourself at the buffet and your fruit tray will be here shortly." The waiter walked away. Vince and Cherish were alone again.

"You know Cherish we've spent a lot of time together these past six months and I've enjoyed every minute of it." Vince moved his chair closer to Cherish and grabbed her left hand.

"I've enjoyed myself too Vince. What's this all about?"

"Excuse me please." The waiter interrupted.

"Here's the coffee you ordered Miss." The waiter placed the coffee pot and cup on the table. He politely poured Cherish a nice hot cup of joe and left for the inside of the restaurant.

"Cherish, I've fallen in love with you. Actually, I've loved you from the first day I saw you but I knew you didn't feel the same way. I want to commit to you. I want to build a relationship. I want to marry you, Cherish. I've never felt this way about anyone in my life. The age difference means nothing to me. You are a young beautiful woman to me and I want you to be mine and mine alone. I don't know much about your past life because you haven't shared much with me but none of that matters I know you here and now and that's all I need or want to know."

Cherish was overwhelmed. She didn't know what to think or say. She wasn't prepared for this. She knew Vince had a little thing for her but she always thought their age was enough to keep them separate. She knew they traveled a lot together but that type of stuff was not unusual for Vince. She'd met many men and women who traveled places with him. Vince always loved a crowd and a party. But she noticed that lately the parties were reduced to

Vince and her alone. Before she could respond, she was saved by the waiter.

"Excuse me but your Champaign is chilled and ready to be served." The waiter placed two chilled Champagne glasses on the table, popped the cork and poured two glasses of bubbly.

"Thank you. The Champaign is right on time." After the waiter left, Vince raised his glass to propose a toast but Cherish was obviously hesitant.

"You're not going to toast this moment with me Cherish?"

"Vince, I don't quite understand what this moment it about. I don't know what it is I'm toasting too!"

"To our love Cherish. Let's toast to an opportunity for you to find in me the love I've found in you."

"But, I haven't thought of you in that way. I always thought we were just having a good time. That's why I always tried to mind my business, stay in separate rooms and let you do your own thing."

"But you're my thing Cherish. I love you. I don't need to be intimate with you to know I love you. All that will come later. The sermon today was just perfect. He called the love a man should have for his wife a "profound mystery" and that's what it is with me Cherish, a profound mystery. I can't explain it but I love you." Cherish was speechless. She didn't know what to say or think. She sat back in her chair and wished she were home so she could light a joint. Instead, she took a large gulp of the Champaign.

"Cherish talk to me. Let me know what you're thinking."

"I'm thinking about you and me. I'm 12 years older than you. You have young children. You don't own your own home. I have no idea about what you do for a living. I know nothing about you and you know nothing about me but you talk about love. I don't understand Vince."

"I know all the things you said and I hope sharing this truth with you doesn't destroy our friendship?"

"I really want to go home, Vince. This has all been too much for me."

"Home! Cherish at least finish the wine with me. I have another surprise for you."

"Vince, I really want to go now. So please, let's leave." Cherish got up from the table and was ready to leave when Vince pulled out a small red box with a large gold bow. He placed himself on one knee to stop Cherish from leaving and presented her with the box.

"What's this?"

"Open it and find out." Vince answered.

"Why are you on the floor?" Cherish backed away from the box as if it were the plague.

"Take the box and open it Cherish." By now everyone on the inside was looking out at the spectacle on the porch and everyone outside stopped what they were doing to get a glance at what was in the red box.

Cherish sat in her seat and poured another drink. Vince was still on one knee in front of her begging her to open the box. She drank the wine and then opened the box. Cherish nearly fell out the chair. Inside were two rings, an engagement ring with a large two carat diamond and a wedding band with four large diamonds that easily equated to three carats. The diamonds were brilliant. Their reflection in the light seemed to put Cherish under a spell. She had never desired diamonds. She always associated them with South Africa and oppression but she found herself mesmerized by them.

"I don't understand Vince. What are you saying?"

"Marry me Cherish, that's what I'm saying, marry me! It doesn't have to be tomorrow but promise me that you're mine and mine alone. I want to wash your feet and show you love." Cherish looked around and all eyes were on she and Vince. It would be like him to do something like this in public. She felt uncomfortable. She didn't want to embarrass Vince and he knew that.

"This is not something to do in public."

225

"But Cherish, I want to pledge my love for you public. You don't have to answer me now. Keep the rings. They're for you. I bought them for you."

"I can't keep the rings Vince." Cherish looked around and could tell that the audience thought the whole thing was taking too long.

"Okay, I'll keep the rings while I think about it. So get up off your knees, please." As Vince rose, the crowd began to applaud. They assumed that everything went well because Vince was off his knees and Cherish had the rings in her hand. Cherish quickly and quietly exited the porch while Vince shook hands with the waiter and paid the bill. The ride home was quiet and long for Cherish. Vince parked the car in front of her house.

"Do you want me to wait for you and take you to the gym?"

"No, that's okay. All the commotion has made me tired. I'll talk to you tomorrow." For once Vince didn't force himself on Cherish.

"Okay Cherish, I'll call you tomorrow. Good night my love. Will you please think about what I said today?" Cherish quickly climbed the steps to her apartment. She didn't know what just happened. She sat by the front window, rolled a spliff and thought about everything.

Her mom recently moved to Atlanta to live with her son and help with the grandchildren. She was basically alone in that big house except for the tenants. She needed help with the property and Vince was always there to help. Cherish thought, there's a young handsome man that loves you and wants to marry you. You're tired of being alone and you need help with this property. How bad could it be to marry a young and handsome man? Cherish had a lot of questions for Vince. They arranged a meeting to discuss the whole marriage proposal.

"I don't understand this proposal. We're not in a relationship like that and we haven't been intimate with each other. I thought we were friends just having a good

226

time together. I appreciate all the time you spent with me. I needed the company but I didn't plan for this to happen."

"Cherish, spending time with you only sealed my feelings. I can't explain it and I don't want to try to understand it. It just feels right me being with you. I've know many women Cherish but I've never felt this way before." Cherish could feel and see his sincerity.

"I don't know what to say. I am attracted to you, Vince. You're an attractive man. You make me laugh and you treat me well but I'm not sure that we have a love that deserves a marriage? And we've never had sex!"

"Cherish, I have enough love for the both of us. I know that we'll be good with each other sexually. Give me a chance. Let me make you as happy as you make me." Cherish had a few more questions for Vince. She asked him about his career, children, and financial status. Vince told Cherish that he was an Electrical Engineer and was injured on his job. The injury left him unable to walk he totally rehabilitated himself and learned to walk again. The woman he was with at the time left him alone and helpless. So he was forced him to move in with his mother and he never left. Presently, he had a lawsuit that would be resolved with a lump sum payment for his pain and suffering over the years.

Cherish was satisfied with all that he told her. She had more questions but didn't care to ask them. She had to remind herself that she was doing something different. She wasn't going to give of herself this time and love him more than he loved her. She couldn't afford anymore hurt and pain.

Cherish and Vince remained celibate. They received counseling from Pastor Kane prior to their wedding and spent more time together. There may not have been any sex but there was plenty of sexual contact. They spent hours petting, kissing and caressing each other. Cherish loved it. She had never been with such a passionate and attentive man. She couldn't wait for the sex. Cherish was excited. All she could think about was diamond rings and the wedding day.

She did notice a few odd things prior to their marriage. Vince said he was at work during the nights but every time he called her there was background noise of a bar. Prior to the engagement, Cherish didn't care or think about where Vince was or what he was doing. She didn't really care now but she was naturally curious about most things in life. She would ask him about it and he would say,

"Oh baby, we just stopped to have a drink and get something to eat." Cherish knew something else was up but it didn't concern her. She knew that after they were married, Vince would work nights and she would work days. They would spend weekends together as they did now and she would still have a lot of time to be alone with herself. She also noticed that Vince really did suffer with a lot of back pain. Often times the pain would obviously be unbearable for him and during these episodes Vince would consume large amounts of beer, cognac and pills to relieve the pain.

The big day arrived. Cherish invited a couple of people from her job and two close friends. She didn't invite her son, mother or members of her family. Her marriage was a secret. She didn't know how things would work out. She was taking a chance on being seen as a fool once again. She didn't want too many people involved in this precarious decision of her.

Chapter Ten

Cherish and Vince did consummate their marriage and for the first year everything was great but soon after things began to fall apart. Vince was arrested on a gun charge and the incident opened Pandora's Box. Cherish learned that Vince was under Federal probation after spending several years in a Federal Penitentiary. He didn't have a legitimate job. His income came from the family illegal number business and because of the arrest he had to stop. There was no lump sum of money. Additionally, he'd gotten a dirty drug test from his probation officer and was forced to attend an alcohol and drug program for his addictions.

"Vince you going to your counselor today at the rehab?"

"Yeah, Why?"

"Well, I would like to go with you sometime. Maybe, it can help me help you? Because right now I feel helpless and you continue to withdraw from me."

"Cherish, I got this. Give me some fuckin time to get myself together, please. You fucking with me about everything don't help."

"I don't mean to fuck with you Vince. I'm your wife but you acting like I'm a stranger."

Vince was deeply depressed. He began to spend more time with his family and friends and less time with Cherish. He didn't think Cherish would understand what he was going through. She didn't know the type of lifestyle he was use to in the past and this wasn't it. He did love Cherish but he wanted more. He wanted more money, more travel and more drugs and alcohol. They no longer made love and slept in separate rooms because Vince would come home early in the morning or not all.

Cherish didn't know what to do. She and Vince were growing apart. Their lives were separate and the love making rarely existed. Cherish wasn't willing to go through any more struggle to be left alone once again. She decided to cut her loss sooner rather than later. The marriage was over for Cherish.

***

Vince came home early in the morning as he usually did but this morning he got in the bed with Cherish as opposed to watching TV and sleeping on the couch. Cherish no longer cared or hoped for a sexual relationship with Vince. She became close friends with her bullet. Her relationship with Vince was purely platonic. Once Vince got in the bed, Cherish pretended as if she were asleep, then she decided tonight is the night. She spoke to Vince without turning her body towards him.

"Vince we need to have a talk. Let's set aside a time now. Because with my two jobs, the gym we need to schedule this talk."

"I got time to talk now, Cherish. Let's talk. That's what we need to do Cherish, talk. I love you Cherish. I know I haven't been the best husband but I do love you and I hope you know that."

"Tomorrow Vince, tomorrow afternoon, I'll come home before I go to the gym. So let me get some sleep, I have to get up early and go to work."

***

Cherish couldn't concentrate at work the next day. She wondered how she would say what was needed to be said. She couldn't accept his lies and his life style. She didn't love him enough to struggle with him. She had no more fight left for anyone but herself.

"Vince, you here?" Cherish yelled out as she opened the door.

"Yes, I'm in the back watching TV." Cherish walked to the back room and Vince was in his normal spot, the couch.

"How was your day?"

"I worried all day about what you wanted to talk to me about." Vince said with tears welling in his eyes. He knew the subject.

230

"It's not working for me."

"What's not working baby?"

"You and me, it's not working"

"Baby I love you. This lifestyle change has been difficult for me. And this gun charge has put another thing on my plate to deal with. Give me some more time Cherish. It's hard to change your whole life. You can't leave me now. I love you." Cherish could hear the pain in his voice.

"Vince I'm not willing to wait for anything anymore. You lied to me and didn't give me a choice. I'm sorry but I should've never married you. It wasn't fair to me or you. Please accept my apology?" Vince was sobbing by now.

"No Cherish we can make it. I love you enough for the both of us. I will change. Give me a little time and I'll show you what I can do."

"Vince, you're a young man and you have changed for the better. Get yourself a young girl and have a few babies. Let the next woman benefit from your maturity."

"Who the fuck do you think you are to tell me to get someone else? Fuck you Cherish, I'll have who and whatever I want!" Vince stormed out the house. Vince was never violent with Cherish but she still worried about what he might do. She didn't try to stop him. She knew he was deeply hurt. A lot was going on in his life. Cherish felt there was nothing else she could do for him. She knew he needed a place to stay. She already decided that she would allow him to remain in the apartment for a few more months until something changed for him. She picked up her gym bag and headed for the YMCA.

Cherish stayed at the gym until closing. The sauna was total relaxation for her and she needed relaxation because having the talk was the first step of more emotional stress to come. When she left the gym, it was dusk. It was early spring so plenty of people were still on the street. She made it home quickly. Both the bus and trolley cooperated and arrived on schedule. She walked the half a block toward her house. The street was empty. She did try to be aware of her surroundings.

She made it to the top of her front steps and walked toward the door. As she put the key in the door, she felt someone behind her. She turned to look and saw two tall men with mask coming toward her. She knew right away it was a robbery.

"What do you want? Please don't hurt me! God Help! Jesus! Jesus! Help me!" One of the men held a gun to her side and whispered in her ear, "Be quite."

"Jesus! Jesus! Help! Help!" Cherish yelled again but this time louder. The next thing Cherish remembers is the other man pulls out a Taser gun, tased her left arm and she falls to the ground. He snatched her cell phone from her waist and both men run down the steps and disappeared. She lay on the porch for a few seconds, when she heard several police cars pull up in front of the house. Cherish was in shock. She didn't feel any pain from the Taser.

She knew God was with her because her life had been spared. As she stood up and tried to gather herself, she could see that all her neighbors were outside. Everyone was standing around to see what was happening. Charlie from across the street ran out from the crowd and gave Cherish a hug. Charlie had AIDS. He loved Cherish because she always took the time to talk with him and give him a big hug. Physical contact was something he missed and Cherish showed him love not fear.

"I heard you scream Cherish and called the police! My window was open and I heard you scream! Are you okay?"

"Yes Charlie, I'm fine. Praise God you heard me. I don't know what would have happened. Praise God! Praise God!" One of the police men walked up to Cherish.

"Miss I'm sorry to interrupt you but you're gonna have to come to the police station and answer a few questions. Your neighbor pointed the directions that the bastards ran so we got that covered. Are you hurt? Do you need an ambulance?"

232

"They took my cell phone and I'm not hurt. I'm just a little shook up. Can I use a phone to call my husband?" Cherish didn't see Vince's car out front. He didn't seem to be at home.

"Sure but let me call your cell phone first. What is your number, Miss?" The police officer dialed Cherish's cell phone but no one answered. He passed his phone to Cherish.

"Here you are Miss. Call whoever you want. We'll be leaving for the Precinct in a few." Cherish dialed Vince's number. The phone didn't seem to ring. Vince answered the phone immediately as if he knew she was calling at that particular time.

"What's wrong Cherish?"

"I was robbed at gunpoint. I'm going to the police station to make a report. I don't know how long I will be."

"I just called your phone and some man answered. I was wondering what that was all about. I should be home by the time you get back." Cherish thought to herself. He didn't seem too shocked or upset. He didn't even ask me if I was hurt. Maybe she thought too much of herself and he was happy to get rid of her old ass.

As the Dean of students at Mayer Middle, many visits to the precinct were required to make police reports about events that happened at the school. The detectives knew and respected her. They knew her reputation for honesty and equity so Cherish was able to get home as quickly as possible. By the time Cherish returned home, Vince was still not there. She opened the door and entered the apartment. Everything was quiet. No Vince. She was afraid and alone. She opened her bible, read the Psalms and fell asleep on the couch.

She woke the next morning still a nervous wreck. She picked up the phone to call out from work but gave it a second thought and decided to go. The job was always an emotional relief for her. When she was at work, there wasn't time to think about her own problems. Her only

233

thoughts were on her students and their problems. Cherish knew that people felt she did so much for the students but only she knew how much they'd done for her personal sanity.

Cherish thought about last night's events. The house was quiet. She didn't know if Vince was home or not. She slept on the couch and didn't hear a sound. Cherish walked lightly toward the bedroom to see if Vince was in the bed. She peeked inside the bedroom door. He was sound asleep.

Cherish walked toward the front room, picked up the house phone and began to dial her own cell number. She intended to dial the cell phone company to cancel the service because she forgot to do it last night. There was no reason to dial her own cell number but her spirit said dial and she was following her inner thoughts more in her life.

After dialing, she heard the vibration of her cell phone. She walked toward the sound and the phone stopped ringing in her ear and vibrating in the apartment. So she dialed it again. The vibrating started and she began to follow the vibration once again. It led her to the closet in the hallway and Vince's coat pocket.

There it was her cell phone! Terror struck her heart! How did the phone get into Vince's pocket? Maybe that explained why he wasn't surprised when she called about the robbery. She wondered what was this all about. Was he trying to have her murdered or was it a threat? Cherish could hear a noise from the bedroom. It was Vince.

"Cherish is that you. Are you awake?" Vince appeared in the hall way just as Cherish closed the closet door and returned to the couch. She needed to keep her composure. She didn't want to show any fear in front of Vince.

"Yes, it's me."

"How are you feeling baby? That shit must have been a trip. You're blessed that more didn't happen to you. You're not going to work are you?" Cherish tried to remain calm. She didn't want Vince to know she had spotted her cell phone in his pocket.

"Yeah, I'm going in. I'll feel better if I have something to occupy my mind. Anyway, you know how the love for my kids sooths my soul."

"Let me sooth your soul, Cherish. You know how much I love you. I'm so happy to know that you are alright. Let me protect you. Remember I am your husband no matter what."

"Did you forget about our conversation last night, Vince? Nothing has changed."

"I didn't think so Cherish but you need someone to protect you. And that someone is me." Cherish spoke before thinking.

"Who do I need protection from Vince, you?"

"What do you mean Cherish? You don't think I had anything to do with what happen last night?"

"I didn't say that Vince. I just feel afraid."

"Are you afraid of me? Why are you afraid of me? You don't have anything to be afraid of. I'm here to protect you not hurt you. You should know that Cherish. I need you to know that I would never hurt you in a million years. I love you too much."

"Okay, Vince. I hear you but do you hear me? Nothing changed since last night; I don't need your protection. God is my protector. He's protected me all this time, not you!" Cherish headed for the bathroom to shower and dress for work. She didn't want to appear as if she was in a hurry but she was and she couldn't wait to get out of there. She felt she was in real danger. Why did he have her cell phone in his pocket? He definitely had something to do with the crime. What was she going to do?

Once in the shower, she prayed to God for strength and wisdom. She finished washing and got dressed. She had no more conversation for Vince and he knew not to say anything else to her. She walked out the door and as she closed the door she could hear Vince.

235

"See you when you get home. Be safe baby." Be safe! How could she feel safe knowing that someone she so close to her was trying to hurt her? What would she do? She couldn't go to her family that would mean guns, trouble, and possible death for many innocent people. This was her problem not anyone else's.

Fortunately, she never shared all of her life with Vince or anyone else. He knew she went to college in New York but that's all he knew. Cherish headed for the 30th Street Station to get the first train out of town. She needed to call her job and her best friend, Jill. They had raised their sons together many years ago in New York. When Jill needed help, it was Cherish she called and now Cherish needed her friend, Jill.

What she really needed was a cell phone. So she skipped the 30th street stop on the trolley and headed downtown. She picked up a cheap pay as you go phone, quickly made the purchase and headed for the train station. Once in the station, she purchased a ticket for New York. She sat down on the bench before the train's departure and took out her new cell phone and called her friend Jill.

"Jill it's me Cherish. I'm so glad you picked up the telephone."

"I didn't go to work today. I just didn't feel like it. I may go in later. What's up my sister?"

"I'm coming to New York today."

"What's wrong Cherish?"

"Nothing, well not anything I want to talk about on the phone. I should be there in a few hours. Will you be there?"

"For you babe, I'll be there." Cherish called the job and spoke to her principal. She shared the robbery story with her and said she would be out for the rest of the week. She boarded the train and said a prayer to thank God for her safely so far.

The train ride was relaxing. She tried not to think about what was going on and what she was going to do. She did manage to get some sleep on the ride to New York. The train stopped and she could hear the conductor yelling, "Penn Station! New York, New York." Cherish woke to the sound of the conductors voice. She picked up her hand bag and headed for the door. New York, New York the big apple, that's what ran through her mind as she entered the crowd in Penn Station and headed for the A train to Harlem.

***

Jill lived in Sugar Hill. The area got its name in the 1920's when rich black people moved to the "sweet and expensive" area. Cherish got off the A train at 155th street. She walked up the stairs and landed at 155th and Amsterdam. Cherish walked two blocks up the street and one block left to 157th and Edgecombe Avenue, the corner of Jill's block.

It was a relief to be out of Philadelphia. Cherish lived in New York for 10 years and she enjoyed every minute of it. She left because she had a child to raise and New York was not the place for that. She knew that life had enough of its own ups and downs, so to add the struggle of living in New York to child's existence was not fair. She knew better and would do better for her child.

New York was a place for consenting adults. She loved its anonymous lifestyle. In Philly, someone always thought they knew you. She didn't experience that in New York. Every neighborhood was like going to a different city. She could get away in New York and she had gotten away. Cherish rang Jill's bell, announced herself and the buzzer rang that opened the front door. As she entered the lobby, there sat the security guard sitting at a desk.

"Hello Miss. Who are you going to visit?"

"Ms. Jill Walker."

"I should have guessed that because her friends are always just as beautiful as she is. Just sign the book right here and leave your digits if you so desire." The security guard said with a smile on his face.

237

"I'll just be signing the book today brother, if that's okay with you." Cherish smiled, signed the book and headed for the elevators. Jill lived on the 6th floor. She usually walked the flights but not today. She was emotionally stressed. She didn't realize how stressed until she knocked on Jill's front door.

"I'm coming. Let me put something on first." Jill opened the door and Cherish broke down in tears.

"What's wrong Cherish? Whatever it is don't worry about it. You're with your sister now. Sit down let me get you some tea and a joint." Cherish sat on Jill's black leather sofa. She could feel her body relax. She was safe.

"What's going on baby girl?" Jill said in a concerned manner.

"Jill you won't believe the shit I been through in the past 24 hours." Cherish told Jill everything that happened in the last few months.

"Well I can say one thing for you Cherish when you get into some shit it's never little. You a crazy Bitch for marrying that Muthafucka anyway." Both girls laughed.

"What are you going to do Cherish?"

"Smoke this joint and drink this tea." Both women laughed. Their togetherness gave Cherish the strength she needed to persevere. Cherish and Jill spent the evening talking about anything else but Philadelphia and Vince. They both slept well and woke to a new day and new beginnings.

"Cherish!" Jill called out as her friend slept.

"I'm going to work. Enjoy your day. Wilson's bakery is closed now but there's a new bakery and café on 153rd and Edgecombe. Try it out and if you feel like it meet me downtown for drinks after work. I'll find us a sponsor for the night." Jill never paid for anything when she went out in the city. She always had sponsors, men who took care of the tabs.

"Wilson's closed! What is the world coming to? I'll call you later about the after work plans." Cherish woke up when she heard that Wilson's was closed, that was her favorite breakfast spot in Harlem. Cherish was alone in the apartment. Her mind went back to the events at hand. What would she do? Where could she go? She decided to call the job to see if Vince called. She dialed the job and as the phone rang she prayed her friend Dee would answer.

"Good morning, Mayer Middle School. How may I help you?"

"Dee, this is Cherish?'

"Cherish where you are? You're husband's been calling here all morning. Are you okay girlfriend?"

"Yeah Dee, I'm okay. Did anyone else get the calls?"

"No Cherish. I don't let these nosey Bitches in this office know any of your business. But is everything okay? Are you sure you're alright?"

"What did Vince have to say?"

"He just said that you didn't come home last night and was worried about you."

"Well if he calls again, tell him that you talked to me and that I took the rest of the year off."

"Okay Cherish, whatever you want Sis. You know how we roll. Girl, I wouldn't have passed the test to keep this job without your help."

"Dee, the pleasure was all mine. Did anyone else call for me because I have a new cell number now?"

"Yes, this guy named Jessie called. He left his number. Do you want it?"

"No Dee, that's alright. I have his number but let me give you my new cell number but promise me that you'll give it to no one."

"Shit girl you got my word and remember word is bond."

"Okay Dee, I'll keep in touch. I won't be back to work. I just got to think of a way to say out."

"There's always disability Cherish. Emotional stress! Remember emotional stress."

239

"Good job Dee. Talk to you next week." Cherish hung up the phone. *Emotional stress, that's it I'll apply for emotional stress.* She got up, took a shower and put her clothes on. Cherish thought about the past 48 hours and realized what a difference a few days could make. She had to deal with the present because she knew that it is a gift from God. She was alive and safe, so the next thing to do was to make lemonade out of these lemons as her grandmother would say.

As she left for her morning adventure, Cherish closed and locked Jill's apartment door. You really needed to be a lock specialist when you lived in New York because everyone had at least three double locks on their doors. After finishing the lock ritual, Cherish walked down the six flights of stairs to Jill's apartment lobby. Seeing the large marble floor of the old rich building reminded Cherish of another time in Sugar Hill. She walked down Edgecombe Avenue with the Harlem River to her left and exquisite old buildings to her right, and headed towards the new bakery that Jill raved about.

She thought about life and how nothing remains the same. The only thing that is constant is change. The coffee and Danish were excellent. The café was owned by people from the Middle East. They were very kind but it still wasn't Wilson's. Happy to be in New York, Cherish decided to walk downtown. She loved the neighborhoods. She headed down Lennox Ave towards the heart of Harlem. She decided that she would at least walk to 125th street and shop. When she arrived, after walking more than 25 blocks, she was surprised to see that the vendors were gone.

"Excuse me brother but where are the vendors?" Cherish asked an older black man standing on the corner waiting for the street light to change.

"Where you been? They been gone a long time now. Ever since the big state office building went up and Clinton moved in, everybody had to move." The old man answered in a perplexed tone. At that moment, Cherish took the time to really look at her surrounding and realized that things had changed on 125th street. The stores that she was use to seeing on the street were replaced with places such as Starbucks and TJ Maxx.

She really wasn't surprised by the change when she took the time to remember how much the people protested over the construction of the state office building on the famous strip. The protesters built a shanty town and lived on the construction site for months to delay the building. But as fate would have it, the building was complete and with its completion came change.

"There's an underground entrance to the building from the subway and parking lot so that the people in the building never have to see 125th street if they don't want to but as you can see a few don't want to be underground." As the old man spoke, two young white men walked pass and headed across the street to Starbucks. Cherish's cell phone rang and bought her mind back to her mission.

"Would you please excuse me sir while I take this call?" She didn't want to be impolite to the old man.

"That's okay baby. You young people and your phones. What would you do without them? I was headed uptown when you stopped me anyway. God bless you young lady." The old man continued to walk up the street and Cherish called out.

"God bless you too and thanks for the talk."

"Hello" Cherish said in a cheerful tone as she answered her phone.

"Cherish? This is Dee. You okay?" Cherish noticed that Dee had a very serious tone as she spoke.

"Yeah Dee, I'm alright. In fact, I'm better than alright. I'm great. What's up?"

"A friend of yours name Byron called the school today and it seems like he really wants to get in touch with you. I didn't take the call but from what I could hear, it sounded like some type of an emergency."

241

"Thanks Dee for looking out. Did Miss Jones take his number when he called?"

"Yes she did and yes I have the number for you. Do you have a pen?"

"Hold on a minute. I'm in the street. In fact, I'm on 125th street in Harlem."

"That's what I love about you girl, you always going someplace different. Only place I ever go is to Lancaster Avenue and back. You ready Cherish?"

"Yeah, give me the number." Cherish wrote the number down and tried not to think about why Byron would be calling her. Byron was her girlfriend Angel's husband. He and Cherish were only friendly with each other because of Angel. Actually Bryon thought that Cherish liked him as a friend but she really didn't. She didn't think he was good enough for her dear friend. That girl really deserved her name because if there are angels on earth, she was one.

Cherish thought about the last time she saw Angel. It was the weekend before all this shit happened. Cherish woke early that morning with Angel on her mind. Vincent was out of town and the apartment was peaceful and so was her mood. The phone rang.

"Cherish I'm glad I got in touch with you. How are things going with you and Vince?" Angel had been one of the few attendees at her weddings.

"Nothing changed too much. I'm still waiting for the right time to tell him. What's up with you Angel?"

"I know everything is going to be alright. Cherish, you remember my brother Earl that lives in California?"

"Yeah the real evil one. The Capricorn that acts like Scott, my ex."

"Yes, that's the one. Well he's moving back to Cape May to stay with mom."

"Really! That's a switch. I thought he wasn't into the family thing. What's going on? I know he was sick the other day. Is he better?"

242

Surviving This Thing Called Life

"That's part of it Cherish, his sickness. He's on dialysis and living in Los Angeles can be very brutal without family and friends. So, I'm going down to help Mom prepare for the return of the prodigal son. Rochelle got to Cape May last night and I'm going to leave sometime this morning. You game? We can shop on the way down!" Angel knew how much they both enjoyed stopping at every discount strip mall on the way to Cape May. Of course they always took the scenic route where Angel could smoke her cigarettes and Cherish her ganja.

"You know I can't pass up a weekend with Mom and Cape May. I should be able to get the 10 o'clock train to Mays Landing if I hang up now. So see you soon. I'll call when I get closer to you.

***

"Thanks again, Dee and once again, good lookin out."

"Sis, I'm gonna hang up because everybody's coming in from lunch and you know how noisy these Bitches are."

"Okay Dee. I'll definitely see you next week because I'm going have to get some kind of doctor's note to stay out of work longer."

"God bless, Cherish." They both hung up the phone. Cherish tried not to focus on what was going on in her life because she knew that nothing outside provided her with security or happiness. She knew that peace is deep inside your soul and you must find it and learn to hold on to it. Cherish looked at the time and decided to eat something before she headed downtown to meet Jill.

She knew that Sylvia's Soul Food Restaurant was still around because it was now a famous tourist stop where busloads of people come daily to eat. She remembered when it was a small eat-in spot with a counter that sat 4 or 5 people and two tables that seated two each. Most customers ordered their food for takeout because there were so many junkies in the place you couldn't eat in peace. She walked down 125th street to Malcolm X Boulevard, turned left and headed for Sylvia's Soul Food

243

Restaurant. She was greeted politely and seated at a small table in the back. That was perfect for Cherish because she felt she really needed to call Byron.

"What are you having today Miss? Would you like to hear today's specials?" The waitress greeted Cherish with a smile. Cherish came to restaurant because of the memories. She had forgotten that she no longer ate 90% of all the things on the menu.

"Are your Collard Greens cooked with meat?"

"Yes they are."

"Do you have any vegetables not cooked in meat?"

"Miss, this is a soul food restaurant and everything is cooked with meat. We have added some vegetables cooked with turkey instead of pork but that's it Miss." The waitress was obviously irritated with Cherish and she understood why. She was right. Cherish was a vegetarian and this was not the restaurant for her.

"I'll tell you what. Give me some of that nice Peach Cobbler y'all have and I'll be happy."

"Now that I can do for you. Would you like a cup of coffee with that?"

"Yes I that would be nice. Thank You." The waitress walked away happily. Cherish took out her phone to call Byron.

"Hello." The voice at the other end sounded depressed and broken.

"Byron is that you? This is Cherish. What's going on?"

"Cherish where are you right now?"

"I'm in New York at a restaurant"

"Are you sitting down?"

"Yes I am. What's going on Bryon?"

"Angel is dead."

"What do you mean Angel is dead? I don't understand. What do you mean?"

"Cherish can you get here. I need you here. You were so close to her. I know I'll feel better if you're here."

"Of course, I'll be there as soon as I can but what happened?"

"Talk to Rochelle." Byron spoke tearfully on the phone. Cherish could tell that he was totally devastated, just as she was.

"Hi, Cherish. This is Rochelle. J.T. came home from work and found Angel dead in the bed. From all that the doctors are saying, it appears to have been a stroke but they're going to perform an autopsy to be sure."

"How are you doing Rochelle?" Cherish was sobbing by now. It was all too much for her.

"I'm okay. Are there people you know near you Cherish?" Rochelle sounded concerned because she knew how close she and Angel were. They were truly spiritual sisters.

"No. I'm in a restaurant." Cherish sobbed into the telephone.

"I'm sorry Cherish but we knew that you'd want to know as soon as possible. I wish I were there with you."

"I'll be okay. You will definitely see me soon. Is Taliah there yet?" Cherish was starting to get herself together. She knew there would be plenty of time to mourn her friend's death and now was not the time.

"No, she scheduled to get in tomorrow night from St Thomas. She took it very hard too. We all did. It was so sudden." Rochelle's voice was beginning to break on the phone. I love you Rochelle and I'll get there as soon as possible." Cherish hung up the phone. She was in complete shock. How could her best friend be dead? She had escaped death and Angel hadn't been so lucky.

"Excuse me Miss. Here's your Peach Cobbler. Is there anything wrong? Can I get you something?" Cherish was sitting at the table with her head held in her hands sobbing quietly when the waitress arrived. She lifted her head and the waitress could see her red and swollen eyes.

"I'll be okay, I just found out that someone very dear to me passed away. Thanks for the concern." Cherish sat up straight and wiped her eyes with a napkin.

"The pie looks good." Cherish said trying to change the subject.

"I'm so sorry to hear that. Are you sure I can't get you something?"

"Does this restaurant have a bar?"

"Why yes it does. What would you like? It's on the house." The waitress said cheerfully

"I'll have a Hennessy straight up with water on the side." Cherish was sounding better but inside she was looking for that peace she so desperately needed right now. While the waitress was away she took time to pray and ask God for strength and wisdom. She thought about her Grandma saying that everything comes in three's. First, that shit with Vince, then Angel, what next. The waitress returned with a double shot for Cherish.

"Take your time. Relax and get yourself together. If you need anything don't hesitate to ask."

"Thanks again for your kindness." Cherish took a sip of the Hennessey and felt the warmth roll down her throat. She knew she needed to get to South Jersey but she had to take care of herself first. She needed to calm herself and remember that life and death are partners. Without life there wouldn't be death. She just wanted to grow old with Angel but it wasn't her decision to make.

Cherish knew that she shouldn't become too emotional over things she didn't control. Eventually, Cherish got up from the table. She found the polite waitress and thanked her for her kindness and headed out door. She still hadn't called Jill. She looked at the time on her cell phone. Jill would be getting out of work any time now. Cherish dialed her friend's number.

"Jill, it's me Cherish."

"Where you been Heifer? You were supposed to be my excuse for leaving early today."

"I'm sorry Jill. I got some real fucked up news today."

"What happened?"

"Do you remember my good friend Angel from South Jersey that I talk about sometime?"

"Yes I think I do. You always said how peaceful she was. Yes I remember her. What happened?"

"She's dead!"

"What do you mean, she's dead?"

"That's the same question I asked when they told me, Jill."

"You okay though, right?" Jill knew about finding inner peace and not allowing emotions to rule your life. Her son was serving a life sentence in prison. He was one of the first to suffer under the three strikes you're out act. The new law stated that anyone who committed three felonies was considered a career criminal and deserved to be locked up for the rest of their life. Jill visited him twice a month in upstate Pennsylvania. As long as she knew Jill, Cherish never heard her complain about any circumstance in her life.

"Yes, I'm okay. I gotta be, alright?"

"Well come on down town. We gonna have a drink for the Sister. She's in a better place than our muthafuckin asses."

"You right about that. I already had one drink but you're right I could use another."

"Where are you?"

"I just left Sylvia's and I was on my way to you."

"Cherish don't come downtown. Let's meet at Lennox Lounge. You know the place. They're havin an after work jazz set this evening."

"That sounds like a bet, Jill. I'm on my way there now. It's better for me because it's only a few blocks away and I still need to chill."

"Did you eat?"

"No."

"You should find something you like on their menu. It's changed a lot because the White people from the State Office building frequent the place. We might even see Bill Clinton himself."

"I'd love to see that sexy Muthafucka, Jill! I'll see you when you get there. If Bill and I are talking, don't interrupt." Both women laughed and hung up the phone. Cherish turned right and walked down Malcolm X Boulevard, formerly known as Lennox Avenue to the famous Lennox Lounge.

As she entered the bar, she noticed that nothing much had changed. The large bar to the right, small tables to the left and a small stage in front of the tables that could be seen from outside. She walked over to the bar and was greeted by a bronze young man with beautiful Dreadlocks.

"Love your Locks, Miss. What can I get you?"

"Love yours too. Give me a Hennessey straight up with water on the side. I haven't been here in a long time. The place looks the same."

"You didn't notice the new dining room in the back, did you?" Cherish took another look towards the back and saw a large wooden door.

"It's a larger room for dining and jazz. As a matter of fact, we're having an after work set today. It's a local group but they're bad, Sister."

"I'm meeting my girlfriend here for drinks. Do we need to reserves a table or it doesn't get that crowded?"

"There are speakers in the bar so you can hear the music from anywhere in the place."

"Well, I think it's going to be me and you tonight because I ain't moving." They both laughed.

"Would you like to see a menu? We have great appetizers."

"Yes I would. I'm so hungry I could eat a bear. Well, I don't eat meat so I should say I'm so hungry I could eat a cabbage."

"There're a few things on the menu I know you'll like. Here, have a look." Cherish studied the menu and the bartender was right. The menu was sufficient enough to suit anyone's taste. She ordered vegetarian spring rolls with hot mustard and waited for Jill to arrive. Before long, Jill arrived at Lennox Lounge and joined Cherish at the bar.

"I see you didn't have any trouble finding the place. You alright?"

"Yeah girl, I'm fine. Have a drink on me." Cherish called the handsome bartender.

"Excuse me, Jabril. Me and my girlfriend need another drink."

"Not a problem. And what can I get you lovely ladies?"

"I'll have the same. I don't know what Jill is going to have." Cherish turned and faced Jill to see her eyes light up while she glared at the handsome bartender.

"I'll have you if you're on the menu." The bartender blushed as he looked into Jill's beautiful dark eyes.
"But we can discuss that later. Right now I'll have a Margarita straight up with no salt."

"Coming right up ladies."

"Girl, why didn't you call me and tell me that the bartender was so fine?"

"I couldn't even see what the man looked like. I only wanted a seat, some food and a drink."

"You feel better Cherish?"

"Yes I do. I'll feel much better when the jazz begins to play. You know music soothes the soul."

"You'll be okay Cherish. There's a lot ahead for you so let's have a good time this evening and let tomorrow take care of itself." So, the women enjoyed themselves that evening. They drank, listened to music, talked shit and flirted until the wee hours of the morning. The next morning, Cherish woke thankful for life and breath. She didn't make it to South Jersey as she had hoped but she realized that she wasn't in any shape to travel yesterday. She did need to buy some clothes today. Jill had provided

249

S. D. Laurence

her with everything she needed so far but it was time to get some clothes of her own. Cherish could hear Jill in the kitchen.

"Hey Jill, what's up. We got in so late last night. How did you manage to get up so early?"

"It's not early girl. I'm late for work. That's why I'm fixing a little something to eat because I won't have time to stop this morning. What some food?"

"No, I'm not hungry right now. I'm going to get an early start so I'll eat while I'm out. I need to get some clothes. My trifling ass been wearing your clothes for three days now. That's if you let me wear something again today?" Cherish said in a sexy way.

"Don't get sweet with me. I like dick and you know anything that's mine is yours. Except for my dicks! Look in my closet and see what you want to wear."

"You treat me so good. You sure you don't want to be my man?" Cherish laughed as she spoke.

"I told you neither one of us got what's necessary to get it on. You need a D.I.C.K. and a big one I might add." Jill laughed and continued her conversation with Cherish.

"By the way did you see all them handsome men at the bar last night. I thought the bartender was cute but as the night went on I found some better sponsors." Jill strutted around in her kitchen, remembering the good time they had last night.

"I don't remember too much but the music." Cherish didn't want to get sad. There was nothing to be sad about. Angel was dead and that was God's decision not hers. So why be sad. It was out of her control.

"But did you get any digits last night Jill. They all seemed like a good time?"

"Yes, the real chocolate one in the red shirt. He had some kind of accent. You know them accents turn me on girl!" Cherish remembered Wisdom. Oh, how she wished he was there for her today. He would know what to say to make her feel better. But she didn't know where he was

250

because they had lost contact. Wisdom was a big star in Europe now. He never had a permanent address as long as Cherish knew him. Even with all the money, Cherish was sure nothing had changed.

"Well Jill, it's been great as usual and thank you for everything. You are a true friend and you know I love you." Cherish extended her arms out to give Jill a big hug.

"I love you too Cherish. If you ever need anything, call me. I might not have all that you need but I'll always do whatever I can." Jill answered as she return Cherish's embrace.

"I got to go Cherish. I don't want to be too late because I'm leaving work early today to meet up with Chocolate." Jill smiled as she spoke.

"You too much girl! I'm going to shop a little before I leave town and then head for South Jersey. I'll call you later and let you know how things are going."

"Cherish don't forget to call me now. I know how you feel about that God protects me stuff but as your friend I want to know what's going"

"I'll keep in touch. I don't know when I'll call but I'm telling you now, I'll call you!" Cherish tried to reassure her friend because she knew how she was. Cherish could leave today and Jill not hear from her for 3 to 6 months from now. Both women prepared for the day. They left the apartment together and boarded the A train headed downtown. Cherish was the first to leave the train.

"Well Jill this is it for now. Talk to you soon but I'll see you later. God bless." Cherish walked away from the platform and headed for Penn Station. She decided to go straight to South Jersey. She forget that there were plenty of discount shops a few blocks from the new train station. Angel took her there at the end of the summer before school started.

Angel was gone and now it was time to celebrate her life. She thought of life and how quickly things were changing in her life. She knew that Father God would continue to

251

guide and protect her. She said a prayer of protection for herself and boarded the train. The ride to South Jersey was peaceful. Cherish loved riding the train. She began to think about her days in South Jersey and how she convinced her friend Angel to move there from Philadelphia.

***

When Cherish's son turned four, she began to remind Scott of his promise to leave New York before their child attended elementary school. Cherish didn't want to raise her son in the city and Scott knew that. Everything was fine for pre-school because she found a dynamic day care center where she worked while her son attended school. But that situation was coming to an end and something else needed to happen.

Scott refused to move. He was young and New York still had a lot of excitement for him. Cherish decided just after their son was born that she wouldn't have any more children for Scott. He wasn't the parent she thought he would be. Besides if things didn't work out, it would be easier for her to take care of one child as an opposed to two or more.

When a person decides to become a parent, it's a great responsibility. Scott could choose not to be involved in his son's life but Cherish was dedicated. She was determined to do the best that she could for the person God permitted to come into the world through her.

So Cherish left Scott and headed back home to Philadelphia. She got an apartment in the Mount Airy section of the city. This part of the city was greener than other parts of the city. Most of the houses were semi-detached or totally detached with large lawns. The streets were still tree lined and children could go outside and play on the sidewalks.

Cherish was enjoying her return to Philadelphia. She left there 10 years ago when she married Scott and moved to New York. Cherish was blessed again in Philadelphia with the opportunity of working in the same school that her son attended.

The Philadelphia School District was not hiring teachers at the time she moved back to the city. All positions were filled and their waiting list was sufficient. So Cherish found a job in a private Muslim school and that's where she met Angel. Angel and Cherish had so much in common. They were Aries, graduate students, and single parents with one child. Their children were the same ages and they were not Muslim.

The not being Muslim part was their first attraction because they were the only two people in the building that were not Muslim. Their classrooms were right across the hallway from each other on the first floor of the building. The large room where Juma Prayer was held each Friday was adjacent to both of their classrooms. So every Friday, Cherish and Angel would put their two classes together and wait for the time when the children could enter the prayer room. Juma Prayer is held every Friday at the MasJid. Muslims pray five times a day to Allah and every Friday at noon prayer is performed in unison. In Islam, men, women and children are always separated during prayer. The men were seated in the front, and the children in the back.

Cherish and Angel would peek out the classroom doors and watch all the men as they entered in droves for prayer. In Philadelphia, becoming a Muslim was almost clique. Maybe it was because so many of the men in Philly spent time in jail or prison and were introduced to the religion there. Mostly men attended Juma Prayer on Friday. The men were often unemployed or the self employed. But most unemployed brothers got some type of work from other brothers in the congregation and also by selling newspapers and bean pies.

Cherish and Angel spent two great years together in Philadelphia as friends. They spent most of their Sunday's together with their children going to the beach, park, the zoo or the museums. They would baby sit for each other also but it was usually Cherish that went out at night. Angel was never the type who liked to hang out like Cherish did but Angel judged no one or their lifestyle. Both Cherish and Angel were carefree in their attitudes towards life but each woman acted it out differently.

While in Philly, Cherish started to date her husband, Scott who was still living in New York. She stuck to her guns. She would not get back together with him until he left New York for a better location to raise their son. She didn't care where but definitely not New York. Scott finally got the picture and brought a home in a small town in South Jersey for his wife and son. So Cherish moved from Philly to unite with Scott as a family.

"Angel you should come and join me down here. There are a few jobs in the middle school. You have your Master's degree now with a few years experience so you would start with a pretty good salary. Besides, I miss my friend. I'm down here in the boonies all by myself." Cherish was trying desperately to convince her friend to leave Philly and head for the woods.

"Cherish you know my family has a couple of summer homes in Ocean City and it can get pretty boring down there in the winter. But the job thing sounds good. Check it out for me and let me know what I have to do." Angel got the job and relocated to Atlantic City which was only a few miles away from Egg Harbor Township. They worked and played together for the next eight years. Cherish moved away after their children, Tyreek and Taliah graduated from high school but Angel stayed.

A year after Cherish and Scott moved, Angel married Byron and now she was dead. Cherish never liked Byron. She knew that he had something to do with her death. If he didn't kill her directly, he definitely put enough stress in her life to kill anyone. Cherish remembered Angel telling her how Byron was arrested late one night on some back street near the bay in Atlantic City with a woman, liquor and a crack vile in the car. He told Angel that the woman was having trouble with her husband and he was counseling her. As for the crack pipe, he claimed it didn't belong to him but to a friend. Cherish knew all of that was bull shit but Angel believed and loved her husband. She would continue to support him even after he failed three drug test, lost his teaching job and his license to teach in the state of New Jersey.

The entire incident was a complete embarrassment to Angel. She would never intentionally involve herself in any of this kind of behavior. Angel would share stories with Cherish about Byron staying out late and sometimes not returning for days. Cherish told her dear friend that only drugs or a woman would make any man act so foolish. Now Angel was dead and Byron was alive. The train was nearing Atlantic City so Cherish called her friend Esther to pick her up from the station.

"Hey Esther, it's me Cherish."

"Cherish I'm so glad to hear your voice. I guess you know our girl died." Esther spoke sadly.

"Yeah I know. I'm on my way down now. In fact, I should be getting into the train station in Atlantic City in about 30 minutes. Can you pick me up?"

"Sure I can but why don't you get off in Mays Landing and that way we'll be closer to Angel's house. You are going there aren't you?" Esther sounded like herself again. Cherish was with Esther when she buried one of her daughters and Esther was strong then so Cherish knew she would be strong now.

"That's a better idea. I suppose I should be there in about 25 minutes. Don't rush. I don't mind waiting for you."

"I'll be there as soon as I can. You know I miss you girl. Can't wait to see you." Esther hung up the phone. Cherish continued the train ride until she heard the conductor yell, "Mays Landing! Next stop Mays Landing!" Cherish exited from the train to the smells and sounds of South Jersey,

255

sea gulls and Back Bay water. She loved her time there. She remembered the Sunday walks on the boardwalk with her friend Angel and their two children.

"Hey girl?" Esther called out to Cherish.

"Esther! How you doing? Ain't this shit Esther, our girl left us?" Cherish reached out to hung her friend. They hadn't seen each other for a long time.

"Yeah girl but what you gonna do? We all live to die." Esther spoke in a melancholy tone.

"You been over the house yet?"

"Yeah I been there. That Bitch is acting like he lost his life. I mean Cherish we're all sad but he's taking this shit out to lunch. It's because he's so fuckin guilty about the way he treated her all these years. You would come and go but I was here with Angel all the time and believe me, he made life miserable for her. He fucked around like a wild dog and drugs, forget about it." It was obvious that Esther was disgusted by Byron's behavior.

"I had a little idea about what was going on. Angel would ask me some things and I was honest with her. I let her know that I thought he was either messing with drugs or another woman." It sadden Cherish to think that her dear friend suffered so much during her short time on earth.

"I told her many times to leave him but she always went to her Buddhist beliefs of looking within and trying to work things it out." Cherish said seriously.

"Cherish it's really hard for me to be kind to that Nigga but I know Angel wouldn't want me to act up. So, I'm behavin for Angel." Esther looked toward the sky and repeated her statement.

"You hear me Angel? I'm behavin for you." They both laughed as each woman remembered the good times they all had together over the years.

"Where's the fourth member of our crew?" Cherish asked.

"You mean Christine? She and Aaron are so important that no one sees them anymore. You know I'm retired so I see Christine at the school board meetings sometimes and Aaron is a big time Vice President at one the casinos."

"Has she been over the house yet Esther?"

"I heard they were the first to come. You know Byron can't stand them because after he was arrested, they totally separated themselves from him and Angel. It really broke Angel's heart because you know the four of us use to hang tough back in the day." Esther said as she remembered the past.

"Yeah Esther! Everything changes, nothing remains the same." Both women sat quietly on the drive to Angel's house. As they entered the driveway, Cherish thought about how this would be the first time coming to her friend's house knowing that she'll never see her again. Tears began to gather in her eyes but she was determine not to cry. She heard a voice deep down in her soul telling her to stay strong because a lot of people are depending on you to be strong.

Esther and Cherish exited the car and walked up the front steps to the door. Both women were silent. Cherish knocked on the door, opened it and they walked in. There was no one in the living room. Byron and Rochelle were sitting at the kitchen table drinking coffee.

"Hey y'all! What's going on?" Cherish spoke in a cheerful voice.

"Cherish, I'm so glad you're here." Byron said as tears rolled down his face.

"She's gone, Cherish. Angel left me and I don't know what I'm going to do. After she died, I realized how much I depended on her for everything. What am I going to do without her Cherish?"

"What are we going to do without her, Byron? We all miss Angel but we'll survive this, God willing." Cherish took her attention away from Byron and headed toward Rochelle. She grabbed her and gave her a tight squeeze.

257

"How you doing Rochelle?"

"As well as can be expected. Taliah is due at the airport in about 20 minutes. Do you want to ride with me to pick her up? I know she'll be happy to see you when she arrives." Rochelle had it together. Cherish could tell. Angel's family was tight but not overbearing towards one another.

"Yes that would be lovely. Do you want to ride with us Esther?" Cherish turned to see where Esther was in the house.

"No, I'll stay here with Byron and start to get things ready for the mobs of people that are about to come through. Remember Charlene's funeral, Cherish?" Esther said as she walked toward the coffee pot and poured herself a cup.

"Yes I do Esther and you're right there were people on top of people. Then we're on our way to pick up Taliah. Anyone need anything from the store while we're gone?" Both women walked quietly out the door and headed for the car. The ride to the airport was short because Atlantic City now had its own International airport. But the airport was so small that Rochelle and Cherish nearly missed its one entrance. The airport had one terminal and two large doors, one in and one out. So it was easy for them to spot Taliah standing at the curbside waiting.

Cherish hadn't seen Taliah for a few years but she looked the same chocolate, petite and beautiful. Taliah always looked like a little teenage girl no matter how old she got. Her youthful looks really helped her as an aspiring actor.

"Hey y'all!" Taliah spoke cheerfully as she entered the car with one small bag and took a seat.

"Hey Baby!" Cherish said as she reached over the front seat to hug her.

"Hey Sweetie!" Rochelle cooed as she threw her niece a kiss through the rear view mirror.

"Are there many people over the house yet?"

"Not yet darling but they'll be soon. There's a lot to do baby. Are you up for the challenge?" Rochelle inquired of her niece.

"Yeah, I'm as ready as I'll ever be but whose ever ready for this kinda stuff, Auntie? Tanisha spoke candidly.

"I guess you're right. But Grandma seemed ready! Did I tell you how we told grandma about your Mom's passing?"

"No tell me Auntie."

"Well Byron and I didn't want to tell her on the telephone. So after I finally got here from Philly, we both decided to drive to her house. Byron was a mess. He couldn't drive or talk. All he could do was cry and moan. I know you both remember how much it rained that night?"

"Yes I do Rochelle. It was the world mourning the loss of a beautiful soul but go on tell the story." Cherish said anxiously.

"I thanked God that the two of us made it in one piece because neither of us were capable of going anywhere. As we pulled into the driveway, we could see candles lit in the living room from the side window. We got out the car, walked across the driveway, up the steps and opened the front. Mama was sitting on the sofa as if she was waiting for us."

"You mean like she knew something?" Taliah asked.

"No like she knew that Angel had passed on. Let me finish telling you. She greeted us with a hug and kiss. Asked us to take a seat and said she already knew that her daughter was gone and that it was alright." Rochelle was holding back her tears as she spoke.

"On the coffee table, sat her bible and crucifix along with several burning candle. Then she began to tell us how she was sitting on the back porch enjoying her garden this evening when an Angel came to her. She said she wasn't surprised by the Angel because she had visited her before. But this time it was different, the Angel spoke to her. She said the Angel told her that her oldest daughter was with

God. She said God took his child because she was tired and needed rest." Rochelle was crying now.

"And by the time me and Byron left, she was consoling us. Without the strength that she gave us that evening, we wouldn't have been able to drive home safety."

"Pull over on the shoulder Rochelle and let me drive. I shouldn't have let you drive anyway." Cherish looked in the back seat and noticed that Taliah was also weeping.

"Okay Cherish. You drive. I'll sit in the back with my sweetheart of a niece." Rochelle pulled off to the shoulder of the road and the two woman changed positions. Rochelle climbed in the back seat of the car next to her niece and squeezed her tight. The two women sat together in the rear of the car mourning the loss of their sister and mother.

Angel was so young and her dying was the last thing on anyone's mind. Cherish drove the car in silence and allowed them their time together. This time when Cherish drove into the driveway there were many more cars.

"It looks as though Angel's Buddhist friends had arrived. They came last evening to chant for Angel and they're here again this evening. I suppose that's what they do?" Rochelle said as she prepared to exit the car.

"We all okay?" Cherish asked the group, including herself before they went inside.

"Yes, I'm ready." A small voice came from the back seat. The three women reached out their arms to gather whatever part of a grip they could of each other for strength. Today was the beginning of more days to come when they would hold on to each other for strength and support.

As they entered the house, there were at least ten Buddhist in the Gahanza room chanting, "Nam Oyo Ran key Oyo". You could see the incense and hear the ringing of bells as the Buddhist held to their repetitive chant. Cherish didn't feel spiritually motivated from the practice.

Maybe this was an opportunity for her to feel what her friend Angel might have felt.

So Cherish took off her shoes and joined the gathered Buddhist to chant. She sat in her yoga position and began to chant as best she could. Cherish sat next to what looked like a peaceful and reflective young lady. She never chanted because she refused to say something that she didn't fully understand. She knew word were power. But tonight it didn't matter; the chanting was for her dear friend, Angel. There she sat chanting and crying for the lost of her spiritual sister, when suddenly she felt a sharp pinch on her thigh. She looked over and it was the peaceful, reflective soul pinching her hard.

"You must not chant. You don't know chant." The woman spoke in broken English. Cherish opened her teary eyes and looked in her direction. She tried to ignore the woman but she persisted.

"You don't know chant! You must not chant!" At that moment, Cherish realized what was going on. It was obvious that she didn't know how to say the chant properly and Miss Peaceful and Reflective wasn't having it. Cherish burst out laughing and left the room. She ran to find Taliah so she could tell her the joke. Everyone knew that Cherish loved to make people laugh especially when times were sad.

"Taliah, Taliah where are you?" Cherish called out as she walked down the hallway where the three bedrooms of the house were located.

"Aunt Cherish, I'm in my room." Cherish walked to the end of the hallway. To the right was Taliah's room and to the left was Angel and Byron's bedroom. She turned right, walked in Taliah's bedroom and sat down.

"Taliah, I have to tell you what happened!" Cherish was laughing as she tried to share the story with her.

"What happened Aunt Cherish or should I say, what did you do?"

"You saw me go in the Gahanza room didn't you?"

"Yes I did but I had no idea what you were doing. I've known you long enough to know to expect anything from you Aunt Cherish."

"Well anyway, I went in there to feel my Sister. My spirit said go and be Angel for now, feel what she felt and say what say would say. So I sat next to this little Japanese lady that looked calm, peaceful and spiritual. I began to chant and cry. Suddenly, I felt this strong pinch on my leg and the girl saying, no chant, you can't chant. I busted out laughing and ran out the room because it was my first experience with a Nazi Buddhist." Both Cherish and Taliah burst out laughing.

"Taliah you okay. I'd thought I'd try and give you a little laugh."

"I'm as best as can be expected Aunt Cherish. It's all so unreal to me right now. I'm waiting for mom to call us and tell us that tea is ready. You know how much she likes tea Aunt Cherish?"

"Yes baby. You know that I loved her like a sister. In fact, she was my Spiritual Sister."

"She felt the same about you Aunt Cherish."

"She died in her bedroom didn't she Taliah?"

"Yes"

"Have you been in the room yet?"

"No"

"Do you want to go in? I'll go with you, Taliah."

"No, I'm not prepared to go in the room yet but thanks anyway." Rochelle heard the conversation as she entered the room.

"You know no one has been in Angel's room since the coroner. Byron has been sleeping on the couch and I've been sleeping in J.T.'s room." Rochelle spoke in a matter of fact tone. There was dead silence in the room. Each of the women thought about Angel in their different ways.

"You know what girls. I'm going to sleep in her bed tonight. My spirit is telling me to be Angel tonight. I need to know what she wants from us while preparing her life

262

celebration." Cherish was excited. She understood what she must do and she was ready to do it. Rochelle and Taliah both looked at Cherish with surprised faces.

"You're going to sleep in the room Aunt Cherish or the bed?" Taliah asked.

"Did she die in the bed, Rochelle?"

"Yes she did."

"Then that's where I'm going to sleep tonight." Cherish left both women standing in surprise. She turned, walked out the room and headed for Angel's bedroom. The bed was still unmade. She could tell that something happened in the room but she wasn't afraid. She needed to feel her friend's spirit. They talked about death while they were both alive and agreed that whoever left first would find some way to contact the other. Cherish prayed for that contact now. She wanted Angel's going home celebration to be everything that she wanted it to be.

Cherish went to the dresser found Angel's pajamas and put them on. She prayed and thanked God for everything especially strength and wisdom and went to sleep. There had been contact. It wasn't anything spooky but she had a feeling in her soul. Cherish was ready to begin everything that she thought she needed to do for Angel. She went about the business of finding pictures and special quotes that Angel would want to share.

By the end of the day, the house was filled with thoughts and pictures to remind you of Angel. Everyone that came in the house commented on how much Cherish reminded them of Angel. It appeared to Cherish that everyone could see Angel through her and she didn't mind at all. The celebration of Angel's life was a success. Everyone and everything was as it should be. As the celebration ended, Cherish stood alone and thought about how much she would miss her friend.

"You alright Cherish? I don't know if anyone else noticed but I know you been working your ass off these last couple of days. You must be tired." Esther walked up to Cherish and put her arms around her.

"Why don't you come and stay at my house tonight. You've done enough. You must be tired?"

"I'm not tired, Esther. It's just that I need to be alone and I know this house is going to be full of people."

"Then we're going to my house. You can have my grandson's room."

"Thanks, Esther. I really appreciate this." The two women drove silently to Esther's home. Once in the house, Cherish showered and prepared for bed. She hadn't checked the messages on her house phone since she left. It was easy enough to hear her message from a remote location so she decided to use Esther's house phone to call home. There were one unheard message but one touched her heart.

"Cherish, just left my mom's house. I tried your cell phone and it's not working. I know everything's alright with you. Just thought about you and decided to give to a call. Well Cherish, I'm on my way home. I'm not there yet Cherish but I'm on my way home. I love You Cherish. Bye, Angel" The next day Angel was dead. She said she was on her way home. Cherish thought to herself I wonder if she knew?

Chapter Eleven

Cherish boarded the train to Philadelphia. She was headed back to she didn't know what. But she did know that she needed a place to stay and food to eat. The train would give her time to think or not think. She knew everything was going to be alright because it always was. She thanked God for life and breath. She knew as long as you have life, you have hope and that was more than she could say for her dear friend, Angel.

"May I have your ticket Miss?" The conductor asked politely. Cherish took the ticket out of her jacket pocket and presented it to the conductor. She also pulled out her generous smile.

"Hope you're having a great day so far?"

"I'm just starting out. I hope I have a good day too, thank you"

"You will." The conductor moved on with a smile on her face also. Cherish listened as the constant, repetitive motion of the train. It put her in a trance. As she was gazed out of the window, she saw a man at one the station stops that looked exactly like Wisdom.

"That couldn't be him, I'm just trippin." she thought! The conductor was walking through the car yelling, "30th Street Station! Next stop, 30th Street Station, Philadelphia." Cherish gathered her belonging. As she exited the train and headed up the stairs, she remembered Philadelphia and Vince.

He'd tried to kill her and that's why she left but now it was time to return. All of her fear disappeared; she knew the only thing to fear was fear itself. She pulled out her cell phone and dialed Jessie's number, he only lived a few blocks away and it was still early. Jessie and she were friends since high school. They were as cool as cool could be. He always said that they should marry because of the adventuresome spirit they both shared.

265

"Hey Jessie, its Cherish. I'm in your neighborhood and I'd thought I'd stop by and say hello."

"Cherish, I don't know what it is about you. I don't see for months but when I see you I always need you. Get your ass over her girl. Where are you? Do you want me to pick you up?"

"No, man! You know I love to walk. I'm at 30th Street Station. It's only a five minute walk and I need it after the train ride. See you in a few." Cherish hung up the phone and proceeded to walk to her friend's abode.

Jessie was an entrepreneur and one of his ventures was to provide the best ganja in the city to a select group of people. Everyone didn't get an invitation to Jessie's home only the selected few and Cherish was one among the few. She walked up the steps of Jessie's four story brick home, a few blocks away from the art museum and Fairmount Park, two of Cherish's favorite places in Philadelphia, and knocked on the door.

"Cherish, I'm so happy to see you." Jessie greeted Cherish and held her tightly.

"What's up man?" Cherish held Jessie tightly also because it was obvious that they both needed the love. After the hug session, Cherish proceeded to the couch and opened the weed box and lit a joint.

"You want a drink with that Cherish? I have brandy, wine, juice, water. What you need?"

"I'll take whatever you fix; I know it'll be good."

"Be careful now Cherish. You know I always wanted that pussy so I might spike your drink and eat the shit out of that pussy tonight."

"Oh Jessie, please don't spike my drink too much, just enough for me to forget our friendship and not refuse! As a matter of fact, I need my pussy ate right now!" Both friends laughed loudly and lovingly while Jessie prepared his friend a warm Cognac.

"What brings you my way this evening, Cherish?" Jessie asked as they both sipped the warm drinks.

266

"My vibe. I just got back from South Jersey. I had business to take care down there. You don't want to know my drama right now because it's too complicated."

"No, Cherish, I'm the one that has drama, not you. You know I told you that you know just when to surface?"

"Well, let me hear your shit, it will get me out of my shit for awhile."

"I got cancer Cherish! I've accepted it and prepared to move on and do what's necessary to save my life. I went to the best, the Mayo Clinic. They've given me two choices: a complete prostate removal or chemotherapy. I've chosen the prostate removal. It's more radical but more decisive. Right now, I'm trying to save my life."

"Jessie, I'm sorry to hear that but I'm happy to hear your fighting spirit. If there's anything I can do for you, don't hesitate to ask." Cherish spoke passionately to her friend.

"As a matter of fact, there is. Cherish, I need someone to stay with me while I recover. I won't be able get up and down these stairs after surgery and my diet is a very important part of my recover. So I can't be nuking shit in my room. I have a dietician that's going to fix my meals weekly but I need someone to heat them up and bring it up the stairs to me. My housekeeper, Wanda, is helping me by taking care of my father at his house. So her time is split and she can't be here as much as I need her to be." Jessie paused to wait for a response from Cherish. But one didn't come soon enough so he proceeded to talk.

"You won't have to cook, clean or anything just heat up a couple of meals a day. You can stay in the fourth floor apartment. Cherish you know I just can't have anyone stay in my home. You know the sensitivity of my business relationships." Jessie stopped talking and looked at Cherish while he waited for her response.

"Jessie, all I can tell you right now is that God is good and all knowing. I will be here for you as long as you need me. You just don't know how you're helping me!" Cherish and Jessie reached out simultaneously to hold on to each other.

"Okay, that's enough of that shit, Cherish. I don't want a pity party. I'm a man of action and faith. So when you gonna bring your shit over here? Have you seen the top floor apartment? Man you're gonna love it. It has the best view of the art museum and the parkway." Jessie spoke fast and enthusiastically so the combination of the two sometimes made him hard to understand.

"Hold your horses Jessie. You said something about clothes and the top floor but I didn't get it all. Let's just chill for a few and we'll deal with the details later. But I'm definitely staying tonight and I hope you said I'm staying in that fly apartment on the top floor." The two laughed and continued to enjoy their time together.

Cherish awoke early as usual the next morning. But this time, she awoke to the beautiful view of Fairmount Park and the world famous Philadelphia Art Museum. She took a moment to reflect but not too much. There were too many things that needed to be accomplished today and it was never her custom to focus too much on the past.

She had to find a doctor and get what she needed for a medical leave that would last until the end of the school year. She smelled freshly brewed coffee throughout the house. She knew that Jessie was an early riser like herself and that he had the morning Joe brewing. She looked in the closet and saw a red silk robe that she decided to wear it to the kitchen.

She never realized how large Jessie's home really was until she began to take the trip downstairs to the kitchen. The top floor where she slept was a large living area with a couch and bed. There was also an enormous bathroom with a Jacuzzi. The third floor was Jessie's personal bedroom suite that included a living area and an even more fabulous bathroom. Jessie's office space was also in the third floor. Cherish thought that arrangement was perfect for Jessie's recovery because he had everything needed on one floor.

The second floor was the main living area. This space was open and spacious. It included various pieces of art that Jessie collected during his travels around the world. The ground floor was a massive kitchen with professional style appliances. There was also a grand dining area and sliding doors that opened to a private backyard that included a small waterfall amongst beautiful foliage. Cherish finally made it down the spiral staircase to the kitchen to find Jessie, as she imagined, pouring two large mugs of coffee.

"I was just about to call you to invite you for morning coffee." Jessie smiled as he greeted his friend.
"Man I never saw that red robe look better!"

"Thanks. I hope you don't mind that I borrowed someone's robe? It was the smell of coffee that forced me to rush down stairs without dressing." Cherish sat down at the table and waited for Jessie to join her.

"The robe is for my house guest. Enjoy! Well Cherish, did you sleep well?"

"Yes I did Jessie. I didn't realize how tired I was until I laid my head down on the pillow. The view from the third floor is fabulous. I'm really going to enjoy being here with you."

"I pray so Cherish. You don't know how much you're helping me. You said last night that I was helping you also. What's that about?" Jessie had a serious look on his face. He was ready to hear his friend's drama. He thought last night was his night and today was her day. Cherish began to fill Jessie in with all the details about the wedding, the robbery and her dear friend's death.

"Cherish your safe here. You need a car. I'd feel much better if I knew you were driving around in a car instead of taking public transportation." Jessie spoke in a serious tone to his friend.

"Jessie you know I like the freedom of walking and not having to deal with automobiles and parking spaces."

"Cherish, I know how you feel but I'm going to need your help for at least three months and I don't want to have to kill a Muthafucka for messing with my help!" Jessie laughed

"Oh, now I'm just the hired help. What happened to my status as future wife?" Cherish was laughing also.

"So you start driving the Volvo today!"

"Jessie I have to visit my doctor's office at 40th and Market today and parking is always a bitch in that area. It's actually in walking distance and I was planning to walk."

"Cherish take the car and park in the lot. Here's some cash for your pocket and I won't take no for an answer." Jessie pulled out a roll of cash and handed it to Cherish. It looked like a roll of twenties but Cherish could only see the top bill.

"Take the money, take the car keys and call me on my cell when you get to the doctor's office and when you leave."

"Jessie, I'll take the car and the cash but I can't guarantee the phone calls. I'm not good at that keeping in touch stuff. You know that Jessie." Cherish was serious now.

"Okay, I'm happy with the cash and car. But call me if you plan to stay out at night. Can you do that for me?"

"Yes Baby! Mommy can call Daddy and let him know that she won't be home at night." Cherish finished her coffee and headed upstairs to dress for her doctors visit. She didn't call to make an appointment. She decided to go to the office and hope that someone cancelled their appointment for the day. Getting dressed forced her to think about clothes. Her clothes were at her apartment and she needed them. But she didn't have time for that just yet. She thought, only one thing at a time.

Cherish picked up the car keys and headed out the door. She didn't hear or see Jessie so she assumed he was relaxing in his room and she didn't want to disturb him. As she walked out the front door, she looked around to see if anyone was in her immediate surroundings. That's when she realized that she was a bit spooked by the entire incident and being back in Philly was reminding her of how she felt that evening when she was attacked. She made it safely to the car that was parked in the middle of the block

"Cherish get yourself together!! You're in Philly and nothing is going to happen to you. The devil is a liar and you are protected!" Cherish spoke to out loud. She needed herself to hear what she had to say. She started the car and headed for the doctor's office. As she entered the physician's suite, she was greeted by the receptionist.

"Hello Cherish. How are you? I don't remember seeing you on the appointment list today?"

"I'm not. I was hoping you could fit me in today."

"Well let me see what I can do for you, Miss Cherish. Yes there was a cancellation. Dr. Smith can see you at noon today. Is that okay with you?"

"Thanks for looking out. I'll be back in a couple of hours." As Cherish walked away, she wondered how she would spend her time while waiting for the appointment. She decided to drive past her house and see if Vince's car was in front. His car wasn't there so she decided to call her tenant.

"Hello."

"Hey Juanita, its Cherish."

"Cherish, I'm so glad to hear your voice. I heard what happened the other night. I've been worried about and afraid for myself at the same time. I haven't heard Vince upstairs either. Is everything okay?" Juanita spoke fast because she knew she might not hear from Cherish again for a long time. They had an agreement as tenant and landlord. Every month Juanita deposited her rent in Cherish's bank account and if she needed repair work there was a handyman hired by Cherish that took care of everything.

271

"Yes, everything is okay, thanks for asking. But you don't have to worry about anything. What happened was personal and that's all I'm going to say right now. To your knowledge, is Vince upstairs?" Juanita lived on the second floor. The first floor was vacant because Cherish's mother was scheduled to return home from Georgia soon.

"No, I haven't heard him at all the last couple of days. In fact, it's been quite lonely in this big house."

"Well, I'm right outside and I'm going upstairs to pick up a few things."

"Where are you going Cherish? What's happening?" Juanita was the type to panic and Cherish didn't want to bring that spirit out in her.

"Everything's okay. You know me! I'm doing something different now. It's nothing else, believe me! My mom is moving back so you'll have more company than you'll ever need! I'm staying with a sick friend but please don't share my business with anyone. As far as you're concerned, you haven't heard from me."

"Mum's the word, Cherish. And yes, I do know you. Remember, I love you and please check in with me from time to time and keep me informed." Juanita did love Cherish. She helped her through her heroine addiction.

They were coworkers and Cherish knew Juanita had a drug problem. Cherish witnessed lots of heroin addicts during her time in New York and Juanita had all the characteristics of an addict. She confronted Juanita and when she needed a place to stay after rehab so she didn't have to move back in with her addicted husband, Cherish was there for her.

"Thanks sweetie, I knew you'd understand. I'll keep in touch. So the next sound you hear will be me moving a bunch of shit around!" Cherish laughed. She couldn't take too many serious moments without a little laugh to follow.

"If you need help, Cherish, I'm right downstairs. You know that. Right?"

"I may ask to help me carry some things to the car but I'll call and let you know." Cherish got everything out of the apartment that she needed. She did use Juanita's help to make the process go quickly because the last thing she needed was to run into Vince. She also grabbed the one picture that Vince had of her and her five caret diamond wedding band and engagement ring.

"Thanks again for your help Juanita. And remember, you haven't seen or heard from me."

"See you later Cherish. Take care of yourself." The two women embraced. Cherish got in her car and headed back to the doctor's office. She was glad she had the car now. She thought, "Maybe I should listen to other people more often?" She thought again, "Maybe not!" She had to laugh at herself. She pulled into the parking garage and the attendant recognized her.

"Didn't you just leave here about an hour ago?"

"Yes I did."

"Do you happen to have your receipt?"

"Why yes I do."

"If you left less than an hour ago, you may not have to pay again."

"Well let's stop talking because we're wasting precious time." The attendant looked at the ticket.

"You're good to go but in two more minutes it would be too late." Cherish was grateful. She had a couple hundred bucks that Jessie gave her but she needed to be frugal because things were still in limbo. She needed the doctor's note to get paid for her time off. She hadn't been to work for two weeks now. She boarded the elevator and headed for the doctor's office. She exited the elevator and walked toward the receptionist.

"Hello Ms. Davis. You're right on time. The doctor will see you in a few minutes. Take a seat and we'll be right with you."

273

"Thanks" Cherish was pleased. Everything seemed to be working out perfectly but she knew that shit could change in a flash.

"Ms. Davis, the doctor will see you now." Cherish walked to the back. Her weight, blood pressure and pulse were taken by the doctor's assistant and she was escorted to the small patient room to wait for Dr. Smith.

"Hello Ms. Davis. Long time no see but that's good right?"

"Yes it is good."

"How can I help you today?"

"Well, I haven't been to work for about two weeks and I need a doctor's note when I'm out past three days in order to get paid." Cherish was blunt with the doctor.

"That's all well and good but don't I need a reason to write down?" Dr. Smith knew Cherish and expected this kind of response.

"A few things have happened Dr. Smith. I wasn't at work because I was robbed at gunpoint and my best girlfriend died suddenly from a massive stroke. I just got back in town from the funeral yesterday and I'm staying with a friend because I'm afraid to go home as a result of the robbery." Cherish said it all in a very matter of fact tone.

"Wow Cherish! You said all of that quite casually but you may have some side effects from so much happening to you in such a short period of time. How do you feel now that you're back in Philadelphia?"

"Actually, when I arrived in town I did feel an overwhelming sense of fear. But I put that thought to the back of my mind because I have business to take care of."

"Cherish, have you ever heard of Post Traumatic Stress Syndrome? We discussed it extensively at the physician's conference in Arizona this year. It's becoming a prevalent condition for people living in big cities. You definitely fit the profile with so much life trauma in a short period of time."

274

"Is that possible? I was feeling afraid but I thought those feeling would be normal after what I experienced"

"It is normal for you to feel fear but I'd rather you deal with this now so that it doesn't affect you later in life. You see it's not only the violence in your personal life but there's violence all around you. You work at Mayer Middle School don't you?"

"Yes, I do. Why does that matter?"

"You could use a break Ms. Davis! Why don't you take this time as an opportunity to relax and let someone listen to you instead of you solving all the problems in the neighborhood?" Dr. Smith knew Cherish's drive and work ethic. Cherish felt she didn't have Post Traumatic Stress Syndrome but what the heck. She needed more time off from the job so why not play along. Dr. Smith was from the hood but she didn't live in the hood anymore. And she frankly couldn't understand why Cherish still worked and lived in the city.

"You may have a good point Dr. Smith. What do you think I should do about it?"

"You need more time off from work and I'm going to recommend you see a Psychologist to discuss any issues that may come up. Do you have the papers I need to fill out from your employer?"

"Dr. Smith, I forgot all about that and everything was going so well."

"What do you mean Cherish?"

"Nothing, Doc. I still have time to get to the school and get the forms today if I leave now."

"Get going then. I'll leave the referral for the Psychologist at the receptionist. You get the forms and leave them with her. I'll fill them out and you can pick them up tomorrow."

"Thanks again, Dr. Smith." Cherish got up to leave the office.

"Cherish, don't forget your follow up visit in two weeks." Dr. Smith called out as Cherish exited the door.

275

Two weeks, Cherish thought, I wonder how long I can make this thing last. She needed to get to the Double M before 3 o'clock. She pulled out her cell phone and dialed the school as she walked to the elevator.

"Good Afternoon, Mayer Middle School. How can I help you?"

"Dee is that you?" Cherish knew it was Dee.

"Cherish, yes it's me. How are you?"

"I'm okay. I'm leaving the doctor's office. She giving me more time off because she says I have Post Traumatic Stress Syndrome."

"That shit sounds good to me Cherish. So you must need the papers for her to fill out?"

"Yeah, that's why I'm calling. Is there any way I can get the paper without coming to the job. I really don't feel like talking to anyone right about now."

"Sure Cherish. I can pick them up and meet you somewhere after work."

"That sounds like a plan. Why don't we meet on the Avenue? You know the bar where my cousin Dana works, Sir Richard's?"

"Yes, I know the place. What time will you get there?"

"I'm on my way now. I'll be there when you get there. Thanks Dee. See you soon." Cherish hung up the cell phone and walked down the steps to the parking garage. She got in her car and drove to the attendant.

"Thanks a lot for looking out. I wish I could give you a tip but I know there are cameras everywhere."

"That's okay, Sister. I know every good deed done will be returned sometime."

"Your right you know. That's exactly why I always try to do the right thing. Thanks again and have a great day." Cherish drove out the lot and headed for Lancaster Avenue. She checked the car doors at two stop lights and thought maybe there is something to this Post Traumatic Stress Syndrome stuff. But she drove on and put it all in the back of her mind. She had too much to do to be stressed. As a matter of fact, she was too blessed to be stressed and that was a fact. She parked the car in front of the bar and went inside hoping to find Dana behind the bar.

"Where the fuck you been!" Dana yelled out to Cherish as she entered. There were four customers inside and Dana was playing a computer game at the end of the bar.

"Here, there and everywhere." Cherish didn't want to give Dana any details because shit like this could start a small war. Cherish did not want to be responsible for anyone's life.

"You look good as usual, Cuz. What you drinking?"

"It's early but what the fuck! Give me a Hennessey. It's cocktail time somewhere in the world."

"No really Cherish, where you been? I haven't seen a sister in a minute."

"Dana, nothing's changed with me. I'm still Cherish."

"Your husband was in here the other night. He said he was looking for you. What was that shit all about?"

"Did he say anything else?" Cherish knew that the Nigga was crazy now. He had the nerve to come to his family and ask for her.

"No, what the fuck else could he say? I told him that if he didn't know where you were, then why the fuck did he think I knew? I also said if I knew where you were, I wouldn't fuckin tell him any fuckin way." Dana performed her usual head and hand motions as she spoke.

"Can I get some service sometime today?" A customer yelled down the bar.

"Yes the fuck you can but you betta wait a fuckin minute because I'm busy talkin to my cousin. The other thing you can do is get the fuck out if you not happy with the service in this spot."

"Come on Dana. I'm sorry. Can you please pour me another drink before I get sober?" the customer knew to change his attitude if he wanted anything from Dana.

S.D. Laurence

"That shit is better. Excuse me Cuz, let me make this Muthafucka a drink before he wrecks my nerves." Dana poured Cherish her drink first then walked to the other end of the bar to wait on the drunk customer. Cherish took a sip from her drink, got up and went to the jukebox to play some music.

"You want to hear some music? Don't put no money in that juke box. Which one of you Nigga's gonna to pay for us to listen to music?" The drunken customer volunteered to pay for the music. He put five bucks in the machine and Cherish began to select the songs she wanted to hear. While making the choices, her friend Dee walked through the door.

"Hey Dee. Give me a hug girl. Don't mention anything to my cousin because I didn't tell her. You know I want to keep the drama to a minimum." Cherish whispered in Dee's ear as they hugged.

"Sure, no problem." Dee whispered in return.

"What you drinking Dee? Have a seat at the bar. I'll be right there. Dana this is my friend from work, Dee"

"Peace Dee. Good to meet you. Any friend of Cherish is a friend of mind. What can I get you?"

"It's a little early but what the fuck. Give me a beer from the tap." Cherish returned to the bar and the women enjoyed their drinks and each other's company.

"Well Cherish, I'm about to be out. Here are the forms you asked for. Let your doctor fill them out and mail a copy to the board and a copy to the principal. You have been talking to Ms. Daniels haven't you?"

"Yes I call her every day after I call out on the computer system. She's been very supportive.

"Why the hell wouldn't she. Everyone knows how much of your life you put into that school. You never take time off. You deserve and need a rest."

"Thanks for everything Dee. I'll keep in touch with you and let you know how things are going." Dee left the bar while Dana and Cherish continued to enjoy their time

278

together. Cherish completed all the necessary paperwork for her leave of absence from school. She was glad that everything was taken care of. What she discovered when returning the papers to the job was that Vincent was following her.

"Hey Ms. D! Where you been?" It was one of Cherish's favorite students, Tyrone, but all her students were her favorite.

"Hey Tyrone. I had some things happen in my life that I have to take care of but I have to come by every couple of weeks to turn in some papers so maybe I'll see you when I come by."

"That's cool Ms. D. Hey Ms. D, this man in a blue car been askin about you."

"Really Tyrone. What did he ask you?"

"He asked me if you was working that day. I told him no then he showed up again and asked me again but I was wit my Old Head that day."

"What happened then?"

"Well my Old Head asked me why he was askin me about you and if he came around here again he would have to take care of that Nigga!"

"Whose your Old Head?"

"You know him Ms. D. It's Najee!"

"Oh yes, I know Najee. I use to teach him. Is he still in school?"

"Yes Ms. D. After that, he told me how much he dug you and didn't want no Nigga askin questions because if he had to ask questions about you he didn't need to know anything."

"Well you tell Najee that I said thanks and thank you too. Y'all keep a look out for Ms. D. because you know there's some crazy folks in this world. But don't y'all do anything to him, I don't want you to get into any trouble because of me."

"Don't you worry about that shit Ms. D? Oh, my bag Ms. D. I didn't mean to cuss but don't worry about

279

nothing. We always got your back because you always had ours. You better know it Ms. D."

"I do know it and that's why I love you guys. See you later Tyrone."

"Later Ms. D!" Cherish got in her car and headed to her new home. She missed her children but there was nothing she could do about that right now. God would have to watch over them but she was realizing that God was doing it all the time, not her.

Although she completed the first round paperwork necessary for not returning to work, she had to see a Psychologist to treat her diagnosis of PTSS. As she parked the car, she looked around to be sure there was no one around before exiting the vehicle. She was definitely more observant and now she knew that Vince was trying to find her. Cherish walked up the steps of her new home and put the key in the door. As the door opened, she heard Jessie speak out loud.

"Is that you Cherish?"

"Yes, It's me. I'll be down in a minute." Cherish ran up the stairs, put down her belongings, changed her shoes and ran back down the stairs to join Jessie.

"How did everything go today, Cherish? Did you accomplish your goals?"

"Everything went well, Jessie. As a matter of fact, it went better than I expected because I was also able to get some things from my apartment."

"That's excellent. Let me get Jocko to take the things out of the car for you." Jessie always had people around to perform chores for him. They were always friends that he knew for a long time that could use the extra cash.

"Jocko, go out to the Volvo, get the stuff out and put it in Cherish's room for me." Jessie yelled up the stairs again.

"Sure, Jessie. Hey Cherish how you doing?" Jocko yelled back. He remembered Cherish from high school. He always loved her because she would take time to talk to him.

"I'm good Jocko. Thanks for getting my stuff out the car!" Cherish returned to her conversation with Jessie.

"Yeah, I have to see a Psychologist."

"Did you get a referral from your physician?"

"Yes, I'm calling tomorrow to make an appointment. This should be interesting."

"Just enjoy and participate, Cherish. You may gain something from this experience."

"Yeah, I know! Oh, I'm gonna have a good time! And I'm also gonna keep an open mind about the whole situation. What did you eat for dinner?"

"Look in the oven. There's some bake fish. Then look on top of the stove and you'll see the steamed cabbage."

"Who cooked Jessie?" Cherish spoke as she quickly scampered to the stove to check out the feast.

"Jocko."

"Can he get down, Jessie?" Cherish spoke as she put a fork full of cabbage and salmon in her mouth.

"Oh yeah, he can get down!" This was said as she quickly chewed and swallowed. Cherish and Jessie sat at the dining table and talked while they consumed a few glasses of wine together.

"Well, I'm going to go to bed. I have another big day tomorrow. Good Night Jessie."

"I'll be up soon. Don't forget that my surgery is next Wednesday so try and schedule your appointments around that date."

"I haven't forgotten. I plan to be right here for you Jessie." Cherish and Jessie hugged again tightly before calling it a night.

***

Earlier that evening, Vince entered the apartment and immediately noticed that things were rearranged. It was obvious that Cherish was by because her things were missing. Vince hadn't seen or heard from Cherish since his horrible mistake. He had planned the fake robbery to scare Cherish into needing and wanting him.

281

Why didn't he throw her cell phone away? He didn't throw it away because he wanted to spy on her. He wanted to know if there was another man but he knew it wasn't. It was him or the lack of him that took Cherish away from him. Cherish did nothing but support him financially, physically and emotionally. He missed her. He knew he fucked up. He picked up his cell phone and dialed Juanita's number.

"Hey Juanita. This is Vince from upstairs. How are you?"

"I'm fine Vince. How are you?"

"Okay considering that I'm missing my wife something terrible. Was she by here today to your knowledge?"

"I really don't know Vince. I was out most of the day." Juanita hated lying but she would do almost anything for Cherish because of all she'd done for her.

"Thanks Juanita. I'm not trying to get you into my business. But when I came home and saw things missing, I didn't know what else to do." Vince broke out crying on the phone.

"It'll be okay Vince." Juanita was trying to console Vince. She thought he was a nice guy and it wasn't her business why Cherish chose to break up with him.

"I'm sorry Juanita." Vince was embarrassed. His emotions were unexpected. He hadn't cried until now. Maybe he was crying about everything; the lost of his wife and the messed up decisions in life that landed him where he was today, nowhere.

"Don't be sorry Vince. Everything will be okay. I don't know how or when but I know it will. Are you working your recovery program?"

"How did you know?" Vince was surprised. Cherish never shared much information with anyone so how did Juanita know he was in recovery?

"You know, I'm a recovering addict." Juanita said in a matter of fact tone.

"Cherish asked me for some resources in the area. She said a friend was having some issues that they needed to deal with. She never gave details. You know Cherish."

"Honestly Juanita, it's not going well. I do need to take it more seriously. Maybe I'd have Cherish now if I'd taken it all more seriously."

"Vince, everyday is a new day and a new opportunity. Don't beat yourself up about the past because you can't change that. All you can do is ask God for a new opportunity. So if he wakes you up tomorrow, see it as an opportunity."

"Thanks Juanita for your encouragement. God bless you. Good night."

"Good night Vince." They both hung up. Vince went into his bedroom, got on his knees and prayed to God.

***

Wisdom was scheduled to leave Zurich early the next morning for Jamaica. He hadn't been home in years. He was tired and needed rejuvenation. He missed the white sand beaches, blue sea and the crystal clear river waters of his home. He thought about the last time he and Cherish were in Jamaica together. He always felt sad about their short time together in Jamaica. He knew all of his efforts were directed into getting out of Jamaica and all of Cherish's efforts were directed toward staying.

He missed Cherish. He'd lost touch. He was too involved in his own success to realize what he would be missing without Cherish because she was always there for him no matter what. But Cherish wasn't there now and he didn't know where to find her. He had fame and wealth but they couldn't fill the gap left in his life after losing Cherish.

"Wisdom! Wisdom! It's time fi yuh tu git up. De limo soon come." Wisdom was awakened by Lex, his road manager. His new life was filled with people who were more interested in his money than his soul. Wisdom turned over and opened his eyes. He remembered that life

283

S. D. Laurence

was no longer his own. It consisted of time schedules, appointments and appearances. It belonged to his fans and his management team. His life had been reduced to others telling him what to do and when to do it.

Wisdom was a free spirit. He missed getting up in the morning and allowing his spirit to guide his daily direction. But with money and fame came other things that Wisdom wasn't prepared for. He believed that money would bring him freedom but instead he felt like a prisoner.

"Why yuh breaking mi peace Bredren?"

"Yuh hab de interview wit Jammin' Magazine dis morning. After de interview, deres lunch tu talk about de new tour. Back tu de hotel fi yuh shower an change clothes fi yuh goin away party. Yuh leave tomorrow fi Jamaica." Lex spoke in a matter of fact tone. His new attitude had long been a source of stress for Wisdom. He never understood how money could change a person so thoroughly.

"Have I changed too?" Wisdom thought to himself.

"Man yuh sure know how tu gib Babylon orders real good." Wisdom was obviously annoyed.

"Wisdom it's not dat mi waan tu order yuh around. It's because yuh hab important tings tu do today. Dis interview wit Jammin Magazine is big." Now Lex spoke calmly.

"Mi know man but who changed de schedule. Dis interview wasn't scheduled on de day before mi leave fi yard?" Wisdom's eyes were open but his body hadn't bothered to move yet.

"Wisdom, de interview was scheduled fi next week but dem changed an mi couldn't refuse." Lex yelled from the bathroom as he started the shower for Wisdom.

"What's dis business about lunch wit Brad? Wisdom was annoyed again.

"Come Mon, git up an git goin. Yuh can handle today's schedule. Yuh handled much worst." Lex continued to organize the items Wisdom needed to get dressed as he spoke. Wisdom dragged his body out of the bed and

284

headed for the bathroom. As he entered, the room was filled with steam from the hot water flowing out of the shower head. He took off his robe and entered the steamy shower. As the hot water rolled off his back, he remembered when all he had were cold showers and how much he enjoyed them.

His thoughts turned to Cherish and how much he missed her. Going to Jamaica was forcing him to think about things he had long forgotten. Thinking was something he hadn't done in a while. He was on the go mode; go here, go there, go everywhere. As first it was cool because he couldn't go anywhere in the world he wanted but now all he did was go.

As the water ran across his back, thoughts of Cherish flowed like a waterfall and consumed his entire being. It was a though she was in the shower with him. Wisdom believed in spirit. He'd live his life in harmony with his spirit and now it all out of balance. He needed Cherish. He wanted to give all this shit up. He'd had enough of what people call happiness: money and power. As he exited the shower, he glanced over at the bed to see what Lex had chosen for the day's attire,

"Bredren, where de fuck do yuh tink me goin? Where de fuck did yuh git dis shit from, Lex?"

"Man, yuh need a new look Bredren. Yuh not the youngest dude in de business but yuh need to look current to be current. Ain't dat right brother?" Wisdom didn't respond to Lex. He quietly put on the first pair of jeans he saw with a T shirt and headed out the door. He was done. His heart and soul was telling him, no more, no more! He boarded the elevator and headed for the lobby. As he exited the elevator, he was greeted by the bell hop.

"Mr. Wisdom, what can I do for you?"

"Mi waan a cab tu de airport!" Wisdom never got over the pleasure he felt when white men waited on him. That was one thing he'd miss about Europe.

"Sure thing Mr. Wisdom." The bell hop walked quickly to the doorman and he immediately hailed the next cab. Within seconds, Wisdom was on his way to the airport. As he drove away, he saw Lex standing in the driveway with his hands on his head yelling,

"Wisdom! Wisdom! Where de hell yuh goin?" Wisdom didn't know himself but he did know it was time for a change. Wisdom made it to the airport and headed for the British Airways ticket counter.

"Good morning Miss." Wisdom spoke kindly to the ticket agent. His anger had subsided.

"My name is Wisdom and I have reservations for tomorrow but I need to leave today. Yuh think yuh can help me out?" Wisdom had learned to speak without his Jamaican accent but didn't do it often. This was an occasions where he didn't want to be misunderstood.

"I think I can Mr. Wisdom. What's your destination? Do you have your reservation number by any chance?

"No, I'm sorry I don't."

"That really isn't too much of a problem, Mr. Wisdom. I'm sure I'll be able to accommodate you. Do you have any luggage and may I see your passport?"

"I don't have luggage today. I decided to pick up a few things when I get to my destination but I do have my passport."

"That's fine, Mr. Wisdom. I can get you on the next flight that leaves at 7:05 this evening. You'll get to Montego Bay through Miami and land in Heathrow by 8:55 tomorrow morning. Would you like me to complete your reservation?"

"Thank you very much. You helped me out a lot."

"It's my pleasure. And by the way Mr. Wisdom, I love your music. I'm one of your biggest fans."

"Thanks again for everything." Wisdom paid for his ticket and walked away from the counter feeling great. He would be in Montego Bay tomorrow morning. He headed for the nearest restaurant to get some food and libations.

The first restaurant he saw was a place called, Garfunkel's. After being seated, he ordered Guinness Stout and a fruit plate. He sat quietly and was grateful for his privacy and space.

His mind wandered back to Jamaica. How he missed home. He wondered why he was always running away from what made him happy. Was it because he didn't think he deserved to be happy? That wasn't it at all he thought. An impoverish life made him believe that money was could buy some happiness but his new found wealth let him know that money only complicated the issues of life.

He had a several hours to kill so he decided to leave the airport and go shopping. He needed clothes and gifts for his family and friends when he arrived. He paid his bill and left a generous tip for the waitress and continued to exit the airport. As he reached the doors to go outside, he spotted Lex at the ticket counter obviously inquiring about him. But Wisdom turned, walked in the opposite direction, exited the airport and hailed a cab.

"Where to sir?" The cabbie asked as Wisdom sat in the back seat.

"Tek mi tu de nearest shops."

"Right away, sir. Would it be too much for me to ask what yuh lookin to buy?"

"Mi need clothes an gifts fi dem back home."

"That's easy. We'll be there in a blink of an eye."

"Take yuh time. Mi plane don't leave until seven dis evening."

"Your request is my command." The cabbie answered politely

"Mi like yuh. Can mi hire yuh until mi plane leaves dis evenin?"

"Yes you can. I'll turn off the meter and I'm sure we can agree on the right amount of francs." The cabbie was elated. He was happy to have one client for the day. The two men drove to an old section of town where both sides of the Limmat River are lined with boutiques and antique shops.

Wisdom loved shopping. That was one of the few areas where he and Cherish differed. She was not a shopper. She knew what she wanted and went and got it. Wisdom also loved to window shop and Cherish hated it. Maybe it was because for such a long time that was all Wisdom could do was shop from the window.

He realized that his phone hadn't rung in hours. That was unusual, so he checked his phone to see what was going on. The ringer was turned off. He hadn't turned it back on when he was rudely awakened this morning. Wisdom had too many missed calls to count and most of them were from Lex but two calls were from his daughter, Grace. He immediately returned the call.

"Guidance, mi princess. It's yuh papa callin yuh."

"Hi Daddy. Where are you? I been tryin to call yuh."

"Doin de ting mi love de most, shopping. Yuh know yuh Daddy don't yuh." They both laughed.

"Uncle Lex said you left out early this morning without saying anything and he was worried about yuh. What's goin on?"

"Everyting crisp, dawta. Mi plane leav seven dis evening. Mi be in Montego Bay bout nine inna de morn. Will yuh be dere tu meet yuh old man?

"Nothing can stop me. See yuh tomorrow. Love you Daddy."

"Little More, Grace." Wisdom was happy to hear her daughter's voice.

***

The cell phone woke Cherish. She looked at the caller ID and it was Jessie. He obviously needed something desperately, she thought, or he wouldn't be calling so early.

"Hey Jessie, what's up?" Cherish was stretching as she spoke.

Surviving This Thing Called Life

"I'm sorry to wake you but I can't seem to reach my pain pills and I really need them. I can't imagine how they got so far away."

"No problem. I'll be right down." Cherish quickly got up and put on her robe and slippers. She rushed down the steps and knocked on Jessie's bedroom door.

"Jessie it's me Cherish. Can I come in?"

"Sure Cherish. I'm apologize for disturbing you so early. The pills are on my night stand but the pain to reach them is too much for me right now." Cherish picked up the pills and handed them to Jessie. She picked up a clean cup from the nightstand and filled it with distilled water from the gallon sitting there.

"Here you go Sweetie."

"Thanks Cherish." Jessie popped the pills and water.

"Do you need anything else Jessie?"

"No, I'm cool now. Do you need any ganja Cherish?"

"Why yes I do. How did you know?" Both friends laughed out loud.

"Cherish take this key and open the truck against the opposite wall." Cherish took the key and opened the trunk. It's was filled to the top with colorful ganja buds.

"Now that's what I call ganja!"

"Grab a baggy on the side and put as much as you want for your personal use." Jessie had a business tone in his voice. Jessie was a good friend but Cherish always knew that Jessie didn't mix friendship with business. Cherish grabbed a baggy and put a moderate portion in the bag. She knew she could always get more so why be greedy.

"Thanks Jessie. You want your breakfast now? Because I'm going to make myself a cup of coffee."

"I'll have tea, Cherish. Thanks." Cherish exited the bedroom and went downstairs to the kitchen. She was happy this morning but she was happy most mornings. Cherish fixed coffee for herself and a cup of herbal tea with honey for Jessie. She carefully carried the two mugs up the stairs on a single tray. It reminded her of her

S.D. Laurence

cocktail waitress days in Atlantic City. Cherish had to laugh at herself, what hadn't she done!

"Here's your tea Jessie. I hope it's the right amount of honey?" Jessie sipped the tea.

"Yes, Cherish, it's fine. You know Cherish, I was thinking about a healing trip to Jamaica. Of course, I'll need my nurse with me and that would be you."

"Jamaica, that sounds great, Jessie."

"When are you thinking about going?"

"I have a follow-up visit with my doctor at the Mayo Clinic in a few weeks. I should feel much better by then and hopefully he'll release me to travel. You game Cherish?"

"Yes, I'm game. How long are you planning to stay?"

"I'm thinking three weeks. How does that sit with you Cherish?"

"That sits damn good Jessie."

"I'm going to call my people and see if that Villa in Iron Shore will be available."

"Cool Jessie. I'm going to take a bike ride down Kelly Drive. It's a bit chilly but the suns out and I'll dress properly."

"Be careful Cherish. Don't forget the time you got a concussion from riding your bike on the drive." They both laughed thinking about the time Cherish feel off her bike and ended up in an ambulance to the emergency room. She and Jessie went to a party that weekend and everyone swore that Cherish had been in a fight. The fall left her with a fully blacked left eye.

"I wear a helmet now, if you must know sir."

"Cherish, just be careful anyway! Remember you're my nurse, I don't want to find a nurse for the both of us." Cherish dressed for her bike ride and headed to the multi-use recreational trail on Kelly Drive where folks could walk, run or ride along the river in beautiful Fairmount Park. Cherish really enjoyed physical activity and the solitude and peace of riding outside in God's beauty really

290

set her day off to a great beginning. Cherish returned to the house fixed Jessie's lunch and sat down in her room to make a few phone calls.

"Hello, this is Dr. Hoffman's office. May I help you?" The secretary spoke in a joyous tone.

"Good morning. My name is Cherish Davis. I would like to make an appointment to see Dr. Hoffman. I have a referral from my primary physician."

"That's great Cherish. You don't mind if I call you by your first name?"

"No not at all."

"Alright Cherish, is there any day or time you would prefer seeing the doctor? There will be a few weeks wait anyway you look at it." That was perfect for Cherish. She would visit the Psychologist right before her trip to Jamaica with Jessie, complete her paperwork for the next three to four weeks and be ready to go.

"I prefer mornings but I don't have a preference for the day."

"Well how about Wednesday two weeks from now." The two ladies scheduled the appointment, put the proper dates in their perspective calendars and said good bye. Cherish felt accomplished and relaxed. She puffed on a healthy rolled spliff as she gazed at her beautiful view.

***

Vince woke with a new motivation. He'd visited the doctor to see about his lack of sleep and appetite. He really made the appointment hoping he'd run into Cherish. They went to different doctors but in the same suite of offices. He didn't run into Cherish but his doctor did prescribe medication for his depression, anxiety and lack of appetite. He really didn't want to start taking prescription medication when he was trying to get off the booze. But he knew that the medications would help with his rehabilitation.

Meanwhile, he joined the 4021 Club. This wasn't an ordinary club but a place where recovering alcoholics

291

gathered for a more positive atmosphere. There were Alcoholics Anonymous meetings held there, but it was an independent organization. The club opened noon and closed at 11 p.m. This gave Vince somewhere to be during the day. He knew a part of staying sober was connecting with people that would support him. He missed talking to strangers at the bar but the 4021 Club was an opportunity for him to fill that vacuum.

Vince got dressed quickly and headed for his daily fix at 4021 Walnut Street. It was a nice daily walk for him. He would be at the front door of the club in about twenty or thirty minutes depending on who he met on the way. As he walked up the steps, of what looked like a private residence, he was happy to be there. Inside were people who were concerned about his well being. He wished he'd shown Cherish more appreciation because no one, except for his mother, had ever cared for him as intensely as Cherish. Vince opened the door.

"Hey Vince. Glad you could make it today. What's cookin son?"

"Hey Junebug! What's up with you old head?"

"Nothing much. Just making everyday count to make up for the ones that didn't." Junebug chuckled. He was an older man from the neighborhood that Vince knew from the bars.

"I know what you mean Junebug. I'm going to get me a cup of coffee. Hold my seat for me at your table." Vince purchased two cups of coffee and went back to join his friend.

"Thanks for the coffee man. Did you come to the dance the other night?" The club also had non-alcohol dances on the weekend.

"Naw man. I was home chillin."

"Man you young. You not old like me. You have a long life ahead. Come to one of those dances and get you one of them tender young things."

292

"Junebug, you know I have a wife and I love her. I can't even think about another woman right now."

"I know man but life goes on."

"Yes it does Junebug and my prayer is that God will allow me to live long enough to give Cherish the husband she deserves."

"You doing the right thing man. You keep hope alive, get yourself together and go get that pretty thing that's already yours!" Junebug remembered seeing Cherish with Vince. When he saw them together, he like everyone else knew Cherish was a catch that any man would want to keep.

"Just keep workin your program man. Thank God you got some sense before you got old like me. Keep the faith, man. You know that Faith is like taking the first step even when you don't see the whole staircase." Junebug stroked his gray beard as he spoke to Vince. He was praying for Vince every night. Both men needed each other. Junebug was the father that Vince so desperately wished was alive now and Vince was the son that Junebug lost and never got an opportunity to have a relationship with.

"That's deep Junebug. I never knew you was that deep!" Vince laughed trying to lighten the moment.

"That was a quote from the late great Dr. Martin Luther King Jr. Now that was a man who walked by faith and not by sight."

"You can say that again, Junebug. Is there going to be a meeting this morning?"

"Yeah, they back there settin up the room now. You want go back and help?"

"Yeah, why not?" The two men shared much love and respect for each other and their shared experiences. They got up, hugged each other tightly and proceeded to the back room to help set up the chairs for the morning AA meeting.

293

S.D. Laurence

***

It was the morning of her appointment with the Psychologist. Cherish was cool with her present situation. She tried not to focus on anything but the present, the gift of life. She had no idea about the future and decided to let it take care of itself. She did know that she was scheduled to leave for Jamaica in a few weeks and looking forward to the trip.

Her mind drifted to Wisdom. She hadn't heard from him in months. She thought she could get in touch with him if she really wanted to. But she wasn't interested in contacting him. She didn't want personal drama right now. She wanted peace and quiet. She didn't even miss the kids at school. She was changing. Cherish was dressed and ready to go. She'd left enough time in her schedule to take care of Jessie before she left. Cherish picked up her phone and dialed Jessie.

"Good morning Jessie. I have a doctor's appointment today. I'll be leaving soon. What do you feel like eating this morning?"

"Morning Cherish. Well, I'm feeling like oatmeal, toast, fruit and tea. What doctor are you going to see today?"

"Dr. Hoffman, my Psychologist. He's going to help me with my Post Traumatic Stress Disorder." Cherish laughed.

"Just make sure you get the time off you need for our Jamaica trip. I've improved so much and I know the Jamaica visit will definitely improve things more."

"Believe me Jessie I didn't forget about Jamaica. Remember the nurse needs healing too. Give me a minute to get things ready for you and you'll be eating real soon."

"Okay Love. See you soon." Cherish went downstairs to the kitchen and prepared breakfast for Jessie. She was enjoying her time with Jessie but knew it had to end soon.

"Jessie, I have your breakfast." Cherish knocked on the door as she called to Jessie.

294

"Come in Cherish. I'm not going to have the pleasure of your company this morning? Cherish could hear the disappointment when Jessie spoke.

"Sorry Jessie. I have to be in town by 9:00 this morning." Cherish knew she had to leave Jessie as soon as he recovered.

"I'll be home by lunch. Do you need anything while I'm out in the world?"

"You don't have to rush home Cherish. Shanae will be here today. She's bringing the weekly food and I'm sure she'll fix lunch before she leaves." Jessie always worried about Cherish when she left the house.

"Great! I may try to get some shopping in while I'm downtown. See you later Jessie." Cherish quickly gathered her stuff and headed for the door.

Chapter Twelve

Cherish was awaken by the sun streaming through the front window of her fourth floor apartment. Usually, after she had breakfast with Jessie, she would take a leisurely bike ride around the Schuylkill River in the park but today was different. Her phone rang,

"You up and packed Cherish? The car will be here to pick us up in about an hour."

"Yes, Mon! Mi up and ready fi de trip." Cherish was excited. She hadn't been back to Jamaica since her time with Wisdom and she was looking forward to the change of scenery.

"Cherish, I made breakfast for you today for a change. Come down and have something to eat before we hit the road."

"I'll be right down Jessie. Let me take a quick shower first. Is Jocko around to bring my luggage downstairs for me?"

"Sure thing, Babe. Put your stuff in the hallway and I'll send Jocko up to get it. You know Jocko is going with us too?"

"Oh, I totally forgot that you are the best friend anyone can have!" Cherish laughed.

"No Cherish! You are the best friend anyone can have! Get your ass in the shower and come on down here and have coffee with your best friend." The two hung up the phone and Cherish jumped into the shower. She was more excited than she'd been for some time. She wasn't worried about anything or anyone. Her family was okay. Vince was still living in the apartment and dutifully paying his rent on time. He not only paid his rent, but according to Juanita he was also taking care of any problems in the triplex. She didn't know Vince's state of mind and didn't really care about now.

She knew if she shared this story with people, most would think she was crazy but in her mind she knew everything was going to be alright. She didn't know what that looked like but she did know God. But today was not a day to think; today was a day to do. Cherish finished her shower, put on her clothes and headed downstairs for breakfast with Jessie.

"Good morning Jessie! Thanks for the breakfast!" Jessie had the large dining table fully set with flowers. The presentation was beautiful.

"Have a seat, Princess." Jessie pulled out the chair for Cherish to sit.

"Are you expecting someone else?" Cherish asked Jessie in a quizzical tone.

"Just you and me. I wanted this to be the beginning of me showing you my appreciation for spending this time with me during my recovery. You know that I love you. I mean I L-O-V-E you girl and what you did just put the icing on the cake."

"Jessie, I know. Remember this is a two way street. You're doing something for me too. As a matter of fact, you're doing more for me than I ever could do for you. Enough of that talk! Let's just focus on the good time ahead us. Who else is going with us Jessie?"

"Well, besides you, me and Jocko. There's Wanda, Shanae and my two boys Kyian and Jamir. Wanda and Shanae are riding in the Limo with us to the airport and Kyian and Jamir are meeting us there."

"Limo? Now that's hot!"

"Well, I figure we all deserve this time so let's make it fabulous. Wait until you see the mansion we're staying at in Iron Shore for the next three weeks. You did clear everything up to be away?" Jessie hadn't really talked to Cherish after her doctor's appointment but he figured everything was okay since Cherish didn't say anything different. For the past few weeks he had been busy planning the trip to Jamaica and keeping his doctor's visits.

"Yeah! Everything cool. I don't have to see the doctor until after we return. As a matter of fact, the doctor told

297

me to find someplace where I felt peaceful and spend as much time there as possible. I told him I would. I just didn't tell him it would be in Jamaica." Cherish laughed. She and Jessie finished up their breakfast together and headed upstairs to wait for the Limo.

"Did you say we were staying in Iron Shore?"

"Yeah, you must know the area. It's right outside of Montego Bay."

"Yeah, I know the place. I know a few people who live in the area also. I just hope I don't run into them."

"Why?"

"I don't feel like talking about where I been and what I'm doin now. I'm just not in the mood."

"You shouldn't see anyone Cherish. We have a housekeeper, cook and driver at our disposal and I made arrangements for us to spend our beach days at Riu Beach Hotel and Resort. It's a new all inclusive right down the hill from Iron Shore."

"I know the place." Cherish didn't continue the conversation. She did know the place because Grace, Wisdom's daughter lived in Iron Shore and worked at the Rui Beach Hotel. She just hoped that Wisdom was still somewhere in Europe. She didn't really mind seeing Grace. In fact, she would be happy to see her pretty face.

"The Limo's here!" Jocko yelled into the house from the porch. Everyone was present and ready to go. They all loaded into the Limo and headed for the Philadelphia International Airport.

***

The people waiting for the flight were the usual suspects of returning Jamaican with many suitcases and many more boxes in combination with the tourist waiting to have a good time. Everyone boarded on the plane. Jessie and his party of six were seated in first class. Champagne flowed for the three hour ride from Philadelphia to Montego Bay. By the time the plane landed, Jessie and his comrades were feeling rather good and ready to meet the beautiful island

298

of Jamaica. The group made it through customs and loaded in a van waiting for them outside.

"Welcome, Jessie." The driver greeted Jessie as he grabbed the luggage and began to pack the van.

"Hello, Winston. Glad to be back. Is everything ready at the house?"

"Yes sir. Everything yuh asked for is dere waiting. Florence preparing lunch. It'll be ready by de time we get to Iron Shore." Cherish noticed that Winston had just a little trace of a Jamaican accent. When everyone was loaded in the van and on the way to the house, Cherish took the time to ask Jessie about Winston.

"Is Winston Jamaican?"

"With a name like Winston, what do you think?" Jessie began to laugh.

"I mean he doesn't really have an accent at all. I was just curious."

"He's Jamaican but he spent most of his life in Philly. He was deported back to Jamaica several years ago after a big drug charge. He is good friends with the guy that owns the villa and this is his new job.

"Oh, that explains a lot." Cherish sat back and enjoyed the ride to Iron Shore. The ride brought back memories of her time with Wisdom in Jamaica. She reviewed the entire relationship in her mind, as she often did, and it reinforced that she did the right thing. She didn't want a life following someone else's dreams. She did that in her marriage to Scott and certainly was not going to do it with Wisdom or Vince.

The van pulled into a steep driveway that lead to a fabulous villa. In Jamaica you found the poorest of the poor and the richest of the rich. This villa was owned by one of Jessie's friends that lived in the states. He rented the villa year round to his friends and family.

"Wow, this place is fabulous!" Jocko had never been to Jamaica and he was elated by the entire experience.

299

"Let me take you guys on a tour." Jessie was excited for his friends. The property had a large beautiful pool with an adjacent whirlpool. Inside there were six bedrooms with a full bathroom attached. There was also a large living room, sitting room and kitchen.

"Let me introduce you guys to Florence. She will be cooking for us all week and trust me she's good at what she does." Jessie had been traveling to Jamaica for as many years as Cherish and this was where he stayed all the time. He loved Florence and would send her things from the states all throughout the year.

"Welcome to Jamaica. Lunch soon come." Florence returned to her meal preparation.

"Okay, there are seven of us and six rooms. So Cherish you have to stay in my room with me!" Jessie waited to see what he could get away with.

"How many beds in your room?" Cherish wasn't laughing.

"I'm just joking with you Cherish. Everything has already been decided. Wanda and Shanae will be staying together. They decided to stay together so they won't exhale with one of these Jamaican men." Jessie was laughing but he was serious.

"Let me show you to your assigned rooms. Then let's freshen up and meet on the veranda for lunch in about 30 minutes." Each guest went to their rooms to prepare for lunch.

***

"Wisdom, yuh know de Iron Shore villa dat de Bredren, Run Down rent tu foreigners? Delroy called Wisdom to ask him to accompany him this afternoon.

"Mi know de place, Rasta" Wisdom remembered that Run Down use to live in Philadelphia. He wanted to hear what else Delroy had to say.

"Di place rented, Rasta. Mi gonna tu check pon dem." Delroy knew Jessie because he was a part of his ganja connection in Jamaica.

300

Surviving This Thing Called Life

"Yuh know where de people dem come from?" Wisdom was hoping that Delroy would say Philly. He was feeling Cherish's spirit more than usual.

"Philly, Mon. Dem from Philly. Yuh waan come?" Delroy knew that Wisdom would accompany him to the villa. Wisdom loved Foreigners. It wasn't that he didn't like Jamaican's but he loved talking and socializing with people who traveled outside of Jamaica.

"Yuh Mon. Mi soon come." Wisdom was excited.

***

"Lunch is on the veranda everyone." Jessie yelled. Wanda and Shanae were the first to appear. They both changed into one their many outfits purchased specifically for the trip. It was their first trip out of the country. They shopped for weeks choosing just the right bathing suits, hats, dresses, and every other accessory. In the end, they each had seven bath suit ensembles and twenty other ensembles to choose from during their stay.

"You ladies look lovely. Don't catch no AIDS while you in Jamaica with me!" Jessie laughed.

"Sit your beautiful asses down and eat some food." The rest of the group made it to the table to consume the great meal that Florence prepared for them.

"I thought we would all relax by the pool for the rest of the day and if we feel like it go out on the town tonight." Jessie meticulously planned the trip for his friends. Everyone played an important role in his recover and he wanted them to know how much he loved and appreciated them.

"Man, I feel so blessed just being here. I wouldn't care if all I did was sit by the pool, eat and drink for the entire time. Especially, if Florence is fixing the food! By the way, anyone else beside me want a drink?" Jocko got up from his seat to make a drink at the bar.

"Give me a Guinness, Jocko. What about ganja, Jessie! We in Jamaica and I should be smoking a big spliff by now!" Cherish was laying in a chaise lounge by the pool.

301

"Ganja soon come, Cherish. It's on the way." Jessie felt in control.

"Yeah, how soon will they be here?" Cherish was reluctant to be around whoever it was bringing the ganja to the villa. She felt something in her spirit about the visit.

"You already know Cherish. In Jamaica, it's "no problem" and "soon come" so who knows." Jessie was sipping on the rum punch Jocko prepared for him. Everyone had a drink relaxing at the pool.

"I'm going inside y'all. Mi soon come." Cherish got up and went inside. She followed her spirit. She was getting better at following her inner spirit instead of her mind. From her room, she had a good view of pool. She waited patiently to see who would appear with the ganja.

Wisdom and Delroy drove up the driveway to the front entrance of the house. The duo knew the Americans would be at the pool. Jamaicans didn't really sit in the sun. They lived in the sun so avoided it any chance they could. Wisdom and Delroy took the liberty to walk toward the pool at the back of the property. Cherish heard the car pulling up the driveway and peeked out the shutters to see who was visiting at the pool. Her view wasn't the best but she thought one of the men looked like Wisdom. Her heart began to race. She took another look to be certain and it was him. It was Wisdom.

"Delroy, it's good to see you man. How long has it been?" Jessie got up to greet his friend.

"Dis mi Bredren, Wisdom. Mi nah stay, Star." The men took care of the business they came for and prepared to leave.

"Yuh goin out later?" Delroy and Wisdom stood. Cherish could see the two men stand and was hoping the physical gesture meant they were leaving. She could see them shake hands and Wisdom walk away. Cherish waited for a long time before she returned outside to join the group.

Surviving This Thing Called Life

"Where you been, Cherish? I was getting ready to come check on your ass." Jessie always worried about Cherish cause he loved her so much.

"Just chillin. When you get a minute, Jessie, I want to talk to you."

"I got a minute now. You want to go inside?"

"Yes" Cherish shared with Jessie all that just happened.

"So, you don't want to see Wisdom? Did he physically hurt you?" Jessie couldn't imagine that Cherish would be afraid of anyone unless he hurt her.

"No, we separated from each other, loss contact and never really resolved anything. I don't feel like doing that right now. I came to relax not solve life problems." Cherish smiled. She didn't want Jessie to worry about her. He was on vacation too.

"Well, they have no reason to come here again. So don't worry yourself. Okay that's enough drama for today. Get your ass back to the pool. Eat, drink and be merry and that's an order!" Jessie reassured his friend that everything was going to be alright.

***

Wisdom and Delroy rode silently to their next destination. Wisdom had such a strong feeling while visiting the Americans at the Villa. He didn't know what it was. He didn't recognize any of the people from his time in Philadelphia. Something about the place bothered him and he didn't know what.

"Yuh know dem people, Star?" Wisdom thought maybe it was the vibe of distrust he felt.

"Yes, Mon. Mi know de Bwoy. Him come tu Jamaica fi years now! Di Bwoy do business wit Zerby. Yuh know de white girl!" Delroy continued to drive.

"Zerby ! Mi forgot bout de Sistren! Di Sistren still hab de ganja farm?"

"Yes, man. Di White girl hab de farm."

"Tek mi tu de farm, Rasta." Delroy followed Wisdom's directions and headed for the hills. Wisdom needed to see

303

Zerby maybe she knew where Cherish was because he didn't.

***

Night fall was upon the island and Jessie and his friends were headed for the Hip Strip in Montego Bay. The street name was recently changed after the infamous Margaritaville was added to the selection of nightspots on the street. It was the main street in Montego Bay where most tourist went to eat, drink and be merry.

"You not going out with us Cherish?" Wanda and Shanae had on one of their party ensemble and Cherish was taking pictures of them at various locations in the villa. "No, I'm gonna stay in tonight. I've been to Margaritaville enough for one lifetime." Cherish really didn't want to go out because he didn't want to run into Wisdom. It was unlikely that Wisdom would be there but she didn't think he would be on the island either.

"Okay, Cherish. You know where everything is. We won't be long cause we all kinda tired and we're scheduled to drive to Dunn's River Falls in Ocho Rios in the morning. It's just the first night in Jamaica and these guys want to see the nightlife." Jessie wanted to stay in also but he didn't want to be a party pooper for the excited friends.

"You guys have a drink and a grind on me while you out!" Cherish hugged everyone and sent them on their way. She was happy to be alone. She needed to go over all that happened today. Seeing Wisdom was a real shock. She prayed that she could avoid him during her short stay on the island but if she saw him she would have to deal with it.

Wisdom and Delroy made it safely to Zerby's 40 acre ganja farm in Bruce Hall about 18 miles into the hills. It took the men about 44 minutes to reach the farm. He hadn't seen Zerby since he left Jamaica for England to release the CD. He wondered how her nephew, Justin, was doing. Delroy and Wisdom drove down a dirt road to the house where Zerby stayed while on her farm. Wisdom

304

hoped she was there. Delroy knocked on the door. Knowledge answered.

"Wisdom! Wisdom! Mi so happy fi see yuh!" Knowledge was beyond happy. He really love and respected Wisdom.

"Zerby! Zerby! Yuh nevah know! Come!" Zerby slowly walked down the stairs to see what Knowledge was yelling about. As she entered the living room, one of the three men with Dreadlocks looked like Wisdom.

"Wisdom is that you?" Zerby rushed down the stairs to hug her long lost friend.

"Yuh good, Sistren?"

"Everyting good. We missed you. How's Cherish?" Zerby knew that Cherish left Jamaica before Wisdom returned but she also expected that the two reconnected by now.

"Was prayin dat yuh knew." Wisdom was disappointed but didn't want to show it to his friends.

"After she left, my mother, sister, Justin, Kizzie and myself lived at the property in St. Mary until my home in Morant Bay was built. I heard from her for a little while and then we lost touch. She changed her cell number and we haven't been in contact since." Zerby was hoping that she'd found Wisdom and Cherish.

"Justin good?"Zerby could hear the disappointment in Wisdom's voice.

"Yes, he's fine. He's with Kizzie at my house. You remember that pretty Jamaican girl we took for the Starlite Chalet in the Blue Mountains." Zerby smiled because Kizzie was one of the best cures Wisdom provided for Justin.

"Yes, Mon. Dat good." Wisdom thought, Zerby and Knowledge were still together. Justin even kept his woman! What was wrong with him that he didn't keep his woman? He wondered if the fame was worth it.

"Y'all hungry? Yuh want a drink?" Zerby was excited.

"Mi tek cold Guinness." The newly united friends spent the evening talking and drinking through the night.

305

S.D. Laurence

***

Vince was rapidly losing the faith that his friend Junebug kept reminding him about. He didn't want to disappoint his friend. He couldn't see the staircase and he wasn't walking blind no more. He thought about doing something he had avoided for years. Going to Jamaica and retrieving the money hidden there. Vince had not only buried money in his backyard but had money stashed in Jamaica.

When he was working in Amsterdam, he met a White woman from New Mexico. Of course, they fucked each other but later discussed their individual illegal businesses. The woman was Zerby. They made a deal that Zerby would smuggle large amounts of money to Jamaica for a 20% fee. He knew that money was the source of a lot of his problems. He now understood the saying, money corrupts. But now he thought that money didn't corrupt people. People have good and bad in them, and it's up to you to act on one or another.

He knew he was ready to be good. The money could help him buy a beautiful home for himself and Cherish. He could start some kind of legal business and when Cherish returned he would be and have all the things she knew he wanted. He didn't know how he would get the money out of the country but he knew Zerby would know how to handle it all. He went to the store and brought a calling card to contact Zerby in Jamaica. The phone rang.

"Hello Zerby?"

"Yes, this is she. Whose calling?" Zerby recognized the voice but couldn't put the name with a person.

"Zerby it's me, Vince!" Vince trusted Zerby with a lot. He could only hope and pray she was as honest as she claimed to be.

"Vince, long time no see or hear. It's been years. What happened to you?" Zerby had thought about Vince frequently. Their time in Amsterdam always left a smile on her face.

306

"We still cool with each other?" Vince knew Zerby would know what she was talking about.

"Of course, everything is fine. You should visit me. I built a new house." Zerby was hoping Vince would say yes. She'd love to see her old friend. In Amsterdam, Zerby saw how obnoxious Vince could be sometime but she liked him nevertheless.

"I will take you up on that offer. Let me make reservations and give you a call later." Vince was happy. It seemed like Zerby was an honorable woman.

"Vince land at the Kingston Airport because it's closer to my home. Talk to you soon." Zerby hung up the phone looking forward to seeing her old friend.

***

Cherish was the first to rise. She wondered to the kitchen where Florence was fixing breakfast for the group.

"Good Day, Florence. How are you doing on this beautiful day that God sent?"

"Mi good so far, Miss." Florence liked that the American woman talked about God. She had been cooking for visitors at the villa for years and her observation was that these Americans thought they did everything on their own. It seemed to her that they may have forgotten about God.

"Your meals have been wonderful. Thank you for all the love you put into your cooking. You can taste it yuh know!" Cherish was smiling. She loved to say things to make others feel good.

"Thank yuh, Miss." Florence didn't have time to talk she needed to finish cooking this morning and clean up before she returned home to wash clothes and prepare dinner for her five pinckney. Cherish could tell that Florence didn't want to be disturbed. She wasn't on vacation and had a lot of other things to do today.

"Alright Florence. I'll talk to you later. Is the coffee ready?"

"Yes, Miss." Florence continued to complete her task.

S.D. Laurence

"That's good. I'll wake the others. We going to Dunn's River Falls today." Cherish decided to wake up the group for coffee and breakfast. She went to each bedroom, knocked politely, and told everyone to meet on the veranda for breakfast. Everyone obeyed and met on the veranda in their pajamas and slippers.

"You guys have a good time last night?" Cherish knew they did. Margaritaville was always a good time.

"Yes, we had a great time. The Hip Strip is really hip, Cherish. We went to Margaritaville, Blue Beat and Pier One. We ended up at Pier One for a night meal before returning home. You should've come Cherish. You going today right?" Wanda missed Cherish last night. Everyone knew that Cherish was a good time.

"Yes, I wouldn't miss the Dunn's River Falls trip." Florence brought out the hot coffee and breakfast for the group.

"Thanks, Florence. I'll serve the coffee." Cherish poured coffee for everyone, took a seat and began to eat her meal.

"When is the driver coming, Dad?" Kyian had visited Jamaica with his father before and knew about the Dunn's River Falls. He was excited to return.

"He'll be here about 10 am. The ride to the falls is about 1 ½ hours. So we should get there about 11:30." Jessie knew the day would be fun for all.

"I hope you all remembered to bring some kind of rubber soled shoes with good grips. If not it's gonna cost $7.00 to rent a used pair and $17.00 to buy a new pair of rubber shoes." Jessie was sure that Wanda and Shanae were prepared because they shopped for three weeks for the trip. No one said anything so to Jessie that meant all was good.

Once inside her room, Cherish thought about the trip today. Ocho Rios was not far from where she and Wisdom lived in Jamaica. He was on the island and could be anywhere at any time and she knew that. She was seriously reconsidering the trip to Ocho Rios with the group. She

308

knew everyone would be disappointed but she didn't care at this point. Everyone was prepared to the trip to Ocho Rios except Cherish. You could feel the excitement in the air.

"Where's Cherish?" Jessie saw everyone but her. He hoped she was traveling with them today and not staying behind. He walked to her bedroom door and knocked. "Cherish, Cherish!" Cherish opened the door and invited Jessie inside.

"I don't want to go Jessie. I'm really sorry. I can't risk seeing Wisdom. You know we didn't live too far from Ocho Rios when we lived here together. I'd rather stay here today. I've been to Dunn's River Falls more times than I can count. I am really enjoying myself at the house, Jessie. I'm just glad to be out of Philly." Cherish could see the disappointment in Jessie's face.

"Alright Cherish. You do what's best for you. I'll explain to everyone." Jessie exited the room to inform the group that Cherish would not be attending today's activities.

***

Dunn's River Falls is a 600 foot cascading waterfall of cool spring water surrounded by a beautiful tropical oasis of lush plants and greenery. Getting to the top of the falls is an amazing opportunity to climb up steep boulders, push your way through gushing water and even slide down a natural waterslide.

The tour guides help make the climb fun and also make sure that nobody slips or falls on the rocks. Individuals that don't want to or are unable to climb the falls can walk alongside using the stairs. It took the group about an hour to complete the hike. Afterward, the group purchased a DVD that was made during the climb up the falls.

"Let's go across the street to eat at the Lion's Den." Jessie already knew where he wanted to eat. The place looked like a tourist trap from outside. Once inside the dining room resembled a Rastafarian chapel with hand-carved columns and wicker tree limbs reaching to the

309

ceiling. The menu includes a lot of local specialties. The food was excellent and well-priced. After the meal, the group headed back to Montego Bay to relax and prepare for another night out.

***

Vince landed at Norman Manley International Airport in Kingston, Jamaica. He exited the airport to look for Zerby. He hadn't seen her in many years. He hoped she hadn't changed that much. He looked around but didn't see her. He decided to sit at the bar and have a drink.

His drinking had reduced considerably and the drugs had stopped altogether. He hoped that Zerby would show up to pick him up. He waited patiently. Vince finished his Red Strip when he cited a tall white girl that looked like Zerby. She was a little heavier now but he knew it was her.

"Zerby! Zerby!" Vince called out to get her attention. Zerby heard her old friend and headed toward the bar where he was sitting.

"Vince, it's good to see you! How have you been? Zerby was sincere.

"It's good to see you too Zerby. You really don't want to know what I been through in my life but the important thing is that it's all behind me now. I'm coming down here to collect my belongings and pray for the best." Vince didn't sound the same to Zerby.

"Well, we have to figure out a few things, Vince. Number one, how to get the money back into the states but I have some ideas to share with you later. Let's head for my house." The two jumped into Zerby's Hummer and headed for her house.

***

Cherish was at the Villa alone. Florence cleaned the place and left to complete her chores at home and return in time to cook dinner for the guest. Cherish was sitting at the pool chilling and decided to go inside and rest from the hot sun.

Once inside, she laid down on the bed. After awhile, she heard a knock at the door. She assumed it was Florence. Maybe she forgot or lost her key. Cherish went directly to the door and opened it. Standing in the doorway was Wisdom. Cherish was astonished. She stood there not knowing what to do or what to say.

"Cherish!" Wisdom knew his vibes were correct. When he left Zerby's, the feeling he had that Cherish was on the island didn't go away. He was riding by the villa where he met Jessie and decided to stop by. Maybe someone in the group knew Cherish. He hadn't asked anyone. In fact, he had nothing to say during his short visit with Delroy.

"Wisdom! I thought you were in Europe." She didn't want him to know that she saw him the other day and had been trying to avoid him ever since.

"Yes, Cherish. Mi felt like a prisoner wit everyone telling de I what tu do!" Cherish didn't feel sorry for Wisdom.

"Wisdom when you get back in Jamaica?" Cherish was trying to change the subject.

"Some time now. Mi buildin a house en de Grange Hills. Yuh must love de place. Mi prayed dat one day I an I would be dere together." Wisdom hoped Cherish would be happy about that.

"Mi on de way tu see de house. Come, Cherish." Wisdom was praying on the inside that Cherish would say yes. Cherish didn't know what to do. She remembered how they hooked up. It was a ride that turned into many, many years.

"I don't know Wisdom." Cherish hadn't invited Wisdom in the house yet.

"Cherish, mek mi come in de house." Cherish invited Wisdom inside and the two sat by the pool and talked about old times. The worst was over! They were getting along. Cherish wasn't angry but she didn't feel the same way. The tingling feelings of anticipation she use to feel when she was with him was gone.

311

S.D. Laurence

***

It took Vince and Zerby about 30 minutes to reach her house. The trip from Kingston, St Andrew Parish was straight ride along the shoreline until they reached the coastal town of Bull Bay in St Andrew. The final 10 minutes of the trip was a one mile climb to Eleven Mile in St Thomas. Zerby pulled up to a beautiful log home.

"Come inside, Vince." Zerby and Vince exited the car and entered Zerby's home.

"Let me show you the house. Let's start upstairs." Zerby knew that no one would be home. Justin and Kizzie were on a road trip to Alex's place in the Blue Lagoon. The two of them fell in love with the place and returned frequently.

"There are two bedrooms upstairs. One my nephew and his girl friend and the other for guest."

"This is nice! I love everything. Especially all the natural wood." Vince was impressed.

"Let's go downstairs. There's the living room, dining room, kitchen, and another bedroom with a full bath" Vince followed. Zerby as she walked quickly through that area of the house.

"Follow me Vince! This is something you can't resist." Zerby opened the door to a massive master bedroom. There sat a large California King.

"Come this way!" Zerby lead Vince to a set of sliding doors that led to a large side porch with Platinum Jacuzzi hot tub.

"It gets chilly up here in the evening and I love to get nude in the hot tub before going to bed. It kinda takes the chill off. You waan get in and relax with me after such a long day?" Zerby began taking off her clothes. She had gotten to her bra before Vince could speak.

"Wait! Wait! No disrespect, but I'm here strictly for business. I need this money to make some things right in my life. I just pray God will let me live long enough to do all I need to do. Anyway me fucking you ain't one of the

312

things I need to be doing right now." Vince reached out and gave Zerby a big hug.

"Vince, I appreciate that. You right! I don't know what got into me. I think I was trying to relive the past. I should know better. What's done is done." Zerby smiled.

"We'll leave in the morning for Montego Bay. It'll take us about 3 1/2 to 4 hours to get to MoBay and another 45 minutes to the ganja farm. It's near a small town in the hills called Bruce Hall.

"You hungry?" Vince and Zerby settled in for the night. They woke early to begin their road trip to the ganja farm in Bruce Hill. The first leg of the trip was through the hills. Vince had been to Jamaica several times but this was the first time he would experience the beauty of driving through the hills. Vince and Zerby passed through Denham Town, Spanish Town, Linstead, Lilliput, Palmyra, and finally Montego Bay. Zerby was exhausted and hungry.

"Vince, let's stop at the Dead End Bar in Mobay for some food." The Dead End bar was one of Zerby's favorite spots. Cherish introduced her to the place. Zerby headed down Norman Manley Boulevard to Sunset Boulevard, and turned right onto Kent Avenue. They rode pass Sandals on the right and to the left was a thin ribbon of white sand beaches with calm aquamarine waters. Zerby continued to drive along the road for a couple of minutes and at the end of the road was the Dead End Bar. She parked her Hummer by the sea wall and the duo exited the car and headed for the bar.

"Wha happenin Zerby?" A short man with Dreadlocks yelled out as she and Vince headed for the bar.

"Stumpy! Bredren, mi happy fi see yuh!" Stumpy worked for Zerby from time to time. She was a generous employer, so everyone knew her and her red Hummer.

"Yuh hungry?" Stumpy anxiously pulled out the chair for Zerby to sit.

"Yes, Mon." Zerby and Vince ordered food and drink. It was Vince's first visit to the Dead End Bar. It was obviously a place visited by more locals than tourist.

"We got another 45 minutes to go Vince. You tired?" Zerby was tired.

"I'm not driving Zerby. Are you tired?" Vince was enjoying the Dead End bar. He already had a few drinks and they served him fried chicken. So he was happy.

"I am tired. Let's chill in MoBay tonight. There's a local hotel, Glorianna's on Sunset Blvd. It's a stone's throw away. It has a bar, restaurant, and pool. You'll like the place." Vince and Zerby spent the rest of the day at the Dead End Beach and later that evening, they made their way to Glorianna's and checked in.

After settling in her room, Zerby called Wisdom to let him know she was in town. She'd just found him after a long time and wanted to see more of him.

"Wisdom, it's Zerby. What's happening?" Zerby was glad to hear his voice.

"Wha happen wit yuh?" Wisdom had just returned from seeing Cherish. He didn't want to tell Zerby over the phone. He wanted to see her in person and share the good news.

"I'm staying at Glorianna's for the night. I got a friend with me from Philly and we going to the farm in the morning." Wisdom thought it was kinda of weird that everyone mentioned in the past few days was from Philly. His felt like he needed to hear more about the man from Philly.

"How yuh meet de man?" Wisdom didn't know why he wanted to know more. He just knew he needed to ask these questions. Maybe the man meant harm to Zerby.

"I met Vince in Amsterdam many years ago. He was a model then. We've been out of contact for years. But we did some business together in the past and he's here to visit the island." Wisdom knew it was more to the story but also knew that Zerby wouldn't talk too much over the phone.

"Meet de I at Pier One, Sistren. Dere someting mi waan tell yuh." Wisdom couldn't wait to tell Zerby that he saw Cherish and she's in Montego Bay!

"Okay, I'm going to lie down and take a nap. I'll be there but it will be late." Zerby hung up the phone, laid down and went to sleep. She left Vince at the bar drinking and talking shit.

***

Cherish said good-bye to Wisdom. She knew she would probably see him one more time before she left the island. She returned to the pool to discover that the group had returned from Dunns River Falls.

"Cherish! I'm so glad to see you. You were missed on the trip." Jessie spoke seriously.

"Jessie, let's go inside. I want to tell you something." Cherish told Jessie about Wisdom coming by the villa and surprising her. She also told Jessie how the encounter benefited her. She knew she didn't feel the same about Wisdom. She loved him but loved herself more. She wasn't angry or envious of Wisdom's new life in Jamaica. She was excited and anxious to start her life. She didn't know what God had planned for her but she was waiting on Him to reveal her purpose.

"Well that's good. We going to Pier One tonight. Finally, you can go out! You're not hiding from anyone else are you?" Jessie smiled.

"No I'm not hiding from anyone else! Yes, I can enjoy my time on the island with my friends." Cherish and Jessie joined the others. Later that evening everyone prepared to party at the infamous Pier One in Montego Bay. Jessie and the crew were the first to reach Pier One that evening.

Pier One is located on Howard Cooke Boulevard at the waterfront alongside the Montego Bay Marine Park building. The club has an open-air design and a Pier that extends out to sea. You can walk down the pier and enjoy

315

the lagoon and the twinkling lights of the surrounding hills. Docked at the pier was many luxury yachts moored up alongside to admire.

Once inside the group headed to the back of the bar closer to the pier. The view excited everyone. The crowds were gathered toward the front of the venue closer to the dance floor. Everyone got a drink and started to enjoy themselves. Cherish wasn't dancing. She was sitting at the bar enjoying the view. Suddenly someone kissed her on the neck. It shocked her. She turned around and it was Wisdom.

"What's the likelihood of us seeing each other twice in one day after so much time?" Cherish smiled.

"Happy fi see yuh Cherish. Mi here tu meet Zerby!" Wisdom couldn't hold the good news any longer.

"Zerby! Well tonight will feel like old times with the three of us! Is Justin still with her?" Cherish was surprised and excited.

"Yes, Mon! Justin good! Kizzie still dere bouts too. Dem en Saint Thomas. Zerby bringin a Bredren from Philly."

"Philly?" The hair on Cherish's neck rose. "Philly, you said. How and where did she meet him?"

"Dem met en Amsterdam." Wisdom answered.

"You know his name?"

"Vince. Mi tink, Vince. Yuh know de Mon?" Cherish almost choked on her drink. Her body began to shake. She couldn't believe it. What was the likelihood of Wisdom, Vince and her being at the same place and the same time? What was the Universe trying to tell her?

"Wisdom, take me out of here! I'll explain when we get into the car." Cherish was shaking.

"Wha wrong, Empress?" Wisdom was concerned.

"I'm gonna let Jessie and the others know we're leaving. I'll tell you in the car." Cherish briskly walked to the area of the club where Jessie and the others were dancing and enjoying themselves. She knew Jessie would be upset but he'd have to understand. There was no time to explain.

316

Immediately afterwards, Cherish and Wisdom headed out of Pier One and entered Wisdom's car.

"Yuh gonna tell de I now, Cherish?" Wisdom wanted to know what this was all about.

"No, Wisdom. Drive off and I'll tell you when we get inside the villa." The two drove away and headed toward Iron Shore. After getting inside the villa, Cherish fixed herself a shot of tequila, grabbed a spiff and headed poolside. She didn't offer Wisdom anything. She wasn't thinking about him.

"Wha happenin Cherish?" Wisdom asked again. This time he was persistent. He never witnessed Cherish in this state before. Then he remembered Negril, when they first met. She needed him then and she needed him now!

After drinking the shot and lighting the spliff, Cherish revealed everything to Wisdom. She told him about her marriage to Vince. She told him about being held at gun point and finding the cell phone taken from her in the robbery in Vince's pocket. She told him about Angel dying and how much she missed her. Cherish was sobbing at the end of all the stories.

As she repeated the sequence of events to Wisdom, she surprised herself about how much she'd gone through. All she knew was that she was still standing and it was all due to her Heavenly Father because she alone would have never had the strength to endure all of it.

"Don't stress yuhself, Empress. Yuh, hab de I. Mi tek care of tings fi yuh!" Wisdom held Cherish in his arms while she calmed down. After a short time, Cherish came back to herself.

"Cherish, mi tek care of de ting fi yuh. Remember, Jamaica no problem!" He kissed Cherish on the cheek and headed out the door.

"Jah guide!" Cherish yelled after Wisdom as he headed to Pier One to meet up with Zerby and Vince. She finished her spiff and went to bed. She knew everything was going to be alright.

317

S.D. Laurence

***

Zerby and Vince got to Pier One well after midnight, and found the place alive and bumping with people jammed into the main bar area. They headed toward the back where it was less crowded. Zerby was looking for Wisdom in the crowd as they made their way to the back. Wisdom and Delroy were seated at the bar.

"Wisdom! Delroy! Wha happenin Bredren!" Zerby was happy to see the two men. Vince was getting on her nerves. He was still drunk from earlier. He only slept for a short time on the veranda of his room at Glorianna's. The waitresses told Zerby that he never made it inside his room.

"Wha happenin?" Delroy was the first to respond. Wisdom had given him an update on tonight's events and he was anxious to talk to the American man with Zerby.

"Oh this is a friend and business associate of mine, Vince. Vince, this is Delroy and Wisdom." Zerby could tell that Delroy didn't approve of something. Maybe it was because she was with this American man and she was Knowledge's woman. Delroy was supposed to understand business but none of that mattered to her.

"No disrespect Bredren! Mi tek Zerby pon de pier! Mi soon come!" Zerby grabbed her drink and followed Wisdom down the pier toward the docked yachts.

"What' going on Wisdom? Why are you and Delroy acting so strange?"

"Zerby, Cherish inna Montego Bay!"

"What? Where is she? When can I see her? Is she okay?" Zerby was excited but knew that something else was going on.

"Wha business yuh hab wit de American?"

"What does this have to do with Cherish?"

"Zerby mi hab no time fi questions. De I need answers!" Zerby could tell that Wisdom was serious. So she went along.

318

"A long time ago, this guy sent money to Jamaica for me to hide. All of a sudden he shows up wanting his money."

"Yuh hab de money, Star?"

"Yes, I have his money. So he's here to make arrangements for me to send it to him in the states. Of course I'm going to another 20% on the reverse end of the deal. Can you tell me why now?"

"Listen now!" Wisdom told Zerby the entire story that Cherish told him.

"Where is Cherish now?"

"De Empress en Iron Shore. Cherish good, Star."

"You sure this is the same guy, Wisdom?"

"Dats wha mi gwan find out tonight!" Wisdom and Zerby wandered casually back to the bar. They did smoke a spliff while on the pier to appear that was their main purpose for heading off to be alone.

"Y'all smoked some of the good ganja?" Vince spoke immediately when the two returned. Vince knew nothing about quiet.

"Hey Zerby you remember when we were in Amsterdam smoking that shit there. It was good! I ain't never really been no weed smoker. Now my wife that's another story. She could smoke your whole farm Zerby!" Vince was loud.

"Careful what you say Vince." Zerby had to keep warning Vince about possibly sharing her business with the entire club.

"Sorry! Yeah, like I was saying. Y'all would love my wife. I call her Goldie Locks because she has pretty light brown locks with strands of gold running through it. She would love to be here now. She loves Jamaica." Wisdom's ears perked up.

"What's your wife's name Vince? You weren't married when we met long ago?" Zerby thought she would ask the question she knew Wisdom so desperately needed to know.

"No, I wasn't married then! I hadn't met a woman that could hold my attention until Cherish. I hope you get a

319

S.D. Laurence

chance to meet her Zerby. That's who this trip is all about. I want to get my money and make a home for us. I only hope God lets me live to make things right." Vince called to the bartender for another drink.

"Zerby, mi tink yuh need fi tek de Bwoy tu Glorianna's!" Wisdom heard everything he needed to hear. It was the Vince from Philly that Cherish knew.

"Zerby, mi waan tek de Bwoy tu Negril on a road trip. Mi must git tu know everyting bout de Bwoy. Hem tu drunk fi talk now." Wisdom knew Zerby would agree.

"Vince it's getting late. I want to go to the hotel and get some sleep for the long ride tomorrow. I think we should go to Negril tomorrow and fill out the bank papers needed for all the future money transfers first and then go get the money from the ganja farm." Vince agreed. He was tired also from the drinking, hot sun and traveling.

It was late when Wisdom left Pier One so he didn't disturb Cherish with what he found out. Wisdom was headed to his daughter's house to get some sleep and prepare for the ride to Negril in the morning. From everything Vince told him, they were both in love with the same woman, Cherish.

He understood when Vince said he only hoped God lets me live long enough to make things right with Cherish. Wisdom felt the same way. He hadn't hired someone to point a gun in her side but he did abandon her thinking only of himself. She deserved more.

Before Wisdom entered his bed to sleep, he got on his knees and prayed to Jah for strength and wisdom. He had no idea what tomorrow was going to bring. His plan was to find out what plans Vince had for himself and Cherish. He needed to know if this man meant harm to his lover.

Wisdom woke early the next morning. He thanked God for waking him up with a sane mind. Today he was traveling to Negril with Zerby, Vince and Delroy. His favorite place to stay in Negril was Roots but if he went there he knew everyone would be asking him about

320

Surviving This Thing Called Life

Cherish. He didn't need that today. He stopped and picked up Delroy and headed for Glorianna's to get Zerby and Vince. He knocked on Zerby's hotel room door.

"It's open! Come on in!" Zerby knew it was Wisdom.

"De Bwoy woke yet?" Wisdom knew Vince would still be sleep because of all the booze he put in his body last night.

"No, I don't think so. His room is right next to mine and I don't hear a sound."

"Wha happenin Rasta?" Delroy didn't like Vince. He couldn't understand why Wisdom was spending so much time with him. Wisdom knew that Delroy didn't understand his tactics. Delroy would have taken Vince in the hills last night, murdered him, and left his body there to deteriorate. Many people came to Jamaica and never returned.

"Everyting crisp, Star. I an I gonna wake de Bwoy and git hem ready fi de trip." Wisdom headed for Vince's room and knocked on the door.

"Who it it?" Vince sounded tired.

"Wisdom. Yuh ready fi de trip tu Negril?"

"Give me a few minutes and I'll be ready to go." Vince was really enjoying his time in Jamaica. He liked Wisdom and didn't mind spending more time with him. Wisdom left his car at Glorianna's and the foursome loaded Zerby's Hummer and headed for Negril.

The ride to Negril would take about a 1 ½ hours. They group would drive along the sea coast and pass Hopewell, Lucea, Cousins Cove and Orange Bay before reaching Negril. Norman Manley Blvd is the main street in Negril. As the group traveled down Norman Manley Blvd they passed many hotels.

"This place is beautiful too. Where we gonna stay Zerby!" Vince was ready for more adventure.

"A place called Moon Cliffs."

"The cliffs. Everything looks flat to me." Vince was confused.

321

S.D. Laurence

"Be patient. You'll see Vince." Wisdom continued down Norman Manley Blvd to a roundabout in the road. He made a right turn onto West End Road. The road led the group high into the hills. They pulled into the Moon Cliffs Resort and Spa. The property sat on several acres with 6 Villas. Zerby checked in while the group waited in the car. She was greeted by Tanya

"Zerby, yuh back!" Tanya knew Zerby because of her frequent visits.

"Tanya, I'm so happy to see you. Is Trevor around?" Trevor was the houseman. Each villa included a housekeeper and a houseman. Zerby knew that Tanya and Trevor would take care of their every need.

"Well, this is another winner!" Vince was impressed. The Villas was fully air conditioned with 4 bedrooms, 4 ½ baths, a private garden Jacuzzi, full wet bar, living room, and cable T.V. Tanya went about fixing a meal for the group while Trevor prepared drinks for all. Wisdom and Vince sat together in the garden with drinks. It was time for Wisdom to get to know Vince better.

"Vince, yuh know mi use tu live in Philly." Wisdom thought this bit of information might open Vince up more.

"Yeah, where?" Vince was curious now. He really didn't like Jamaicans. He never trusted anyone Jamaican. He trusted Zerby because she was a White American. She just happen to do business in Jamaica. He knew that with connections, Jamaica was a good place to hide and stash money.

"Mi nevah remember, yuh know! De stay was short den mi move tu New York." Wisdom decided that was enough information about Philly.

"Oh, New York. Yeah, I love New York." Vince lightened his tone. He was relieved that Wisdom wasn't a part of the various Jamaican gangs that his family battled during the '80s. Wisdom could sense Vince relaxing. The two chatted and the more Vince drank the more he opened up.

322

Surviving This Thing Called Life

"Cherish, yuh wife? Yuh love de Empress?" Wisdom needed to know how much this man loved his woman.

"Wisdom I do love her. But I did some real dumb shit that she may never forgive me for. On the other hand, Cherish is the most forgiving person I know. So I figured, if I get this money, put this booze down and make a home for her to come to, she might take me back."

"Wha yuh do dat she nah forgive yuh?"

"It was something real stupid. I feel dumb even telling it!" Vince didn't want to tell Wisdom what he did to Cherish. He was too embarrassed.

"Tell de I." Wisdom hoped Vince would share his story.

"Alright. First of all, she wanted to leave me. She wanted to end the marriage! I couldn't allow that so I asked my two cousins to scare her somehow to make her reconsider living alone in that big house without me. Them Niggas put a fake gun to my wife's side, scared the shit out of her and when she screamed, they tazed her with a taser gun!" Vince looked into Wisdom's eyes to see his reaction. There was no reaction.

"What happened next?" Wisdom waited to hear more.

"She left the next day and I haven't seen her since. I'm still living in her house. The renter on the second floor puts the rent in the bank for Cherish and the first floor apartment is empty." Vince waited for a reaction. There was no reaction.

"Wha yuh plan fi do?" Wisdom couldn't believe this man was still living in Cherish's house. She hadn't told him that part.

"I'm going to get this money from Jamaica and move out of Cherish's house. Maybe she'll feel safe enough to return to her own home. I feel so bad about so much. I only hope God will let me live long enough to make everything up to Cherish." Vince was getting drunk while talking to Wisdom.

"Star, mi tink yuh hearts en de right place. De first ting yuh must do is gib de Sistren de house back." Wisdom felt

323

sorry for Vince. He didn't think he was going to harm Cherish but he also didn't know that Cherish had no place to call home. How much more had his love endured while they were apart?

"Yeah, Wisdom! I'm gonna do the right thing. I promise you and God." Vince was feeling better.

"Wisdom let's exchange telephone numbers and keep in touch." The two exchanged numbers. Wisdom had this man's telephone number and could keep in contact with him to make sure he left Cherish's home. Zerby entered the garden.

"I thought we would go to Rick's Café for drinks. The view is beautiful. You guys down?"

"Let's go!" Vince was excited. This was the best he'd felt in years. Somehow he knew everything was going to be alright. The foursome drove up the hill to Rick's Café located at the top of a cliff on the far west end of Negril.

"This is where you will see the best sunsets in the world, Vince!"

"I don't know Zerby. You know I been around the world a few times!" Vince was drunk and loud again. Upon entering Rick's Café, there were people drinking and chanting while others jumped off the high cliffs. The excitement attracted Vince's attention. He by passed the bar and headed straight for the cliffs. Wisdom followed him while the rest of the crew settled at the bar.

The view from the cliff was absolutely breathtaking.. The highest cliff was about 35 feet. Skilled Jamaican divers were making risky and daring dives from as far as the tops of trees above the actual cliff. The men ask for a donation from the tourist to make these jumps but they wouldn't jump until enough donations are put in pot. Vince and Wisdom returned to the bar and took a seat.

"Now that's exciting!" Vince was an Adrenaline Junkie. He thrived off of a lot of outside stimulation.

324

"You gonna jump, Vince?" Zerby knew that Vince liked excitement. That's how they met but time and stress had taken its toll on Vince.

"Deres de shorter jumps fe yuh tu try, Vince." Wisdom was always cautious. Besides Wisdom saw a lot of tourist injure themselves trying to do what these Jamaican men have done all their lives. The plan was to have drinks and listen to music. Not jump off cliffs!

Vince was becoming more boisterous and drunk as the evening progressed. Wisdom was ready to leave. He gotten all the information he needed from Vince. He didn't feel that Vince was a threat to Cherish but he wasn't sure because Vince didn't seem too stable when he was drinking. When they started the trip earlier, he was sensible and even tolerable. But by the fourth drink, his entire demeanor changed.

"I'm gonna jump y'all!" Vince yelled out.

"I don't think you should Vince. You had too much to drink!" Zerby and Wisdom were concerned. Someone at the bar heard Vince's announcement and the chanting began. Vince needed little persuasion and before anyone could stop him he was headed for the highest jumping point.

Vince should not have jumped for many reasons. None of which anyone in his party knew about. He'd suffered a heart attack recently and had three stents placed in his arteries to restore the blood flow in to his blocked arteries. He also suffered from a degenerative disc in his spin that caused him pain from his back to his buttocks and upper thighs. But when Vince drank, he felt no pain.

Vince jumped in the water in a seated position. He lost his breath under the water and was in extreme agony. He couldn't move. He began feeling an uncomfortable pressure, fullness, pain in the center of the chest. The pain quickly spread to his left arm, neck, and jaw. He thought he was having a heart attack. He vomited and passed out.

S.D. Laurence

When Vance didn't surface, the lifeguards jumped into the water in an attempt to save him

Crowds gathered around as the lifeguard dragged Vince's limp body out of the water. He immediately began to perform CPR. It appeared that Vince was dead! Zerby and Delroy stayed behind. None of them wanted to answer any questions the police might have about Vince. Wisdom edged closer to the commotion to try and hear what was going on. He could see the lifeguard giving Vince CRP but to no avail.

The trio quietly left Rick's Café before the police and ambulance got there. They knew it was nothing else they could do. Vince always carried a backpack with all his personal things where ever he went, so they left his bag at the bar in a place where someone would notice it. If Vince survived, he would call Zerby and Wisdom would pick him up from the hospital and made sure he made it to Philly safely. If he hadn't survived the police would discover who is from his belonging and notify his family in the states.

***

Cherish awoke early in her own bed and her own apartment. She started her morning reading her bible, performing some yoga stretches, and a cup of Blue Mountain coffee. She sat at her window and thought about all the recent happenings in her life. Vince did die from the horrible accident at Ricks Café in Negril and Wisdom moved into his new home. They were in touch but only as friends. And for the next four years, she would have 9,900 dollars deposited in her account monthly by Zerby. Everyone knew that Vince wanted the money to make a better life for Cherish.

Cherish decided to put all thoughts of the past away. She didn't live in the past but the present, God's most precious gift. She knew that God controlled all things and that she'd survived all because of His Grace and Mercy. She knew that he had a plan for her. Life was good but God was the best.

326